Martyr

N.P. Beckwith

To my darling wife Angela, who endured far too many late nights during the writing, and played the role of sounding board in all states of wakefulness (and non-).

And to my precious children, Micah, Isaiah, and Nehemiah, my most gifted gifts from the Deity, who constantly inspire me to imagine and create.

Praise for **Martyr** *by N.P. Beckwith*

"Martyr is a brilliantly-conceived story and a great start to what promises to be an exciting new series! I honestly had trouble putting it down... the pacing is terrific, the action is spectacular, the deep artistry of creative imagination is utterly mesmerizing, and the romantic element is emotionally satisfying. New author N.P. Beckwith delivered a home run on his first attempt! An epic fantasy for a post-modern world!"

- Nicholas Downing, Author of Talon's Test and the Shield of Faith

"I enjoyed Martyr and found it an engaging and fascinating read. I would recommend this book to people who enjoy post-apocalyptic style works, with a hint of survivalist skills, and a healthy dose of good vs. evil."

-Sarah Dalziel, Woad Writer

"Martyr is the impressive debut novel by N.P. Beckwith. Justin Mayer is a young man who finds himself transported... to a lightless cell in a strange and different world. Cities lie in ruins and the survivors of a long ago plague have formed isolated bands of resistance against Magus, a dark power supported by superior armies, technologies and demons... Martyr is well written, with descriptions that made it easy to visualize Justin's new world, and well paced as the story built to its conclusion. The actions scenes were intense; you can't stop reading them in the middle. If you think you know where the story is going, you will be caught off guard... Martyr is for all readers who enjoy themes of good vs evil, dystopian worlds or young adult literature.

- Claudia Epstein, Amazon Review

"Loved how this book weaves a good mix of fantasy and philosophy... Great relief from the overdone formula dribble released in the summer. I am waiting for book 2!"

-Christy Coleman, Amazon Review

Martyr™ by N.P. Beckwith

ISBN-13: 978-0692295410

Copyright © 2014 by N.P. Beckwith

Published by Flagship Fiction™ an imprint of CGI Publishing™

Copyright © 2014 Command Group International LLC

Denver, Colorado, United States of America

www.cgipublishing.com/FlagshipFiction

www.facebook.com/FlagshipFiction

Foreword

Having set out to create a work of "Christian fantasy", I feel compelled to at least attempt a definition. The past half-century has witnessed a shift in thought regarding the "meaning" of a given text. There are voices in literary criticism claiming that a text has no *inherent* meaning, but any number of potential "meanings" that can only be discovered through the reader's interaction with the text. Thus the important matter becomes not what the author meant, but what the story "means to me". Over against this view, I would argue that only a view that respects authorial intent can be seen as consistent with a Christian worldview. In fact, I would argue that the effort to divorce the text from inherent meaning arises from a rejection of that worldview, and ultimately leads to irrationality.

This is heavy stuff, to be sure, but not irrelevant. In simple terms it means that when I write a book, it means what I intend it to mean. So the really important question is, "What am I trying to say with Martyr?" As a work of fantasy, it is on one level telling a story that isn't "true". It's "made up" (at least, as far as you know, and I'm not authorized to tell you otherwise). What is "Christian" about a story that is ultimately a lie? Well, the Bible also contains stories that aren't true. They are called "parables". A parable is a short story intended to illustrate some deeper moral truth. I see Martyr as a novel-length parable. As a parable, it is a form of allegory, but I would seek to distinguish it from the kind of pure allegory that some Christian authors have attempted.

Martyr is not "stealth evangelism". The reader will not find Jesus hiding behind every tree, and shouldn't suspect that everything red is blood, or everything wooden a cross. More than one person has read Martyr cover-to-cover, and been surprised to learn that it is considered Christian or religious fantasy. I would argue that it is not necessary to share my worldview in order to enjoy Martyr as a work of fiction. Nevertheless, it is a deeply philosophical and theological book at its core, a fact I believe many Christian readers will not fail to grasp. Rather than positing a one-to-one correspondence between characters or details in the book and spiritual realities, Martyr explores some of the deep questions of faith: "Is God good?" "Can I trust him?" and some we may hope we never have to consider: "What if he asks me to violate my own conscience, to make an impossible choice?" "Does his goodness require him to stay the hand of evil?"

Whatever else may be said of Martyr, it is my hope that the reader will find their own answers to some of these difficult questions, or at least be spurred to consider them anew. For in my mind, what makes Martyr a work of Christian fantasy is that the way in which these answers are given or implied assumes the ultimate validity of the Christian God and worldview. My greatest hope is that as the final page is turned the reader will feel in a very real sense that "it is finished". But that as the first book in a trilogy, they may also eagerly expect and anticipate a future *consummation*...

I never dreamed. Or if I did, I never remembered. Sleep was anesthesia, a blink of the eyes between awake and awake again. That night I had dreamed, my mind born anew into a world of tangible light and sound. I woke, elation dissolving into panic as I realized my alarm hadn't sounded. The blue-green digits were flashing twelve o'clock, again and again; the power had gone off. A glance at my watch confirmed my fears. I was supposed to be in class in less than twenty minutes. I braced for an icy shower.

A few minutes later, I had one leg in my pants and a trickle of red down my neck from a reckless shave. I tried to remember my dream, but with each cast it receded farther from my grasp. I finished dressing and ran a comb through my hair, pausing before the mirror to inspect the result. I was a junior English major with a minor in philosophy. English as a major was an easy choice. I loved the interplay of words and ideas, and realized early on that a command of language could give me a decisive advantage in life. But philosophy…that was a little harder to explain.

I wasn't especially religious. My family hailed from a long line of non-practicing Methodists, and had conveyed an attitude of extreme indifference with regard to spiritual matters. It was more of a personal quest for truth. I wanted to know what was real, what mattered. I wanted the certainty my upbringing had failed to provide. I wasn't dogmatic about it; on the contrary, every time I was proven wrong brought me one step closer to knowing what was right. I was fine-tuning my belief system, chiseling away the contradictions and fallacies. When it was done, I would either find absolute truth, or nothing. I honestly wasn't sure which would be worse.

I checked my watch again. Seven minutes. It wasn't that I cared about the class. "Politics of Religion" – sacred ground for the

1

pious; battlefield for the profane. Interesting, if only for the limitless mayhem potential. It wasn't that hard, really. All you had to do was suggest that something could be known with certainty, and one side or the other would pounce, eager to shred both the argument, and the person foolish enough to advance it. The real art was in planting the seed without owning it, as in, "I heard someone in the history department say…" Then just sit back and watch the blood flow.

I had a powerful suspicion the professor was wise to my little games of instigation, but he had yet to call me out. He was a real head case, that one. Recently PhDd, arrogance in spades. Textbook narcissist. Humiliation and intimidation were the weapons he wielded to strike down any who questioned his views or methods. This was all out there for anyone to see. Privately, rumors circulated that he was into occultic stuff, but accounts varied widely on the specifics. Almost nothing would have surprised me. No, it wasn't the class that had me trying to cram thirty minutes of hygiene into ten. And it certainly wasn't the professor. It was all about the girl.

Mana. Part-time friend and long-time crush. Raven-haired beauty of some semi-exotic stock. We had bonded over a mutual love of sport, somehow always ending up in the gym at the same time. These were carefully crafted coincidences. I had given her an edge in our first racquetball match, and she had neatly diced me. After that I had always tried, and had lost as often as I'd won. As far as I could tell, Mana didn't suspect my true intentions. She went on a lot of first dates, and few seconds. As soon as the guys realized that she expected them to match wits with her before she'd even consider taking it farther, most never called again, and she was fine with that. So was I. I worried that I might have played the friendship angle a little too well, and become locked into that status. Maybe it was time to do something about that. But now I was going to miss the social window, the crucial few minutes before lecture when everyone found their seats and made their connections.

Breakfast could wait; coffee could not. I nuked the thick stuff still sitting in the pot, spiked it with cream before slipping into my jacket and out the door. I had settled off campus after a less-than-satisfactory first term in the dorms. The never-ending party that was campus life had not been conducive to serious study. I shared a spacious rental house with three other guys who were hardly ever there. This was a blessing. Most days I enjoyed the drive, a mind-calming jaunt through a shadowed glade and along the edge of a sandy-shored pond. Today it was just unwanted minutes. I accelerated, dropping it into fourth as I entered the winding stretch of road that passed through the shadow of the granite bluff called "God's Forehead". The landscape permitted only a truncated view of the road ahead, but the Jeep knew the way. Another quarter mile, and the road would level out, dip under an old railroad bridge, and resume an easterly course toward the University.

Lances of golden sunlight had begun to penetrate the thickness of forest, treetops stark against a copper sky. The dream! It was the same sky I had seen in my dream, triggering a recollection of other details. In the dream, I had been driving on this same road, or one very much like it. But instead of going under the tracks, the bridge had taken me over them. On the other side, the pavement had become cracked and pitted, with tufts of long yellow grass poking through in places. The farther I progressed, the more the state of the road deteriorated, until the Jeep could no longer manage the terrain, and I was forced to proceed on foot. Navigating the uneven ground, I traveled for some time with eyes downcast, until a huff of exhaled breath brought my eyes back to the fore.

There was something in the road. It was a massive, many-pointed thing, silhouetted in golden light. As my eyes adjusted to the glare, I could see that it was some kind of creature, though not like any I

3

had seen before. It was a deer, or something of that nature, but essentially different. It had six legs: four long, delicate forelegs and two heavily-muscled hind legs. It was easily ten feet high at the shoulder, and it held its enormous head well above that. Its antlers branched, and branched again, and again, more like the branches of a tree than anything animal. And they were translucent, capturing and holding the early morning light in a luminous halo about the beast's head. It was entirely white, like new snow, save for four enormous eyes of liquid gold. It was watching me. There came a sound like an old air-raid siren. The creature had thrown back its head, and the noise was issuing from that great, arching throat. It lasted forever. Then the thing was across the road and gone, into the trees.

Were dreams really supposed to mean something, to provide a key to some unresolved conflict in the psyche? The deer was my father, looking at me with censure, the four eyes implying double the disappointment. I laughed at my own pathetic attempt at Freudian analysis. Or the deer could have been Mana, representing all that is beautiful, mysterious, elusive…and perhaps unattainable. Then again, maybe the meaning lay in the numbers: four eyes, six legs, infinite branches; something about my limitless potential? Psychobabble and nonsense. Dreams don't mean anything, I decided. Or they mean whatever you want them to mean. Then I saw another angle. It wasn't about the animal; it was about the bridge, the first departure from the familiar, from the world as I knew it. Every day you take the same path. What if, one day, you took a different one? A bridge over instead of under, down instead of up, right instead of left? Could that change everything? Could you ever go back? Would you want to?

That was it: a different path. I was going to take a leap. I was going to talk to Mana, ask her out. It wasn't quite that simple, of course. But I knew the words would come, as they always did. I'd say that the idea came to me uninvited, when I was thinking about how much fun we always have together. I'd tell her that it

4

surprised me too at first, but when I thought about it, it just felt so right. I'd assure her that it could never jeopardize our friendship, only make it better. And of course, that we owed it to ourselves to find out if there might be something there, and would regret it forever if we didn't try. OK, I'd drop the "forever" part, too melodramatic. But the rest of the pieces were there. What happened today *would* change the dynamic of our relationship forever – for better or worse. I was feeling my nerves, to be sure; but I was also exhilarated. My dream had emboldened me to do something I had wanted to do for a long time. And even if it backfired, it would be better to know than to cling to a hope that was ultimately false. Wouldn't it? I crossed the bridge without even noticing.

2

Arriving on campus, I parked as close to the philosophy building as I dared. I jogged across the lawn, clearing the steps two at a time. I was only a few minutes late when I arrived at the lecture hall, but I paused at the door, edging it open just a crack, enough to see that class was already underway. I waited. A notice board across the hall was plastered with several brightly-colored fliers announcing one of Maitland's pay-per-view lectures. It was entitled, "God's Mistakes: How irregularities in the fabric of the universe argue against cosmic intelligence". No bias there.

When I heard one of the students ask a question, I made my move, slipping through the door and melting into the nearest empty seat, next to an older Asian guy named Hyung who always took notes on his laptop. I hoped the constant tapping would mask the sounds of my entry. Professor Maitland was responding to the question. "So you would say we can't know *anything* unless it is divinely revealed?"

"Yes, because otherwise knowledge would be subjective, and what you know may not be the same as what I know." The questioner was revealed to be a bespectacled young lady with a long braid of mousy brown hair. I had never noticed her before.

Maitland answered with his customary snark. "Then, my dear, you would be wrong, wouldn't you?" This earned an approving laugh from his fan club in the first couple of rows. The professor waited a few seconds for the buzz to subside, then added, "There is of course another possibility…"

The young woman stood defiant, refusing to dignify the professor's comment with a response. He continued. "As I see it, one can grovel and beg for whatever scraps may fall from the gods' table, or…" He clutched the edges of the podium with both hands and cast his gaze around the room. "...he can climb up there and take it for himself, just as the great ones did eons ago."

Instantly, the room was abuzz with whispered conversations. "Take it...," the girl echoed, incredulous, "from the gods? You mean literally?"

"What is a god?" asked Maitland. "Who is a god?" He glanced around the room, perhaps hoping someone would be foolish enough to attempt an answer. "A god," he said, "is simply one who has the will, and the ability, to rise above. The rest are destined to be worshippers, followers...*slaves*."

The questioner was undeterred. "Some say we are all gods," she said.

"And some say we are all winners," Maitland said. "But it is a poor kind of victory that is shared by all. Likewise, godhood that is common to all is of little value. Uniqueness is an essential quality of deity. Consider the Olympians. Of what advantage is the ability to hurl thunderbolts if your siblings are invulnerable?"

I should have held my tongue. Instead I heard myself say, "And what good are siblings, when you could have a few more slaves?"

Maitland smirked. If he was ruffled by my comment, he didn't show it. "As it happens, I have been given students rather than slaves. And the only god-like power I wield is over your grades." A subdued chuckle. "Oh, and the next time you decide to come to my class late, Mayer, please close the door behind you." This yielded a collective "ooh" from the class, as heads turned to see who had just been humiliated. "We'll pick this discussion up tomorrow," he said. "Remember to bring the abstracts for your research papers." He collected his notes and slipped out the back, brushing off the three or four students hoping for an audience with him.

Through the deluge of bodies pressing for the door I spotted Mana. She was still sitting, surrounded by some of her most trusted girlfriends. They appeared to be discussing a text Mana had received. Breaching the perimeter would be no easy task. I had to formulate a strategy, time it perfectly, and…oh, what the heck. "Mana!" I said. One of the girls stepped aside; the rest just turned to look at me with mild amusement. Change of plans. "Got a minute?" I asked.

Mana pocketed her phone, excused herself from the circle of trust. "Sure, Justin," she said.

"Walk with me," I said. Her eyes searched mine for some clue to my intentions, but she smiled and came along. The hallway was bustling with students, too noisy. I led her to the stairwell at the end of the hall, then down the stairs. The basement of the building housed the faculty offices; nobody would bother us there. Halfway down the hall there was a small lounge area off to one side consisting of a couple of chairs and a table scattered with outdated magazines. That was where I led her.

Mana was beginning to look concerned. "Justin, what's going on?" she asked.

"Look, I'm really sorry for being so cryptic, Mana," I said. "I just needed to talk to you alone for a minute."

"OK," she said, still uncertain.

"Can we sit?" I asked, indicating the chairs. She complied. I took the other chair, drew a slow breath. "Mana, we've been friends since first year, right?"

"Yeah," she said. "Ever since I first mopped the racquetball court with your sorry butt." She was obviously trying to break the tension. But was she also trying to remind me of the strictly casual nature of our relationship?

I allowed myself to smile. "Since then," I said. I reached out and rearranged a couple of the magazines on the table. "Mana, that's what I'm trying to say. You have a great sense of humor. I love that we can talk trash with each other like that. I would never want to do anything to jeopardize that."

"Justin," she started. I could see from her body language that she was growing uncomfortable. "Before you say any more, I need to..."

"*You old fool! How dare you presume to tell me...*" It was a shout, from somewhere down the hall. We gaped at each other for half a second, then Mana rose and gestured for me to follow, taking cautious steps. As we approached a darkly stained wooden door the voices resumed, animated but not quite so loud. These were the faculty offices. The brass plate on the door was engraved with the name, "Simon Maitland, PhD".

"...the Board's decision, ultimately," a second voice was saying. "They had proposed an administrative review, in response to some of the liberties you've been taking with the curriculum, but..."

"*Liberties!*" The tone was elevated again. It was definitely Maitland. "That curriculum hasn't been revised in over a decade. The 'liberties' I've taken are the only parts of the program that actually reflect current scholarship!"

"Current scholarship, Dr. Maitland, or your own ideas?" said the other voice.

"Have you taken the time to crack open a journal in the last few years, Rackliff?" Maitland asked. That had to be Bruce Rackliff,

9

Dean of the College of Sciences. "The two are pretty much synonymous."

"Really? One of the other faculty members overheard you saying that Plato and Aristotle aren't even worth reading. It's a philosophy department, Professor!"

"What do you know about philosophy?" asked Maitland. "This department is just rehashing the dead ideas of dead men. I could breathe new life into this school, if you and the Board would stop blocking me at every turn."

"I don't appreciate your tone, Simon," said the Dean. "Given the serious nature of these concerns, I might have expected a more contrite response."

"You mean boot-licking, Dean," said Maitland. "You won't get that from me."

"No matter. In light of these facts I'm afraid I'm going to have to recommend an administrative leave. You can call it a sabbatical."

"*Sabbatical?* You can keep your pity, Rackliff. And you can *get out of my office!*" These last words were laced with menace. I knew the Dean would be exiting presently, and I knew we did not want to be seen to have been eavesdropping. I grabbed Mana's hand and strode briskly toward the nook where we had begun to talk. Just in time, as it happened. Dean Rackliff emerged from the office just as we rounded the corner, and mercifully turned the opposite way, toward the nearer stairwell.

We waited until he had cleared the landing, then followed. We were directly in front of Maitland's office when we heard a click, and the scrape of old wood swollen by time. I hesitated. Mana bolted past, bounded up the stairs and out of sight. Too late for me to do the same, I spun and raced back down the hall, hoping

10

against hope that he would spend some amount of time fumbling with keys, that he would turn the other way. "Mayer?" I heard. I saw a faculty washroom, ducked inside. "*Mayer!*" Curses. Positive identification. He would know that I had heard something. He would make me suffer. There was a lock on the inside of the door. I turned it, heard the clunk of the bolt sliding into place. It might not be safe to go out, but at least he couldn't get in. I'd just wait him out, and eventually... What? He'd stop pacing in front of the door and go in search of easier prey? This was ridiculous. I wasn't going to hide out in the bathroom. Maitland was just a man, and from the sounds of his meeting with the Dean, I wouldn't have to worry about him for a few weeks anyway.

I reached for the lock. The lights flickered. I turned the knob, and heard it click. Another flicker, and then the lights went out entirely. There was no window, the room was completely dark. The power must have been out in the hallway as well, because I couldn't detect even a sliver of light around the edges of the door. I had seen that the door had a large lever style handle, it wouldn't be hard to find. I reached for the handle, but it wasn't where it should have been. Perhaps in the darkness I had taken a step back. I reached further, but encountered nothing. Palms forward now, I advanced a step at a time – three, four, five steps – and still nothing. Panic was beginning to set in. I took one big, lurching step forward, and saw a flash of white light in the darkness as my head met with unyielding stone. The world began to spin, a feeling made worse by the total lack of visual cues. Tumbling, falling, my head met stone a second time, and I slept.

Had I imagined it? I would have thought so, were it not for the unfamiliarity of my waking surroundings. Not just unfamiliar, but in fact quite unpleasant. As I gradually regained the use of my senses, I felt overwhelmingly cold, and realized I was lying naked on damp stone. There was an odor of mildew and urine that caused me to gag as I inhaled deeply. I was unable to determine if my eyesight was impaired, or if there was simply no light in this place. I started to turn in an attempt to raise myself from the cold floor, and felt an intense, throbbing pain in my head, and aches all over. Gritting my teeth against the pain, I forced myself onto my side and managed to get my right arm underneath me. I rose onto hands and knees, then to a seated position. The throb in my head intensified briefly, resisting the change to a vertical posture. I held steady until the pain subsided somewhat, then attempted to stand. I held a hand over my head as I rose, unsure of the dimensions of my current abode. I inched forward, shuffling my feet so I wouldn't encounter any unexpected obstruction and topple in the dark. But the floor appeared to be composed of fairly level cobbling, and the only thing I felt was a wall a few feet forward. A memory was triggered. Maitland…the washroom; what had really happened? I planted both hands on the wall, slid them upward as far as I could – no ceiling that I could reach. I worked my way along the wall to my left, discovered a corner, then an adjacent wall. The stones here were moist and slippery – some sort of fungal growth? Bringing my fingertips near to my nose there could be no doubt: blood. Fresh, not coagulated. I touched my forehead with my other hand and felt, along with the resurging pain, the same moist stickiness. My blood on the wall? Maybe. Probably.

Continuing my exploration of the wall, I came to a line of division. To the left of the line what felt like cold steel, heavily corroded but solid. Sliding my hands up and down along the edge,

13

I found no hinges. I began to slide my hands in large circles over the surface, and found no handle or latch. What I did find, just below eye level, was a narrow, rectangular slit, apparently open and unobstructed. I strained to detect any distant light source through that opening, but saw nothing but the all-consuming blackness. I focused my hearing, but no sound met my ear. Everything about my surroundings suggested a cell of some sort, but there were no clanking chains, no scurrying rodents, no flickering torches – nothing that my lifetime of movie-watching had led me to expect from a proper dungeon. Then, suddenly I did feel something. I felt a warm breath on my ear, accompanied by the unmistakable scent of freshly baked bread. The breath was followed by a sharp, audible inhalation, still inches from my ear.

"Who's there?", I demanded. "Is someone there?"

…Silence…

"Please! I don't know what's going on. I don't know where I am. Won't you…"

"Wait!" A whispered command.

I waited. Before long, muffled footsteps. Not just beyond the door, but close. The sound stopped for a moment, then resumed, receding slowly over a span of seconds that seemed like hours. I wanted to ask again, but heeded the voice that had spoken and kept silent.

"We must move now." A dull clunk, then I felt the door receding from my hands. "Put this on." Something soft was thrown over my shoulders; I felt my way into sleeves and found a belt at the waist – a robe of some sort, a welcome defense against the cold. Something warm was pressed into my hand. "I've brought bread. Eat it quickly."

I didn't need to be told twice. Suddenly aware of a gnawing hunger that had seemed secondary to the pain in my head, I tore into the tough, small loaf. I wasn't about to complain about the texture. "Who are you? What is this place?"

"Not yet."

I had to blink as a blade of light defined the edge of another door. I could see now that the reason I had seen no light was this airtight outer door. It too locked from the outside. That made sense if this was indeed a prison; in the event that the inner door were compromised, the captive would make it no farther. Normally, there would be another guard on the outside door, with a separate key. But it appeared that protocol was not being followed in this case.

As my eyes adjusted, I could make out a dim silhouette of my savior. It was a woman, or more properly a girl, fully two heads shorter than I and dressed...well, not as I expected. In keeping with the dungeon theme, I'd have thought to find her in the simple frock of a scullery maid or serving wench. Instead, she wore faded jeans and a torn, filthy hooded sweatshirt. She had long, wispy, dirty-blond hair, brown eyes, and slightly chubby cheeks. There was something vaguely familiar about her, though I couldn't place it. She took me by the hand and coaxed me into the candle-lit passageway. She pushed the door closed behind us, then led me around a corner where I saw four more doors like the last. The first on the right was ajar, and she guided me toward it. When we entered, she pulled the outer door to within a couple inches of closing, but left it that way.

"A little information, please?" I said.

"Not yet. Quiet."

15

"Please!" I said. "I don't know what's going on! Who are you, at least?"

A slow, irritated sigh…

"OK," she said, "but we don't have much time. My name is Maaike. I'm not important. You are. You've been a captive of lord Magus. Sorry, 'Magus'. I heard them say they just found you in the cell one morning. I don't know why you're alive, and they seem as shocked as I was. I think they are unsure what to do with you, but whatever they decide, it won't be good. We have to go now! A reconnaissance party is waiting to meet us, if I can get you to the east gate. But the sun's nearly up."

"Wait, Maaike, who is Magus? Why am I so important? And why does everyone seem to think I'm supposed to be dead?"

She stared at me for a moment, clearly perplexed. "You…don't remember anything? OK, look, it's not my place to give you those answers. The time will come. But right now, there's *really* no time for this."

"What's going on?!?" We both froze. A third voice, but not from the hallway. It came from the cell at our backs.

Maaike answered. "Nothing! Be quiet, you'll alert the guards."

"Guards? Who are you then? Oh my God, this is an escape! You're taking me with you!"

"No! I mean, we can't, not now. I'll come for you another time."

"No, you'll take me now, or *I'll* alert the guards!"

Another sigh. "Fine. All right. Just be quiet!" Maaike nimbly unlocked the cell. A gaunt man with a sparse goatee joined our

16

party. He was dressed in brown corduroys and a striped jersey. He looked older than he probably was.

"OK, let's go. Be advised, we actually have to pass *through* the lord's chambers in order to get out. I drugged the dogs, but he will still be in there. It's the only part of the plan that is subject to chance. We'll just have to be swift, silent, and hope he's preoccupied."

"Not exactly a fool-proof escape plan, huh?" That from our uninvited guest.

"Yeah, well I didn't exactly have a lot of time to plan. Nobody foresaw this." I wasn't sure what she was referring to, but opted not to further stall the operation.

We turned another corner, and Maaike listened against a heavy-looking wooden door. After a pause, she unlocked it and we proceeded past it, up a short flight of concrete steps, through another door, and into a maroon-carpeted hallway. I heard footsteps. Maaike turned white. She pushed us back through the door and closed it, remaining on the other side. There was silence for a few seconds, then the rumble of a man's voice. It was followed by a female voice; it sounded like Maaike. The man spoke again, and Maaike apparently responded. Then a long pause...

The male voice again. Then light footsteps, receding. Oh no! Maaike had been sent away. I hadn't heard the heavier tread – was he still there? There was silence for a long time. My companion started to say something, but I silenced him with a quick hand. Then the worst thing I had imagined - the rattle of the latch. He was about to descend into the dungeon! I thought of running to the nearest open cell, but knew we'd never make it, would be heard if we did. Then the rattling stopped as quickly as it had started. It seemed he had changed his mind. The next sound was that of heavy footsteps, mercifully receding.

We waited. I had to shush my tag-along once more, but nothing else happened. Maaike didn't come back. But neither did the guard. After a time I made a choice. I cracked open the door. The hallway ran straight ahead, and straight to the right. It appeared to skirt a columned central area. There were no walls on that side, only scarlet curtains that ran floor to ceiling between the columns. There were doors at the ends of the hallway in each direction, but instead I ducked through a gap in the curtain. This appeared to be a sort of lounge, with a bar on one wall and several couches covered with an obscene number of gold-embroidered pillows. There was a full wall on one side, hung with photos of idyllic landscapes, impossibly green and inviting. Adjacent to that wall, another partial wall was interrupted by an arched door. I peeked around the edge of the doorway, and saw a wider hall leading into a similar, but larger, lounge. I motioned my new friend forward.

In the bigger lounge three beasts lay on the floor. I took these to be the "dogs" Maaike had referred to, though they looked like no species I had ever seen. For one thing they were absurdly massive. Lying on their sides as they were, their rib cages rose to the height of my knees at least. They also had a grotesquely exaggerated underbite, which housed four tusk-like canines that the mouth could not contain. They looked to be sleeping, but I knew better. And I was grateful. At one side of this lounge was a big set of double doors. They were not shut completely. I approached them, and as I drew near, I heard the male voice we had heard through the door earlier. I could make out the words of a conversation, and when the other party responded, I was sure it was not a human voice I heard. That wasn't what really caught my attention, though. The man's voice...I knew it, had heard it before somewhere...recently. I tried to listen closer.

"But how is this possible? I watched him die!"

You watched someone die, not him.

"How can this be? I know that face. It has haunted my dreams for three years now."

The face is the same. The man is not. Tal-Makai is dead. Truly do you say you watched him die.

"I don't understand."

Then I shall try to explain it in terms you will understand. Do you know of genetics?

"I have read of the matter."

Strands of DNA, like the coils of a serpent, define each of your traits. Normally, each strand defines its own trait.

"Yes, I understand the concept, but…"

But occasionally, a piece of one strand is exchanged with a piece of another. The results can dramatically alter the resultant organism.

"Are you suggesting that Tal was altered in this way?"

Try to stay with me, mortal…we are talking about worlds. Worlds are like this – disparate strands that are not supposed to cross. But rarely, there is a crossing, an exchange in the substance of reality itself.

Silence…a blank stare…

This is what must have occurred. Tal-Makai is dead in this world. But there has been an intersection of worlds. The Tal-Makai of that other world has come to us. There is no reason for it. It was not anticipated, much less

19

planned. Let's just say the Deity has made a mistake. The only question is, what do we do about it?

"I thought it would be over when I killed him. Even without this, his death has only served to increase his legacy. 'Martyr', they call him. Like it's a badge of honor! He died, I prevailed, and somehow he is the victor! Smirking at me from beyond the grave. Gods! What should I do?"

Tell me what you see as the options.

"I could reveal him to the resistance. Use him to demand their surrender."

But to show what would seem to them a living Tal-Makai…to their simple minds it would seem a resurrection from the dead. It wouldn't matter if you killed him again, the fools would find hope in it; they would wait forever for another resurrection, fighting all the while.

"Indeed. Then it would be no better to stage a public execution. There can be no advantage to retaining him alive. Here is the situation as I see it: the Deity has made a mistake. It falls to me to correct it."

Like lichen creeping over a stone, it dawned on me that I was the object of consideration. I took action. Grabbing my companion (I would have to remember to ask his name when time was not such a key factor), I ran back into the previous chamber, and dived behind one of the larger couches. I heard the fall of heavy feet behind us, but he didn't seem to have detected our presence. I could see his black boots as he passed beyond our chosen hiding spot, and my eyes panned to his face. It was only the briefest of glimpses, but there was little doubt. The voice, the smug look….it was Maitland. He headed for the door to the dungeon. A dungeon he would soon be finding disappointingly empty.

"We need to run."

As soon as we heard the door clamp shut behind him, I edged toward the door at one end of the hallway we first emerged into. I tried it, and found it unlocked. As I pushed it open I encountered some resistance, and discovered why; Maaike was standing on the other side. Clearly relieved, she said, "Oh, thank Chaer-Ul! Come on!" There was another hallway leading to the right, and a high-ceilinged room with big bay windows to the left. That was the way we took. I could see some leafless treetops from the windows, and I drew closer. I was able to see a portion of the building we were in. Not a castle or fortress, it had paned glass windows and a peaked slate roof. The structure itself was constructed of stone. In the front I could make out fragments of asphalt amidst the yellow-brown grass that could have been the remains of an old driveway. It looked like the private mansion once belonging to someone of means, long since neglected. Two guards wearing what looked like mechanics' jumpsuits conferred near a broken stone wall about fifty paces south of the building. They appeared to have swords at their belts.

Maaike took my hand, leading us through another door to the top of a carpeted staircase. Without a sound, she reached a hand behind her to stay us, and we watched as another guard paced slowly to the right on the floor below. We waited until he passed out of view, and a few seconds longer, then Maaike said, "Let's go." We descended the stairs with a few quick steps, turned to the left, and started toward a windowed door. Before we had gone more than a few paces, we heard a shout from above. Turning, we saw the guard we had so cleverly evaded emerge from around a corner and start to run our way. Other guards were flying down the stairs, barely touching the ground, shouting commands. Without a word, we turned again and ran for the door. Maaike didn't bother to fumble for her keys, but met the door with a well-aimed kick without breaking stride. The latch shattered and the door swung wildly on one intact hinge. We burst through and ran

21

straight ahead, toward a stone gate about a hundred paces away. There was a guard between us and the gate, already drawing his sword and readying himself for our arrival. We were unarmed.

Maaike didn't slow her pace. As we ran, she began to speak in short, calculated phrases between gulped breaths: "Beyond the gate…the hill rises…beyond the hill…a party awaits…whatever happens…meet the party….don't stop…don't slow. You must live!" By that point we were a mere ten paces from the gate, and the guard. He held a wide stance, hilt of his blade planted at his hip, tip pointing at us. Before I knew what was happening, Maaike threw herself onto his blade. I saw it emerge from her back, just under her ribs. She wrapped her arms around the guard and pulled him close, receiving the blade fully, and clung to him, unrelenting in her death embrace. She never made a sound. I tried to scream, but no sound emerged from my constricted throat. I stumbled but didn't fall. I remembered her words; I would not let her die in vain. Grasping my companion's sleeve, I mounted the base of the hill. I never looked back. My eyes tried to well, but I fought it, ran harder. Seconds seemed to drag into minutes, until finally, we crested the hill. There, I could see something.

A small group of people stood around a vehicle, an SUV. Dilapidated and many times patched, I was a little surprised when it started. There were three men and a woman. I saw the woman's eyes scanning the hilltop, possibly for pursuers. They ushered us quickly into the back of the vehicle, the men staring at me as if in disbelief. "Maaike …," I started, but one of them, a young, bearded man with dark, curly hair, silenced me with a gesture. "She would have come if she could," he said. "I know what she must have done." At this the woman began to sob bitterly. Then I remembered where I had seen her face before. Add a pair of glasses, a different hairstyle, and she would have looked just like the girl who had challenged Maitland in class. That unhuman voice had spoken of parallel worlds and alter egos; maybe Maaike

22

had been a doppelganger of that girl. I guess she was destined to be brave in any world. My accomplice spoke after a time, extending a hand, "I'm Jeyt."

4

We rode through a dead wood, following a rut that might once have been a road. I had so many questions, but my mind was swimming with the whirlwind of events that had led me to this point, and I couldn't manage to formulate a coherent thought. I suppose I had also lost a fair amount of blood during my imprisonment. Consciousness came and went as it pleased. I saw glimpses of trees, outcroppings of stone, flashes of yellow sunlight. At one point I felt we had stopped, and I tried to look around. We were at an abandoned gas station. Two of the men from our party were bending back some saplings that had erupted through the concrete platform and claimed the pumps. After some investigation it became apparent that the pumps were dry. A pack of crows laughed at us from the roof of the former cash booth. The few vehicles scattered around the lot were in far worse shape than our own, seeming to be made of paper-thin sheets of rust that were perforated in numerous spots, rubber tires almost completely disintegrated. Across the road the remains of two massive oil tanks resembled a pair of beached whales, forever trapped on this sealess strand.

We resumed our progress, and I fought to remain aware. The land descended as we went, our road passing between steep gravel slopes. To the left of the road I spotted a trickle. I didn't notice when it had started, but it grew as we descended to a respectable stream, always following the road. Its water appeared to be clear, perhaps drinkable. I craved it. I asked our female passenger if we could stop, and she reached behind her seat, handing me a liter bottle of dirty-looking water.

"But...", I gestured toward the crystal stream at the roadside.

"This is better. You'll see soon."

We started to slow down, and I looked at the road ahead. The stream, small though it was, had decided to cross the road at last, had been doing so for some time. In the process it had eroded away a big chunk of our road. The neat slice passed completely through the road from left to right and rendered continued passage impossible. Thankfully there was a broad, sloping shoulder off to the right that merged seamlessly with the streambed. We pulled off and began to follow the stream as it had followed us previously. The trees grew more dense as we rode, and after traveling thus for a couple of miles, the stream arced to the left. As we rounded the bend, the trees separated and the sand of the streambed was replaced by gravel as we emerged into a clearing where the water pooled into a shallow pond. On the far shore, roughly fifty yards away, were a series of lumpy, white forms. The vehicle stopped, and the bearded man handed me a pair of binoculars. I focused on the white shapes, and gasped. Four great white deer – just like the one in my dream – lay decomposing by the pool. The woman spoke.

"Magus poisoned all the running water in this area, knowing our camps would draw from it. We lost a number of good people before we realized it. Our secondary water sources are not as clear, but are not tainted, at least not yet."

An older man with uncontrolled salt-and-pepper sideburns and a green vest spoke up. "You met him – Magus – didn't you? Did he say anything…uh…useful?"

"Now is not the time, Denkel," said the bearded man. "When we are safely within the camp…"

The woman spoke up. "Safe! The only safety is on the move. Do you think he is not tracking us already? We won't be able to keep camp here beyond this night."

"I think not," replied the bearded man. "This was already a stretch for Magus; I've never seen him stray so far from the city. No doubt *you* were the reason for his excursion." He was pointing at me.

"And we were lucky for that, Jager. We wouldn't have stood a chance of recovering him if Magus had held him in his stronghold. Chances are, he hadn't held him for long when we received word. He was probably still trying to decide how best to kill him."

"I think you're right about that," I chimed in. "I overheard him talking to someone about the very matter."

"Apologies," said the woman. "We've been talking over you as though you were not here. I'm Kaire." She extended a hand. "This is Jager, Denkel, and that's Tryst at the wheel." He waved over his shoulder with a wink in the rearview mirror. "And I believe you've met Jeyt." The thin ex-con nodded in my direction. "Jeyt," said Kaire, "I was glad to see you. We were coming for you next."

"Of course you were. I was actually a little annoyed that my stay was cut short….was really starting to acquire a taste for the rat."

"Haven't lost that sense of humor, I see."

We rode on beyond the clearing. We reentered some woods, but only for a short time before it opened again, this time revealing a golden field. Here we made our own road, veering to the left and heading for what appeared to be an impenetrable tangle of undergrowth. I looked behind us, and saw that the yellow grass was not matted by our passing, but sprang back to its original height with remarkable resilience. We pulled up before the undergrowth, and stopped. Kaire and Jager jumped out, grabbed handfuls of shrubbery and began pulling. It swung open like a gate, and Tryst wasted no time driving through. Closing the way

26

behind us, Kaire and Jager rejoined us. Our drive proceeded now through a much thicker wood, mostly of towering pines and smaller evergreens. They were the first plant life I had seen thus far that was not yellow. We rode in a deep trench that rarely deviated from a straight course for several miles. Then I felt us start to slow. I looked to the road ahead, and saw two armed guards, one on each side of the road, before an arch made of twisted vines. I stiffened, but Kaire laid a hand on my shoulder.

"Peace, these belong to us."

The guards waved us past, smiling broadly, straining to catch a glimpse of something as we passed. As we continued to drive slowly beyond the gate, several young boys and girls emerged from the trees at either side and ran alongside our vehicle, shouting, "Martyr! Martyr!" Then among the trees tents started to appear, and campfires. The intoxicating scent of roasting meat reached my nostrils. Small groups of people stood here and there in groups of two or three or four, staring at us, then turning inward upon themselves and muttering excitedly. So obvious and so unanimous was this response, that a wave of excitement could be observed passing from one cluster to the next, on both sides, following us as we rode by.

"They're really glad you made it back," I said.

"What you're seeing isn't for us," Kaire answered. "It's for you."

"Yeah...I've been meaning to ask about that. What's all this "martyr" business? Who do these people think I am?"

"I think it best we leave that discussion to the Commander."

"You understand I'm *not* who they think I am, don't you?"

"I understand you don't think you are. I don't know what to think just yet. But I must ask you, for the sake of all of us…"

"Ask me what?"

"To let them think what they will think…at least for now. You don't have to lie. Just don't deny anything. Can you do that? Will you?"

"Look, I'm pretty sure I wouldn't be having this conversation if you guys hadn't rescued me. I'll do whatever you think is best."

"Thank you. Really. It will mean so much to them. And who knows, maybe they're not wrong." I raised an eyebrow at that, but said nothing more.

"In case it comes up, there's a name you may hear, the name of the one they think you are."

"Tal-Makai," I said.

"Yes. How did you…"

I simply smiled. It occurred to me that in spite of being indebted to these people, I really didn't know any of them. And it might just work in my favor to play along, at least until I had a better idea who I could trust.

At last we pulled up before a circle of larger tents, and Denkel motioned for me to get out. He and Tryst led me to a folding chair before one of the tents, while Jager and Kaire remained at the vehicle, conversing. Shortly two young girls arrived and furnished me with a tray containing cuts of roasted flesh and a pitcher of beer. They giggled and twittered, then backed away without removing their gaze from me, turned and skipped off whispering to each other. I didn't dwell on that, but immediately tore into the meat, washing it down with greedy gulps of beer. I nearly spilled the pitcher when another girl, without warning, began to clean my head-wound by dabbing at it with a moist cloth, then applied a salve and wrapped my head with bandages. I had to push it off my eyes so I could see to continue my feast. Another appeared and asked if I had any other wounds; still another whether my pitcher needed refreshing. Just then Kaire emerged from the trees at my back and sent the girls away.

"I'm sorry for leaving you alone like that. They mean well."

"It wasn't a problem, really. It's not every day I'm treated like a returning hero."

"The Commander will be anxious to speak with you, but has not yet returned from the field. I would suggest you get some rest; you may use the tent behind you if you like. A pair of guards will be stationed at your door, just notify them if you have need of anything."

"I will, thank you."

Kaire walked back in the direction from which she had come. I polished off the rest of my meat and ale, and set the tray on the ground. A heretofore unseen girl scurried up and removed it with a smile. I rose, and was surprised to not feel the now familiar throb in my head. Maybe that was a pretty good salve they had, or maybe it was the beer. What I did feel was exhaustion. I dragged myself through the doorway of the tent behind me and collapsed on the blankets laid there for me.

I slept an uneasy sleep, aware of an increasing bustle outside my tent, whispers growing to an excited hum of voices. I tried to sink back into unconsciousness, was successful for a time, but ultimately found myself focusing on the sounds, attempting to separate individual voices. Aware of a presence, I cracked open

29

my eyes and scanned to the tent flap, where a face stood silhouetted against the brightness outside. Seeing me stir, the figure spoke.

"Sir, the Commander has returned." It was one of the serving girls.

Someone had laid a pile of clothes near the doorway. Of course, I was still wearing the bathrobe Maaike had given me. Maaike …such a young girl, gave her life without a thought. I doubted I could ever do what she had done, to give so selflessly. Was there even any cause I believed in so strongly? I pulled on a pair of faded jeans and a coarse cotton shirt with a Nehru style collar. There was also a waist-length brown leather jacket and brown shoes. Everything fit perfectly.

I peeked out of the flap, and the guards stepped aside to allow me to emerge. Kaire approached me. "The clothes suit you well."

"Thanks. I was told the Commander was here?"

"Not here, yet. The party was spotted from one of our surveillance towers, and we were notified by a signal fire. They'll be arriving in the camp shortly. Come this way."

I followed her out of the small circle of tents and into the woods along a wide path, but not the one we had ridden in on. It seemed to be the general direction in which people were moving. About fifty paces ahead, three great forms rose slowly over a rise in the path. Three of those great white deer, each bearing a rider. The riders, and the beasts, were armored, but not in the finely crafted and detailed suits of legend. Their plates were makeshift creations, scraps of metal and plastic secured with pieces of cord. The riders themselves wore what looked like a collection of sporting pads, welders' gloves, and motorcycle helmets. The two riders at the sides carried long spears, and the central one had a great bow on his back. As they drew near, the other two held back while the archer approached us. I now understood the purpose of the stepped wooden structure at the roadside – a necessity for dismounting beasts of this size.

The rider walked right up to me, and I could see now that he was not as large or imposing as he had appeared on his mount. Unsure of the proper protocol, I extended a hand in a gesture of intended goodwill. The rider did not take my hand, but stood staring at me through mirrored glass for several seconds. Then he raised both hands to his head and slowly removed his helmet. Her helmet. It was Mana.

5

It was definitely Mana...those almond eyes were unmistakable. But something was different. Aside from the fact that she was filthy, her dark hair matted from her riding helmet, dried mud caked on her clothing. Aside from her well-tanned skin. She was older somehow, early-30's maybe. And perhaps it was my imagination, but she seemed...healthier, I guess. Stronger, more solid, and more filled-out. The Mana I knew was a wispier thing. This world suited her. I suppose I had known that Mana was of mixed ethnicity, but I was now a little ashamed to realize that I had no idea where her family was from. This Mana was truly exotic, her skin a palette of rich earth tones.

She stared at me for a long moment, as if searching for something. I thought I detected a hint of pain in her eyes before she blinked several times and turned away abruptly. At last she spoke, and as she started to stroll away, it was clear that I was meant to follow her.

"The clothes fit you well."

"Yes, thank you. And is it you I have to thank for the rescue as well?"

"No thanks are necessary. We could not have left you there. You cannot understand how important you are to the resistance." She stopped suddenly, turned to face me. This time her hand was extended. "I'm sorry. You just look so much like him. I'm Reya."

I took her hand. "I'm Justin. Unless there is another name I should answer to..."

"I have mixed feelings about that. I know the people want you to be Tal. But I think it best to be completely honest with them. With myself. You are not Tal-Makai."

I wanted to ask so many questions, and here at last was someone who might be able to tell me everything I needed to know. But this was clearly a touchy subject. I decided to steer toward somewhat safer waters. "Do you know why I am here?"

"Why? No. But I know there is a reason. In the morning, I will take you to a place that may hold some answers. I know it must be difficult, but I would ask you to keep your questions until then. There is much we do not know, either. Walk with me, please."

I followed her to where her mount remained standing. It lowered its head as Reya approached, massive yet somehow incredibly graceful, its many-pointed rack easily spanning 12 feet from side to side. It blinked its pupilless liquid gold eyes twice. Reya scratched under its white goatee and it emitted a soft humming sound. She then released latches on its saddle and bridle and let them fall to the ground. A young boy and girl scurried up and collected the items. "Thank you Bole, Breya." The children giggled and hurried off with the items. The humming continued, and after a moment I realized that Reya was matching the sound. Her voice trailed off, and the creature slowly raised its head again toward the treetops, appeared to steal one last glance at her, then turned and wandered off into the trees in a different direction from which it had come. The others followed suit as they were similarly relieved of their gear.

"They are not stabled?"

"There is no need. They will return when they are needed."

"But how?"

"Long ago, men like us came across animals that were sickly, or injured, and would have died without help. The men nursed and raised them, but did not keep them. The deer are very social creatures, and don't forget kindness. They don't forget wrongs, either. They know the difference between our troops and the enemy's. They are fierce and loyal allies."

I nodded. "I had a dream of one of these before I came to this world. They are unlike any animal where I come from."

"Truer than you know. They are no dumb beasts, but have other…gifts. Even we don't understand them fully, but are glad to consider them friends."

Another mystery. But not the one that concerned me most at the moment. I needed to understand what had happened, why I now found myself in this strange place. The key to that seemed to be the person, the legendary figure, known as Tal-Makai. And I had already been warned that that particular topic was not on the table just yet.

Reya now motioned for me to follow her, back toward the center of the camp. I fell in step beside her. Was Mana that tall? I found myself checking to see if she wore heels, but she did not, just flat canvas shoes cleft between the toes. I was reminded of the footwear I had seen ninja wear in old samurai films. No, her height seemed to be more a function of her stately posture and carriage. I could see in her every movement how these people could see her as a leader. My instinct told me to walk a step behind her, but I held my place at her side.

"I trust you made the acquaintance of your rescuers."

"Yes, I owe them a great debt."

"There is no man or woman here who would not gladly have taken their places. Here is another I would like you to meet."

An oddly-shaped woman approached us, round of body, thin of limbs. She wore a brown coverall, and her short, grey-brown hair was tucked under a dusty baseball cap. Her skin was red and weathered, a mask of creases stretched over her round face. Between those creases her eyes were warm and kind. "Good to see you up and about, sir. How's the head? Understand you took quite a blow to the coconut."

"Much better, thank you. I'm Justin."

This caused a row of new creases to form between the existing ones above her eyes, and a glance to be cast at Reya, who quickly filled the awkward pause, "Justin, this is Greda, one of my most trusted advisors."

Greda clasped my hand in her remarkably firm grip and smiled, which caused her face to be completely consumed in a sea of creases. Somehow, it was an endearing effect. Then, turning to Reya, she said, "Sir, there's something I think you should see."

"Show me." We followed Greda back into camp. Jager, Kaire, and Denkel were standing with a tall, gaunt man who leaned on a long rifle. They appeared to be standing over something, regarding it. A number of other people were milling about, trying to see what was the object of interest. I recognized Jeyt toward the back of the crowd and threw him a nod, which he returned. The circle parted as Reya drew near, and I followed her through the gap. There I beheld a beast, its side streaked with blood from a nasty-looking gash, apparently knife-inflicted. It was dead. Reya stood looking at it for a moment, then turned to me. "Have you seen a creature like this before?"

"Yes, in the place where I was held."

35

"It's not a natural thing. This can only have come from Magus."

Jager spoke up. "Then they know of this camp already. We have to move!"

"No," said the rifleman. "I was hunting some distance to the north and east when it found me. I was taking aim at some fowl and it rushed me from the right." He turned, indicating three neat scratches on his right cheek, too close to his eye. "They are searching, and they are getting closer by the day. We will have to move, but we have some time."

"Good. I'm taking Justin to the hollow in the morning. I'm anxious to learn what he will hear." There was a general buzz just then as all around people broke off into whispered conversation. I was pretty sure I heard the name, "Martyr" a couple more times. "In the meantime, we are alive another day. Eat well, make the acquaintance of our guest, show him how we celebrate. But keep your weapons and equipment at the ready, just in case."

They didn't need another cue. In moments, fires were struck, meat was roasting, and ale was being spilt freely. I met most everybody, eventually; the camp only consisted of about forty people, including children. I didn't remember many names, as most of them were unfamiliar spellings. By the end of the night, I had forgotten my own as well. There was music, from stringed and winded instruments, and dancing of a most vigorous variety. Jeyt pulled off some moves that would have impressed in any club back home, leaping and spinning around the high-licking fires. My head heavy, but no longer paining, I finally excused myself and retreated to my tent. I slept, and I dreamed.

In visions of the night, I found myself suspended. Not in the air, but in fluid. The womb. Warmth and comfort surrounded me. I didn't breathe; I didn't need to. I had no desire but to remain as I was, forever. Time passed, but I was unaware of its passage, or of its length. I could have been there mere seconds, or an age. Then a voice…

"Be born."

It came as a soft rumbling. It was not unkind, but I resisted. "I'm not ready."

The voice smiled. I don't know how I perceived this, as I saw nothing. It wasn't that I saw blackness, it was that sight was not part of the reality I now enjoyed.

"You will be."

Then I felt a breath. I suppose it was a stirring of the fluid that embraced me, but I knew it as a breath. I felt myself rising, and the fluid became thinner, cooler. After an indeterminate amount of time, my head broke the surface of the fluid and I continued to rise. The air was cool, but pleasantly so. It occurred to me to open my eyes. It was too bright at first, but gradually my eyes adapted. I was standing on the surface of the fluid for the briefest of moments, then I began to slowly sink into it. It reached to my waist, my chest, and then to my neck. At this point normal buoyancy took over, and I was floating in a crystal stream. I began to tread water. Looking around, I saw that I was closer to one shore. I made my way toward it. Upon reaching it, I pulled myself out onto the grassy bank. I was not tired. I stood.

The stream flowed in a more or less straight course for as far as I could see in either direction. The landscape was perfectly flat, all similarly covered in downy green grass. Green. Yes. The grasses of this world had not been green. I looked upstream (the water was flowing almost imperceptibly in one direction). As I looked, I saw a light under the water, a few dozen feet ahead. It grew in brightness, and the water there began to ripple. Then suddenly, like a soundless explosion, a geyser of water and light erupted vertically from the surface. It formed a pillar, then it divided. It branched, then branched again, and again, an infinite number of times. A tree of light took shape before my eyes. Like no natural tree, flawless in symmetry, the divisions continued, then began to slow. Already it was broader and taller than even the ancient redwoods back home. As the growth ceased, the branches revealed their final form: a perfect sphere. The entire tree glowed with an ethereal light, like a moon.

"Become."

I woke with that word still rumbling in my head. It had been more vivid, more real, than even the deer dream. And yet, unlike the other dream, I had known I was dreaming. I also knew it had meaning, but I didn't know what it meant. I was suddenly aware that it was still dark. And then I felt a breath in my hair. I tipped my still-groggy head back slowly, and saw a round, white face, and two dark eyes. As my own eyes focused in the dim light, it dawned on me that it was not a face at all, but the snout of one of those great deer. I gasped and instinctively sat up, unwittingly pressing my face for the briefest moment against that cool, wet nose. The beast snorted and exhaled again, feathering my hair for me as it removed its head from my tent. I heard a snicker, and crawled to the flap to peer out. Reya sat atop the mount, clearly pleased with herself.

"Climb up. We've a bit of a ride and not much time."

I withdrew into my tent and determined that I had slept in my clothes, shoes and all. I emerged and stood, looking up at Reya on her mount. I could see her clearly in what I now realized was bright moonlight. The creature kneeled. Reya extended a hand to me and to my surprise hoisted me in one smooth motion onto the back of the beast, behind her. "You'll want to hold on." I reached behind me with both hands and grabbed handfuls of the beast's

38

soft hair. Without waiting the animal righted itself, and I saw my legs fly up over my head as I was tossed backward. Then as quickly as I was thrown, I felt myself being righted. Reya's strong hand had seized my thigh and steadied me. "You'll want to hold on…to *me*." I felt myself flush, but she was only advising me of necessary riding protocol. I heard Reya hum. I wrapped my arms firmly around her waist just as the beast broke into a slow trot.

It was exhilarating; the cool moisture of the air against my face, the warmth of Reya's body as I pressed myself against her, the undulation of the creature's back beneath me. For such a large animal, the ride was surprisingly smooth; its muscular legs seemed to have remarkable shock-absorbing properties. I was initially uneasy, being up so high and moving so fast – faster now as the beast had steadily picked up speed as we began to clear the larger trees. But it moved with such grace and care, seemingly always aware of exactly where it was placing its feet so far below in the darkness. Reya hummed again and the mount increased its velocity further yet. The sensation was that of riding a living projectile. I now tucked my head behind Reya's shoulder, for fear that I would be dislodged or perforated by the impact of some alien version of a June-bug. With my head so protected, I was afforded a view to the south, and I was amazed at how fast the landscape flew past. In the moonlight I was able to make out the contours of valleys and mountains, forests and plains, all cast in shades of black and blue and grey.

I looked down momentarily and saw the blur of rapidly covered terrain; it made my head spin. Suddenly my stomach tightened and I felt a sense of weightlessness. There was a slice of a moment when all was silent. I thought I saw a flash of light and then it was gone, as the soft hoof beats and gravity returned. I righted myself and looked over my shoulder. Our ride had just cleared a wide stream in a single leap; the light I had seen must have been the reflection of the moon in its rippling surface. I vowed not to look down again, and then allowed myself to look at that moon. It was high in the sky, only slightly ahead of us, and appeared to be full. Time had passed, maybe twenty minutes from camp to the time we crossed the stream, and then fifteen or twenty more at full clip. This was truly an amazing species, with stamina to match its size. At last it began to slow, and we came into an area largely devoid of vegetation. The mount found it necessary to pick its way more carefully among sharp, irregular outcroppings of rock, which rose and fell, but the net effect was that of a gradual descent. It became apparent that we were descending one slope of a great valley, which continued to drop for maybe a half mile before rising toward its far brim. Casting my gaze to the north and south, it seemed to extend to either horizon. No water seemed to flow in this natural trough; whatever had carved it had done its work and found a different course, or dried up.

Near the bottom of the groove Reya guided our mount to the south, and I now saw that we traversed not a dried up riverbed, but a jagged fault line. It paced us off to the right as we continued to ride south for another couple of miles. There didn't seem to be any separation of earth, only a meeting of two plates: the healed scar of some ancient tectonic activity. Reya hummed one last directive to our mount and it stopped, folded its legs underneath itself and laid its head on the ground. Apparently the dismounting platforms back at base were a courtesy for these creatures rather than a necessity. Reya informed me that it was ok to release her waist and I flushed again as I did it, hoping the moon wasn't bright enough for her to notice my change in color, but knowing that it was. She climbed down and I followed suit. She took my hand and led me a few paces farther, where I could see the fault line did separate briefly, forming a roughly circular hole about six feet in diameter. I would have thought it a well if not for its peculiar location.

"Here we are."

I looked at Reya with raised eyebrows. "You can't mean that we are going down there?"

"Not 'we', 'you'."

Reya stood looking at me expectantly and offered no further advice.

"What is this place?"

"We call it the hollow," she replied. "It's a place of understanding." As if that clarified things. If there were something I was supposed to understand here, I had missed it. But as I saw no reason why these people would have rescued me at great risk to themselves only to drop me into a hole in the wilderness, I decided not to probe further.

"Do you have any supplies? A rope or harness of some kind? A flashlight, perhaps?"

"You won't need it. Trust – that you will need."

That was about the only thing I had to offer. "Of course I trust you," I said. "But what do I do?"

"Just step into the opening. You won't be harmed. And then wait. And listen." I looked briefly to her mount, which cocked its enormous head to one side and snorted as if to say, "What part of this is difficult for you?" And then I approached the edge of the hole. I expected something – a musty smell wafting from below, a sound as the dust from the edge struck a distant bottom, I don't know just what – but it was just a hole, black and entirely mysterious. I wanted to look back over my shoulder, but knew Reya, and possibly the animal, would just nod encouragement. So I stepped out into the middle of the hole.

I fell quickly at first, but soon felt as though my descent were slowing. I wondered briefly how I could determine this in the absence of sight, then realized that I could, in fact, vaguely make out the walls of the column through which I passed. And they became clearer the deeper I went, softly illuminated in a bluish haze. I could see that I dropped through a roughly cylindrical passageway, varying little in diameter as I descended. After only a few seconds of this sort of motion, the cylinder suddenly exploded into a vast, open chamber. Simultaneously, I was bathed in blue light. I had to blink against it after the recent period of light deprivation. As my eyes adjusted, I saw that I was suspended in the center of a massive, round chamber of stone. The walls of the chamber glowed with a blue luminescence that seemed to pulse rhythmically. It was not clear what force held me in mid-air, but the sensation was like that of floating in a viscous liquid, and the air had a touch of warm moisture to it that was not unpleasant. It was oddly familiar, and then I placed it: my dream. The amniotic stream that had raised me to the surface; here it had slowed my descent and now held me aloft. And then another piece fell into place. The chamber that now surrounded me was a sphere. My memory gradually inverted itself and became superimposed upon my present reality. The tree of my vision! It was the trunk I had fallen through and now I lay in the midst of that lunar sphere of branches I had seen by the shore of the stream. This place was like a negative image of the tree I had seen. Or was it the mold from which such a tree was cast? Was the stream of the vision then the fault-line? Perhaps it was best not to try to find analogues to every detail of my vision. But it could hardly be denied that my present circumstances were foreshadowed.

I expected Reya to call down to me, to ask if I had landed safely. The call never came, and I understood why. She had been down here herself. Maybe every member of her band had at one time. She knew there was no need for fear in this place. I considered calling up to her. But I decided to heed her advice and wait. And listen. For what?

44

"Justin Mayer." The voice from my dream, a soft vibration like distant thunder, but clearly understood. "I know you." The voice seemed to resonate from the walls of the chamber in every direction. It was impossible to identify a source.

"Do I know you?" I ventured. The question sounded foolish in my own ears. It was greeted by kind-hearted laughter of the same rumbling tenor. I hastily mouthed a follow-up question that sounded only slightly less obtuse: "Do you have a name?"

"As many as there are points on a sphere. But you may call me Chaer-Ul." I noted that the blue light continued to pulse rhythmically, but slightly brighter while the voice was speaking.

"Chaer-Ul..." I repeated the name, wondering if the voice would give meaning to the sound. When there was no response, I decided to try a more direct approach, one that I hoped would shed some light on the many questions assailing my mind. "Do you know why I am here?"

"Yes."

"Why am I here?" I wanted to shout the question, but restrained myself out of respect for the force that presently prevented me from plummeting the rest of the way to the chamber floor.

"Because I chose."

Was I asking the wrong questions? Or was this entity being intentionally cryptic? I took a different tack. "Why am I being called 'Martyr'?"

"There was another who bore this name."

"Tal-Makai," I said. This elicited no response. I took this to mean that I was not entirely off-track.

45

"You are not Martyr. But you must become."

I felt a sudden surge of resentment at being shoved into a role I never asked to play. "Become....'Martyr'? What do you mean? If this Tal-Makai gave his life heroically, I'm sure he had a good reason. But I'm not anxious to do the same!"

Silence...

Infuriated more by this, I continued to press my point. "These seem like good people, but I don't want to die for their cause...I'm not even sure what their cause is!"

Silence...

"As you have pointed out, I'm not who they think I am. I don't even belong here! Don't *I* get a choice?!!?" These last words were tinged with the bitterness I was feeling at being dealt such an unfair hand. This time there was again silence, but only for a moment. Then I felt as if my head were cleft by a blade of pure sound – a shriek of such pitch and intensity that my vision was momentarily blurred. When I was again able to focus, the blue light emanating from the walls grew abruptly brighter, whiter. The sound became a deafening roar, and amidst a shower of sand from the passage above the light flashed blindingly bright for but a second, then all was dark and silent. I felt nothing.

Slowly I became aware of a profound stiffness in my neck. I attempted to reposition my head to alleviate the discomfort, but something prevented me. I also began to feel as though my entire body were being jostled about. Presently I pried my eyelids open and glimpsed once again a moving landscape. I was riding behind Reya. The stiffness was a function of my having been strapped to her back in the upright position, head turned to one side. Feeling

46

my respirations grow suddenly deeper against her body, Reya addressed me. "What happened down there?"

"I think I may have angered your god."

"Oh, you think?" she said. "I told you to listen."

"I did! I mean, at first. But he was being incredibly vague, and I have so many very specific questions. Don't I have the right to know why I am here, and what is being asked of me?"

"You're right," she said. "You do, of course. All of this happened so fast, we are all still trying to figure out how to react to your presence here. And this is so hard for me, especially. Don't you realize...no, of course you don't. Ta...Justin. It's painful for me to even look at you...I... I'm sorry, I really am. You can't be expected to understand. But it's also not fair to deprive you of knowledge this way." She began to bring her mount to a slow trot. "So at the risk of my own emotional well-being..." With a flick of both her wrists, the creature assumed the dismounting stance once again. "I think it's time for a little history lesson." She muttered something to the animal then. It sounded something like, "Muur-puurrha", but it came from deep in Reya's throat.

At first I only heard a sort of hum, like the sound heard while walking under high-voltage power lines. Then I thought I saw little sparkling lights before my eyes. No, not before my eyes precisely, but between the many prongs of our mount's antlers. Thousands of tiny sparks, and a crackling sound joined the hum. Then, it seemed as though the air between us and the animal began to shimmer and take on a different aspect. A sphere roughly two meters in diameter hovered in the air before us, essentially green with forms moving within. Suddenly I had a nauseous feeling, of a rapid change in perspective as if accelerating toward that sphere. It grew to envelop me, and then there was no more Reya or beast, only the emerald of a dew-sprinkled hillside.

47

From uphill to my left, dozens of men and women rushed down the slope. They were dressed much like the people of Reya's camp, in soiled and well-worn clothes and scraps of makeshift armor. They carried melee weapons of equally mundane origin: garden rakes, pruning shears, sharpened handles of push-brooms and mops...I even thought I saw a hockey stick in one pair of hands. I directed my view downward and to my right, and saw that they advanced upon a mass of figures that held their position at the base of the hill. These others were noticeably better equipped, wearing uniform, darkly-colored outfits with only a splash of crimson at the left shoulder. They all brandished the same sort of bladed staffs. At a shouted command from somewhere unseen, these soldiers assumed a series of neat rows and positioned their weapons to meet the onrushing horde.

For a series of breathless moments, the troops to my left appeared to be frozen in the instant before the inevitable clash with the army below. Then motion and volume returned in force; the shouts of individual combatants pierced by the spine-shattering screech of steel-on-steel, the sickly-hollow thud of blunted tool against poorly-protected skull. Wave after wave of hapless and ill-prepared troops flung themselves down the hillside, and most of them met a speedy end at the tips of the enemy's weapons. Occasionally someone would breach the enemy line for a moment, and the thick line of dark soldiers would realign itself, new members pouring into the gaps. The effect was like a great, thick, dark serpent healing itself after each insult, repositioning scales to cover areas of exposed flesh. Or like rows of shark's teeth, new ones quickly pushed forward to replace those lost or damaged.

I heard a shout from high above to my left, and squinted in the brilliant sunlight to see the form of a great white steed and its rider high on the hilltop. The valkyrie that issued the shout was Reya, and at a command she was flanked on either side by two neat rows of archers. I saw them raise their bows in unison to point at the first row of enemy troops. Then as I watched they raised their weapons slightly and froze. At a second command from Reya they unleashed their missiles as one. The projectiles flew not at the enemy's front line, but at a point just beyond the last row of soldiers. As each one landed, a small explosion could be seen, followed a micro-second later by its sound. The enemy troops, more heavily armored for a frontal attack, were caught off-guard. Here and there the perfect lines of their formation were disrupted, and the efforts to restore order seemed a bit less organized than before. Some were injured; a few fell. Reya's troops, encouraged by this small victory, pushed with renewed vigor down the slope. The shouts grew louder, weapons and heads held higher.

A warm breeze swept over the hillside, rustling the grass and carrying the smoke from the explosions away. As the haze cleared I saw a stirring on the crest of the next bluff, beyond the enemy. Reya's people saw it too. A second wave of enemy troops. Then a third. They filed in behind their comrades at the base of the hill. The dark serpent was now a veritable sea of black, a great dragon in constant, subtle motion, ever poised to strike. The effect of this newly tripled threat was immediately evident among Reya's troops. Their descent slowed; the battle cries were choked off in their throats; a few warriors actually stumbled. Reya's army was outnumbered to begin with; now the situation had become entirely hopeless. I tried to see how Reya would react to this, and I saw her glance quickly over her shoulder and back, a nervous sort of motion that seemed somehow out of character for her. Reya issued a command for her army to regroup, but even as her voice reached the front lines a change was taking place on the enemy side.

A strange silhouette appeared at the top of the distant hill. A lone figure atop some sort of vehicle, rising over the flattened grass of the hilltop. It continued to rise, and it became apparent that it wasn't a vehicle per se, but a seat, a throne, carried by six or eight

49

bulky warriors. On the throne sat a dark-cloaked figure. The air above and around the figure rippled and shimmered like the heat from a tarred road in summer. As I watched, the dark figure raised his arms high in the air and lowered his head. At the last moment before his head was fully bowed, I detected a glint from his eyes, even shielded as they were by the overhanging hood. Stranger still, I felt certain he had in that moment glanced directly at me. I felt in my bones and my blood the cold cruelty of his smile. The sensation was not easy to shake, even when reason prevailed and I told myself the distance was too far, the shadows too deep...that indeed, I wasn't really there.

Moments later, something else could be seen rising over the hilltop on either side of this figure. Several, perhaps a dozen or so, large creatures began to descend the slope, side-by-side, each about fifty meters from the next. They looked like the animals Reya's people rode, but something was wrong. Their heads were bowed low to the ground, and they lumbered down the hill in a manner entirely unlike the careless grace with which I had seen them move. There was some sort of man-made device strapped to their backs, an extension of which ran up the ridge of their great necks to the base of the skull. A pair of large, metallic cylinders hung on either side of their bodies, and as I strained to get a better look, it became apparent that this equipment was not the only reason for their awkward movement. These creatures had only four legs, the middle pair apparently having been amputated to accommodate the ungainly accoutrements. Their many-pronged antlers crackled with the same sort of sparkling effect I had observed before entering this vision-state, only dimmer. These once-majestic beasts were a sickly shadow of their former selves. Their hides were sunken and pallid, fur fouled and matted, the golden light of their eyes all but extinguished. Occasionally a dejected moan escaped one of their throats.

Reya's men had halted in their tracks several paces short of the enemy's front line. They seemed unsure how to react to this new development, frozen by a mixture of fear, confusion, and an overwhelming feeling of sadness at the wretched state of these animals. Reya, recognizing that this development posed some sort of a threat, immediately ordered a retreat. But it was as though her soldiers heard her only through a dense veil. She repeated the command, louder now, but her troops stood motionless, staring toward the opposing hillside. Incensed, Reya looked more closely at the beasts and saw that the tanks on their sides glowed with rows of orange lights. Were these strange devices exerting some kind of effect on her troops? She stole one final look over her shoulder, then, muttering something softly to her mount, started down the hillside at a fair clip.

As the row of pathetic creatures reached the rear guard of enemy foot soldiers, the formation parted in multiple places to allow their passage. The animals lurched laboriously past row after row of the enemy's legions, finally emerging at the front line. They advanced but a few steps more and then halted facing Reya's army, snouts almost touching the ground, enormous heads swaying hypnotically to and fro. Reya spoke again to her mount and it broke into a full gallop. This was an impressive thing to see, now for the first time as a passive observer. The great white hide revealed an elegant and powerful musculature as the beast worked its six legs, thundering down the steep incline at the top of the hill, leaping over a broad outcropping of rock and landing without breaking stride to resume its gallop on the more even ground at mid-slope. Reya had almost reached her army's right flank when the sparkling in the antlers of the enemy's poor beasts suddenly grew to a blinding flash. Above the head of each beast a tiny sun exploded, sending a devastating wave of energy spreading ahead of the animal, encompassing a broad, cone-shaped area. In that instant, the battlefield was terribly transformed. Wherever the energy had touched, scores of men lay dead. And immediately after the blast, each animal emitted a hollow groan and expired, never to rise again. The orange lights went dark.

51

Reya, despite the incredible momentum of her steed, had not advanced far enough to suffer the effect of the blasts. Her mount reared up high on its hind legs, and she again ordered a retreat. This time her remaining troops seemed to hear, and hastily obeyed. Quickly scanning the area of destruction, she saw that maybe two-thirds of her people had died in that one terrible act. Shaking her head, she turned and led the retreat, back up the hill the way they had come. As she reached the base of the rocky bluff she had cleared earlier, she halted and cocked her head. The thing that apparently gave her pause was a deep rumbling that now reached my ears as well. It grew to an almost deafening din, then the air over Reya's head was filled with a half-dozen or so great, white, soaring shapes as a small band of men on beasts like her own leaped over her position and plunged down the hillside. At their head, an oddly familiar figure. The face was my own. I knew before she cried, "Tal!"

"Tal, no! This fight is lost!" she screamed. He reined in his mount, cutting a sharp left arc, and came up a few dozen paces below Reya.

"Not again!" Tal barked, his face a mask of vengeance. "He must pay for his atrocities! For what he's done to our people. To our friends!" He gestured toward the corpses of the fallen deer-creatures.

"He's too powerful! You can't hurt him! Tal, please! There'll be another day to fight," Reya pleaded.

"Not if I can help it," Tal said . "This ends here. Today! We rout his troops, then I take Magus out. Tonight we celebrate!"

"Don't, Tal!" But he was already racing to rejoin his brothers in the fray. Racing past disorganized groups of retreating soldiers in twos and threes, Tal came at last to the first row of enemy foot soldiers. His companions had already split and were hungrily

52

assaulting the flanks. Tal-Makai met the enemy head-on. These seven men, and their mounts, were noticeably better-armored and better-equipped than most of the soldiers of Reya's camp, if not than Magus' army. That and the ease with which they proceeded to dispatch the enemy led me to believe that they represented an elite corps of warriors, the strongest and finest of those who fought on Reya's side. They passed along the leading edges of the enemy army, and as they rode, their blades flickered gold in the late-afternoon sun. In their wake the enemy lay like cut grass. As they decimated the first row, they wheeled about and made for a second pass. Tal-Makai now sat atop his mount in the center of the action surrounded by dark soldiers. But his stance was not a defensive one. As his mount turned in slow circles, his bladed staff flashed and spun, felling enemies with each swing as though they offered no resistance.

Awestruck by this display of military prowess, I didn't immediately perceive the change that then began to take place within the enemy ranks. Gradually I became aware of a different sort of movement outside the immediate circle of Tal's struggle. While most of the troops held their positions, individual soldiers freed themselves from the collective and began to push inward toward Tal, squeezing past their fellows. From my vantage it looked like a reverse starburst, a large circle of points converging inexorably upon a single point, and that point was Tal-Makai. As they reached the inner ring of soldiers, they seemed momentarily to draw back a step, then lunged forward as one. At the same instant their weapons simultaneously extended, nearly doubling in length, perforating Tal's mount in numerous places, while the tips of other blades pressed into Tal's flesh and against his throat, immobilizing him without inflicting serious harm.

"No!" screamed Reya. The air thundered with booming laughter that seemed to come from everywhere, but undoubtedly originated from that cloaked figure that still stood unmoving at the top of the hill. The noise reverberated around the entire valley for a moment, then suddenly localized to a point directly before the face of Tal-Makai. As it did, a wisp of vapor coalesced there into the form of a man. The vaguely human face addressed Tal then with the voice of my former teacher, the one known to these people as "Magus". The cloaked figure hadn't moved from his place high above.

"Tal-Makai." He attempted to suppress a chuckle but failed, erupting into a disgusting cackle that sounded like an infected cough. His perverted glee was echoed among his troops with a sound like the chittering of countless insects. "The great warrior!" More laughter. "I must say this is better than I could have hoped." The mist-figure drifted slowly around the pinned and helpless Tal, examining his catch from all directions before returning to rest before him. Shouts could be heard from farther afield, where I looked to see that other soldiers held the remaining members of Tal's pack at bay. "You see? There's no help for you now. Kialam-Tal..." He let his voice trail off as the word-play had its desired effect and a wave of renewed snickering passed through the watching troops. Tal-Makai – "One who rises", twisted to become Kialam-Tal – "Pierced One" – a vile parody of his present predicament and probable end.

"I have no desire to delay your death. However, as an event long anticipated, I do have very particular designs regarding its manner." Caught up again momentarily in his gagging chuckle, he then began to incant something in a strange tongue. As he spoke, a reddish-orange hue was cast across the entire scene. It grew extremely quiet for but a moment. Then...

I heard a growing rumbling noise, and the vapor-being dissipated. The spot over which it had hovered began to pull together and rise, as though an invisible cord from somewhere far above tugged at the very earth, causing it to pucker and peak. Rocks and roots and clods of topsoil rolled together, adding their mass to the forming mound. As it grew it constantly writhed and twisted inward upon itself, stones clacking against each other, roots and branches forming sinewy extensions. All the while, the pulling of earth continued, drawing more and more raw material from which to fashion – whatever it was that was being fashioned. This roiling sod pile grew to the height of a man, and then quite a bit more, and then the extensions could be seen to be forming themselves into crude arms and legs. In various places, larger chunks of rock or wood began to stabilize and hold fast, forming a suit of natural armor. Around these pieces the remaining material constantly stirred and rearranged itself.

Finally, there stood before Tal a humanoid monster of massive bulk and proportion. It held one earthy hand before its face, then stretched it skyward. The extremity elongated to form a great lance of wood and stone, which it brought slowly to bear, not on Tal-Makai, but on his mount. Positioning its point at the center of the creature's breast, it thrust its arm forward, impaling the beast through nearly the entire length of its body cavity, and killing it instantly. Tal was horrified, but could do nothing. The blades of enemy weapons held him fast. The monster withdrew the lance and it resumed the shape of a hand. Then, placing both hands together at the newly-formed hole in the creature's chest, it pried the animal's chest apart, ripping through bone and flesh as if it were soft cloth. Reaching one enormous hand deep into the chest, it withdrew a long, flat, whitish object – the animal's breastbone. Small stones and grains of sand from the monster's body spiraled down the arm and flowed over the bone, grinding it clean of flesh and blood. The demon again stretched the hand over its head, and it became a weapon once more, the breastbone forming a long, broad blade of exceptional sharpness. It drew back and swung its new weapon once in a broad, horizontal arc, neatly decapitating the already lifeless beast. It then performed a similar bone-cleaning process with the animal's skull, accomplishing this with remarkable speed and efficiency. This it fastened to its other arm with roots from its own substance to wield as a gigantic shield.

"Do it now!" The booming voice commanded from somewhere indeterminate.

The monster righted itself, drew back its great blade-arm, and drove it straight through the heart of Tal-Makai. He stiffened, and was gone. Somewhere far away, Reya's hysterical screams could be heard. The soldiers now withdrew their weapons, and the bodies of rider and beast slumped to the ground. Blood gushed from Tal's wound in hot spurts and spilled on the earth. Reya pulled herself together enough to shout a final command to her surviving troops and then they all beat a speedy retreat, back up the way they had come. Back in the valley I saw the blood of Tal-Makai form rivulets upon the ground. Then I saw these trickles flow toward the monster. As the blood reached its feet, it began to be absorbed into its body, imparting a red stain to the ever-writhing earth-flesh.

Thinking the horrors at an end, I tried to shake my head free of the vision, but it wasn't done with me. I heard again a rumbling of earth, and watched as the body of Tal-Makai was drawn toward the monster, rolling over tiny stones and pebbles. As it came near, roots from the monster's body reached eagerly to receive it. Stone plates were shifted aside as the body of Tal-Makai was taken into the monster's body. Dirt and stones filled in around it, essentially burying him in a living tomb. The lifeless eyes of Tal-Makai stared out through a slit between the stones of the demon's face, lit with an unnatural orange glow. And everywhere, the cruel and mocking laughter.

Suddenly I was back in the present, with Reya. She was crying. Shocked, I realized that I had not only been watching the scene unfold, but had known Tal-Makai's thoughts and feelings. I even thought I felt for a moment the sting of that horrible blade in my chest. I was also surprised to realize that I knew how Tal had felt about Reya. Instinctively I put an arm around her to comfort her. She leaned her head against me and sobbed softly. After a few moments, she composed herself, gently lifted my arm from her shoulder, and turned to face me. "It was a long time ago," she said. "It's just hard to see it again. Tal was desperate to stop Magus. We all were. You cannot begin to imagine the horrors he has unleashed on the world. Tal, like all of us, just wanted it to end. In his desperation, Tal made a tactical error. It cost him his life and weakened the resistance. It also made Magus that much more powerful."

"That...thing..."

"Is not Tal. Tal is dead. Yet it somehow draws strength from his body, perhaps from his essence. Just pray you never come face-to-face with it. It is enough for now that you have seen what you have seen. We'd better be on our way. We can talk more about all of this when we reach camp."

"Wait, one more thing I just realized...the grass was green in the vision."

"Yeah, Magus did that too. He cursed the vegetation hoping to starve the puurr-deer. He knew they were our most powerful allies."

"Puurr-deer? So that's what they're called. And....wait....are you saying we have *other* allies like them?"

"Not like them, but those who resist Magus are more than you might think. C'mon, we need to get going."

We had no sooner resumed our journey than we heard a buzzing sound that started softly and far away, but quickly grew to a deafening roar. It was a jarring sound, but one that I recognized from my own world. Seconds later my suspicions were confirmed, as a helicopter passed over us in the clearing where we had stopped, billowing thick smoke and barely clearing the treetops. A few seconds after it passed out of sight, there was a single loud scraping sound punctuated by several sharp cracks, and then silence. Reya turned our mount in the direction we had seen it go and headed out.

7

The chopper had come to rest in a small clearing amidst a grove of spruce saplings. The landing had snapped a few of the smaller saplings and the vehicle smoldered still, but appeared largely intact save for some cosmetic scratches raked into the weathered paint of the fuselage. The fact that it ended up in a space scarcely larger than the craft itself was a testimony either to exceptional piloting, or incredible luck. It looked like the kind of helicopter I remembered seeing in films of the Vietnam War. Reya brought the mount up to within a few meters of it, then slowly reached down and drew her bow from the sling along the animal's side where it hung, all the while watching for any movement. She nocked an arrow and brought the weapon to bear on the cabin of the vehicle.

She didn't have to wait for long. A bulky figure dropped to the earth on the far side of the 'copter, and presently the cockpit hatch on our side opened. A more graceful frame slipped nimbly from the pilot's seat and dropped the few feet to the ground, landing in a feline crouch. For half a second I thought she was trailing a black cape, but immediately realized my mistake as an impossible quantity of thick, dark hair settled about her shoulders and around her small face a couple of moments after her body touched down. She wore an oversized military helmet covered in green camouflage material, and a matching vest covered with dozens of pockets of various sizes, every one of which bulged with something interesting. A few odd apparati jutted out of their respective pockets, revealing buttons, knobs, and dials galore. The remainder of her lithe form was covered in a close-fitting black jumpsuit, the base a clunky-looking pair of late-issue canvas and leather army boots. It looked as if she had just come from the going-out-of-business sale at a military surplus store and had bought the lot.

As she stood, I momentarily lost her soot- and grease-streaked face in the black cloud of hair that floated around its periphery. As she took a few steps in our direction a breeze wafted it back and I could see that she wore a filthy pair of goggles of the kind worn in high school wood-shop classes and usually labeled "protective eyewear". She tried in vain to wipe the blackened lenses with her two index fingers, a comical gesture that reminded me of a pair of tiny windshield wipers working frantically to restore visibility during a heavy downpour. She then abandoned this effort and instead pulled the goggles away from her face entirely and set them to rest on the front of her helmet. Her eyes were the same almond shape as Reya-Mana's, only larger, softer, and of a decidedly brown-gold hue. Framed by her dark lashes and brows, and set off as they were against the sooty blackness of the surrounding skin, they were stunning.

My eyes flicked to Reya, who met my gaze for the briefest of moments then turned her attention quickly back to the scene before us. Even from my skewed perspective at her back, Reya seemed for the first time in my experience somehow other than entirely sure of herself. But she lowered her bow and muttered the command to our mount, and we both descended to meet the newcomers. By this time the other passenger had come up to stand beside this odd female. He was a giant of a man, clad more simply than she in a surprisingly clean white tank, brown slacks, and army boots of a more vintage style. Spotting a dirty flak jacket on the ground behind him, I realized that he must have stripped it off after exiting. He was dark and brooding, all rippling muscle topped by a neatly-shaved head. A heavy brow and chiseled jaw dominated his countenance. Reya extended a shaky hand, never breaking eye contact with the younger woman. The latter clasped the offered hand tightly in both of hers and shook it enthusiastically, if a little too much so. Then in a somewhat husky but cheerful voice, she declared, "I'm Maya! This is Doog. We're resistance!"

"Uh...," Reya shook her head once briskly as if to dismiss a thought and then resumed, "Yes....Yes, of course. I assumed as much, but...where did you get *that*?" indicating with a little jerk of her chin the downed chopper.

"Oh! I found it! *We* found it, Doog and I!" And then, dropping her head toward her left shoulder, she squinted one giant eye and peered up at Reya with the other, then continued in a small voice, "I mean we stole it." Then suddenly louder, "But we stole it from Magus!"

"Well then, *that* crime is officially pardoned!" replied Reya. Everyone chuckled, and it went a long way toward relieving some of the tension. "Sorry, I should have said...I'm Reya. And this is Justin. We're not far from our camp. You could..."

"I know," answered Maya, "I saw your tents from the air. I was trying to bring 'er in there, but...," she screwed her face up and simultaneously shrugged in a goofy yet slightly adorable way, then, "I'm a *lot* better at take-offs!"

"I'm not about to complain," said Reya. "You're already one-hundred percent more pilot - and more air support – than we had a few minutes ago." Her eyes scanned the clearing. "And I think you're a fair bit better at landings than you let on. My men will come back and see what can be done about this bird. Just make sure you take the keys, and follow us."

"Sure, but how are we supposed to..."

Just then Reya tilted her head back and produced a hollow sound deep in her throat. The beast mimicked the sound, both of them tossing their heads back in unison, an unearthly tone filling the woods. Before long we could hear the cracking of small branches and a second puurr-deer burst into the clearing. Gesturing toward it, Reya stated matter-of-factly, "Your ride awaits."

61

At the pace of the massive deer we were entering the outskirts of the camp a mere few minutes later. As before, we were thronged by members of Reya's entourage, but I was spared the awed exclamations of my initial visit, as they seemed eager to extend hospitality to their new guests. I was of course attended to, and more than a couple of giggling children carried my travel packs away and offered me food and drink. When we had all dismounted Reya allowed the crowd to envelop Maya and Doog, who were quick enough to make their own introductions. As they moved away en masse, I saw two people approach Reya. I recognized them as Greda and Denkel. They each drew close to her in turn and hushed conversations ensued. I was not able to catch enough words to know what was being discussed, but it didn't seem to have anything to do with the new arrivals. One after the other they finished their business with Reya and bustled off to disparate points within the camp.

Reya turned her head to me but kept her eyes fixed on a clod of topsoil on the ground between us. "Lots to do tomorrow. Best get something to eat and get some sleep." She turned as if to head off toward the main camp.

Lunging, I caught hold of her sleeve at the elbow and stayed her. "Not so fast! What aren't you telling me?"

She drew her lips into a tight line and made as if to pull away and continue on her intended path, as if she hadn't quite heard me. But I held her fast, and so she soon relented, sighing and turning back to face me. "OK, but not here. Walk with me." She led me along the main road I had first come in on, away from the noise of the camp. "Greda thinks we need to move soon. There have been more sightings of unnatural creatures like those dogs. And Denkel was just telling me…"

"Not about that!" I interrupted. "That girl. Maya. She looks just like you! A slightly disheveled version, maybe, but it's unmistakable. And you acted strange when you saw her. It's *not* a coincidence, is it? Do you know her?"

A pause. Then, "She's my daughter."

"But she doesn't seem to know you."

"She *doesn't* know me. That's probably why she's still alive. And I'd like to keep it that way. I just wish she hadn't come here."

"I don't understand. How could you not be happy to see your own child?"

Reya answered sharply, "Be careful what you say, Justin." Her voice edged with pain. "There are things you don't know yet."

"I'm sorry, I didn't mean anything by it. There's a lot I don't know yet. I'm trying to understand."

The fire slowly burned out of her voice as she continued. "There was a plague, a virus. Almost a hundred years ago. It was worldwide. Almost everybody was touched. In a matter of weeks all but a very tiny portion of the world's population was dead. It was the greatest tragedy in the history of the world. Only the strong survived, those who had some kind of natural immunity or resistance to the bug. I'm guessing this didn't happen in your world?"

"No, thank God," I said. "Not yet, anyway."

Reya continued, "A broken people who had trusted in science now turned once more to religion for answers, for hope. Many trusted the Deity of ancient times, the One believed to have made the worlds. We know him as Chaer-Ul. A few chose rather to blame him for what had happened. So it is to this day. Magus was one who preached a new religion. A religion of his own making. He proclaimed that Chaer-Ul had not only permitted the disaster to occur, he had actually initiated it, a sort of population control plan. He discovered old and forbidden ways of reaching into the realm of spirits. He spoke with lesser gods and they lent him their powers."

"This explains a lot, but what does it have to do with your daughter?" I probed.

"I was married years ago, before I met Tal. I came to trust in Chaer-Ul, but my husband did not. I persuaded him to let us join with a resistance group for mutual protection. In those days, as now, most of the resistance consisted of Chaer-Ul's faithful, but some number simply wanted to be free, and saw Magus' cult as the greater threat to that freedom. My husband was a natural leader, and easily rallied men who were willing to fight – and die if necessary – to remain free. Our camp grew too large, and eventually attracted the attention of Magus' spies. When he learned that my husband was amassing a small army, Magus made him a prime target of his offensive. He reserved his greatest hatred for the followers of Chaer-Ul, but would tolerate no form of heresy."

"Which he defined as any deviation from his teachings," I offered.

"Exactly," she replied. "He sent assassins – fiercely loyal members of his cult, whether from faith or fear – and attempts were made on my husband's life. He managed to evade them at first, but they were persistent. Ultimately, one of his own inner circle betrayed him, and he was slain one moonless night. Shortly afterward I discovered I was pregnant."

"With Maya," I said.

Reya nodded. "The attacks didn't stop, and when they realized I had assumed the mantle of leadership in the wake of my husband's death, I found myself in the crosshairs."

"I think I'm starting to understand," I said.

"The idea of being away from my baby was unthinkable. But Magus' spy network was extremely efficient, and as the months passed he came to be aware that I had had a child. One night we captured one of his men inside the camp. Not here, but an earlier camp, farther to the east. He carried blankets and changing cloths. It was a kidnapping attempt. He hadn't been able to find Maya, but it was too close. I was forced to consider the fact that this child would ever be in danger as long as she was near us. I had family living just outside one of the great cities to the south. It was a quiet place, quite secluded. I brought her there to live, and my family raised her as their own. She was to learn nothing of us, the resistance, or Magus. But as she grew, she proved to be an exceedingly clever child. And Magus' infamy grew; it was impossible for her not to learn of him, and of the good people who refused to submit to his new law. She knew nothing of me or of her father, but when she came to be of age she joined her local resistance movement."

"She is a remarkably bright girl," she went on. "My family has sent me regular updates over the years. And a few times…," here her voice was thin, cracked a little, "…I traveled there and watched her, unseen, from a distance." Now the corners of her eyes were moist, I could see her swallowing hard. Collecting herself she added, "She is amazing with machines and gadgets. No doubt she got that chopper running. Magus doesn't have any sophisticated aircraft, and nobody with the knowledge to fix them. That kind of technology was lost with those who died from the plague. This could be a *huge* tactical advantage for us. But now…," she trailed off, sighed deeply, "chance has brought her right back into harm's way."

"Chance?" I asked. "Or choice? Don't your people believe that the Chaer-Ul has something to say about what does and does not transpire?"

She looked surprised. Then a warm smile spread across her tear-glazed face, and she breathed more easily. "We do indeed."

8

Nobody asked me about what had happened in the wilderness. I kind of expected that they would, at least those who had known where Reya was taking me. Instead I got a few knowing smiles, as if they thought I had received some great revelation, that I had now become enlightened, self-aware, knowing my true identity and purpose. I hadn't. I looked away whenever I encountered these faces. I was not "Martyr", or Tal-Makai. I was no warrior or hero, and had no intention of "becoming" any of that. I had learned a fair bit more about this world to which I had come, but it seemed the only one who knew why I was here rather than snug in my dorm room bed was a mysterious entity called Chaer-Ul, and he or it seemed content to keep me in shadows over the matter.

After my chat with Reya, I had made my way back into the camp as she busied herself with the mundane tasks of running a rebel camp. Jeyt caught up with me and offered to lend me his expertise in spear-handling with a couple of free lessons. I promised to take him up on that later, as he had clearly already had a few draughts and throwing pointy things in his present condition didn't seem the best idea. I joined the broad circle of faces around the bonfire, where Maya was entertaining with tales of vehicle theft and the latest news from the south. The people watched with rapt attention, as many of them had friends or loved ones in other camps. I spotted Doog sitting on the far side of the circle, looking stoic and detached. It occurred to me that I hadn't heard him speak since our forest meeting earlier.

I let my gaze drift to Maya, who was acting out her adventures with dramatic gestures in the center of the clearing. She had found opportunity to refresh herself since we had parted, and I was able to make a better analysis of her features. The eyes were Reya, no doubt, but without the soot I could see that there were more differences than I had at first suspected. Her face was smaller than Reya's, nose more delicate, lips a bit fuller and more shaped. And efforts had been made to tame all of that hair - a long braid down each side of her face and the rest pulled back into a thick ponytail. A few wavy strands danced about the corners of her forehead. And all of it shimmered in the firelight. She was beautiful. Maya was a few centimeters shorter than her mother, but still quite tall and stately, if a bit wiry. As she painted her tales in dramatic pantomimed strokes, her bodily movements mirrored in flickering shadows on the dusty earth, the effect was intoxicating. An hour passed without notice. When at last I caught myself nodding, I removed myself to my tent.

Sleep came fast and easy. I dreamed. Not the horrific images of Tal-Makai's final moments that I might have expected, but a vision of serenity. I stood as if emerging from a dense forest that stretched for miles behind me and to either side. Before me the trees ended abruptly as a towering slope of soft-grassed green rose before me, almost to the clouds. At its peak, the great tree of my former vision. At its sight all the lesser trees of the forest bent in reverent genuflexion. I felt compelled to do the same, but a voice said, "Come up." I began to climb the steepness before me, and found it surprisingly effortless. Gold-edged clouds drifted slowly over my head from beyond the mountain, sailing through a lavender-hued sky. As I drew at last near the enormous tree that dominated this surreal landscape, I paused, as I saw several armored figures approaching its trunk.

As I drew closer still, I saw that the men and their armor were fashioned of carved wood, and the axes they carried were made of bark. With these they began to hack at the base of the tree. The tree's trunk, I could see now, was made of unpolished steel, and the arboreal implements quite naturally shattered as they struck its impervious surface. The men paused, looked at one another in wonder, then they too splintered and flew apart as if struck by unseen bolts of lightning. The voice was the thunder: "Become!"

Startled, I woke suddenly and sat up. At once I thought I saw a shadow pass across the front of my tent. A moment later it was followed by a pair of feet. Crawling to the flap I pulled it cautiously aside and in the dim glow from the dying fire saw Maya, followed closely by Doog, stalking through the camp in the direction of the fallen chopper. Doog carried armfuls of mechanical parts, Maya a large toolbox. I dressed hastily and followed them at a distance, stepping carefully to avoid twigs that would betray my presence.

They moved through the camp with care, but more swiftly once they reached the woods. There was a moon in the sky, but it passed in and out of cloud cover, so I struggled to keep their dark forms in sight without tailing close enough to be heard. Finally I decided it would be safer to let them slip out of view and only follow the sounds of their passage. I fell back, and when the snapping of branches and crinkling of leaves was but a distant whisper, I resumed my pursuit. Whenever the sounds grew almost inaudible, I picked up the pace momentarily. I found it necessary to do this more and more frequently. How fast could they run with all that heavy equipment? And this seemed a lot farther on foot. I was sweating as I raced faster and faster, now a bit terrified of losing the sounds entirely and being lost in these woods, unable to find my way either to the helicopter or back to camp. Why had I come out here after them again? I ran on, panting heavily, then gasping, lungs aching. Then suddenly, unexpectedly, all sounds stopped. I froze. Had they reached the clearing? Had I lost them? I waited a long couple of minutes, then heard the sounds abruptly resume, far ahead and slightly to my left. I dashed in that direction and felt something solid knock me in the windpipe. I went down, flat on my back, gulping air. I knew it hadn't been a tree branch. I lifted my head and looked up, straining to make out shapes in the darkness, expecting to see the hulking form of Doog towering over me. Instead my eyes met Maya's, which looked back with a scolding expression. "Why are you following us?" she demanded.

69

"Why are you being sneaky?" I asked.

"We're not *being* sneaky, we're being *smart*. Magus' people will be looking for that 'copter. If they find it before we get it running again they'll take it back, and then he'll have air power too. They don't sleep, so why should we?"

I felt quite foolish of a sudden. "Makes sense. Sorry about the following and all. I just wanted to know what was going on."

"Mm-hm." She turned to Doog, who had come back to examine Maya's handiwork. "This one's curious," she said, tipping her head in my general direction. Doog smiled and returned the nod, but said nothing. "I once summoned a big cat to kill a curious guy."

"I don't think that's how that saying goes," I said.

"Saying?" Maya replied, looking genuinely confused. I felt a tiny chill pass through me, and decided to direct the conversation elsewhere. First I picked myself up off the ground.

"So, as long as I'm here, is there anything I can do to help?"

"Not likely," she said. "Unless of course you have a degree in aviation repair."

"Sorry, no. Does Doog?" I asked, expecting a negative response.

"No. But he is strong enough to carry heavy things. Which I can see you are not." That one stung a little. "Anyway, I've heard some strange things about you over the course of the evening. That you've come back from the dead, or from another planet or something. That you're really important. Aren't you supposed to be supervised at all times?"

"I'm nobody special. And I can take care of myself," I said.

70

"Still, I don't think Reya'd be too happy if I let you wander about in the woods alone at night. You'd better stick with me 'n' Doog for now."

It became my job to keep watch, for either Magus' scouts or unwelcome company from the camp. I climbed a medium-sized white pine that had taken root amidst the smaller spruce, and found myself a comfortable perch that afforded views in all directions. Maya set about fixing the chopper, occasionally asking Doog for a part or handing him one she'd removed. At first it was too dark to see much of anything, unless someone happened our way with a torch. But by now dawn was already frosting the horizon beyond the farthest treetops, and soon beams of sunlight were penetrating every gap in the forest's cover and warming its leafy carpet. I could easily see a quarter mile into the surrounding woods in any given direction. I spotted a small herd of puurr-deer grazing on the budding upper foliage to the southwest, and a family of pheasants just to our west. Otherwise, nothing stirred. Below me, Maya continued her work, which to my untrained eyes looked more like dismantling than repairing. But she had gotten it in the air and flown it here, so I presumed she knew what she was doing. Her face and hands were starting to collect streaks of grease anew.

Suddenly she shouted. "Oh no!" I nearly fell from the tree. When I recovered, I quickly scanned the surrounding woods for an approaching threat, but saw nothing.

"What's the matter?" I called down.

"The black tube thingy is ruined! It's melted right through, I don't think I can fix it."

"So is that it?" I asked. "No more air support?"

71

"Well, I saw a town on my way in, just a couple of miles to the south. Looked like an old mill town. It won't have helicopter parts, of course, but we may be able to find something that will work."

"Are towns safe?" I asked.

"Not always. Most of the cities are patrolled periodically by a contingent of Magus' troops. But smaller towns can be kind of a mixed bag. Usually not Magus' people, but the locals sometimes have their own agendas. This was a pretty small town I saw, so it might be abandoned, or it might be OK," Maya said.

"Or it might not," I added helpfully.

"Or it might not. But we've got Doog. That's a pretty good backup plan right there." Doog was smiling.

"OK," I said. "Now the question of transport. I saw some puurr-deer nearby. But we don't know how…" I was almost toppled from my perch again as a startling but familiar, hollow sound issued forth from the lungs of the young woman below me. "I thought your faction weren't familiar with the puurr-deer?"

"Of course we know them!" exclaimed Maya. "We wouldn't have lasted as long as we have against Magus' hordes if we didn't. I just normally prefer mechanical forms of mobility." That seemed somehow fitting.

A pair of the great animals trotted into view. "How'd you happen to get two?" I asked.

"'You don't speak puurr-deer? I clearly said, 'Two, please'." I could've sworn she winked at me. Maya mounted one deer and Doog the other. "He's heavy," she said. "You'll have to ride with me." Not particularly disappointed, I made my way down the trunk of my tree and then, taking her hand, directly onto the animal without touching the ground. Maya made a burbling sound to her mount and we were off. I skipped the bashful routine in favor of not being thrown to my death, and held on to her tightly. "A man of action, not words, I see," Maya chided.

"Actually, I am a man of words. I study language. Or I used to, anyway."

"Maybe battle tactics would've been better," she replied. "Magus isn't much for negotiation."

"I don't plan to be here long enough to find out," I said.

Maya looked back over her shoulder at me, one eyebrow raised. "When do you expect the mothership to come back for you?"

"Funny. And I'm not from another planet. But I definitely don't belong here."

No, obviously not," she said. "But the kind of thing you're talking about, only Chaer-Ul can help you with that. Maybe if you talk to him…" She seemed to be genuinely trying to help.

"I tried that," I replied. "I don't think I did it right."

"You spoke with Chaer-Ul?!!?" What did he say? What do you mean, 'didn't do it right'? All you have to do is listen. Whatever he said, just do *that*!"

"Yeah," I said. "That's the part I screwed up. The listening."

"He doesn't talk to just *anyone*, you know. Maybe you *are* a little special." It was a nice thing to say. She had her moments.

"Maybe," I conceded. "I just know I'll try a different tack if I ever manage to get a second audience." The forest was a blur of yellow leaves and walnut trunks as we raced toward our destination. To our right the other animal and its rider periodically passed into and again out of my field of vision. "So Doog…does he…," I began.

Maya finished the thought, "Doog is mute. He used to work for my family from time to time, mostly building things around the farm. He has always been kind of a big brother figure to me, ever since I was little; always had a certain affection for me, an innate desire to protect me. He's a great man."

"So…" I began.

"He's just a friend," she finished. I saw her ears turn a pinker shade.

9

The path we traveled merged onto an overgrown logging road. Once broad enough to allow big trucks to pass with their payloads of lumber, it was now a barely-discernible thoroughfare where the trees were not quite so close together, or so large, and where more yellow grass than moss prevailed. After a time it was intersected by a much wider swath of grass that had been the route of a set of powerlines that led up the side of a small mountain to our east. The enormous utility poles with their many criss-crossing beams stood bent, wireless and corroded, the defeated skeletons of an army of metallic titans that once traversed this valley. We paused here to rest and refresh ourselves from the canteen Maya had taken from the chopper. The sun was by this time high in the eastern sky, and clusters of wispy clouds occasionally obscured its face.

"So," Maya began, breaking the silence. "Tell me something about this place you come from. Was yours a large clan?"

I chuckled a little. "There were no clans. There was no plague. There are still billions of people in my world."

"Billions?!!?" Her eyes grew wide. "That must have been awful!"

"Awful? No, it...I mean...yes, I suppose in some ways it was. But there were still lots of places you could go to be alone, places where you could ride through the woods forever and never see another soul."

"That many people...all living in peace...it's hard to imagine," Maya mused.

"Oh, I never said my world was at peace," I corrected her. "There are wars and smaller skirmishes going on all the time. It's just that they rarely involve more than a couple of countries. I guess that's one way the population keeps itself in check."

"Have they looked into plagues? They can be very effective," she offered, a wry grin appearing in the corner of her mouth. So, she had a dark sense of humor. I liked that.

Joining into the game, I replied, "I believe they're working on it. Now all we need is an egomaniacal evil magician."

"You can have ours!" she said cheerfully. "Really, we're done with him." We both laughed, and afterward her gaze held mine for a couple of seconds before dropping abruptly to study a fascinating blade of grass between her feet.

We were interrupted by a snort from one of the puurr-deer. Shortly the sound was echoed by the other animal. Looking down the hillside to the southwest, we saw another deer with a rider, galloping our way.

The rider was an Asian man who appeared to be in his mid-50's. Upon seeing us his brow furrowed, then his face registered surprise, but he didn't inquire about our destination or our reason for being so far from base. I didn't recognize him from camp, but there was an air of familiarity about him; perhaps I had seen him in the vision of Tal-Makai's final battle. "Water spotter," he explained. "There was a report of a clean spring somewhere west of here."

"Did you find it?" asked Maya.

"No, will look again tomorrow," he said, already prodding his ride to motion. He rode up the mountainside to the first utility pole before veering off to the north toward camp.

"Hm...," said Maya, "He wasn't looking for water, he was looking for us."

"How can you be sure?" I asked.

"Because he wouldn't have quit searching so early in the day. Plus, water spotters usually travel in pairs, for safety. They keep searching until they find water or it is too dark to look any more."

"Interesting," I said. "So what do you think it means?"

"Isn't it obvious?" she asked. "Reya's keeping tabs on you." I wasn't at all sure that I was the one she was worried about, but didn't voice my suspicions. If Reya wanted to reveal Maya's genetic affiliation, she would do it in her own time. And if she didn't, then it wasn't my place to do it.

"Yeah, probably," I said.

"You're perfectly safe with Doog and me, but I can understand why she'd want to protect you. If you're as important to the resistance as everyone seems to think you are, you'll be a high-priority target for Magus." She looked off in the direction the rider had gone. A soft breeze tugged at an unbound spiral of hair at her temple. "I doubt we'll see anyone else today, but they'll try to track us in the morning. Let's get to that town and try to find what we need before the sun gets much higher. I'd not want to have to make camp in a strange town. No way to watch the perimeter."

As we rode on, Maya engaged me once again. As grateful as she was for Doog's oversight, it was clear that she longed for good old-fashioned verbal communication. "Sorry if I gave you a bit of a hard time earlier about your 'chosen one' status. I'd really like to know more about where you came from, and how you came to be here."

"As would I," I said. "I can only tell you what I know, and it isn't much. But I'm happy to share if you're really interested. Maybe you can find some sense in it that I couldn't.

"Try me," she said with a smile.

"As I said before, there is war in my world too, constantly. There are even those who, like Magus, seek to destroy all who oppose them. But where I lived was at peace, for the most part. Not everyone trained for war, only those who chose to. There were buildings - houses, schools, hospitals, places of commerce - all of the places that lie in ruins in this world. But there they are still used and lived in. If you need a tube thingy for your helicopter, there are stores where you can buy it new. If you need to, you can get it from the other side of the world in a matter of days."

Maya's eyes grew wide. "What manner of magic can accomplish this?!!?", she gasped.

"Not magic," I explained. "We have thousands of people and vehicles that deliver..." I saw her dumbfounded expression melt into a devilish grin. "You were joking."

"I was joking," she replied. "Sorry again. I couldn't resist. Yeah, I know all about the post. I read it in a children's book I found. What remains of libraries isn't in good condition, but it's of no practical use to the looters, so sometimes you can find some interesting stuff. My parents taught me to read. The others thought it was a waste of time, but they valued the written word, and I'm thankful for it."

"So you're something of a student too," I said.

"I guess. That's also how I learned to fix stuff, so that's why it's important to me. Anyway, you were telling me about your world."

79

"Yeah, if you haven't already read this story," I teased. She wrinkled her brow and pursed her lips in an expression of mild impatience mingled with interest, and I continued. "My world seems to resemble yours in many ways, but with a few subtle differences. It's not even exactly the same landscape, so I'm not sure if places here correspond to ones in my world. There are different types of animals, and no puurr-deer. And no magic. Or if there is, it is a largely forgotten art."

"In my experience, magic is more trouble than it's worth. A world without it would be a world without Magus. A world where he could never have come to possess the kind of power he has here."

"You may be right. But there is a man in my world who wears Magus' face. I knew him, he was one of my teachers."

This time her face displayed genuine shock. "Your teacher! What, exactly, were you learning?"

"Nothing especially important," I assured her. "Certainly nothing dangerous. If the man I knew is the Magus of our world, then I'd say we have very little to fear. He had the ego, but that's about it."

Not looking totally convinced, she changed the subject. "So you were a student. What were you planning to do with the knowledge you acquired?"

I didn't answer immediately. I began to imagine how the life of an American college student must appear to someone who lived in a world where all knowledge must have a practical purpose. I weighed my words with care. "I had hoped to write books, to teach others about philosophy, about theology."

"Theology?"

"The study of the Deity."

"So you knew Chaer-Ul in your world too?" Her face was aglow with the excitement of innocence.

"I knew more about him than most," I said, trying to inject an appropriate amount of humility.

"Knew *about* him? I don't understand. Why didn't you just talk to him? Don't people in your world *know* him, as we do here?"

So much for impressing her with my theological qualifications. "Of course...I mean, some people claim to know him, but most people think he can't be known in that way. Actually, a lot of people don't even believe he exists."

Maya looked at me in a way that could only be interpreted as pity. "Your world suddenly doesn't sound that nice to me." She didn't mean it in a hurtful way, but I felt as though she had penetrated to my core and found it sad and empty. "Wait...you said you knew your world's version of Magus. Are you saying that every person in my world has a double in yours?"

"Apparently. I knew Reya in my world, too. Only she wasn't called Reya."

"And me?" she asked playfully, batting her lashes, "Do I also remind you of someone back home?"

"No, sorry," I said. "Nobody that I knew."

"Don't you think it's just a tiny bit convenient that in your first few days here you happened to run across some of the same people you knew from your world of billions?"

"I hadn't really thought about it, but now that you mention it, it doesn't exactly seem random. But that doesn't get me any closer to knowing why this happened in the first place."

"Did it occur to you that maybe it didn't happen at all?" she asked. "I mean, maybe you're dreaming all of this, and you'll wake up pretty soon in your own world. Lots of times, in dreams, you see things that are familiar, but not quite."

"Now look who's waxing philosophical! As a matter of fact, that possibility did occur to me, but I've never had a dream that went on for so long, and with so much detail. So I don't think that's what is going on. Anyway, are you saying that you might just be a figment of my nocturnal imagination? How then would you account for your memories, your self-awareness? If it's a dream, then from your perspective it would make more sense that you were the dreamer, and I, the object of your dreams."

"Hmph. *In* your dreams," she said smugly.

At that moment our trail rose sharply, and we could see nothing beyond the birches lining the ridgetop ahead. "Wait here," Maya said. She dismounted and scaled the last few meters of earth to gain a better vantage. "Come on up," she said, waving us forward. Doog and I dismounted as well, and clambered up to where she stood.

Before us a narrow valley stretched between two great peaks. The weathered remains of a small town straddled the trickle of a stream that wound through its center. It must once have been a rushing torrent to have cut such a deep cleft through solid granite, but now only fed a taut band of fertile green along its margins. Green. New growth was green. So even Magus' poison couldn't kill everything...not for good, anyway. The town's most defining attribute was a monstrous structure of brick and steel that loped a third of the way up the eastern slope - an old paper mill. It stood

82

in stark contrast to the valley in which it sat; a foreign geometry amidst the natural curves of river and mountain. Incredibly, its ancient brick smokestack remained intact, though no smoke had issued from its blackened depths for ages.

"There," Maya said, pointing to a straight line amidst the crumbling buildings that paralleled the river's edge. "That will be Main Street. If anything is left of the old shops, we'll find them there. And if we can't find anything useful there...," her fingertip drifted up and toward the behemoth resting on the eastern mountainside, "Then we may just have to look in *there*."

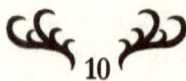

It was a strange feeling, standing there in the middle of a deserted town, expecting to hear...something...but only an unsettling stillness confronted the senses. There would once have been cars traversing the streets, a few pedestrians bustling to and fro, and over it all the rumble and hum of an active paper mill. And more than the sounds, all of the small movements, the visual cues; signs of life. All of that was absent here, and it didn't feel right. I had seen ghost towns before, but they were usually much smaller than this, tiny communities overly dependent upon a single industry, like the coal mining towns of long ago. When supply or demand tapered off, the inhabitants migrated elsewhere. It made all the difference in the world knowing that the reason for this town's solitude was the sudden and speedy extermination of its residents by plague. And all the more knowing that almost every city, town, and village in this tragic world had fallen victim to the same fate.

We noted the types of businesses that fronted the main thoroughfare: a bank, women's clothing, sporting goods, a pizzeria. They could be identified by their architecture, by fragments of their original signage, and by the few pieces of ancient furniture that had not been completely broken down by the ravages of weather and time. All of the windows were broken, and in most cases large portions of the upper floors or roofing of the structures had collapsed. Maya dismissed the animals, and we began to walk slowly along the street, inspecting the contents of the storefronts for any indication that they might conceal something useful. We passed a number of buildings without success, their contents having long ago been thoroughly scavenged. Then, a bit farther down the street, we found what we were looking for: what was left of an old hardware store.

It was dark inside, under the overhang of a dangerously sloping roof. The remnants of a checkout counter sat to our right. The store extended straight back for the first few steps, then angled ninety degrees to the left. Once around this corner the only meager light came from a small, glassless window far in the back. From what we could tell, there wasn't a lot left. Whole rows of shelves had been knocked over or had crumbled. Those still standing were bare or covered with a uniform layer of silt not disturbed for at least a decade. There were a few heavily corroded metal objects on the floor in various places, their presence indicated by an irregular disruption of the floor's own sediment and a rust-colored stain. They were not what we needed, and wouldn't have been in workable condition anyway. A filing cabinet lay on its side, suspended a few inches off the floor as a result of having fallen against a low piece of moulding. Doog kicked it aside to reveal a random assortment of bolts, rusted into a single huge chunk of orange slag.

"There's nothing here," Maya said. We turned to make our way back toward the front of the building, and a fleeting shadow momentarily blotted out our light. Something had moved across the tiny window at the back of the building. Maya whipped something from under her vest and swung her arm around to point at the window. With a quick snap the piece of dark shininess in her hand unfolded to form a crossbow barely larger than a long pistol. Doog instinctively pulled a matching pair of fierce-looking throwing axes from where they were sheathed at his thighs and took position at Maya's back, facing the entrance. I pressed myself against the wall to avoid taking a bolt to the head in the event Maya saw any new movement at the window. I promised myself to ask where I could get a weapon of my own before tagging along on any more crazy adventures.

We stood frozen this way for another pair of seconds, then Maya whispered, "Let's move!" We bustled toward the street the same way we had come, but now the objects on the floor and the dangling sections of ceiling resisted our attempt at more rapid egress. Once back in daylight, it took a moment for our eyes to adjust, but Doog pointed with one of his axes and I looked in time to see a ragged figure slip between two buildings on the opposite side of the street. Doog tensed to give chase but Maya, who stood before him, put out her free arm to stay him. "It could be a trap," she said. "Come on!" Rather than follow the figure up the alley, she led us farther down the street until we reached an intersection. We headed up the hill on the adjacent street. Here the storefronts of Main Street gave way to dilapidated houses with immensely overgrown yards. The rusted husks of ancient cars adorned some of the driveways. In many places new trees and other plant life had grown up through the ruins of homes. It looked like a photo of a forest superimposed on a photo of a town. I wondered how many of the families that once occupied this town had remained when the plague struck. I wondered how many of these homes still entombed the bones of their doomed owners.

As we worked our way up the hill, we constantly glanced between homes and trees on our left, hoping to catch another glimpse of our spy. In most places there were barely any gaps between houses that were not filled with trees or rubble. Still above us and now to our left towered the old mill. As one of the only brick structures above the main street, and certainly the largest, it seemed a likely destination for whoever had been watching us. Unfortunately, if we had to approach and enter that mill, we would be extremely vulnerable to anyone who decided we weren't welcome there. We came at last to another cross street paralleling the main street. This one led to the lumber yard directly before the mill. We didn't see anyone dash across this street into the mill, but they would almost certainly have reached the mill before we got to our current position if that's what they were trying for. We turned down Mill Street.

On the right side of the street was a fallen wall. The forest flora had expanded its jurisdiction over the wall and now reached well into the street with thorny tendrils. This forced us uncomfortably close to the back walls of destroyed homes on the left. These houses had front yards on the downhill side, but no back yards. Residents had apparently parked on the street; the skeleton of one old pick-up still rested behind one of the houses. Maya led the way, stalking stealthily to the edge of each building and pointing her crossbow at the narrow gaps between houses as she came up to them. I was in the middle, and Doog watched the rear. Progress was slow and uneasy, as at any moment someone - or something – could spring from behind the next building, and it was unlikely we would have enough advance notice to effectively defend ourselves. I began to understand why Maya had said that towns could be unsafe. I had certainly felt more secure in a tent in the woods than here in these claustrophobic streets.

As we came up to the old pick-up truck, something bright flashed through the sky and stuck fast in the beam of the house next to it. It was an arrow, wrapped in oil-drenched rags and set ablaze. It had come from an upper window of the mill. Maya and Doog steadied their weapons, trying to pinpoint the precise origin of the projectile, but soon similar flames could be seen in several windows, no doubt trained on us. Shadows stirred beneath the canopy of trees to our right, and the tips of bows and spears slowly came into view, followed by the faces that bore them. At last a half-dozen or so armed men stepped forth from within and between the very houses we had just passed, cutting off any potential retreat. A smallish man of ruddy complexion moved to the forefront. He had a large, unkempt moustache, and a port wine stain dominated most of the left half of his face. In an unexpectedly hoarse and high-pitched voice he said simply, "Lower your weapons". We were vastly outnumbered. We complied and Maya and Doog were relieved of their arms.

We were led to the base of the mill, where the small man conferred briefly with a guard, who then waved us past toward one of three large bay doors that opened as we approached. Once inside, it was immediately apparent that this was no grass-roots, would-be militia. The mill was a stronghold, and these people formed a small but well-organized army. The inside walls of the mill had been fortified with additional layers of brick and stone, and wooden ladders and catwalks had been constructed all about the interior, providing easy access to most of the windows for surveillance, as well as to an enclosed upper section at the far end of the building. All of the machinery that had once processed lumber had been removed. Along one wall were a series of sectored-off rooms that served for such mundane but essential tasks as food preparation and laundry. And all of this was accomplished without betraying the mill's secrets to any passing observer. It was an impressive operation for such a small town.

We passed several more "checkpoints", at the last of which our captors handed our seized weaponry to one of the guards, who hastened the items into a room with a very solid-looking metal door. Opening a locked gate, the small man led us up what appeared to be the building's only original staircase toward the enclosed section on the second level. The stairway was open on one side, but we were flanked by a pair of big, staff-wielding guards, and were at all times carefully watched by archers posted on the upper walkways. At the top of the stairs we were ushered into a long, torch-lit room with no windows. It had the feel of a hunting lodge, with animal skin rugs and heavy-looking, hand-hewn furniture. There were several large chairs and a round table, and at the far end a tall hutch filled with various collected trinkets, most notably a collection of knives and several large globes of green and blue colored glass. A rifle and a sword leaned against its side. Hand-drawn maps and diagrams covered the table's surface.

Our guards were dismissed, and we were invited to sit. The little man wasted no time in formalities. "What business brings you to Milltown?" he asked bluntly. I wondered if that was the town's original name, or one conferred more recently by its current inhabitants. It was logical, if not overly creative.

"We were only looking for supplies. What business do *you* have taking us prisoner?" Maya demanded.

The ginger-mustached man feigned offense. "Oh! You're not our prisoners, you're our *guests!*"

"Funny way to treat guests," I added.

He chuckled. "We had to be certain you were on the right side. You *are* on the right *side*, aren't you?"

"That depends," said Maya. "Who do you work for?"

"The one true Deity, of course. Allow me to introduce myself. My name is Ormond. My people call me the Caretaker." He extended his hand in an artificially magnanimous manner and indulged in a shallow bow. It might have been regal in a more impressive man, but in this tiny red man it just looked absurd.

Maya did not reciprocate, but responded instead, "We fight against Magus. If you are true to Chaer-Ul, then Magus is our common foe."

The unblemished half of his face flared hot, Maya's omission clearly graveling him. His voice grated through clenched teeth, now pitched even higher than before, "*Magus*...yes, indeed, Magus...he is a fool and a heretic. Our battle is against *all* forms of unbelief."

"Good, then we have no quarrel with you. I would appreciate it if you'd return our weapons, and we'll be on our way."

"In good time, my dear. Now it is almost time for our daily assembly, and I'd *very* much enjoy your feedback."

"Thanks just the same, but we have quite a ride to get back to our camp before dark." Maya was choosing not to acknowledge the decidedly non-optional nature of the invitation. She apparently did gather that it was not an ideal time to ask about borrowing a tube thingy.

"I *insist*," he barked, a twitch in his right eyelid belying his insincere grin. He rapped twice on the big table and the two guards entered at once. "Boys, kindly show our new friends to the assembly hall."

"Yes, Caretaker," they replied in unison.

"Oh, and one more thing," he said as we were about to leave the room. "We would have you be as comfortable as possible while within our walls." Ormond caught the eye of one of his guards and nodded toward Maya. The guard moved as if to remove her utility vest, and she raised one index finger between herself and him, drew her lips taut and moved her head ever-so-subtly back and forth. He withdrew a step and shrugged, eyes darting to Ormond for guidance. He said nothing, as Maya had already begun to remove the vest herself. She handed it to the guard, who then draped it over his arm. Maya flashed him a sarcastic smile and curtsied.

We were bustled rather *un*kindly down the staircase, and then fell in among others who were making their way toward a previously unseen doorway hidden in an alcove at the rear corner of the building. We passed through the door and then down a half-flight of granite steps into an adjoining room.

It felt as though I had just stepped into the middle of an evangelical church service back home. All of the essential trappings were in place: the pews, the pulpit, the altar adorned with white cloth and ceremonial bowls. The only things lacking were the stained glass windows, but dozens of the colored glass

90

spheres like the ones we had observed in Ormond's chamber were suspended from the ceiling, all of differing sizes and dangling at various heights. The pews were simplistic and purely functional. The pulpit, in contrast, was much higher and more elaborately carved than any I remembered seeing before. It spoke of a vast chasm between the preacher and the common man.

We were ushered toward the front of the sanctuary, and directed to sit in the third pew, directly in front of the pulpit. Two armed men already sat at the far end, and those attending to us indicated that we were to take a place near the middle of the pew. The two guards that had come with us then sat down as well, neatly sandwiching us between the two pairs. An additional guard stood at each end. We wouldn't have gotten far if we'd tried to jump pews to the front or back, either, as everywhere more people were pouring into the room and filling every available seat. The ambient hum of excited whispers became the dominant sound. I turned to Maya to ask if she had formulated a plan, and felt a painful thud as the butt of a spear was driven into my shoulder blade. I threw an unappreciative glare over my shoulder at the one who had delivered the blow, and he raised it as if to strike again, so I returned my gaze to the front and assumed a more reverent posture.

Just then the chatter subsided and an awed hush fell over the gathered throng. I knew something was happening at the back of the room but didn't dare chance another backward glance. I suspected that the Caretaker had entered the room, and I was right. If I had expected him to be adorned with sumptuous priestly vestments or to inspire veneration with the majesty of his presence, I would have been disappointed. He wore what appeared to be an oversized Navy dress uniform, minus the cap. It was adorned with an unlikely number of medals and insignia that he hadn't earned, but must have been collected from various other uniforms and assembled here. The sleeves and pantlegs had been cut and hemmed, but the obvious excess of material and span of

91

the shoulders gave him the sense of a child playing dress-up. He carried a sword of non-Navy issue at his belt. The Caretaker ascended to his lofty pulpit, drew the sword, then bowed and swung it in a wide, slow arc over the heads of all his congregants. They understood this as a directive to be seated, and did so. We were already sitting.

The Caretaker began to preach. "People of Milltown, today is a special day!" Nobody made a sound as he rasped his message in his high and grating voice. "The Deity has sent us a sign!" He raised his sword again and let his arm drift until it rested over our heads. "How mysterious are his ways...how wondrous his plan!" He let his arm return to his side, then slowly sheathed his sword, and instead clutched the rim of the pulpit with both hands. "That he can accomplish his purposes through the means of such *broken...useless...unworthy* vessels." Each word was enunciated sharply and punctuated with a sharp rap of his fist on the surface of the pulpit. "They come as thieves...in broad daylight! They come to take what they want, what they think they *need...*" His face manufactured a look of absolute astonishment. "...to further a conflict against a *man*...a fight that the Deity has not ordained!" I saw Maya's eyes narrow to slits. Doog gripped the edge of his seat so tightly that I half-expected the wood to splinter. "And what did they bring as an offering in exchange for the things they wished to steal?" He spat the words: "Treachery and violence!" He spun wildly to his left, arm outflung, and everyone watched as one of his men stepped forward on a podium situated below and behind the pulpit, but still above the level of the congregation. He held Doog's and Maya's weapons high above his head for all to see. The parishioners gasped and grumbled. As if every one of them wasn't also armed.

Maya leaned forward slightly, her hands sliding slowly down the front of her thighs toward her knees. The guard to her left must have detected the motion out of the corner of his eyes, as he turned his head to look at her. Maya hastily covered the

92

movement by pretending to stretch and performing an exaggerated yawn. The guard looked her once up and down, apparently deciding at length that she posed little threat without her many-pocketed vest, and then returned his adoring gaze to the Caretaker.

Ormond's anger melted into a face of enlightened calm, eyes cast ceilingward. He spoke slowly and intentionally, "But...The Deity...is... merciful..." He held his expression for several uncomfortable seconds, then looked back out over the crowd and spoke with crazed excitement. "He has spoken to me!" This was met with reverent oohs and ahs. When it subsided, the Caretaker continued. "And he has told me...," his hands still clutching the pulpit, he lifted one finger to point at Maya, "that he has sent this woman to us in fulfillment of the ancient prophecies! She is the second *Eve*!" An awestruck wail from somewhere in the back. "And just as the first Eve brought death, so the second shall be a giver of life, the Mother of a new humanity!"

Maya's outraged, "What?!!?" was barely heard over the shouts and cheers of the lunatic mob. She tried to stand and was forcibly shoved back into her seat. Doog did manage to stand, and paid for it with a spirited beating from several of the men around him. I took a moment to scan the room, and realized for the first time that there were no women present. I hadn't seen any on the way in, either. It seemed as though this was an oversight they hoped to rectify immediately. It had been a mistake coming here.

I saw Maya's knees rubbing against each other. At first I thought it was just an outward manifestation of the vortex of rage swirling within. But then she raised one knee higher than the other, and I heard a small "click". Nobody else seemed to notice it. It was followed by a tiny mechanical whirring that grew in pitch as the seconds passed. Then I saw it. A tiny device of wheels and gears speeding across the floor toward the left side of the pulpit. Apparently not all of her secrets were tucked into her vest. When the apparatus reached the side of the pulpit it stopped moving forward and began to spin in place. At the same time it started giving off sparks, while the noise it was emitting increased to a frenzied pitch. For all of that, it took a couple of moments for anyone to notice it over the cultish chants of the assembled congregants. When it happened, startled and confused eyes looked as one in that general direction, trying to determine the source of the chaos. Maya took full advantage of the distraction. She sprang from her seat as no less than five sharpened blades perforated the space she had just occupied. I saw one of her boots alight upon the top of the pew before us, and then she was sailing through the air, easily clearing the remaining pews and landing in the open space just under the pulpit. Ormond, face flaming, screeched an incomprehensible command to some of his nearest guards. Maya leaped again, and I saw the guard next to me draw back, preparing to skewer her with a launched spear. I tackled him, grasping his spear tightly to prevent him from throwing it and struggling to wrest it from his hands. Maya made for the place behind the pulpit where the guard had retreated with their weapons, but the way was now cut off by some more of Ormond's goons. She darted nimbly toward the other side of the pulpit, dodging jabbing spears as she sought a way to reach her seized property. Meanwhile Doog lowered his head and drove his leading shoulder into the nearest guard, using his superior strength to push him into the person beside him. He continued to shove one person into another until they were packed so tightly that nobody could move. This created a momentary gap directly in front of me, and I sprinted through it before vaulting myself up onto the podium.

My timely arrival startled a fleeing Ormond, the clear part of his face flushing pale as he looked around himself and realized that all of his guards had either joined the fray below or preceded him behind the safety of the heavy door at the back of the podium. His delay bought me enough time to get to my feet and lunge for him. I managed to grab hold of both of his pantlegs as he dove through the rapidly closing door. Owing to the generous cut of his

94

trousers, he was able to wiggle free and scamper through the opening just before his men pulled it tight. I heard the clunk of a heavy bolt, and found myself sitting outside the door clutching a small pair of Navy-colored pants. The only saving grace was that the pants had been held aloft by a thick leather belt, and on that belt hung the Caretaker's still-sheathed sword. At least I was finally armed. I ripped the belt out of the loops and slung the whole thing over one shoulder. I was about to try the door that Ormond had slipped through when I heard Maya shriek. I turned to find that the guards had at last managed to contain her, though to her credit it was occupying the full attention of no less than four full-grown men. I saw her land a solid bite on the arm to her left, and the angry guard grabbed a thick shock of her hair, knotted his hand up in it, and pulled back hard. She winced with the pain, and spotting me, shouted, "Justin!" Already at the edge of the podium, I launched myself into the air, simultaneously withdrawing the sword from where it rested behind my shoulder blade. I swung it around my head in a wide circle, shattering several of the large glass globes. The shards radiated outward, missing Maya and her assailants but blinding or disorienting a number of those around them. I landed in a crouch, sword held in my right hand, its blade over my left shoulder. I immediately sprung and directed the hilt at the man who held Maya by the hair, and delivered a jarring blow to his forehead. He loosed his grip, stiffened and fell, sprawling over the first pew. I turned the tip of my blade on those who still grappled with her arms and legs, and was about to rush them when suddenly...the room imploded.

At both sides of the sanctuary the brick walls bowed inward in slow motion and disintegrated into chunks of mortar and billowing clouds of reddish dust, as a sonic boom deprived me of all sound except a shrill ringing. Every remaining globe burst instantaneously, filling the air with a shimmering mist of glass. Everyone in the room cringed and covered their faces, protecting their eyes and trying not to inhale the deadly fragments. Before the debris could begin to settle, shadows materialized out of the lingering haze. Dark commandos in gas masks strode fearlessly into the chaotic fray and dispassionately disemboweled the first hapless worshippers they encountered. There was a moment of shocked disbelief, then hearing returned with a vengeance as the entire room erupted in hysterical screams. The black-and-scarlet-clad death squad tore into the panicked swarm with an insatiable bloodlust, and one after another the bodies fell, the best of the Caretaker's guards offering only a prolonged defense before succumbing to the unrelenting brutality of the attacks. There was a secondary explosion at the back of the sanctuary, and I turned to see two of the assassins rushing into the dust and through the jagged aperture that now occupied the place of the Caretaker's escape hatch.

I turned back to the anarchy unfolding in the center of the room and scanned the mass of clashing combatants in an attempt to locate my friends. I couldn't see them, and began to fear that they might have fallen. I joined the mad rush of people pressing toward the door through which we had entered, back into the mill. I thought perhaps Maya and Doog had already made it out, and were waiting for me. The Caretaker's men were too concerned to escape the scene of slaughter at their backs to notice or care about me. Then I saw it: several more dark soldiers standing as gatekeepers just outside the door, cutting down everyone that made it that far. The other people didn't seem to notice them, so blinded with fear of the known evil behind them. The force of the torrent of human bodies that carried me along could not be stopped. And the pile of slain bodies at the door kept rising. I began to feel a rush of panic and tried to dig my feet in, to work my way to the outer edge of the stream and to freedom, but to no avail. Then a strong hand grabbed me by the arm and held me fast, an anchor amidst the crush of luckless souls that swept around me. Slowly, I felt myself being pulled to the side. When I emerged from the death surge, it was Maya's face that greeted me, pulling me to safety as she clung to a pillar with her other hand. I opened my mouth to speak, and she interrupted, "Just returning the favor."

Maya pointed to one of the new holes that the dark warriors had blasted through the wall of the sanctuary. It was presently unguarded. "Follow me!" she said. She hadn't let go of my hand, so it didn't seem like I had much choice. Not that I minded. We dashed for the outlet, and I glanced back to see that several of the cultists had also seen the opening and were following our lead. I watched as the tip of a blade emerged from the abdomen of a man at the center of the pack. He was lifted from the ground momentarily, legs still pumping, then slammed back down as his murderer planted the head of his bladed staff in the earth and, without losing momentum, vaulted over the heads of the man's companions. As he landed, he swung his weapon behind him without looking, and neatly lopped off the heads of the remaining men. Then, removing a small object from his belt, he tossed it over his shoulder, back through the hole into the sanctuary. Black smoke billowed from where it landed, and I could hear people inside coughing and gasping as the nerve gas started to take effect. Thankfully, Maya hadn't stopped running, and hadn't let go. But soon he was in fast pursuit, and rapidly gaining ground. As we neared the treeline behind the mill, Maya called out to the puurr-deer. Almost immediately three of the great animals burst from among the trees and circled toward us. Anticipating my question, Maya panted, "I figured you were ready to drive." The foremost two deer edged up beside us and matched our pace. Lowering their heads, they allowed us to grab onto their antlers and fluidly swept us up onto their backs. The third deer followed closely. "We have to go back for Doog!" Maya shouted. The deer cut a broad arc, making sure to stay well ahead of the dark soldier that pursued us. Their path brought them to a raised wall of earth that may have formed part of the mill's outer perimeter of defense. As it loomed closer I realized that it marked one shore of a now-dry river that must once have run alongside the mill. Arriving at the obstacle Maya's deer leaped, landing easily on the far side. I was

97

next. My mount needed no instruction, instinctively following the first. But I was accustomed to clinging to a slender waist, not to a puurr-deer's substantial neck with its covering of silky fur. So when my ride struck down on the other side of the mound, I slipped just a bit to the side of its neck. At this precise moment a bladed weapon, thrown with pinpoint accuracy, spun through the air and glanced off a point of my deer's rack, just where my head had been a second before. The staff clanged to the ground as I righted myself and reaffirmed my grip. I didn't have time to contemplate the possibility of luck in a theistic universe.

As we pulled along the far side of the mill, I heard Maya yell, "Doog!" He was crouching on a low windowsill covering his mouth and nose with one forearm, black smoke curling out from the top of the window over his head. When he saw us he held Maya's crossbow aloft in his other hand and shook it victoriously. As we came closer we could see that he also had his axes strapped to his thighs, and he tossed Maya her vest as she raced past his position. "Doog, you got 'em! Great work!" Doog jumped onto the back of the third deer as we passed under the window, and immediately we peeled away, choosing a path that hugged the forest's edge and led back toward our camp in the north. The shadows under the mill coalesced into three dark shapes that continued to pursue us on foot. Magus' assassins were frighteningly fast and seemingly inexhaustible, both in physical prowess and sheer numbers. But they were no match for a healthy puurr-deer at full gallop. We quickly put a half a kilometer between them and us, and were well out of throwing reach. I looked back one last time to see with relief that the mill-fortress had once again become a rather small and pathetic-looking thing, a rusted and decaying symbol of a long-lost economy. And now the scene of a bloody massacre and the tomb of a misguided sect. As I turned my head back to the road that lay before us, I thought I saw a glint of light in one of the high windows. A realization flashed through my mind like lightning, and with it a renewed wave of fear. But not for me. In an eye blink, I threw my weight against the side of my deer's neck, causing it to veer to the right, placing myself between Maya and the mill. A second later I felt a punch like a jackhammer in my back, followed by the most profound agony I had ever experienced. My body hit the ground, twitched once, then lay still. The thunder of hooves grew distant.

The puurr-deer could not stop quickly when traveling at full speed. By the time Maya and Doog realized what had happened and began to turn back for me, the three dark warriors were almost upon me. Maya screamed, "No!" and pressed her mount once more into a full gallop, this time back toward me. She raised her crossbow and took aim, trying desperately to steady her hand against the jarring movements of the deer. She released a bolt and dropped one of the soldiers dead in his tracks; shakily nocked a second. Thoot! Another went down. The third was already upon me. Raising his staff over me, he plunged the bladed head under my ribs then levered it back, angling the tip upward. I felt the blade penetrate; felt an irregular throb, then a spreading warmth. My vision became hazy. The last thing I saw was the bolt of a crossbow entering his throat.

11

My eyes came slowly to focus on Maya's pretty face, inches from my own. Something different...no, not Maya; it was Reya. She pulled away. Stood up, rather. I was lying on my back on the ground, head propped up with soft cushions. The canvas background told me that I was in my own tent, or one very like it. "How are you feeling?" she asked. My peripheral vision kicked in, and I could make out the faces of Denkel and Jeyt behind her on my right, Maya and Doog on the left. The gas mask from one of Magus' assassins dangled from her right hip with its bug-eyed lenses and breathing hose. A black tube thingy. I smiled. My back should have ached, but didn't. Cautiously I raised my head to examine the gaping wound in my belly, fearful of what I'd see. I was covered with a blanket, so the damage was not immediately evident. But since this small movement elicited no stabbing pain, I chanced another. I raised myself to one elbow, and with the other arm threw the covering aside. As it turned out nobody had bothered to re-clothe me after presumably tending to my injuries. I quickly pulled the blanket back over my lower half. Reya smiled and raised her eyebrows. Maya reddened and her eyes hastily inspected the tent flaps in the corner for signs of leakage. I would have been mortified, were I not distracted by the fact that there was no wound, no pustulent gash, no sign of an amateur stitching job. No indication, in fact, that anything had happened at all! I sat up, careful to gather the blanket around me as I did.

"My wound..." I began. I turned to my friends. "Maya, you saw...Doog..."

"Oh, we saw!" Maya responded. I thought for a moment she was still referring to my recent exposure, but the tell-tale pinkening was absent, and genuine excitement tinged her voice. "Doog had to pull the weapon out, it was so deeply embedded." Her voice grew thin. "We didn't expect you to survive the ride back to camp."

"There was also this," Reya added. She presented the sheathed sword I had taken from Ormond. The sword...that I had slung over my back! She turned it over to reveal an irregularity in the contour of the scabbard, an indentation clearly made by a bullet of considerable caliber. "This may have saved you from the impact of the projectile. But I have no explanation for what happened with your wound. Is there something we should know about healing times in your world?"

"Yeah," I said. "They take a lot longer than this, and you don't heal from this kind of injury. Nobody does."

"You did," Maya said warmly.

I returned her smile.

"I don't know what this means," Reya said. Denkel cleared his throat as if to speak, but Reya continued, initially louder, "It will require careful consideration. More importantly, it was extremely dangerous," she said to me, then her eyes darted to Maya, "and foolish, for you to go there. The risks were enormous. We survive, only because we are united in our resistance. If you have need of something, we can formulate a plan to acquire it...together. When we act alone, we play Magus' game. He would divide us, and then destroy us, one by one. This incident was a perfect example. Magus knew you were going to be there. That means we have a little security breach. If any of you knows or suspects anything, you must confer with me at once."

Maya began, "There was a man, out in the field, before we reached Milltown."

"Not here," Reya said. "We'll talk later, in private. Now, Justin," she returned her attention to me. "Maya told me how you helped in the battle. I think you may have an aptitude for combat, but you'll need some training. Since you've already made Maya's acquaintance, I'd like you to shadow her. I'll give her specific instructions as to what skills you need to master. First lesson: riding. And not just riding, but everything about the puurr-deer; how to communicate with them, what special capabilities they have. However..." her voice took on a weightier tone, "You are to remain within strict boundaries, and observe the timelines I prescribe." Reya turned to address me. "I'd have a word with you alone, when the moment presents itself."

"My clothes...," I started, and she gestured with her head to the corner behind me, where a fresh stack lay folded for me. Reya exited the tent, the meeting adjourned. The others filed out silently behind her, Maya lingering only for a moment.

"I'll wait outside," she said, then followed the rest. I waited until she had refastened the flap and then I inspected the garments Reya had left. It was an entirely new set of clothes, but I liked them: jeans with a heavy belt, black jersey, black riding boots of a sort I might have admired back home, but would never have dared to wear on campus. I hastily dressed before anyone else decided to pay me a visit, and found that these clothes fit as well as the previous set. I was not entirely surprised.

As promised, Maya was standing just outside the entrance. "Let's take a walk," she said as I emerged.

I fell into step beside her. "So I guess you're stuck with me for a while," I said, smiling.

She looked me up and down quickly through half-closed lids, her right cheek dimpling cutely as she half-smiled, "I suppose you'll have to do."

102

We strolled through a yellow wood on one of the less traveled paths out of the camp, heading in the general direction of the helicopter. Maya began, "So, did you feel it?"

Assuming she was referring to the giant blade that had so recently skewered me, I replied, "Yeah, I felt it good. I didn't like it."

"Oh...yes, of course you felt that! But I meant after that, on the ride back to camp."

"I can't say that I felt anything after that. I was pretty much out of it," I said. "What did you feel?"

"I don't know how to describe it; sort of an awareness of something good. It was as though someone spoke softly to me and told me everything was going to be all right. But I heard no voice. It was the presence of Chaer-Ul."

"How do you know it was the Deity? The human mind has an amazing ability to supply what is needed in times of great duress."

She looked at me with pity. "You have spoken with Chaer-Ul and yet you do not believe..."

"It's not that I don't believe, I just don't necessarily think every breath and every sensation is an act of God."

Her eyes grew wide, she stopped in place and turned to face me, touching my cheek gently with one hand. I recognized in the gesture not pity, but a heartfelt desire to help me see. "But that's *exactly* where he is found!" Her words shook me, made me pause to question my own sometimes cynical and doubt-riddled approach to religion. Maya's child-like naivety was at once repellant to my modern mind and possessed of a fragile and elusive beauty, like something long forgotten.

103

It was a conflict I didn't care to resolve at the moment, so I returned the conversation to the practical matters at hand. "If you are to train me, what about your work on the chopper?" I asked. "What about Doog?"

"He actually prefers to work alone when it comes to mechanical things," she said. "He would never ask me to leave him alone, but he just sometimes gets...I don't know...*quieter.*" I tried to imagine what that would sound like. "Anyway, he has a lot more experience fixing things on that scale. I mostly tinker with gadgets or get old bikes up and running."

"Bikes?" I asked, my interest level peaking.

"Yeah, you know, motorcycles. I've worked on Kawasakis, Suzukis...a few Harleys...I even once found a sweet Ducati! It was kept in mint condition while the owner was alive - covered and in a dry garage – she almost turned over when I tried the key..." Her voice trailed off sadly, eyes fixed on a distant cloud where I presumed the bike was now parked.

"What happened to it?" I asked.

Returning to reality she looked at me and said, "I traded it because my family needed some supplies. I never let myself think that I could keep it. I pretty much never keep anything that I can't carry on me. It's safer – and less painful – that way."

"Hence the pockets," I added.

"Hence the pockets," she echoed, noticeably cheered. "Anyway, we'll check in on Doog every day, while we're training. When it's done I'll take you both for a little spin...with your mom's permission, of course."

I smiled, partly because of the irony of her comment, but also happy for the lighter turn the conversation was taking. "So where is your home, anyway? Is it far from here?"

"A couple hundred kilometers to the south," she said.

"Then how did you end up this far north?"

"The base where I found the 'copter was east of there. Magus had just discovered it and was trying to figure out how to move it. His armies are all along the east coast...for the most part. I was pursued as I tried to escape. They had some kind of energy weapon that can slice the sky. The chopper took damage, but I could still keep her in the air and was able to pull out of range of the weapon's beam. Then we saw two small aircraft taking off below us. Not sure what they're called, basically a single pilot in an open seat, a motor, and gliding wings made out of cloth. They weren't very fast, but we couldn't pull ahead quick enough to lose them entirely. I wasn't gonna lead them straight to my family and the rebel base, so I steered north for as long as I dared. When we couldn't see them anymore, I banked toward the west. They must have either continued to follow our last known trajectory, or turned back and reported to their superiors. I suspect the latter, as I doubt those things carry much fuel, and we had already come a long way.

"Anyway, by that time I was getting low too, and I knew I couldn't make it home, so I started looking for someplace to set the 'copter down and cover it with brush. Just then I spotted the big smokestack of Milltown poking over the crest of the ridge ahead. We passed over it once, just looking for human activity. When I made to circle back for a second pass, Doog pointed to a funny little cloud on the horizon. I figured it was smoke from a rebel camp, as we were a long way from the coast. I thought it was a better bet than Milltown – too many hiding places there. We were flying on fumes by the time you guys saw us."

"Maya," I said, "You don't have to do this. Train me, I mean. I'm sure Reya has other people who could do it."

She became indignant. "Oh I see! Other *men*, you mean! Can't possibly learn such *manly* arts from a woman!"

"No, that's not what I meant! I just thought..." I saw the amusement in her eyes.

"Boy, one of these days maybe you'll figure out how to read me," she said as she jabbed an elbow between my ribs. "That can be your final exam!"

"Maya...," I said seriously, "I thought you'd want to be getting back to your family once the chopper was air-worthy again."

She stopped, turned to face me again, and there was no hidden jest in her smile. "Justin, I love my family. But my resistance activities put them at risk. For now, the farther I am away from them, the better. It's easier if I think of the resistance as my new family. I already had a brother in Doog, and now I have another. Reya talked to me while you were unconscious, she asked for my help. It was my choice. I'm staying here."

I tried not to show the sudden relief I felt.

"Besides," she continued, "I'm anxious to see what you're capable of."

We stopped by the landing site, where Doog was busy inside an open panel on the helicopter's near side. Maya whistled, and he turned, a big-toothed smile etching its way across his grease-stained face. She tossed him the gas mask, and he caught it with a nod, setting it on the inside floor of the vehicle until he was ready to install it.

106

"I'm gonna be working with Justin for a while, teaching him fighting and stuff," she informed him. He shrugged and wobbled his head back and forth in a display of indifference, but this quickly dissolved into a stern glare and a pointed finger. I thought for a second it was directed at me, but immediately realized it was meant for Maya. "Don't worry, I'll be careful. You just make sure nothing happens to this bird!" Doog rolled his eyes and brushed us away with a flick of his wrist before returning to his work. He was clearly relieved to learn that he would be working solo.

Walking on a little farther, Maya asked me, "So, shall we get started?"

"You're the teacher," I replied.

She made her deer-summoning sound and we waited. Soon enough two healthy specimens trotted into view. They approached and sniffed us, then began to lower their heads and position themselves for mounting. But before we could climb up, a cracking of branches could be heard, and the deer raised their heads once more, curious, not alarmed. A moment later Reya burst through the trees on her own deer, describing a circle around us and the two unmounted animals.

"Didn't want you two to get too far before we'd had a chance to chat," she said. "Go ahead, mount up. We'll ride together for the first bit."

We did so, and soon we were riding three abreast. Reya led us up the gradual incline of a wide, grassy hill, the trees thinning as we neared its crest. From the top we could see a pond, its surface mottled with wind-blown whitecaps. We descended the far side of the hill and paralleled the near shore of the pond, where dense yellow-brown reed beds obscured our view of the water. Here we slowed, and Reya introduced the business at hand.

107

"I have no desire to prevent you from beginning your training," she said to me, then addressing Maya as well, "But I must know what you know about the potential security breach. Tell me about the man you saw. Leave no detail out, however small." We proceeded to describe the man we had seen by the powerlines, and the strangeness of his demeanor. We expected her to identify him immediately, as distinctive as he had been. But her look was rather one of puzzlement.

"Do you know who it was?" I asked finally.

"No," she said. Maya and I looked at each other, surprised. "That means it could have been one of Magus' men in disguise, or it could have been a traitor entrenched in one of the other rebel camps. I'll send word to trusted agents within the camps I know of, and see if they have anyone matching this description. It's also *possible*," she continued, "that he really was just a rebel looking for water, however strange his behavior may appear. I *don't* believe, however, that the attack at Milltown was a case of 'wrong place, wrong time'. It was too convenient. Magus knew you were there. And that means that *somewhere*, we have a traitor."

"How are traitors dealt with?" I asked.

"They'll be given a trial," she said. "We're not beasts like Magus's men. But the sad fact is, we don't have enough men to keep prisoners of war under watch, and we can't afford to let them return to Magus with any information they may have stolen. If we manage to catch someone involved in treachery, the only realistic option is termination."

I felt a chill, and saw that Maya was equally unsettled. But Reya was right, if this was a war, then even the good guys might have to make some distasteful choices now and then.

108

"Was there anything else that might be helpful?" Reya asked. Maya and I both shook our heads. "Then I won't detain you longer." Turning to me, "Get to know the Puurr-deer. Magus can only employ them through coercion. They have a will, and they reserve their greatest gifts for their friends. We count ourselves lucky to share that status." Then to Maya, with a bit of menace, "And do be careful to observe the boundaries I spoke of previously."

"Of course," said Maya. Warbling to her deer, Reya turned about and galloped back along the shore and up over the hill, out of our sight.

I returned my gaze to Maya. "So what's the first lesson?"

A devious smile spread slowly across her face, still staring at the distant hilltop. "Lessons can wait," she said. "You recently survived a fatal attack. Aren't you the least bit curious what that means?"

"Of course I am. But I don't see how I'm going to find out, short of…" My mind was beginning to go down the path hers had so recently traveled. "You want me to go talk to the Deity again."

She was nodding. "Chaer-Ul. He will know."

"But Reya…," I started.

"…Is not my mom," she finished. Then she made the vocalization and her deer exploded into motion. At a loss for alternatives, I imitated the sound awkwardly, and to my astonishment, mine took up chase.

109

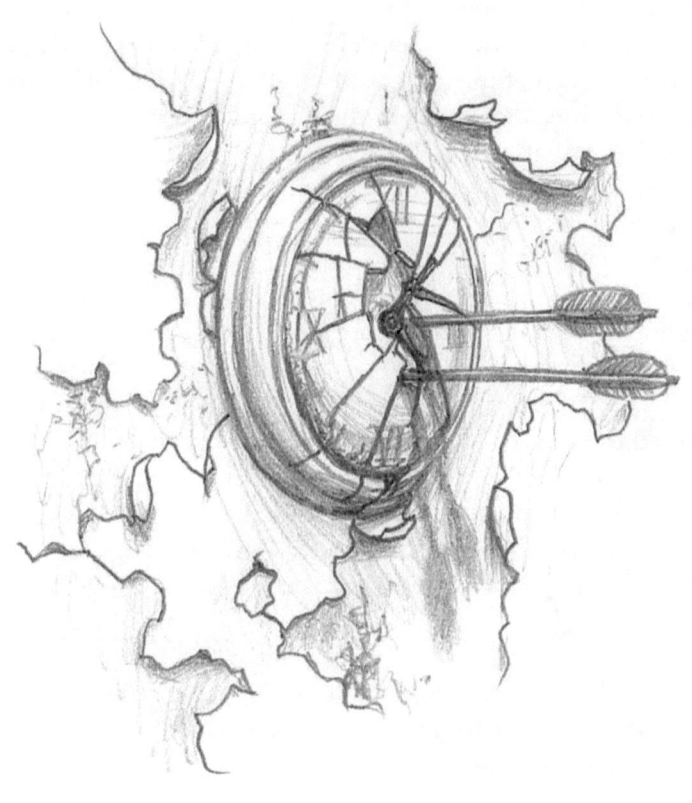

12

It was gone. The hole, the gap between the tectonic plates that formed the fault-line, was gone. I walked a couple hundred meters in each direction trying to find it, but to no avail. I was sure that was the spot, but the cleft through which I had descended to that spherical chamber was not to be found; there was no way in. I turned to Maya, still mounted on her deer. "You knew of this place. Did people from your camp come here too?"

"Yes. Chaer-Ul can be sought anywhere, he knows no physical limitations. But only here has anyone ever spoken with him face-to-face, at least as far as we know."

"And you have been here too?" I asked.

"Yes, but not for myself. All of the leaders of the resistance agreed that this place should only be accessed under very special circumstances. That it should not become a 'wishing well' for every curious supplicant wondering if the girl he liked fancied him too."

"But we didn't have authorization to come here now. Maybe it opens only at appropriate times," I suggested.

"Possibly, but I don't think so," said Maya. "For one thing, I think this is a *very* appropriate occasion. I'm surprised Reya didn't suggest it. And in my experience, Chaer-Ul doesn't respect the customs and restrictions of men. Many have come here to seek his counsel and been met with only darkness and the sound of their own breathing. But the hole remained; the gravity anomaly was intact." A creeping sense of guilt nagged at my mind. Had my outburst merited a permanent end to this mode of communion with the Deity? Not just for me but for everyone?

"What do we do now?" I asked.

"Well, I guess we head back," said Maya. "But we should rest the deer first. There's a glade with a spring not far from here. I came across it on a previous trip. The deer should be able to refresh themselves. Us too. There's sometimes berries!"

We set off almost directly east, rather than following the fault-line north to intersect the normal trail. Immediately we entered a forested area. The density of trees and undergrowth that might have hindered a horse proved no obstacle for the puurr-deer, for whom thick vegetation was home turf. They bounded over low shrubbery and dodged tree trunks with great facility, and the remarkable resilience of their long legs made for a mostly smooth ride. Maya's long, dark hair whipped about in her wake like a windblown flag. I focused on this fluid movement as the yellow foliage smeared into a blur in my peripheral vision, leaves occasionally brushing my cheeks. It became a golden tunnel through which we raced, and the serpentine swirling of Maya's hair lulled me into a state of relative relaxation.

So entranced was I that I didn't at once notice that the tunnel had grown narrower, the forms of Maya and her deer smaller. Only as the leaves began to touch my face more frequently, and with a less gentle caress, did I begin to realize that Maya had pulled a good bit farther ahead, and the forest had become markedly denser. When I did notice the change, I shook myself out of my motion-trance and called to Maya. She didn't appear to hear me over the rustling of leaves and the steady thumping of hooves against the forest floor. I shouted to her again, with similar result. The forest canopy high above had now grown so thickly intertwined that the light touched the earth only here and there, and all was cast in twilight tones.

The braches pulled harder now against my clothes, and it seemed at last that my deer began to strain against the increasing

112

resistance. When the darkness was nearly absolute, I felt my legs slipping against the body of my mount. I squeezed my thighs hard against its sides in an effort to remain in place, but too late; its snow-fleeced haunches disappeared into the thickness of brush before me. Still I didn't fall; the branches held me fast, suspended well above the ground. I twisted and pulled against the restraining tendrils, but the tips of countless branches bent by my passage recoiled, lifting my body, contrary to gravity, higher into the prickly overgrowth. I squinted my eyes tightly against the probing twigs that scraped my face. When I felt myself achieve a sort of equilibrium, I waited, listening for the sound of Maya and the deer returning.

Instead, there was a faint, irregular crackling and snapping from somewhere high above. Cautiously, I pried one eye open, then the other. Directly over my head, maybe ten meters above me, a tiny spark had kindled the very tips of the branches where they came together. There was no flame, but an orange glow began to spread slowly outward from the point of ignition. Where it had already burned, the branches turned completely to ash and crumbled, sprinkling me and the lower foliage with a shower of fine, glittering ash. As a larger area was scorched by the unseen conflagration, a cavity of branchlessness appeared and grew; a hollow sphere the bounds of which were described by countless tiny brands that continued to burn orange-hot. When the branch-tips immediately around my head had been similarly seared, the progression of the burning ceased. Dozens of tiny match-tips smoldered around my face, but I felt no heat.

Then I heard again the voice from the subterranean chamber.

"Justin Mayer. You sought me, but it is you who are found." With each uttered syllable the branch tips flared a brighter orange, as if blown upon by an unseen breath.

113

"Chaer-Ul...," I intoned softly, but the name on my lips felt as if taken without consent. Inexplicably I experienced shame. "I'm sorry for the way I acted before," I added awkwardly.

"Your mind hasn't made enough room for me yet. Your mind *hasn't* enough room for me. What can you understand?" the voice said.

"I understand that you are a god. *The* god of this world, or at least the greatest. The people who follow you speak of other, 'lesser gods'."

The smoldering tips flared white hot, pulsed to the sound of rumbling laughter. There was amusement, not anger in the words that followed. "I am *not* the god of this world. I am the god of *worlds*," he said.

"You brought me here, right?" I asked. "What exactly is it that you want me to do? To *become?*"

"I only expect you to *be*. What you may become is in my hand," he said simply.

"Can I go home?" I tried.

"Do you want to?"

I didn't answer right away. The pulsing embers accented a chuckle that grew into a hearty laugh. I couldn't completely suppress a smile. "I have to admit, I am a little curious where this is all going."

The laughter tapered off into a rumbling "Mmmm..." that sounded suspiciously of satisfaction. "That sounds like teleology," he said. The embers beamed and smirked.

I wasn't convinced that this was the same god of the dead religions of my world. Had anyone ever truly spoken with him as I did now? Was this a god of penance and reprobation? I suspected that Chaer-Ul could extinguish my life as easily as one of these embers. I also had a feeling he wouldn't. That gave me the confidence to press a little farther. "Look, I need to understand what is happening to me. I need to know why I survived that blade. Was that bullet just luck, or something more?"

"It is *always* something more. That you live…that is because of who you are. That you are untouched…that is because of who you must become.."

This Deity had an amazing way of using a lot of words to say absolutely nothing. I wasn't ready to give up just yet. "Am I immortal?" I asked. It seemed like a fair question.

"A belief in one's immortality has a way of making heroes into martyrs," he said.

"And is that what you'd have me become – a martyr in this fight against Magus?" There was no response. Only the sound of a long, slow exhalation that I took for an exasperated sigh. As it finished, the orange glow of a thousand burning branches faded to black and sent tiny trails of smoke wiggling into every small gap in the dark canopy above. It was very dark for a moment, and very quiet. Then without warning the limbs that supported me cracked and sent me plummeting toward the forest floor. I landed on the back of my mount in full stride, and blinked at brilliant rays of sunlight beaming through the leaf cover. Grabbing thick handfuls of the deer's shaggy coat, I turned to look back at where I'd been. It didn't look particularly dark, or dense, and focusing on my arms I saw no trace of ash. I turned my view to the fore once again, and was relieved to see Maya's entrancing locks swirling before me.

115

She turned to glance at me over her shoulder and smiled warmly. "We're almost to the clearing!" she shouted. Then her smile grew wider and her eyes took on an ever-so-slightly unfocused appearance as she added, to no one in particular, "Berries!"

As it turned out, there *were* a few berries by the spring. I was hungry, but I let her have them all. It was fun watching her eat, her mannerisms at once primal and child-like. By the end her lips and fingertips were all stained red-purple from the juice. I sat on a big, mossy rock dappled with patchy sunlight. Crystalline water burbled from under some overhanging roots behind me and to my left, flowing between Maya and me. All around us the ground was spongy green moss, decorated with fallen yellow leaves. Here and there a patch of tender new grass or ferns poked through and vied for a place in the sun. It was a scene of incredible serenity, and I wished we could stay there, unmoving, forever. My reverie was interrupted as one of the deer approached and sniffed the water tentatively, then tasted it. Maya stood from the spot where she was crouched opposite me and removed a pair of canteens from her pack, tossing me one. We filled them and drank, filled them again. The deer drank freely and nibbled blissfully upon the rare greens.

Since Maya made no comment on my recent temporary absence I asked. "Did you notice anything unusual since we left the fault?"

"Like what?"

"I think I had kind of a vision," I explained. "I was lifted right off of my deer and…and Chaer-Ul spoke to me."

"Chaer-Ul! What did he say?!!?" she asked excitedly.

"Very little that I understood."

116

She nodded, unperturbed. "That's his way. But it always has meaning. Come here, tell me, and maybe I can help you understand it."

Actually, that seemed like a good idea. I hopped over the narrow stream and we both sat down on a broad, flat rock. I began, "I don't remember it word-for-word, and a lot of it was just riddles, non-answers. I tried to press him for an answer about why I didn't die from that assassin's blade..."

Maya thinned her lips and tilted her head at me in a mildly scolding manner. I explained further, "I wasn't disrespectful, I tried to ask in a nicer way this time." This softened her features. "The part I remember is that he said something about those who think they are immortal becoming martyrs." I knew the wording wasn't right, but hoped that it was close enough for her to make something of it. She smiled and began to nod her head. "This means something to you?" I asked.

She continued to nod, her mouth fell open slightly and at length she said, "...no." I grunted, but she hastily added, "But often Chaer-Ul gives a piece that doesn't look like anything, and only later gives the key that unlocks it. Other times he gives the key first. And sometimes..." I could tell she was winding up to a dramatic conclusion. "...sometimes...you already *have* the key and don't know it! Do you already have the key?!!? You *have* the key!!!" She was so genuinely thrilled that I hated to let her down.

"Sorry, no. I don't think so," I said. I thought she might experience a bipolar crash, but her smile endured. I don't think she totally believed me.

Maya picked up tiny pebbles and tossed them one by one into the stream. "You seem to be doing all right with your deer," she said. "I mean, except for that one part where you fell clean off her and had a vision." I squinted my eyes tightly and grimaced, letting her

117

have her fun. "Anyway, there's still a lot of daylight left. Let's work on some more riding skills, and we can still be back before Reya would start to miss us."

"You're the teacher," I said.

"Good," she said. "Let's start with some communication. You've heard some of the sounds we make to get them to come, to go, and so on. You did it yourself, as we were leaving camp, right?"

"Right," I said.

"You probably assumed that there were specific commands for each action. It's not exactly like that. The puurr-deer communicate in tones, like the ones you've heard. The sounds are essential for understanding to occur. But the tone itself is not the message. It is only a vessel for the message."

"Watch," Maya said. She leaned in close to her deer's face and scratched it gently under its chin. An aside to me, "The touch isn't essential, they just like it." I nodded, but she was intent on what she was doing. She started to hum in low, vibratory tones. Shortly, the deer pulled away, turned, and trotted across the clearing. Foraging behind some low shrubbery, it came up with a sprig of berries in its mouth, returned and presented it to Maya. "See," she said, "I knew I had missed some! I just asked it if it had seen any."

"Neat trick," I said, impressed.

"We use the same technique to issue commands while riding. Watch this." She started humming again, her big, brown eyes locked into its golden ones. In her concentration she pushed her lips forward in a way that was surely not intrinsic to the technique, but entirely fetching nonetheless. This woman such an amazing mix of grace and strength, wisdom and innocence. Completely lovely. She blushed suddenly. "Oh! I'm sorry, I

118

should have said this first. The humming is used to issue specific directives. But even without it they can read the general sense of our thoughts." I was visibly confused, so she continued. "And they also spontaneously broadcast them to any nearby deer, and thereby to any humans currently in communion with them." Oh. Oh! Now I felt my face getting warm. Sensing my discomfort, she quickly added, "Just watch this," and returned to humming. There was the beginning of a smile in the corner of her mouth. The deer lowered its head and bowed its forelegs, enabling Maya to mount. "Your turn," she said.

"So, I just hum, and think what I want it to do?"

"Sort of. Think it, and feel it. Imagine it already happening."

"But I did it before," I said. "Without even trying."

"No, you didn't. You just made the sound. I willed both deer into motion the last time." Oh. "But it isn't hard, it just takes a few tries the first time. Most people can do it, but some can't. You have to have some amount of imagination. Some people just can't see something that is not. Why don't you try it?"

"I'll give it a shot," I said. I imitated the sound Maya had made. Nothing happened. "Oh, I forgot to envision it. Let me try again." I hummed again, and this time summoned an image of a deer lowering its head. I waited until I ran out of breath, but nothing happened. "What am I doing wrong?" I asked Maya.

"Did you see your deer performing the action? In your head I mean?"

"Yes. I had just seen you do it, so I pictured the exact same thing."

"A-ha!" Maya exclaimed. "That's the problem. You imagined a deer lowering its head. You have to imagine *your* deer doing it. For that reason it's necessary to know your mount a little bit. You don't have to stare into its eyes like I did, but you must familiarize yourself with its unique characteristics and mannerisms, its personality. Try it once more."

I wasn't aware that deer had personalities. I looked mine over. I compared it with Maya's. Mine had a curlier patch of fur right in the middle of its chest. It also had little brownish flecks around the perimeter of its eyes. I noticed that it chewed on its upper lip periodically. It seemed slightly younger than Maya's, and perhaps a bit hyper...it repositioned its feet several times as it stood waiting. Little differences, things a casual observer might not notice. But was that enough? I started to hum. I saw a vision of my deer lowering its head, upper lip held fast in its teeth. Vision and reality became one, as my mount proceeded to genuflect before me. I felt elated. I climbed onto its back.

"Nice work!" said Maya. "Now get it to run. I'll let you go first, so you know it's you doing it." No sooner had I pictured six hyper hooves stamping out a beat than I was compelled to grab hold of my beast's neck as it lunged forward rhythmically. Soon Maya pulled abreast of me on her own deer. She was beaming with pride at the speedy progress of her new student. Catching breaths between hoofbeats she said, "That's quite an accomplishment, but that's actually the easy part. The hard part is controlling which thoughts the deer will receive. That's imperative. You have to learn to section off a part of your mind solely for communication with the deer. They don't *try* to read your thoughts, they do it instinctively. Human emotions are almost palpable to them. I'm sure you can understand why that is important."

My first thought was the recent embarrassing incident when I was musing a little too loudly on Maya's finer attributes. But then a darker thing occurred to me. "Can *anyone* commune with the puurr-deer? Even if the deer don't want it?"

120

"Yeah, that's the concern," she said. "Magus has tried many times to invade their minds, to eavesdrop on us rebels. There is no telling what kind of information he could extract if he were able to do it. He's no doubt tried every sort of sorcery and machine he can think of, but as far as we know, he's never gotten in. It seems the deer have to be willing participants in the union. And they can read enough of him to know he's no good. But that doesn't mean he'll never figure out a way to do it, so you should start practicing walling off your thoughts. I can show you a few simple exercises to get you started."

"Thanks, that would be helpful," I said.

We were riding pretty much due north, the sun just beginning its long westward arc overhead. Maya addressed me again, "Why don't you give the deer a series of commands? It doesn't matter where we go, as long as we are heading generally back toward camp. The precise route is up to you. My deer will follow your lead." I did that. It was exhilarating, and I started to feel a modicum of control over the direction of my life for a change. Up to this point, I realized, I had been along for the ride, following the lead of others. At least now I was making decisions. I led us east, and the land dipped down to follow a dry riverbed flanked by birch saplings. We veered south over some low-lying hills and then skirted the rim of an abandoned gravel pit. Then east again, across a broad plain toward a row of majestic willows whose branches swept the ground as they were stirred by a southerly breeze. To the north, at the far limits of our sight, indigo mountains marched along the horizon's edge. Against the backdrop of this captivating scenery, I remembered the words of Chaer-Ul. I looked back at Maya, as exhilarated as I, her face touched by the afternoon sun. Maybe I didn't have to leave just yet.

13

Drawing near the place where the helicopter had come to rest, the unmistakable high-pitched sound of its engine reached us through the trees, alternately rising to a peak and then receding. A small flock of white birds took flight from the treetops, startled by the noise. Our deer were wary of the sound as well. We decided to dismount where we were and walk the remaining distance. We did so, and the deer trotted back the way we had come without a backward glance. When the noise crescendoed again, they broke into a gallop and disappeared into the trees. When we reached the clearing we could see Doog sitting in the pilot's seat, having reclaimed his flight jacket. The rotors were now turning in a lazy arc. He didn't notice us until we were right beside him on the ground. Then he gave an enthusiastic double thumbs-up. Maya approached the cockpit. She placed one foot on the chopper's landing gear and opened the door, sliding it back in its grooves along the vehicle's fuselage. She then nimbly swung herself into the chopper's now open side. I couldn't hear what she was saying over the engine noise, but I saw her offer her canteen to Doog, who received it gratefully and drank.

As I watched this exchange, a hand touched me on the shoulder, startling me. A familiar-looking, dark-haired man had entered the clearing and walked up behind me, from the direction of the main camp. He had a closely-trimmed beard and wore a tight leather vest over a red shirt with somewhat billowy sleeves. After a moment I remembered where I had seen him before. He had been among those who had rescued me when I first arrived in this world. I wondered momentarily why I hadn't seen him since. Dipping into my memory of that day I recalled his name: Jager. "Reya wishes to see you," he said curtly. Maya and Doog had seen him by now and were looking down. "All of you." They couldn't hear him, but he had accentuated his words with sharp and unambiguous hand gestures, and they got the message.

A small crowd of people were standing near the front of Reya's tent as we approached. Reya was pacing, looking worried. She waved us over. "I heard the helicopter's engine. How soon will it be able to fly?"

Maya looked at Doog, who responded with a couple of simple hand gestures. Maya spoke for him. "Within a week, we hope," she said.

"Good," Reya continued. "There's been an attack." Immediately my mind conjured images of the horrific slaughter at Milltown, but nothing of that caliber appeared to have happened here. "My hunters came across a pair of Magus' hell-hounds. They were feeding on something they had recently killed. When they saw the men they fled, one of them dragging a portion of a carcass. The hunters took up pursuit and felled the dogs with two quick shots before they got very far. When they investigated the remains of the kill, it was clear that they were human, an adult and a child, too disfigured for easy identification. A headcount was taken upon the hunters' return to camp, and it was determined that a father and son had gone to fish in a nearby brook. He left a wife and another young child; she grieves for him now."

There was a moment of stunned silence before she continued. "And we all grieve with the family. Yet, as terrible and tragic as this occurrence is, we must consider the broader implications. It was not without reason that I used the word 'attack', rather than 'accident'. I believe Magus is very close to learning the location of our camp, if he hasn't already. This attack occurred frighteningly close to home, a mere half-day's walk to the northeast. We cannot delay our search for a new base camp any longer." She turned to Doog. "That helicopter will greatly assist us in locating an ideal spot. I want to be notified the moment it is ready." Doog nodded and saluted, a formal gesture that was probably not necessary but seemed appropriate enough. "There's a mountain range far to the southwest. It's about as far as I've ever ridden. I think that's a good place to start, as a base in the mountains will offer good visibility and will be more easily defensible. I don't want you to go alone; you'll need help should you encounter any unfriendly forces."

Suddenly Jeyt squeezed through the crowd, hand raised. "I'd like to help in any way I can," he volunteered.

"Thank you, Jeyt," said Reya. "I know I can always count on you. But I've already selected people for this mission, and I have need of you here."

Nodding acceptance, Jeyt lowered his hand in two jerky stages and stepped back into the crowd, trying not to look too dejected.

"Kaire, Jager, come along," said Reya. Oh yes, Kaire; another familiar face from my rescue party. She was somewhat stocky – not as tall as either Reya or Maya – and strong-looking. Not unattractive, but she definitely looked the part of a warrior, solid and formidable. Her hair was closely cropped and she sported multiple tattoos on her forearms. She and Jager fell into step beside us as Reya led us away from other ears. "Solely for the information of those now present," she made eye contact with each of us individually to ensure we understood the confidentiality of this discussion, "I have sent messengers to each of the nearest resistance outposts with a note regarding the suspected traitor. I have already heard back from the nearest two, and will keep you updated as more information comes in. So far, nothing fruitful. Furthermore, I have no intention of sending you to the mountains in the southwest. That was an attempt to lure the traitor into revealing him- or herself. Whether or not this ploy will succeed may only be seen with time. I do have an intended flight plan, but it will be revealed only to you five, and only a moment before you take off.

She stopped, as we were now well out of hearing range of the tents or other people, turned and said to Maya and me, "Continue to work on riding skills. Our flight from this place will transpire as soon as you've found an adequate location for a new base. Once we are resettled you will have ample time to develop proficiency in combat. Your present company," she indicated Jager and Kaire, "will assist Maya in that important role. I assure you they are well up to the task." She eyed Doog's massive biceps. "I imagine Doog can teach you a thing or two as well." Doog grinned, deeply creasing his eyes. "And one more thing. Kaire and Jager will alternate guarding of the helicopter until it is ready to fly. It is integral to our plan, and we can't afford to leave opportunity for sabotage. Further, I have more guards than usual assigned to watch the perimeter of the present camp. All trusted men. There is no need to worry about being caught unawares. That is all. Get some rest and take up your training in the morning."

Reya, Kaire and Jager turned back in the direction of camp while the rest of us remained standing. Doog wanted to keep working on the chopper well into the night, but Maya forbade him, charging him to get enough sleep lest he cross a pair of important wires. Reluctantly he trudged off toward the tent that Reya had provided for him. "Any idea who the traitor might be?" I asked Maya. "See any nervous twitches during Reya's speech?"

"As a matter of fact, you looked rather uncomfortable," she gibed.

"If so, it was only because I suspected she knew where we had been," I replied.

"Seriously, though, no," Maya said. "I have no idea, especially since I hardly know these people. I would even be wary of Jager and Kaire, but I have to trust that Reya knows her own people, at least those closest to her. It would suck if one of them decided to sabotage the chopper while we're in it, though."

"That would indeed suck," I agreed. I made a mental note to be hyper-aware of what everyone was doing while in flight.

Maya continued to stand there for a minute, as though she wanted to say something else, but she didn't. I couldn't think of anything more to say either, so after a slightly awkward moment I put my hand on her shoulder and said, "Well, good night," and turned to go to my tent.

Maya grabbed my arm, spinning me around to face her once more. "Justin..."

"What is it?" I asked.

"I think we should sleep together." I swallowed hard, but she seemed deadly serious.

I cleared my throat, but my voice still cracked. "Sleep together?"

"Yeah. Somewhere in this camp we have a traitor who's loyal to Magus. We already know Magus wants you dead because you didn't stay dead the first time." I wasn't sure if she was referring to the death of Tal-Makai or to the attempt on my life at Milltown. I decided not to ask. She went on, "I've been charged with your care. Therefore I don't feel safe leaving you alone. I have a slightly bigger tent, so...it just makes sense."

Normally I wouldn't have balked if a beautiful woman unexpectedly invited me to bed (not that I had often had opportunity to test the theory), but somehow I was relieved to realize that she apparently didn't mean it in that way. Maya wasn't like other girls I'd known. There was a purity about her that was so rare, that I felt it shouldn't be so readily spoiled. I think something in my picture of her would have been tainted if she'd really meant it that way.

"You don't feel safe leaving *me* alone…or *you* don't feel safe?" I teased.

"Don't make me throw you right here," she said. "We both know you haven't started your combat training yet."

I smiled. "I'll get my bed linens," I said. I gathered what I needed and met Maya in front of my tent.

"Seal up your tent so no one goes poking around," she said.

"Good idea." I did so, then followed her, tip-toeing around the outskirts of the camp until we came up behind her tent. I understood the need for discretion: not that she was concerned about what people might think, but because we wished to maintain the illusion that I slept in my regular tent, and to conceal my actual location. Her tent was indeed larger, and I set up my bedding on the opposite side from where Maya's lay. She sealed the entrance behind us and lay down on her side of the tent, utility vest and all. I lay down on my side, also clothed. I stared at the shadows in the roof of the tent, listening to the sounds of night insects, hoping that was all I would hear this night.

After a time, Maya turned her head to look at me. "I do feel safer, too," she said. I smiled. I don't think she could see it in the dark.

14

We rose early, before anyone else, so it wasn't necessary for me to try to sneak back to my tent. Still, we checked it each morning for any signs of disturbance. On the third day I saw what looked like fresh tracks in front of and around one side to the back of my tent. It was the side that would have been least visible to the rest of the camp. It gave me a chill, but I found no evidence that anyone had actually tried to get in. The ground wasn't soft enough to try to determine the size or shape of the feet that had made the tracks.

We rode every day. Packing only water, since it could be scarce in the field, Maya would always find something edible growing, or kill a rabbit or bird with her crossbow and prepare it. She carried small pieces of flint and steel that she used in combination with a piece of charred linen to make a fire when needed. Her survival skills put my old boy scout training to shame. We set off in a different direction each day, but never far, and never to the east. Maya would teach me how to perform increasingly difficult maneuvers with my deer, and after a few days I began to feel as though it would take more than another bullet to dislodge me from my mount. The deer would be a different one each time, usually, so I'd have to "learn" the deer's personality each time to make the connection essential to riding. Each evening we'd check in on Doog, and every time he'd assure us that the work was almost done.

On the fifth day I told Maya about the vision Reya had allowed me to see through the instrumentality of the deer. She asked me to recount it in detail, so during one of our lunch breaks I did. "Wow," she said. "So that's what happened to Tal-Makai. And that must be why they call him 'Martyr'." She inhaled slowly, then blew it out with puffed cheeks. "What a legacy to have to live up

128

to. It's really not fair, you know, that so much has been put on your shoulders."

"Tell me about it," I said. "That's why I'm not trying to fill Tal-Makai's shoes. Besides the fact that I'm *wearing* them, of course."

Maya laughed. "Ah, the irony!"

"Maya," I said, "Can you show me how to do that vision thing that Reya did with the deer?"

"I can. It may come in handy at some point, so it's important for you to learn it. But you should also know that it is very strenuous, both for you and for the deer. It saps a lot of the deer's energy temporarily, so it should not be overused. But for you it is more of an emotional strain. It draws out memories that are bound to deep-seated emotions and lays them bare for another to see. In everyday life we are not so open with our hearts, even if we think we are. It's also done differently from all of the other commands. You can't just hum, this requires a very specific sound."

"How did anyone ever figure that out?" I asked.

"Good question. In ancient times the people already realized that the puurr-deer were intelligent. I suppose someone long ago just stumbled on this ability when making various sounds to try to communicate with them. It must have been quite a shock when images started to materialize in front of their eyes! Anyway, the first tricky part is forming the right sound, as it is not comfortable for the human throat and tongue to form. It sounds something like this:" Then she made the same throaty "Muur-puurrha" sound that Reya had made before. Both deer grew alert and gazed at her, apparently expecting something more. But Maya stopped making the sound to give me further instruction. "Then comes the second tricky part. After the initial command, you have to make the humming sound as at other times, but you have to keep it up for as long as you want the vision to persist. Obviously you have to breathe, but you have to take short, infrequent breaths, or else the vision will be disrupted. It's something like what a horn player has to do when performing a piece that doesn't have pauses; just breathe when you can."

"I don't remember Reya doing that during the vision she shared with me," I said.

"No, you wouldn't have. As soon as you are pulled into the vision, your senses only detect stimuli from the memory-vision itself. So even if someone touches you, you won't feel it. That obviously means that you are quite vulnerable while experiencing someone else's vision. It is therefore imperative that a degree of trust exists between you and that person."

"That makes sense," I said. "Also, I did play trumpet for a couple of years, so I think I can do the timed breathing thing."

"Yes," she said. "But at the same time you have to concentrate pretty deeply, as you try to recall the desired memory. It has to be your own memory. You can't summon a vision of an event you haven't experienced first-hand. That might seem unfortunate, as there is much you could learn from someone else's memories, but it also means that nobody else can see anything in your head that you don't want them to. Unless you're careless with your thoughts while communing with the deer. By the way, have you been practicing walling off your thoughts?"

"I have. You haven't been catching any of my subconscious thoughts while we've been riding together, have you?"

"No," Maya said. "Just when you talk in your sleep." I waited for a smile that didn't come. I *really* hoped she was pulling a good poker face. She continued with the instruction. "One other important point. Just because it is your memory doesn't mean you have to remember it perfectly. It is like a dream in a way. In dreams your mind fills in gaps that would otherwise jar you out of the trance state. A similar thing happens with these visions. Sometimes you can see things in the vision that you couldn't possibly have seen from your perspective in the original moment. But unlike in dreams, the transitions are usually accurate to the original events. No one knows for sure where this information comes from if not from your mind. Some philosophers have theorized that the deer themselves fill in the gaps. That doesn't really answer the question, as then you are left with another question: 'how do the deer know what happened?'. Most people aren't prepared to say that the puurr-deer are omniscient, so a little bit of mystery still surrounds that debate."

"That's really interesting, from a metaphysical standpoint," I said.

"Isn't it?" She said. "Also, what is 'metaphysical'?"

"Oh, sorry. That's the theologian in me talking. It isn't really important right now. So, other than the command word, the humming, and all, you just try to remember the events that you want to share, and the other person will see them?"

"Pretty much. It's a completely voluntary sharing of information, so you decide where it starts, where it ends, and what you want to leave out in between. Again, this requires a fair degree of control over your own thoughts. You can even temporarily suspend the action if there's something you want to point out or emphasize."

"Pause. Like video." This time I realized instantly that she had no framework for understanding the reference. "Sorry again. It's a device…"

She interrupted, "That transmits visual images electronically from storage media such as a disc or hard drive to a viewing screen, mostly for entertainment purposes. Am I close?"

131

"Frighteningly," I said. "You…"

"*Read*. Right," she said. "I also tried to get one working once, using battery power, but I think the battery was too weak, or the machine was just too old, too many corroded parts."

I shook my head, smiling. "You never cease to amaze," I said. "I'll try really hard not to underestimate you again."

"Please do," she replied, with no ill intent. "So, are you ready to give it a try? I mean, if you trust me enough."

"Why not?" I said. "What do you want to see?"

"How about we start with just a short memory? Nothing emotionally traumatic, just an event that you remember vividly. Don't jump around, just show me a few consecutive minutes of a time you remember fondly. And don't feel bad if it takes a few attempts. This is harder than anything else we've tried."

"OK," I said. And after a few seconds' thought, "I think I have something. This is a family trip to Florida, quite a few years back."

"Show me," Maya said eagerly.

I said the magic words, "Muur-puurrha". I tried to pronounce them as Reya and Maya had, but I realized right away that I was forming words with my lips. These weren't words, they were sounds. I pushed the sounds farther back in my throat and tried again. "Muur-puurrha…" I was careful this time to slur the last sound into a steady hum, breathing like a trumpet player. When I was comfortable with this rhythm, I pressed my mental 'play' button, and heard a faint crackling sound.

Suddenly, I was strapped into the back seat of our family minivan, my younger brother on my left, Dad driving, Mom reclining in the passenger seat, window rolled down, her right foot resting on the side mirror. Dad said something about wasting AC, as a traffic light changed and we crossed a busy intersection, then over a bridge spanning the Intracoastal Waterway. Turning right at the far side of the bridge we drove south with the ocean on the left, all white sand, palms, and boardwalks slicing through thick copses of sea grape. On the right side a jungle of tropical vegetation. Lush, beautiful greenery swayed to an unseasonably warm April breeze, and the late-afternoon sun graced us with a shadow across my side of the car. On both sides of the thoroughfare broad sidewalks played host to countless roller-bladers, bicyclists, and fellow vacationers recognizable as much by their armfuls of tote bags and folding chairs as by their pasty limbs. Dad selected a bikini-clad skater as the latest object of his disdain, commenting on her obvious lack of modesty and piety. So deep was his disgust that he continued to monitor the skater in the rear-view mirror for several seconds after we passed. I cut the vision short, having forgotten how much baggage we had taken on that trip.

I was back in the present with Maya. "That wasn't quite the way I remembered it," I said.

"It never is," Maya replied. "That's not important. What is important is that you *did* it! You know, it's funny, as many things as I've heard and read about life before the plague, I could never really imagine it fully. There were so many people! That was weird. It made me a little nervous. And all of those cars, still working, full of people who couldn't care less about anyone else. They weren't allies or friends, but they didn't want to kill each other either. You *do* come from a different world. By the way, I see the memory the way you want me to see it. You could have presented it as if I were an outside observer, able to see you as well. But you didn't; you showed me exactly what you had seen. Was that intentional?"

133

"Not really, at least I don't think so. But you're right, I remember seeing Reya in her own vision. I guess it just didn't occur to me to do that."

"You should realize that that only applies to sight," Maya explained. "What you were thinking and feeling, all of that I experienced. You were with your family in a beautiful location. But you weren't happy. You were looking for something. What it was, I don't know, because you didn't know."

"Sometimes I'm still not sure," I said. "But I think my biggest problem was that I was looking in the wrong place."

Maya watched my eyes for several seconds, perhaps wondering if I'd elaborate, but I didn't. She continued, "So, that was a single memory. The next test will be a little harder. I want you to show me a series of chosen glimpses. What I've already seen of your world intrigues me. Why don't you show me snapshots of some of the most beautiful and interesting things you've seen in your world."

I thought about that for a second, decided that I could probably do that. "Ready?" I asked.

"After you," she said cheerfully. I started the whole process again. Command, humming, crackling, we were in. I showed her everything I could think of that I thought she might like. Waves crashing against barnacle-encrusted rocks on the coast of Maine. Times Square with more people in five seconds than she'd likely met in her life. Taking off in a 747. Cathedrals and statues and fountains of clean, drinkable water, all in pristine condition, not crumbled and eroded from decades of neglect and warfare. Then I had a sudden inspiration. I had been to a motorcycle convention once. I recalled it in all its glory. From restored classics to concept prototypes, they were all there. Row upon row of beautiful bikes in every imaginable color and all in excellent repair. It was my grand finale. The vision dissolved. Maya was smiling from ear to ear. Her breathing was notably faster. "Thank you," she said. "That was really great. *Really*. But…" But? What was the 'but…' when I had just shown her some of the best things my world had to offer? "Now I've seen a lot of your world, but almost nothing about *you*. Try it again, only this time, let me see you. And I'm not talking about the viewing angle. I want to see a piece of your life."

"Is that essential to learning the technique?" I pleaded.

"It is if I'm your teacher. Let me know when you're ready."

This was going to take a bit more finesse. The last personal memory was not as sparkly as I'd expected it to be. It would be wise to avoid touchy areas. But what to show her?

"Time's up…let's go!" she said. Pressure. OK, I threw a few things together that seemed relatively innocuous, but which I hoped would satisfy her curiosity. The vision began. First, cruising down the main drag in my hometown on my own Kawasaki Ninja. Receiving an academic honor, my family visible in the front row, cheering me on. Then, me on the wrestling team, one of the matches I'd won, of course. Springboarding off of this idea I remembered that I had taken a Kendo class and I let her see that. For most of these memories I allowed her to see me from a third-person perspective. And lastly, not wanting it to appear as though I'd only selected the most macho moments, I showed her a typical day in class. This time I restricted it to first person, as I knew I'd often run out the door to class in sweats and holey T-shirts. I wasn't sure how she'd take it, but I'd chosen Maitland's class. It's not like he was the megalomaniacal evil sorcerer she knew. Most of the time my view was not of him and the front of the class anyway, as I was turning frequently to my right to dissect what he was saying with a classmate. I thought it would provide an interesting slice of my daily life. I was right. But I realized my

135

mistake a second too late. In the vision, I turned unexpectedly to my left, where Mana was sitting one seat over and one forward. Oh no. My gaze lingered on her profile just a moment before I aborted the vision.

When I came back into full possession of my faculties, I turned to Maya. Her mouth was hanging open, and her face was white. I knew it had nothing to do with having seen Magus lecturing on the doctrine of inspiration. I could see disparate thoughts rapidly assembling themselves in her mind. She spoke, at first in broken fragments. "Reya...so young...she looked so different...she looked like me...your thoughts, your feelings...you loved her...you love Reya...Reya...*Reya is my mother!*"

There were so many things wrong with that series of utterances, so many things I wanted to correct. But it wasn't all wrong, and I didn't know where to start. I knew one thing for sure: Reya was not going to be happy with me. And just then, I cared a heck of a lot more what Maya thought. "Maya...," I tried, sheepishly. She sent me a look that was equal parts fire and ice, then stood without warning, hummed to her deer, mounted quickly and took off. "Maya, wait!" I tried, but I knew it was pointless. I mounted and followed as fast as I could get my deer to go.

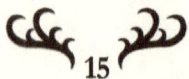

There was never a chance of catching Maya if she didn't want to be caught. She had grown up riding deer and could form a connection with one without having to think about it first. And if there was a way to milk a little more speed out of them, she knew it. For a short time I thought I was following the movement of recently disturbed branches swinging back to conceal her wake, but after a couple of minutes it seemed like they weren't moving any more than the other branches all around me. There was after all a pretty steady wind blowing through the forest. It would have been foolish to just keep going straight, as I had no way of knowing whether she had done the same, and if she were intent on losing me she certainly wouldn't have. I did know the way back to camp, though, and that seemed the most likely place to start looking. Given a choice between the helicopter and camp, I figured she was probably going to confront Reya, so I headed straight there.

When I got close I sent my deer away and walked, not wanting to make as big a scene as she was about to. I may have blown Reya's secret prematurely, but now that it was out, the manner of engagement was up to Maya. Once inside the perimeter of camp, I walked briskly toward Reya's tent. I was about to clear the corner of a large tent used as a meeting place when I heard voices talking softly. One of them sounded like Reya. I drew up short and backed up several paces as quietly as I could, trying to hear what was being said. "That was my intention," the voice said. It was definitely Reya. "I wanted to give him enough rope to hang himself."

"I don't like it." A gruff voice. Denkel. "It's very risky. He could lead them straight into a trap. He could seize the opportunity to kill them and report to his master."

"Do you think I would leave something like this to chance? That's why I've placed one of my most trusted within the party. There is a small risk, but believe me, I've thought out every contingency. If he's the one, we can't lose this opportunity to catch him. If the traitor isn't exposed before we relocate, there's no reason to leave. It will only be a matter of time before Magus knows the location of our new base as well."

"Well then, if you won't listen to reason, I'd like to go on record..."

Reya, interrupting, "*I know better than anyone* what's at stake. But it's my decision. Should anything go wrong I alone will bear the guilt. Your hands are clean."

I backed farther away, stepping carefully. When I was sure I was out of earshot I turned and ran. There was no way I could have beaten Maya to camp. And she obviously wasn't talking to Reya. She must have gone to the chopper. It wasn't far enough to warrant summoning a deer, so I ran, but what had seemed a short walk before now felt like hours. When I finally entered the clearing, I saw Maya, talking with Jager and Doog. Kaire, squatting on a low limb of a willow tree, dropped to the ground, I assumed in response to my arrival. I was startled by a voice directly behind me, just stepping out of the trees. It was Reya.

"My messenger informed me. The helicopter is ready," she said. How had she gotten here so quickly? Had she seen me before I came here? I looked to Maya, who was trying to avoid eye contact with either me or Reya. She was completely successful with me, but I saw her steal a look at Reya before returning her gaze to her feet.

Finally Jager spoke. "Yes, and it appears we are all here...not a moment too soon." He looked at me. I tried to read something in his eyes. What exactly did treachery look like? Jager...the traitor?

I supposed I shouldn't assume the worst just because of his shady locks and devil-red shirt. I felt like I should say something, warn Maya and Doog. But for one thing I didn't have the chance to do it privately, even if Maya were willing to listen to me. And Reya was going to have enough reason to be angry with me whenever Maya decided to talk to her, so I kept my mouth shut.

"Who's piloting?" Reya asked.

"I am, of course," said Maya. She wasn't her usual chipper self. Doog didn't look the least bit offended, or surprised.

"OK," said Reya. "I've drawn a map." She pulled out a scrap of paper and proceeded to unfold it until a surprisingly large, well-worn chart emerged. "I want you to head due west-northwest." She pointed to the left side of the map. I tried to peek over her shoulder to see what she was indicating. "This shows every important landmark that has been discovered along your flight path. Most of them I've been to personally." She then slid her finger to an area in the upper left corner where nothing was drawn. "This is farther than anyone has been. It's more than two days by deer, riding full-out. But you should be able to reach it easily within a day using the helicopter. I don't know what's there. No one does. Just fill in what you see. Jager and Kaire are excellent tacticians; they will know what will make for an ideal military base. It has to be big, with plenty of potential for growth, and well-fortified. At least fortifiable." Maya reached for the map, but Reya turned and handed it to me instead, along with a pencil.

Maya objected, "Doog is my co-pilot…"

"Not this time," Reya said. "Training doesn't stop just because you're on a mission. It's more important now than ever. It's a good idea for Justin to learn to fly, just in case." She turned, looked me straight in the eye. "I want you to stay by Maya's side at all times." She held my gaze until I nodded, then after a pause,

140

"Good." Maya noisily blew a wisp of hair out of her eyes. Reya addressed Kaire and Jager, softly, "Complete the mission. Keep them safe." The two warriors nodded.

"We'll keep *them* safe," Maya said loudly.

For a second Reya had the look of a parent whose toddler has just said something defiant, but incredibly cute. She composed herself. "You do that," she said to Maya. Then to all of us, "Chaer-Ul goes before you. Now go." Kaire and Jager sprang into action immediately, climbing into the helicopter. They were obviously more conditioned to follow orders. The rest of us followed closely behind. I entered the chopper last, and by the time I did Maya already had the blades spinning. I took one last look at Reya, then slid the hatch closed. It seemed very dark all of a sudden. Had we just sealed our fate as well? I squeezed past Doog and Kaire to take my place in the cockpit. Maya didn't turn to acknowledge my arrival.

The beat of the rotors and the pitch of the engine increased, and then at last lift began to take effect. The chopper wobbled a bit as it rose, but finally found an equilibrium, and rose above the tallest of the trees. I leaned to try to catch one last view of Reya or the camp, but we were facing the wrong way, and I could see only forest. Clear of the treetops, Maya pushed the stick forward and the chopper followed her lead, pitching forward into the great unknown.

I turned to see where the others had taken up position, and was relieved to see that Doog had propped himself against the inside wall of the vehicle, arms crossed, a last line of defense against any potential threats.

Confident that the noise from the engine would cover the sound of our voices, I spoke to Maya. "I need to talk to you."

141

"Now is not the time," she replied curtly.

"It's not about what you think. It's really important."

"*I said not now!*" she snapped. It was as close to not-nice as I had ever seen her, but it came from a place of pain, not real anger. Then, more controlled; "I need to concentrate until we have reached our target speed and elevation. Please don't distract me unless it's related to the mission."

I respected her wishes and saved it for later. I saw some of the places Maya and I had ridden together. A glade, a lake, a big, open field. The remains of an ancient stone wall where we had sat for one of our picnic lunches. I opened the map Reya had given me, and incredibly, most of these things were etched on its surface with tiny, precise lines. There were, of course, huge stretches of nothing but yellow forest, and these were indicated on the map by shaded areas with a few symbolic, not-to-scale trees drawn in here and there. The path we flew ran almost parallel to the blue mountains we had earlier seen to the north, but not quite; they creeped slowly closer the farther west we went. I saw on the map that our trajectory eventually took us beyond them, but we had a long way to go. Thinking of the distance, I experienced a moment of panic when I remembered Maya telling me that they had been nearly out of fuel when the helicopter came down near camp. Scanning the control panel I located a fuel gauge, and saw with relief that it was nearly full. Reya's people must have filled it at some point while Maya and I were out, from the limited reserves they had collected here and there, or perhaps had made by combining more readily available substances. I understood how rare and precious something like that was here. Reya was banking a lot on this mission.

More yellow forests, broken up occasionally by a dry riverbed or an overgrown field. Here and there a crumbling homestead, a barely-perceptible road. I wondered when a vehicle had last used those routes. More yellow trees. It all started to look the same. At some point, I dozed off. I woke again after what had seemed a long while, but taking a quick scan of the horizon I determined that we were still this side of the mountains, that we had in fact only covered a fraction of the distance. I allowed myself to drift off again.

I dreamed about yellow trees. They sat on the bank of a circular lake, reflected in its surface. But the image inverted in the lake was clear and still, the trees above wavered. Six ravens sat in the tops of the trees, only one of them was not a raven. The rippling of the trees sent the six birds into flight. They flew at first in different directions, but then found a common path and fell into a line. They circled the treetops once, twice, three times, each arc wider than the last. As the birds completed their final pass, they ascended one by one to a higher altitude. As each bird reached a certain height, they dove, one after another, straight toward the crystal surface of the lake. The first bird punctured the water's surface like a dagger through flesh, and like flesh the water buckled before permitting the projectile to enter its tender depths. The skin-like surface then recoiled and assumed its planar form in preparation for the next bird. Each remaining raven entered the lake in exactly the same way, until they were all beneath, and there remained no sign that they had ever been. As I continued to watch, the water began to bubble and froth in the center of the lake. Then a pillar of water erupted from its surface, rising toward the sky. Its movement as it rose was sluggish, as of a substance more viscous than water. My sleeping mind grasped for a memory that would explain the familiarity of this image, but it found nothing solid to hold. From somewhere came the idea that the pillar should branch and become a tree, and so it began to do, cleaving itself into two equal halves. But there did the arboreal resemblance end, as each half did not then likewise split, but became at its edges like many quivering fingers, and the whole substance of the two branches vibrated with the shivering of many fine tendrils. Each of the two halves then stretched itself wider

143

and flatter in a single great pulsing spasm, forming two enormous, arcing wings, the gelatinous tubercles fraying into translucent feathers. The wings expanded to enormous proportions, and then, catching the wind, consumed the sky.

I woke with a start to look upon a landscape, not of yellow forests, but of rocky crags; we were passing over the northern mountain range. From this perspective the mountains were not a series of flat blue triangles, but a rich tapestry of color and texture, from green-grassed plateaus to frosted peaks to deeply shadowed clefts. We drifted over some of the higher places close enough to see vast herds of puurr-deer grazing on the flat places between peaks, and once another kind of animal, resembling a big cat with the armor plating of a rhinoceros or armadillo, but of massive proportions.

As the mountains began to recede, giving way to foothills to the north, I saw in several places small flocks, or perhaps herds, of large, grey, ostrich-like animals. Noteworthy was the presence of a thick, squat tail, and short arms in the place of wings. I wanted to ask Maya what they were called, but thought the better of it. These foothills were on Reya's map, but they were one of the last things she had drawn. Beyond that was a narrow strip of what looked like grassland, then a few scattered fir trees sketched in a line to indicate a border at the far end of the plains. Presumably Reya had at some point ridden far enough to see the beginning of a forest beyond the flatland, but had not explored its extent. The far side of those first trees was quite literally a blank page. I found this realization exhilarating, like discovering a whole new world. In all likelihood, there was a whole lot more of the same – trees, fields, and the like – beyond that first row of trees. But maybe not. Maybe there was a perfect site for a new base, or a secret weapon that would turn the tide in the war against Magus, just sitting there waiting to be discovered. Whatever was there, it had never been seen by anyone I'd met or seen since I arrived. And maybe, just maybe, whatever was there had managed to escape detection in the years since the plague, and unlike almost everything else in this world, had not yet been thoroughly picked clean of anything useful. Better yet, perhaps there lay beyond those trees a place where everything could be made right again between Maya and me.

We were leaving the foothills and flying over what did in fact turn out to be a vast yellow plain. From this point onward I scanned the horizon constantly, looking for even a single evergreen that might indicate the presence of a whole lot more of its kind. I did this in vain for the better part of an hour, twice or thrice nearly falling asleep again. Then at last, I saw something. Not a single tree, but the whole row of trees, just as Reya had drawn it. But unlike Reya, we had a bird's eye view, so it wasn't long before we could begin to get an idea of the extent of that coniferous forest. Straight ahead, it continued on for as far as the eye could see. But just a little to the west it was much thinner, maybe only a few hundred meters at one point. And beyond that...buildings. Houses in a neighborhood, and after that, what had to be an industrial park. In the distance I could see a huge mall, restaurants, highway overpasses. It was not a very big city, but it was a city, and it didn't appear to be occupied. Then again, neither had Milltown. I started to draw.

Maya pitched the chopper to avoid flying directly over the city, just in case somebody did live there and happened to have come into possession of a fully functional rocket launcher. I doubted it since anyone who lived there had already been hearing our approach for some time, and as we were not an everyday occurrence, surely someone would have stepped outside to take a peek. We curved around to the west of the city, following a river that formed its border on that side. Maya silently decided not to look for a place near the city to set down. She didn't have to explain her reasons, even if she had been talking to me. We were all still apprehensive about what might lurk behind the walls of all of those buildings. We stayed with the river, moving upstream, to

145

where it emerged from between steep-walled cliffs. Maya took us a little higher and passed over the tops of the cliffs, tracing the winding canyon that the river had carved long ago. I was busy working it into my piece of the map when I heard Maya gasp.

Jager and Kaire pressed themselves against Doog as all three heads vied for a view. I looked up to see a massive wall of solid concrete spanning the entire canyon. At its top a sparkling lake was held at bay, behind a row of formidable concrete towers. It was a massive dam, and apparently it was still doing its job. It was the perfect fortress. Even if somebody did live in the town below, the dam's elevation made it virtually impossible to assail. The only relatively easy access would be from the two sides, and the towers had good line of sight at both ends, plus the approach could be fortified, set with additional guard posts and even traps.

Maya circled a couple of times. Nobody made their presence known below. It appeared as though the only place big enough to allow a landing near the dam was the old parking lot on the east shore, but it was situated too close to the dam for comfort. A small group of armed men bursting forth suddenly from the entrance to the dam could seize the chopper. Maya hovered and turned the helicopter around in a slow 360□ arc as we all scanned for an alternative landing site. At once several of us made exclamations as a clear, grassy hill was spotted a short distance to the east.

Soon we were on the ground, the chopper's engine cooling, rotors making a few last determined rounds. Kaire spoke first. "We'll need deer. Even though it isn't too far back to the dam, we may need to get back here in a hurry if anything seems amiss. There's not much else up here except the dam. If it's empty, the only likely threats would have to take the long way up from the town." She took the liberty of calling deer for all of us. There was no need to double up. I hadn't seen deer from the sky for some time, but they

146

were pretty much ubiquitous here, it seemed there were always a few within hearing.

Sure enough, five fine specimens were seen emerging from the trees at the base of the hill and ascending to our position. "For safety's sake, we should split up. Two teams should do it," said Kaire.

"I'll ride with Doog," Maya said.

"Sorry," said Jager, "That's not an option. You heard Reya. You and Justin are to stick together. The teams are..." He looked back and forth between us, as if weighing the strategic advantages of different pairings. "Kaire and Doog, one team. I'll ride with you two." I really wasn't sure about this. Was he trying to isolate us from the group? Trying to make sure we didn't have a chance to speak privately? Why was I assuming the worst? Maybe Reya's hunch was wrong. I hoped for our sakes it was. We didn't seem to have much choice at this point. "If anything goes wrong, we regroup here. Understand?" Everybody agreed.

Once we were all mounted, we set off in the direction of the dam. Kaire and Doog cut a fairly straight path, while Jager led Maya and I a little bit farther north before turning toward the west. He said that he wanted to skirt the lakeshore for a while to see if any other outbuildings were visible above the dam. We followed his lead. From our lofty viewpoint in the helicopter, the hill had seemed quite close to the dam. In reality, it was a few miles. And it was pretty heavily forested terrain. We had ridden for just a few minutes, long enough to have penetrated the forest enough that we could see neither the hill where the chopper sat nor the dam or even the lake.

That's when we heard a hunting horn. It echoed through the forest, the sound bouncing off trees in a way that made it impossible to determine its source, sending chills down all of our

147

spines. Instantly, Jager spun his deer around and shouted, "Back to the helicopter!" Maya and I fell in behind him, inciting our deer to speed. The horn sounded again, much closer. This time we could tell that it came from somewhere off our left flank. We weren't left to wonder for long. Two more puurr-deer materialized out of the trees to our left, each driven by one of Magus' black-and-scarlet-clad assassins. They pulled along beside us and matched our speed, then began to narrow the gap. Without a moment's delay, Jager flung a throwing knife at the head of the first rider, apparently trying for the soft spot at his neck. The knife missed its mark, glancing off the rider's helmet.

The second rider was dropping behind us, already swinging something over his head. I was the weakest rider of the three of us, and I was in the rear. I saw a spinning mass of cords and stones entangle itself around my deer's front legs, binding them. Its balance offset, it plowed into the ground, launching me into a nearby tree. When Jager realized what had happened the first rider was already on the ground. A moment later he was standing over my aching body. He hauled me to my feet with a single powerful gathering motion and clutched me to his chest, an unseen dagger pressed under my chin. Then with his free hand he drew a long blade and pointed it at Jager, who had circled back. The point of the blade followed Jager's movements, keeping him at bay as his deer paced just outside of its reach. I detected a quick movement behind him, and saw Maya draw her crossbow, only to have it struck from her hand by the other dark rider, who then immobilized her as well.

Jager bluffed, "Two of you, three of us. Unfortunately for you, I'm the one who is free. Even if you kill them, I'll still kill you both before you have time to make another move."

The rider who held Maya hissed through the vent in his helmet, "We all know you won't let that happen."

Jager continued to pace. The dark soldiers held their positions. After a time Jager shouted, "What are you going to do?!!?"

The rider who had spoken before replied coldly, "Wait for the final scene."

A crackling could be heard, growing louder. Shortly two more dark warriors approached, prodding Doog and Kaire, hands bound, ahead of them at the point of their weapons. When they reached the spot where we stood at impasse, they each kicked their quarry in the back of the knees and sent them sprawling to the forest floor, not far from my position. One of the soldiers growled at Jager, "Now, *dismount!*"

After a quick pause, Jager complied. Apparently satisfied, the dark soldier slowly removed his helmet. Maya and I gasped simultaneously. It was the man we had seen on our way to Milltown! The old Asian man who'd said he was looking for water. I looked to Jager, whose face registered recognition. When he found words, he said, "You son of a...!" Then his rage was replaced by a friendly smile.

Approaching Jager, the man returned the smile, embraced him warmly and replied, "How the heck have you been?"

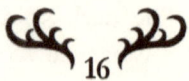

16

The realization of ultimate betrayal hit me. Reya had been right. "Traitor!" I shouted, finger pointed accusingly at Jager.

Jager laughed. "Traitor, no. I'm quite loyal, in fact. But I can understand the confusion." Then to the old man, "Look who we've brought you!" He denoted me with a dramatic sweep of his arm, his scarlet sleeve cutting the air like a backstabber's knife.

His friend looked at me, took a step closer. His jaw dropped. Then to his men, "Cut them loose." That they did, and the soldier holding me released his grip and withdrew his knife from my throat. Immediately I spun around, relieving him of the dagger, then closed the distance between me and Jager with one lunging step, twisted his arm behind his back, and introduced the tip of the blade to his ribs.

He laughed again. "Well done, friend. Reminds me of someone I used to know. But..." And then he stomped hard on my right foot, just where the first metatarsals start. I heard the sharp pop of a joint dislocating, followed by a stabbing pain, and instinctively withdrew the foot to guard the injury. Jager took advantage of my sudden instability and sprang forward, placing distance between himself and the knife, and simultaneously twisting to put slack in the arm I held. Already balancing on one foot I was unable to maintain my grip without toppling, so I released him. Before I fully regained my balance his own sword tip was pointed at my nose. "Sorry for the painful lesson, but there are two things I want you to take away. First, know the limitations of your abilities. I trust I have adequately demonstrated that. You have some innate skill, but you have a lot yet to learn. I don't suggest you try to play the hero again until you have a lot more training under your belt. How's the foot?"

It was a strange question to ask of one he had so recently crippled, but when I focused on it, I realized that the pain didn't feel quite so sharp any more. I wiggled it a little, set it down gently. Gradually I allowed my body weight to be distributed evenly between my two feet. A dull ache, nothing more. Incredulous, I slipped out of my right boot, and saw no swelling or bruising of any kind. "It's not too bad," I said.

"That's lesson two. Know your strengths. One of yours appears to be an amazing ability to heal. It is not by chance that we happened upon these men. We have been gifted with a unique opportunity. Kaire and I can help you learn exactly what you are capable of, and also what you are not. And I think you will find that this old fellow," he said, indicating the Asian man, "will be able to give you some of the answers you have so desperately sought, but which have eluded you so far. In short, he can help you understand who you are, and why you are here."

Slowly it began to dawn on me that perhaps everything was not as it had seemed. Clearly these were not Magus' men. Yes, they had recently tripped my ride, causing me to interact painfully with the broad side of a tree. They had subsequently held various pointy objects to key parts of my anatomy. And yes, one of them had just tried to break my foot. But their leader had ordered us untied, and Jager was now trying to teach me things, promising the one thing I desired above all else: answers. Maybe Reya had been wrong after all. "Who exactly are you people?" I asked bluntly.

"Kind of a mixed bag," said Jager. "This old fool is Kuro. He was the one who first taught me the fighting arts. He had another student as well back then, a man by the name of Tal-Makai."

"Heard of him," I said. "But if he trained Tal-Makai, then why didn't Reya know him from our description?"

151

"For one thing, Reya never met him. Tal met Reya a couple of years after we completed our training. Kuro doesn't exactly make the regular social circuits. And besides, most people, myself included, believed him dead. I'm glad we were wrong." Kuro nodded. "Kuro, you'll have to introduce your current batch. I doubt there are any familiar faces."

"Pleasure," said Kuro. He pointed to one of the soldiers, whom I now saw was not wearing the same sort of armor as the others, but instead something custom, with lots of hinges and attachments that must have served some purpose not readily apparent. One such purpose was quickly discovered, as the soldier touched a place near the collarbone and the helmet separated and folded multiple times, finally disappearing into a place at the back of her neck. She was a thin-faced woman of African descent, with swept-back features that gave the appearance of having ridden into the wind as she was formed. Her hair was gathered into thick ropes and pinned back to her scalp "That's Charr. She makes mechanical things you wouldn't believe. She's also quite a good shot with the crossbow. She's developed a repeat-fire model." My eyes darted to Maya, who was gazing at Charr with what could only be awe. "Bit of an odd bird, though, kind of does her own thing." Charr made no sound; I guess she took this as a compliment.

"That's Knox," he said, pointing to the soldier who stood to my left. Knox had removed his helmet a moment before. He looked solid, but not as heavily-muscled as Doog. He was tan and fair-haired. "Knox is a good all-around warrior, but his strength lies in sheer power. That and swordplay. He is a master of bladed weapons, and particularly the ability to wield two blades at once." This I had witnessed firsthand.

"And that leaves Corvus." All eyes turned to the last warrior who stood detached, still in full armor. "Corvus. Helmet." Corvus slowly removed his helmet, not looking at anyone in particular. He

152

had a terrible scar that dominated the left side of his face. It began above his mouth, drawing the lip up on that side, and continued up his face, spreading wider as it went. The skin within the scar was a dark reddish-pink. It consumed the entire left eye, the iris a sightless pearly white, and it turned a wide swath of his straight, longish hair silver-white on that side. From what remained of his original face, he appeared to have been rather handsome, dark-featured. "Corvus kills. Quite efficiently, I might add. He's very loyal. It's a good idea to have him on your side." I was pretty sure he was the one who had taken down my deer.

Addressing his team, Kuro pointed in my direction and said, "And *that* is the one I told you to expect. That's *Martyr*."

I narrowed my eyes slightly, "Justin," I said. "I usually just go by Justin."

Jager took the initiative to introduce the rest of us, then spoke to Kuro, "Was the rough handling really necessary? And what's with impersonating Magus' assassins?"

"Yeah, sorry about the first bit. I didn't know these two, and my men couldn't have known who the rest of you are. Plus it's been a while, hasn't it? I'm not as young as I used to be. Didn't even recognize that one (tipping his head in my direction) till I got real close. As for the armor...spoils of battle. I figure it's more humane than taking scalps. And it can't be denied that Magus equips his soldiers with the best armor around. Infuses it with magic to make it extra strong." He rapped on his breastplate.

An intentionally loud "Hmph!" from Charr. "Unholy stuff," she said. "I won't wear it. You shouldn't either," she said to the old man. "Maybe Magus can control you through it, get into your mind. It's already not so sharp."

"Certainly not as sharp as your tongue, Charr," he retorted.

153

"You might want to at least consider painting the armor a different color," said Jager. You're going to scare the wits out of any resistance members you come across, dressed like that. As you did us."

"That's a risk that's well worth it for the few seconds of uncertainty it buys us when we encounter Magus' actual troops," the old man said.

"I suppose," said Jager. "I'm assuming you use the dam as home base?"

"That's right," said Kuro. "You immediately recognized its strategic potential. That was always your gift."

Jager accepted the praise with a humble smile. "How would you feel about a whole lot more company?" he asked. Kuro frowned, the idea obviously distasteful to him. He didn't respond right away. When he did, it wasn't an answer to Jager's question. "Have you eaten?"

Jager shook his head. "Not recently."

Kuro smiled and spoke to Knox. "Head over to the dam and fire up the grills. We feast!"

Maya excused herself, saying she'd left her pack in the chopper. "Not alone," Kaire said. "Justin will go with you."

"Fine," said Maya flatly.

"I'll go too," added Kaire.

"That's really not necessary," said Maya.

154

Kaire started to object, but Charr said, "These are *our* woods. There's really nothing to fear. Besides us, of course."

"Anyway," added Maya, "The chopper isn't far."

Kaire finally conceded, but said firmly, "Don't delay."

As the others made their way toward the dam, Maya said to me, "Let's take deer." My deer had been freed from its entanglements, but had promptly bounded off into the woods, having had its fill of human company for a while. Maya's was still nearby. As she mounted she said, "Why don't you call one for yourself?" As I turned to do so, she hummed her deer into motion, taking off in the direction of the chopper. I shouted for her to wait, but she didn't slow. I called my deer, and began already running after Maya before it came. When it arrived a few seconds later I rode it hard after her.

This time I was able to keep her in sight most of the time. When I did lose her only for a moment my deer was able to find the trail again. Maya veered left, and my direction-sense told me she was no longer heading for the helicopter. Soon the forest thinned, and rocky outcroppings began to appear here and there. Maya steered around one, behind another. The outcroppings grew larger, began to dominate the landscape. It was becoming increasingly difficult to find a path between them. At the same time, the ground we traversed was becoming more uneven, and her deer was having a little trouble as it reached these places before mine did. This enabled me to gain on her steadily. Suddenly the ground rose steeply just as the stony protrusions converged to create only a single, narrow path between granite cliffs. Maya's deer squeezed between them and I followed closely. It was a dead end; a natural amphitheatre surrounded by high rock walls.

Realizing she was trapped, she spun her deer about quickly, startled to find me blocking her escape. *"Why are you here?!!?"* she yelled.

"Why are *you* here?" I retorted. "This doesn't look like the chopper."

Defeated, she slid off her deer to the ground, dropped to sit on the hard stone floor. She drew a long, shaky breath, slumped her shoulders, and sobbed. I dismounted as well, approached her cautiously. I wanted so badly to hold her, to comfort her. "Maya…"

"I don't know what to think about all of this," she said. "It's just too much. Reya's my mother. Why didn't she tell me? Why didn't she want me? How could she just send me off to live with strangers? Those are the only parents I've ever known. Now I don't even know who they are!"

"They're not strangers. They really *are* family, they just aren't really your parents," I explained.

She looked up at me with big, watery eyes. Her mouth opened and her anger flared up again, "You knew! You knew all along and you didn't tell me!" She burst into heaving sobs.

"Maya, please understand, Reya forbade me to say anything; it was not my place. She had reasons for doing what she did, I know that much. She didn't just abandon you, she loved you…*loves* you, more than you know."

"How do *you* know?" she demanded. "Did she tell you that?"

"She didn't need to. I *felt* it, when I shared her vision. It *killed* her to leave you there! I knew her pain. I saw it in her eyes."

The sobbing slowed. Her breathing grew a bit more regular. "In her eyes," she mused. "She's beautiful, Reya, isn't she?"

I chose my words with care. "I suppose she is…for a woman of her age," I tried. I saw a hint of a smile linger momentarily in the corner of her mouth.

"The young Reya, the one from your world…"

"Mana," I said.

"*Ma-na*," she repeated, trying to make the name sound unpretty. "Did you love her?" She allowed her eyes to flicker briefly to my face.

"No…," I said, realizing I was telling the truth. "No…love? *No!* I didn't love her. I've never loved *anyone* before."

"Before…," she repeated. The fragment of a smile appeared again. Then she gulped an uneven breath. "Reya's my mother. That means Tal-Makai was my father! Who *are* you, Justin? Are you my *father?* Is it wrong for me to even *think*…"

"Tal-Makai was not your father," I explained. "Reya told me your father died before you were even born. She only met Tal later, after you had gone to live with her family. Anyway, I'm not Tal-Makai. I may or may not be 'Martyr', but Tal-Makai and I are not the same person, any more than Reya and Mana are."

I could see Maya's eyes welling up again at the mention of these names. I dropped to sit beside her, shuffled close. "Maya, I don't love Reya, and she doesn't love me. And I never loved Mana."

She was quiet for a moment, apparently thinking, and then, quietly, "Mana…what was she like?"

157

"I don't remember," I said. Maya turned her face to me, her eyes filling with a different kind of tears, and pressed her lips warmly against mine.

17

The ride back to the dam was infinitely more pleasant than the last one; we shared a deer, and Maya let me drive. She was very chatty all of a sudden. "I *am* still a little mad at Reya - my mother," she said. "And I want to know more about my Dad."

"Of course," I said. " Give Reya a chance to explain herself. Maybe you can at least make up for lost time with her."

"I'll think about it," Maya said. "Justin, your foot really doesn't hurt any more? I may have been upset with you, but I never wanted to see you hurt like that."

"Like that? You had a better idea how to punish me?"

"Oh, I had *plenty* of ideas! Just none I would have actually inflicted. I felt bad enough about the way I knew I was hurting you with my silence. I was still trying to figure out Jager's game at that point, and when he did that I *so* wanted to put a few crossbow bolts through him!"

"Thanks," I said. "But if you were that worried about me, why'd you leave me to fend for myself against the ravages of the wild when you first found out about your mother?"

"Idiot, do you really think I would have done that? I was doubly bound by my heart and my sense of duty to keep you safe. I circled around behind you as soon as I was sure I was out of your sight. Then I followed at a stealthy distance, fuming all the while. I saw that you were headed to camp, and when I was sure you were safely there, I backed off and made for the chopper instead. I would never just leave you, know that."

159

"Oh." I was touched. "And just now? You knew I would be able to keep up?"

"I *made sure* you could keep up. Had to practically make my deer walk on its knees to do it, too. Yeah, I *wanted* you to follow me."

"I will always come for you, know *that*," I said.

"I *do* know that," she replied cheerfully. And after a moment, "I wanted to thank you for all the things you showed me through your vision. Especially the bits from your life, girlfriend notwithstanding. How come you never told me you had done combat training?"

"Honestly, it wasn't exactly combat training. In my world lots of people do that sort of thing for fun, and to get in shape."

"To get in shape...for combat," she said.

"No, just to be strong," I said. She looked puzzled. The concept of training the body as an end in itself was completely foreign to her. I couldn't think of a better way to explain it without making my world seem like an incredibly shallow place.

"Well anyway," she said, "I was impressed with the way you moved, the control you had over your body." I felt her thighs momentarily tense against mine and then relax. "That strength and training can certainly be applied to real combat."

"It can't hurt," I agreed.

"If you wouldn't mind, I would like to see more of your life sometime. You know, since I don't get to meet your family and all."

160

"Sure," I said. But immediately I began to question the wisdom of this idea. Maya was the person she was at least in part because of the circumstances of her life. I had to wonder if she would have retained the same child-like innocence had she grown up in my neighborhood. I doubted it. I changed the subject.

"So, how many of them do you think there are? In Kuro's camp, I mean."

Maya shrugged. "Beats me. But I've seen plans for a similar type of dam, and there isn't a ton of space inside. Most of it has to be solid concrete. Perhaps most of them stay in the town below."

As we neared the dam we could already smell the aroma of roasting meat. Knox was tending to a pair of large, barrel-style steel grills, while Jager and Kaire chatted with Kuro nearby. Corvus leaned against the wall next to the dam entrance, tracing lines in the sand at his feet with the tip of a spear.

Unexpectedly, Maya raised both of her hands in the air. "*My beloved and I are one,*" she declared, loud enough for all to hear.

"*And one in Him,*" the others said in unison. Only Corvus remained silent.

"OK, that was…different," I said. "What was that all about?"

Maya gave me a pinch, more playful than painful. "What do you *think*? I was announcing our marriage!"

"Announcing our…I'm sorry, what now?"

"Our *marriage*, silly. Announcing it."

161

"Yeah, um…ok," I said. "We can start talking about that, maybe eventually set a date…obviously, not right now, there's so much going on, what with the war, and the end of civilization…"

Another pinch. Less playful. More painful. "*Sweetheart*," she said, speaking with slow deliberation, "I was announcing our marriage." She caught my vacant expression, so she clarified. "I was announcing *that we are married*."

My jaw must have dropped a little. I don't think she liked that, judging from the third pinch. "That we are…um…*Darling*, can we talk about this?"

"Justin! Haven't you ever seen a marriage before?" she asked. I didn't get a chance to answer, as Corvus chose that moment to interrogate Maya.

"Where's your pack?" he inquired without lifting his head.

"Not that it's any of your concern, but I got what I needed," answered Maya. That was true enough. He didn't need to know that she was referring to her emotional needs. Corvus' permanently snarling lip lifted a little higher, but he said nothing more.

Kuro shot him a warning glance and stepped past him to where Maya and I stood. "Come, friends, I want to give you the tour," he said to us. We followed him into a lobby of sorts, itself surprisingly large. Near the far end was a wall spanning the width of the chamber, clearly not in keeping with the room's architecture, and of more recent origin. It seemed to be pieced together out of steel scrap, a patchwork of welds, rivets, and bolts. Despite its makeshift appearance, it seemed quite sturdy. In its center was a large, round hatch that resembled the door to a bank vault. For all I knew, that was where it had come from. Kuro opened it with a swing of the handle and swung it outward, then

162

ushered us through. Beyond was a second, smaller chamber, another, less formidable door, and then a long, curving hallway that followed the contour of the dam. A yellow light issued from far down the hall, just out of sight beyond the bend of the passage. There opened several steel doors off of this hallway at regular intervals, but Kuro pointed us instead to a lift close at hand.

"That can't still work," I said. Kuro pressed a button on the panel, and a mechanical rumbling issued from somewhere deep within the concrete walls. After a short pause, the door slid open, and Charr stood within.

"Oh!" she exclaimed, not really surprised. "I was just trading up." She held a short but very sharp-looking silver blade before her face, turned it to catch the light, smiled, then stepped out and waited for us to enter.

"Anything can work if Charr has a hand in it," Kuro boasted as the door slid shut once more. We descended to an indeterminate depth, and emerged into another long hallway. This time I could see the first light, and it appeared to be electrical. I hadn't seen a lot of that since I'd left home. I supposed if it could survive anywhere, it would be here where there was a constant natural source of energy. Kuro led us past a number of doors before directing us to a door on the right, and we entered a room whose walls appeared to be composed entirely of bladed weapons of every conceivable kind. A closer inspection revealed that this was not entirely true, as tucked in among them here and there could be found various wooden staffs, clubs, long bows, and a few crossbows. A few items exceeded my working knowledge of ancient weaponry.

Unnecessarily, Kuro announced, "This is our weapon room." He looked at me specifically. "You will be trained in all manner of weapons and fighting styles. Ultimately, you must find a weapon

163

that feels right for you. You may choose anything from this room, and switch at your leisure. Charr keeps her private collection elsewhere." I saw Maya trying to edge closer to the door through which we had entered, as Kuro's attention was presently focused on me. I was already unbuckling my belt to remove the Caretaker's blade, which was outshined by pretty much everything in this room. I let it drop with a clang to the concrete floor, and selected a broad, two-handed staff with a curving blade that extended almost halfway down the length of the weapon. It was like the one I had seen Tal-Makai wield in Reya's vision-memory. I looked up at Kuro, who was grinning. "Nice weapon," he said. "You're welcome to hold on to it, but I want you to start..." He strode across the chamber and chose a straight, duel-edged sword with an unassuming guard. "...with this." He tossed it to me and I caught it by the hilt, hefted it. It was surprisingly light and well-balanced for its length. "Maya...," he started, suddenly aware of her again a fraction of a second after she had reappeared in the doorway, grinning suspiciously. "You're welcome to choose something for yourself as well, though I suspect you already have a good idea how to use most of them." Maya nodded. "Your big friend as well," he added, obviously referring to Doog. "What's his weapon of choice?"

"He likes to throw sharp, heavy things," she said. "Axes mostly, or knives if they have enough heft. If the target is advancing toward him, he wants to stop it in its tracks. Or preferably send it back a few steps." I shuddered to imagine the force of a throw that would actually reverse the forward progress of a running opponent. But if anyone was capable of throwing an axe that hard, it was Doog.

"You should be able to find something like that here as well," said Kuro. "And for all of you, Charr can customize something if you don't find the perfect match. A weapon should feel like an extension of not just your body, but also of your mind and spirit. With your preference for the crossbow," he lifted his chin at

164

Maya, "I imagine Charr will take great delight in making something special for you. Maybe let you see how she does it, if you're lucky." Maya grinned widely. "So," he concluded, "you can access this room at any time as long as you are staying with us. I just ask that you don't take more at any one time than you plan to carry. We don't want any weapons going unaccounted for." I knew that wouldn't be an issue for Maya, whose modus operandi was to only keep what she could physically carry on her person. "The sleeping quarters are down here as well. You can basically just find any empty room and make it your own."

"Where is everyone else?" I asked abruptly.

Kuro looked confused. "Everyone else?"

"Yeah, the rest of your camp," I clarified. "Surely you few are not the only resistance in this region."

"Let me make myself clear about this," Kuro said. "We don't belong to any camp. We are not affiliated with any other resistance group. Here there is just me, and my students."

"Why?" Maya piped in. "You and your soldiers are exceptionally strong and skilled, but is there not an even greater strength in solidarity? Why not join with others of like mind?"

"Well, now, there you've hit it precisely on the head," said Kuro. "There *are* no others of like mind."

"What do you mean?" I asked.

Kuro explained, "We represent the last remnant of an ancient sect that is all but forgotten. As you may know, the religion of Chaer-Ul has never been bound to the written word. Chaer-Ul communes with men at his own times, and in his own ways. The faith has always been passed down verbally; parents to children

165

around the hearth, open sharing of information between camps. The message has thereby been preserved with a high degree of accuracy, and through the instrumentality of the puurr-deer, faithfully passed even to the most remote outposts. Thus what may be known of Chaer-Ul is readily available to any who would seek it without impure motive." Maya and I looked at each other. Nobody had to say that Magus' motives were less than pure.

Kuro continued, "However, long ago a manuscript was found. The details of its discovery have been lost with time, and at some point, the manuscript itself disappeared. It was believed to pre-date any known verbal communication from Chaer-Ul."

"What did it say?" Maya asked, wide-eyed and enthralled.

Kuro didn't directly address her question, saying instead, "Most of the followers of Chaer-Ul rejected the manuscript as a forgery, and those who did choose to believe it were branded as heretics, ridiculed and abused."

"Why didn't someone just *ask* Chaer-Ul if it was true?" I asked.

"Have you ever tried to ask Chaer-Ul a direct question?" Kuro challenged me. I had, and the point was well taken. He went on, "I didn't ask. Chaer-Ul told me the message was from him. He warned me not to share it with anyone, but it was like trying to extinguish a fire with gasoline. I think he knew I would preach it, and that he intended the inevitable result – my separation from the rest of the resistance, and my formation of this small group."

I glanced at Maya, whose teeth and fists were clenched, and who looked as though she were about to explode with suspense. I asked her question again. "What did the manuscript say?"

"It was a series of prophecies about a man whom Chaer-Ul would call from beyond this world to aid us in our time of greatest need.

166

It foretold the coming of the one who would be called 'Martyr'. I believe it was about you," he said. Maya's eyes turned to me, scrutinized me. I got the distinct impression that she took Kuro's words at face value, that the information resonated with something she already knew, and that she was merely probing me now in an attempt to determine whether I knew it too. "The real question," Kuro said, "is what you believe."

"I'm not really sure what to believe," I said. "Some pretty strange stuff has happened to me recently, so I'm open to being convinced. As far as being 'The Promised One', I'm not so sure. It's hard enough to come to terms with possibly being the reincarnation of a legendary hero; this information adds a whole extra layer of hype. I don't look forward to the day when the masses screaming my name come to the painful realization that I wasn't who they had thought I was after all."

"That day isn't going to come," Kuro said with a smile and what seemed to me an unfounded confidence. "That I trust you'll see soon enough."

I let that one go. "So, does *anyone* live in the town below the dam?"

"Not anymore. Not since the plague. This whole area north of the mountains appears to have been hit early and hard by it. It spread extremely quickly and killed almost everyone in the town. There is some evidence of a few people trying to flee, but they too died before getting very far. It is not known whether the majority that remained were unable to leave in time, or simply unwilling. We also don't know if there was something that made these people more vulnerable than others. Very little is known about the mode of transmission of the virus; the science that might have uncovered that knowledge was lost with most of the world's population. That town down there is a massive tomb. The bones of the dead still litter its streets and houses. We have cleared them

167

from the places that we needed to use, but the idea of giving the population of an entire small city a 'proper' burial was simply untenable. It's kind of creepy, at first, but you get used to it. The mall isn't much fun, more for the sheer number of skeletons you have to step over to get anything done than for any lingering emotional impact. You might see it differently through fresh eyes, though."

Maya and I were a bit freaked out, so Kuro went on, "The good news is, because of the sudden manner of this area's demise, the town has never been plundered. There's a lot of useful stuff down there, much of which is still just waiting to be found. Charr keeps her workshop down there. I don't like it, as she spends an awful lot of time there. It's much safer up here. But she found a place that was set up perfectly for the kind of fabrication she likes to do, and it would have been an enormous undertaking to dismantle it and haul it all up here. She's always careful, and she's sound-proofed and booby-trapped that place to the point that I'm scared to drop in on her without warning. It's never been a problem. For that matter, we've been here for a couple of years now, and we've never had an unfriendly visitor, thanks be to Chaer-Ul. It seems as if Magus is yet unaware of this place, and that's a huge tactical advantage. We train here, and when we do venture out, it is for the purpose of surveillance and gathering of intel on Magus' movements. Occasionally a raid, but we just don't have the numbers for a large-scale operation."

His tone suddenly brighter, Kuro said, "Anyway, enough about death and war for now. I'm hungry! Who else is hungry?" We both voiced our assent, and the three of us started out of the room. I leaned my new staff against the wall near the door, where I was sure I'd remember to look for it, sheathed the sword Kuro had given me, and we headed for the lift.

As we made to step out of the elevator on the upper level, I was almost bowled over by Doog, running down the hallway with a long folding table under each arm. We followed him out, and shortly Charr emerged behind us carrying flatware, utensils, and cloth napkins, then Jager with a big steel drum and some ceramic mugs. Kaire was assisting Knox with the grills. Seeing her, Kuro waved her inside for a private word. Corvus still leaned near the door outside. It was he who addressed me. "So, I understand you bleed just like the rest of us. Feel pain too. Those are weaknesses Magus is bound to exploit," he sneered.

I stopped in my tracks and spun to confront him. "What is your problem?" I asked. "I mean, besides...?" I made a not-so-subtle motion with my finger to indicate the portion of my face that mirrored his scarred half. Corvus drew his sword in one lightning-quick motion and brought it to bear on me. I met its tip with my own, almost as quick. I noticed that he had returned his spear to a sheath on his back.

"I have an eye for weakness." While his seeing eye stayed fixed on me, the dead one darted this way and that, as if that side of his face were asleep and dreaming. The effect was quite unsettling. He began to side-step, circling me slowly. I matched his movement, stepping in the opposite direction, not allowing him to gain a position of advantage. "I identify weakness in my enemy, and I turn it against him. Magus does the same. Your ability to be injured, but not killed, is a liability, not an advantage. Were Magus to capture you, he could torture you in ways not possible with a normal man, to extract information or to put pressure on the resistance." We continued to rotate in a slow, counter-clockwise circle, blades poised, keeping one another in check.

Jager, having relieved himself of his burden, drew his sword and advanced cautiously. Charr stepped into his path. "Don't interfere," she said softly. "Corvus will not harm him." And louder, for Corvus' ears, "Kuro would have his head, he knows that." Jager took a step back, but kept his sword in hand.

169

Corvus growled, not removing his one good eye from me, and said, "You have another weakness as well, a greater one." He steered the tip of his blade to the side and pointed with it, directly at Maya. "A true warrior avoids romantic entanglements. Your feelings for her put us all at risk on the battlefield. You would be better off...*without her.*" He spun free of the circle we had been tracing and drew back his sword arm to strike. At the same moment Kuro emerged from the dam, having apparently finished his business with Kaire. Assessing the situation in a flash, he shouted, "No Corvus! Not like this!" But even as he spoke Corvus' sword sliced through the air toward Maya; Kuro was too late to intervene. I on the other hand was not. I lunged and met his blade mid-swing, diverting its tip from his intended target. But my parry had thrown me off balance, and I was slow to recover. Without a doubt his skills with a sword far exceeded my own, and now he turned them against me. With a quick, spiraling motion around my blade, followed by a flick of his wrist, I was disarmed, my sword flying through the air behind me. There was no time to retrieve it. Maya stood unarmed and in shock, as he raised his blade high into the air, then brought it down with vicious strength in an arc that meant to sever her head from her body. Instinctively, desperately, I thrust my unprotected arm between him and Maya in an attempt to intercept the razor edge of his sword. As the milliseconds stretched, I waited for the sick sound of steel cleaving bone and sinew, and the agony that was sure to follow. As expected, the blade contacted my arm, but instead of pain there was a brilliant flash of white light, and his sword rebounded from my arm with such force that it flew from his hands, and he was sent sprawling to the ground at Kuro's feet, where he landed hard on his back. For several seconds I simply held my arm aloft, waiting, I suppose, for a red line to appear, and the end of my arm to slough to the ground. Or at least for something to hurt. But it didn't happen. Slowly, I withdrew my arm, then stepped to Maya and placed it around her shoulders. She was shaking. She lifted her eyes to mine and with shuddering breath whispered, "Martyr".

Every face was touched with awe, save for that of Kuro, who displayed only a knowing smile. "So at last you become in the flesh that which in fact you are."

"Now you speak like Chaer-Ul," I said. "I've had enough of mysteries and cloudy premonitions. Speak plainly what you know."

"Oh, no worries friend," said Kuro, pausing as he approached me to offer Corvus a hand. Corvus accepted, then hastened to retrieve his sword. Kuro continued, "The time has come for that which was hidden to be revealed. I apologize for the manner of enlightenment;" he narrowed his eyes and tipped his head in Corvus' direction without actually looking at him, "Corvus can be a bit over-zealous at times. I hate to imagine how this might have played out if he – and I – had been wrong. But clearly that was not the case." Kuro reached the place where I stood, turned and gestured with a broad sweep of his arm to include all now present in his address. "In the beginning, when Chaer-Ul formed the worlds, he made men, and populated his worlds. He drew a limit for the years of a man's life, and prescribed a law: that all men must die, but once. When the law was made, man knew nothing of the existence of other worlds, countless beyond number, but all within the scope of Chaer-Ul's creation and dominion...and *plan*. Neither has anyone ever passed from one world to the next, but only from his own world into the place prepared by Chaer-Ul for those departed from this life. But now, in our day, and as you are all witness today, he has brought a man from another world to aid us in our own world's time of greatest affliction."

I scanned the faces of those standing nearby. All listened intently, weighing the words as if to determine their worth. Not yet fully convinced of their veracity, but eager to hear what Kuro had to say. There was a measure of doubt in every face, but also a new thing: *hope*. Kuro went on, "In Chaer-Ul's wisdom, he was pleased to make, among his myriad worlds, degrees of variation. It followed that while some worlds would vary greatly from one another, there were others that differed only in the minutest degrees, perhaps even imperceptibly. In two such worlds, there could be said to be duplicates of every individual, such that in another world you could find another Kuro, another Charr, another Jager, and so forth. These copies could be identical down to the smallest components, what science once called the 'genetic code'. Thus it could be said in truth that any such pair described different variants of the same person, though the circumstances of their lives, their decisions and thoughts, even their age at a given time could vary considerably. Because of fine differences in each world's cosmos, time would flow differently in each world."

I realized that he was talking about me and Tal-Makai, had even suspected something of this nature, but the skeptic in me spoke first. "With all due respect, all of this sounds pretty specific for a prophecy. Are you suggesting that these ancient writings of yours – conveniently missing as they are – contained details about genetics and parallel worlds? I've spent a fair amount of time studying the prophecies and parables of many different religions, and I can tell you that they are never so clear, except to their followers, and after the fact."

"A very astute observation, my boy," said Kuro. "And I'd have been just a little disappointed if you *hadn't* picked up on that fact. True enough, the words I speak now were not all contained in the original manuscript. They represent my own musings on the text and its implications, combined with fragments pieced together from the spoken words of Chaer-Ul – those spoken to myself and to others." At this point Kuro mistakenly interpreted my uncertainty for something else. "Perhaps he has told you something as well?"

"No," I said. "I mean, he's spoken to me, but he's never said anything of substance. Just things like, 'You will become what you will become'...you know, very circular stuff that was probably just meant to make me think." But as I said this, I recalled with shocking clarity one thing that Chaer-Ul had told me. "Wait!" I said. "He did say, 'That you live...is because of who you are. That you are untouched...is because of who you must become.' Does that mean anything to you? Why did he make such a distinction?"

Kuro stared at me blankly for a moment, then suddenly burst out laughing, and slammed the butt of his spear against a stone at his feet several times. "Oh yes!" he said at last. "I dare say that one thing says it all! And this confirms a great deal of my speculation on the precise meaning of the prophecy." He walked to a spot in the middle of the gathering, and head lowered, took a slow, deep breath before proceeding. "Jager and Kaire have been telling me the details of your encounter with Magus' men at Milltown, and the terrible things you endured. Your gear deflected a bullet, and you were subsequently skewered by a blade, is that right?"

"That's how I remember it," I said dryly.

"Was there anything different about the bullet? Did you expect it? Do you remember what you were thinking in the seconds before it struck you?"

I gave him a look that I hoped conveyed my complete lack of appreciation for being forced to re-live any portion of those events. But when I made a genuine effort, the shards of memories reassembled themselves to form a true picture of what had happened. So I told him, "I had glanced over my shoulder and seen a fleeting glint of light. I knew at once that it had to be a reflection from the scope of the sniper rifle we had seen in the Caretaker's war room. I steered my deer...I was..." When I realized it, I shouted the words, "*I was trying to protect Maya!*"

174

A grin from ear to ear, Kuro added, "As you were today."

The implications were slow in their advance upon my psyche. "So…I'm untouchable…when I'm protecting Maya?"

"That, yes, but that understanding is far too narrow", said Kuro. Then he repeated the words that Chaer-Ul had given me. " *'That you live…is because of who you are. That you are untouched…is because of who you must become.'* You cannot die, because *you*, in the form of Tal-Makai, have already died in this world. A man may only die once." And while that was only starting to sink in, he finished, "And you cannot be touched, are absolutely incorruptible and effectively invincible, because you are Martyr, or rather, *when you become* Martyr. That is, when you lay your own life down for what you know to be right, for what you believe. When your self-interest is eclipsed by your concern for others, to the point that you will not cling to your own life when theirs are at stake. That is what it means to become Martyr."

Corvus interrupted, "Unfortunately, the only thing he believes in now is a *girl*. What if she's not around to protect when the enemy comes for him?"

This time Kuro spun angrily and snapped, "Corvus, you are out of line! We have yet to discuss your reckless behavior here a moment ago. *And we certainly will*," he added with ominous tone. Corvus did not fail to appreciate the sincerity of his words, receded a half step. Then to me Kuro said, "But Corvus has a point. You have not yet fully 'become'. Your training must now focus not only on the acquisition of skills, but more specifically on unlocking that which lies within. I do not know exactly what Martyr must do, or how you will be instrumental in the redemption of our world. On such matters the prophecies are silent. But you must be willing to act; to do whatever it is that Chaer-Ul requires of you."

175

Here Jager chimed in. "There is also wisdom in what Corvus said before, though his manner may not have been right. If you are not able to understand the true nature of what you must become, if you cannot master not only the sword, but also your own heart...then these unique abilities will become a liability, a weakness that Magus can and will exploit."

"Your inability to be killed," Kuro said, nodding acknowledgement of what Jager had said, "is a fact; a function of the manner in which you, and not Tal-Makai, came to be in this world. *But* – and never forget this – your invulnerability, the fact that you can be effectively 'bulletproof', is not intrinsic to your circumstances. It is a *gift* from Chaer-Ul, a thing that he has been pleased to bestow, and which should not be taken for granted. You *could not be* Martyr if you had not come to occupy the place of Tal-Makai – one particularly set apart by Chaer-Ul. But you *are* Martyr – whatever that title means or may come to mean – only because Chaer-Ul decrees it. It is not because you live while Tal does not; it is by *his will alone*. Martyr...is a creation of Chaer-Ul. I may not know what he has in store for you, but I cannot believe that he brought you here for nothing. This is a new thing that Chaer-Ul does today; such things have never been seen before."

It was a lot to take in. If it were even true. But the things I had seen seemed to lend credibility to Kuro's words, as much as it bolstered his faith. "There's something I think you should know," I said. "You've been away for a long time, and I'm not sure the views you hold are still as heretical as they may once have been seen to be. The name of 'Martyr' is on the lips of many. I heard it when I first entered Reya's camp, and on several occasions thereafter. The people are desperate for something to believe in, for someone to follow."

"I don't think so," said Kuro. "I didn't leave because of the whispered insults or the condemning stares. I've never had a care for what people think of me. I'd have been perfectly happy to

176

dwell in enmity with my neighbors, knowing my conscience was clear before Chaer-Ul. No. The camps breed complacency. Warriors go soft, begin to care more about what's coming up on the community social calendar than about formulating a plan to reclaim our world. I was sickened by those who were content to hear the voice of Chaer-Ul through others more willing to seek him out. They've lost purpose, wandering through life with blinders, pretending that it might go on this way indefinitely. Look at this world! It's a wasteland, devastated by plague, and now Magus would burn up any good that remains with his vile sorcery and allegiances with dark powers. I couldn't countenance the apathy I saw around me! If I were to be the only one to stand against Magus, I had to try. And finally, after long months of searching, I managed to gather these few who were ready to give all, even their very lives if necessary, for the name of Chaer-Ul."

"Things *have* changed, Kuro," said Kaire. "You speak of a time when the camps had grown complacent. That was in the beginning, when Magus first began his campaign against Chaer-Ul. Nobody could have anticipated the kind of power he would amass, nor the depths of depravity to which he would descend. And nobody thought we'd still be fighting him to this day. After you left, Magus' attacks grew ever more frequent and widespread as his dark army grew. The people were afraid at first, but grew tired of living in fear. The camps demanded strong leadership, and through that leadership they came to be far more organized and disciplined. Today the settlements that are militarized far outnumber those that are not. But the attacks were relentless, and many good people have been lost. Those that survived to continue the fight grow weary and begin to lose hope. The whisperings about Martyr, a hero-redeemer sent by Chaer-Ul, started to be viewed less as the mad rantings of heresy, and more as a source of hope."

"It's true, Kuro," I added. "If you believe that I am Martyr, maybe they will too. Perhaps I can be, if not a hero, at least a symbol

177

under which all of the resistance can unite. Your faithful few, however strong, cannot stand alone against Magus' thousands.

Corvus had by this time collected what remained of his dignity and drawn near Kuro's side. Kuro addressed him. "Well, what do *you* think now?"

"With all due respect, I think this 'gift' is nothing more than good armor. A defensive advantage, maybe. Invulnerability won't slay Magus' legions. *He can't fight!* I may not be able to stop a blade with flesh, but I don't have to. I just have to make sure the enemy's sword never makes it that far."

Kuro pressed him. "*Do you believe* he is the one Chaer-Ul told us to expect? Do you believe he is Martyr?"

Corvus huffed derisively. "I don't know. I don't see how he offers anything we don't already have. If he is Martyr...then I have to say I'm a bit disappointed."

A second later the tip of Kuro's blade hovered millimeters from Corvus' good eye. Corvus made no attempt to defend, his arms never moving from his sides. This was not a failure to act, but evidence of exceptional discipline. He would not act against his master even at the cost of his life. Had I tried the same trick, the response would have been quite different. "Words should be weighed before they are meted out," Kuro said, sword still menacingly poised. After a prolonged pause he added, "fortunately for you, I don't believe faith should be coerced," and withdrew his weapon slowly. "You expected Chaer-Ul's Martyr to appear in the clouds as a conquering hero. Is it not like Chaer-Ul to act in precisely the manner that is least expected?" Corvus remained thoughtfully silent, his opalescent eye flicking once to me, and then back to Kuro.

"Knox!" Kuro shouted unexpectedly. Knox trotted dutifully to the fore. "Justin's training will begin with you. Starting with the morning light, you will teach him everything you have learned about the handling of bladed weapons. Work him hard. When he is broken, work him harder."

"Sir!" Knox replied with a salutatory nod.

"You'll eat when we eat, sleep when we sleep," Kuro told me. "When the sun sets, the evening time is yours. I suggest you avail yourself of that time to seek the counsel of Chaer-Ul. In any case, don't be out too late or you sleep under the stars. Once the vault is closed for the night, it stays that way. You will alternate training days with each one of us, as every member of my team has unique skills to share." I was already not looking forward to working with Corvus. "That includes myself. And I assume Jager and Kaire will want their share of your time as well."

"Indeed!" Kaire said. "We found him first." A couple of people chuckled at that. "Besides, it will be sort of like old times, won't it?" I wasn't sure exactly what she meant, but filed it for a later conversation.

"Good enough!" Kuro exclaimed. "Now, everybody eat up. Then, select your rooms and get some rest. Morning comes early up here." As per his instructions, we feasted heartily. I was reluctant to leave Maya's side, but presently Kuro ushered Corvus inside the dam for what could not be a pleasant chat. A lot of the tension left with them, and soon even Maya was smiling again. We ate, and talked about lighter things, and by the time Corvus rejoined the group there was little he could do to dampen our mood. In fact, he seemed just a little less cocky than before. That might have been the beer. Anyway, he didn't offer an apology, as I hadn't expected him to. The night was cool, but not cold, as darkness settled upon us, and a mist from the lake filled in the spaces between the trees. Nobody tried to engage me in

179

conversation, but I was happy enough with Maya's company. At some point, when everyone else seemed sufficiently distracted, Maya took me by the hand and led me through the shadows cast by the flickering firelight to the dam entrance.

As soon as the elevator door closed, Maya pulled me close and kissed me passionately. I held her softly, one hand cupping her head, the other navigating the silky waves of her hair, finally finding rest in the small of her back. The door opened altogether too soon. I wanted to remain as we were, but she reached behind her back and took my hand, then reluctantly interrupted the kiss and led me down the hallway past several identical-looking doors before stopping at one. "I saw this one earlier," she said. Her back to the door, she kissed me once more, releasing my hand as she pushed the door open with one foot. She stepped backward into the room and out of the hallway's light, temporarily silhouetted against the dimmer light cast by the room's single bulb. I hesitated, wondering if I should begin to look for a room of my own. Maya's hands reached from the shadows and found mine, and interlacing the fingers of both hands with mine she drew me in behind her, our lips reuniting. "You weren't going to leave me all alone, with Magus' assassins about, were you?" she asked.

"I...no, I...of course I wouldn't...," then I caught the sparkle in her eye, the trace of a smile.

"Your place is with me, *husband*," she said firmly. I lacked the will to object. I entered, securing the door behind me. The room was sparsely furnished save for a single, large bed. Removing only our boots, and Maya her vest, we tumbled onto the mattress. Maya turned to me, shared one last prolonged kiss, then rolled away, pulling my arm over her as she did. Curling herself into a smaller form, I could feel that she was shuddering, though it wasn't cold. "Hold me," she said. "Never let go." I did just that, and she exhaled slowly, emitting a small, satisfied sound as she did. My passion surrendered to her more pressing need. Content in a way

180

I'd never been, and too exhausted to dwell on the day's startling revelations, I was soon asleep.

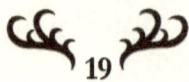

19

I didn't dream this time. In fact, it seemed to me that I had only just closed my eyes when there came a sharp rap at the door. I cracked the door open a sliver to see that it was Knox, armed and in full armor save for the helmet, which he carried under his arm. Latching the door quietly behind me, I followed him to the elevator. As we reached the lobby, I saw the parts of a suit of armor like Knox's laid out for me. He assisted me in putting it on and securing it properly. I was surprised at how light it really was, and how mobile; there was virtually no restriction to my range of motion. I had brought along the weapon Kuro had selected for me, and that I now fastened at my waist. We stepped out to a brisk morning. There was just the faintest premonition of dawn beginning to warm the eastern horizon. We walked across the top of the dam to the far shore of the lake, then called deer and rode through a still-misty canyon which eventually opened to a massive natural arena that dwarfed the one Maya and I had happened upon earlier. It was dominated by an expanse of flat, level ground, but there were also a number of large, wooden structures apparently designed to simulate an array of potential battlefield conditions. The most prominent of these had the appearance of a tower, from which two straw archers kept permanent watch.

"I thought maybe there'd be coffee," I said, hoping to draw Knox into conversation, as he seemed to be all business this morning.

Clearly not appreciating the subtleties of my humor, he answered simply, "Your meals will have to be earned from now on. Adequate progress, and you eat. Unsatisfactory performance, and you don't."

So that was the game. Well, I was already hungry, so I wasted no more time and drew my sword. "Put that away!" Knox said. I almost dropped it. Mildly irritated, I returned my weapon to its sheath and awaited his next order. "You only did two things wrong when you fought with Corvus. You failed to stand, and you failed to keep your sword. Both problems stem from the same source: stability. Firm footing and a firm grip, balance and strength, don't come from your hands and feet, they come from your core." He indicated with both hands the general area of his belly. "When this is strong, your feet will remain where you place them, your hands firmly on the hilt of your blade." I was tempted to say that my core would feel a lot more stable if it had some food in it, but didn't. "I am going to come at you," he said. "Withstand me."

It would have been considerate of him to give me a few seconds to mentally prepare, to concentrate on stabilizing my core. That obviously wasn't his tack. He charged with the force of a bull, at the last moment tucking his head and jamming his shoulder into my abdomen, and with an upward thrust sending me temporarily skyward. The angle of my launch was such that it was impossible to right myself while airborne; I landed flat on my back on the gravelly floor of the arena. I shot him a look that I hoped conveyed the sense of "cheap trick" as I rose and dusted myself off. Remarkably, the armor had absorbed most of the shock of both impact and landing, and I felt really none the worse for it. "What was that intended to teach me?" I inquired.

"The importance of balance, first," he said. "And second, of readiness. You must learn to exist in a state of constant expectation of attack. In the beginning, this will undoubtedly lead to a degree of stress, as this is not a normal or comfortable place for the human mind to dwell. However, among those whose reality includes the constant threat of war, it becomes second nature. Indeed, almost every other species lives this way, as all must find a balance between eating and avoiding being eaten. If you think about it all the time, it will drive you insane with fear. It must become instinctual, as it is with the beast."

"Try me again," I said.

"Listen, I may not have the element of surprise the second time, but in terms of pure combat ability, you're no better off than you were two minutes ago. Now is not the time to get cocky."

"Just one more time," I said.

Ignoring me entirely, he continued with his intended lesson. "Now, let's start by taking a look at your stance. See how you..."

"*Come at me!*" I shouted. My voice echoed around the granite amphitheatre like a roar. Knox stopped mid-sentence, cocked his head to one side, and exploded into motion. He was not a tall man, but solidly built; he rushed me with the force of a freight train. A sliver of a second before he reached me I dropped to a low crouch, placing my center of gravity below his. Then, precisely at the moment of contact, I shrugged upward into the bulk of his torso, then righted myself fully, flipping his substantial mass up and over me so that he landed on his tailbone behind me. More shocked than hurt, he lifted himself slowly to his feet, took the time to examine his armor and stretch his hamstrings before he finally permitted his eyes to make contact with mine. Having locked me in with his gaze, he charged again. This time he didn't employ the same maneuver, nor had I expected him to. It looked as though he intended to tackle me outright. As his hands prepared to grab my shoulders, I arched my back and swung my right shoulder to my rear, placing my upper body just out of his current path. As I did so I took hold of his right arm firmly with both of my hands. Simultaneously I replanted my right foot farther to my rear and pivoted on my left heel. This enabled me to swing him just far enough off his course to unbalance him. Having done so, I released my grip suddenly and let his momentum do the rest. A minute later he was brushing himself off once again. I could see that he was slightly winded from the exertion and did not plan to launch a third assault.

184

"Where did you learn those moves?" he demanded.

"I didn't," I said. "It just seemed like the right thing to do."

"With all due respect, I have been trained in warfare all my life. Nobody who has had no such training just *happens* to best me."

I shrugged, said nothing. I didn't mean it to be disrespectful, but it probably was. "So what now?"

"Well," Knox sounded a bit confounded, "You just saved us an entire morning of training."

"Good. Lunch, then?"

Knox's eyes narrowed as his face reddened. "*Draw...your...weapon,*" he growled. The time for joking had passed.

My blade was in my hand. Knox lunged for my chest, I parried it easily. This was a feint; he immediately took advantage of the extended position of my sword arm and attempted to disarm me in the manner that Corvus had. I was having none of that. I held my weapon fast by the hilt and drew it back quickly to guard my body. He came at me with a series of powerful blows directed at my abdomen. It was all I could do to deflect each strike and prepare for the next. The attacks did not seem particularly intent on making contact with flesh, only on keeping me on defense, and at that they were quite effective. He continued to press his assault, and as I defended, I found that I could trust my arm to keep me safe. For a strange moment my mind detached itself from the business at the end of my sword, and as the action commenced I was free to observe other aspects of Knox's fighting style. It was as though a silent narrator had paused the scene, and was now advancing it frame by frame, pointing out key elements of my opponent's form and holding. I became aware that the focus of his onslaught had shifted upward, to the area of my chest.

185

So it was that when I noticed a small twitch in the muscles of his neck, a slight elevation of his unencumbered shoulder, I knew instinctively that the nature of the attack was about to change. As he landed the next blow, not unlike the last, I pushed his sword forcibly off to the side, then swiftly brought my blade to bear on the second, smaller blade that appeared in his other hand, and which had already begun the motion that would bury it deep in my abdomen. My sword contacted his close to the hilt, and with such a shearing force across the plane of his thrust, that his thumb was loosed and the weapon flipped out of his grasp, burying itself in the gravel at his side. Knox paused, shocked by the unexpected speed and efficiency of my defense. When he did, I launched my offense. But I didn't employ a series of similar strokes as he had; rather, I tried to mix it up a bit, going first for the legs, then for the head, now for the gut. He managed to parry each attack with his remaining blade, but just barely. His response time slowed as I refused to let up, and I could hear his breath coming in gasps between moves. Once I grazed his shoulder, another time sliced partway through the leather belt that held his sheaths. I made his blade dance, forcing it repeatedly away from his core, keeping him feeling exposed, vulnerable.

I saw numerous opportunities to strike at a vital spot and end the fight, but opted rather to prolong it, exhausting him, knowing *he* would realize that I could have finished it but didn't. I wanted him to feel that. It was a point I wanted to make sure I wouldn't have to make twice. To earn not only his respect, but a healthy degree of fear. I slowed my assault to match his wavering defense. When he made a half-hearted downward slash I raised my foot and stomped down hard on the tip of his descending blade, forcing the weapon out of his anemic grasp. Shoulders slumped, panting heavily, he made no attempt to reclaim it. I gave him a minute to catch his breath, then said, "You tried to stab me."

"The armor," he said between labored breaths, "would have protected you…from lethal injury."

"So you planned to inflict the non-lethal kind," I said. "Thoughtful."

"You heard Kuro. We're not supposed to take it easy on you. And apparently it wasn't necessary, was it? I thought you hadn't had any training. Where the heck did you pull those moves out of?"

"I have no idea," I said. "I've never learned them, but it had a familiar feeling, like skiing for the first time in the season." His expression informed me that the analogy was completely lost on him. "I mean, it was a little trial and error at first, but it felt like something I had done before, but had just gotten a bit rusty." Corrosion was something anyone in this world could appreciate.

"Well, whatever the reason, you obviously know how to fight," Knox said. "Our task, then, is just to knock the rust off of the rest of your weapons. But hey…don't feel the need to go all out in every skirmish. You'll wear yourself out too quickly." He had removed his helmet by now, and the wet mop of hair underneath suggested that perhaps I wasn't the one who needed to worry about fatiguing myself, but I didn't say it. "Let's kill something and eat it."

It was a welcome thought, and at one point we scared up a pair of brightly-colored pheasants, but Knox's thrown knife fell shy of its mark. It really wasn't the right tool for bird hunting. Doog wouldn't have missed, I was sure. At one point I asked, "I take it we don't eat deer?"

Knox looked at me judgmentally. "I *hope* you're kidding."

"Of course I was," I mumbled, as my mind created the scent of roasting venison. We came across a patch of something like wild

187

asparagus, and dismounted. The younger shoots were sweet and even tasty, but there were few of those, and the larger ones were impossibly fibrous.

"I think this may have to do it for now," Knox said. We'll eat better back at the base this evening. We need to get through some more exercises before we lose daylight." They might have been the most disappointing words I had ever heard. We headed back to the training arena. We had only ridden for a few minutes when the air was split by a horrific guttural bellow. The deer froze instantly, ears twitching this way and that, trying to determine the direction and proximity of the sound, or rather, of *whatever* had produced it.

"What *was* that?" I asked Knox, my voice sounding too loud even to me.

He shushed me quickly and voiced only a muted, "After me!" He veered sharply to the right and my deer followed suit. As we raced through the trees, I was amazed at how little noise the deer made as they ran. Maybe the extra pair of legs helped distribute their weight better. I kept expecting to hear the roar again, closer, but it never came. I might have actually been able to breathe a sigh of relief if we'd heard it coming from farther away, but that didn't happen, either. I didn't have a super sense of direction, but I was fairly sure we weren't heading back toward the arena. After a time I expressed my concerns. More anxious than annoyed, Knox replied in hushed tones, "Training is over for the day. We need to get to the dam. *Fast.*" We burst into a clearing, and it was immediately apparent that the thing that stood there had other plans for us.

It was a massive armored feline, like the one I had seen from the chopper, up in the mountains. It was wider than it was high, its tough hide folded into interlocking natural armor plates like a rhino. It was black or almost-black, and mostly hairless except for sparse patches of short, bristly hair in a few places. Its legs were huge and wide-set, ending in rows of claws that were more reminiscent of extinct theropod than cat. It bellowed again, and I was momentarily deafened. Knox shouted something at me, but it was lost to the ringing in my ears. Both of our deer reared up and beat the air with their front hooves. Knox managed to maintain his hold upon his animal when that happened. I was not so lucky. I landed in some shrubbery at the base of a large rock. My deer bounded off through the trees. Apparently the creature didn't see me fall. It leapt to the top of the rock above me, then soared over me in pursuit of the deer; a great, dark shape that reminded me most of a monster truck taking a jump to clear a row of school buses. No doubt it weighed at least as much – the beast was enormous. Built for strength and stability, not speed, the deer easily outpaced it, and the creature was smart enough to realize the chase was futile.

It turned back to see what morsels remained for the picking. A pair of great, red, tri-pupilled eyes scanned the area, saw Knox on his deer, skirting the far perimeter of the clearing. Its limbs tensed, preparing to launch itself in that direction, when I saw the skin of its snout wrinkle, its nostrils flare. A colossal, black head the approximate size and mass of an engine block swung to face me, demonic eyes confirming what it already knew through olfactory means. Rightly surmising that I lacked the capability of rapid flight, it stalked hungrily toward me, taking its time to savor the experience. I clambered up the side of the big rock, but I had seen it leap; I knew I wasn't safe there. I jumped from the rock to a branch of a small tree nearby, and tried to place as much height between myself and the monster as possible before it arrived. I theorized, based on its stocky build, that it wasn't much of a climber. I hoped I was right. Reaching the base of the rock, the cat hopped effortlessly to its top, and located me on my perch high above.

189

Just then Knox shouted something to try to distract the animal, but it spared him not a glance. The creature didn't look straight up at me, but cocked its head at an odd angle and peered at me sidelong with one eye. It seemed that the thick, armored skin of its neck didn't make for easy upward glancing. Judging by its size this hadn't prevented it from finding enough to eat. The big cat returned its head to level, paused, then abruptly lashed out with one huge paw and whacked the trunk of the tree to which I clung. The whole tree shook wildly, the top bowing first one way, then the other. For a second I thought it would bend in two and deposit me on the ground before the beast – an easy meal. The tree held, but I was already looking for a more secure place to roost. The only other tree within reach was only slightly larger in diameter than the current one, but I didn't have a lot of other options.

I was still suspended halfway between the two tree trunks when I heard a sharp crack, and felt the smaller tree give way under my weight. I experienced a brief sensation of panic like falling in a dream, but my dubious grip on the second tree proved true, and I pulled myself to it fully, quickly finding better purchase. I looked down to see that the cat had bitten cleanly through the trunk of the tree, and was now discarding it and taking stock of my new situation. It batted the trunk twice in rapid succession, and the larger tree shook violently but didn't bend. I wasn't at all sure that it couldn't bite through the new trunk almost as easily as the first, and I began to consider my options. There were no other trees of any size that I could jump to. Even if I thought I could land on a moving deer, there was no way Knox could get close enough without exposing himself and his deer to the creature's wrath. While I was still wracking my brain for a solution that wouldn't involve me serving myself up to the cat, I heard another loud crack, and was almost shaken from the tree as the animal took one huge bite out of the second tree. Now it swayed precariously, and I knew a second bite would finish it, and me. I chose an option that my mind had rejected a moment earlier, having deemed it extremely ill-advised.

Loosening my grip on the tree, I slid down a few feet. Then, when I was close enough, and just as the cat took his next bite of hardwood, I pushed off from the tree trunk and landed , crouching, on the animal's back. It was temporarily stunned by the impact, which gave me the chance to turn myself around to face its head, and firmly grip the edge of one of its armor plates above its shoulders. I saw now that it was tougher than a rhino's skin; more akin to a tortoise's shell, possibly composed of bone covered with skin. It cocked its head to one side, then the other, raised a paw and swatted the air a couple of times, then apparently realized it couldn't reach me, and took off at a run. The great cat roared angrily, and I was deafened again for a little while. It threw its body against tree trunks as it barreled along, trying to dislodge me. But it was just too big; my legs were straddling it widely, but still didn't come close to its sides. It roared again, once, twice, sounding higher and more desperate than before. Then its speed increased quite suddenly, and I lifted my head to see the reason. Up ahead the land dropped down to form a natural gully between walls of topsoil held in place by an interwoven network of roots from the surrounding trees. The ravine was wide enough to allow the creature to pass through safely, but about halfway through there was an enormous tree trunk fallen across the gap. The cat would be able to slip underneath, but I would not. I would be brushed clear and would fall to the base of the ditch to await its return. Most likely I'd be rendered unconscious by the blow and the resultant fall. Then I'd be eaten.

I considered jumping, but the log was too high to clear, and I'd never have time to climb the roots to the top of the gully before the cat was upon me. I looked behind me, but Knox was nowhere to be seen. So much for a rescue. Out of options once again, I drew my sword. I only had seconds to act before we would reach the fallen tree. Finding the spot where the armor of the creature's

191

neck met that of its head, I drew back with a two-handed grip and plunged the tip of my blade into the spot. The cat shrieked and lost a bit of its momentum, but didn't deviate from its course. I summoned all of my strength and attempted to push the blade deeper, hoping to reach its brainstem. It shrieked again, but my sword didn't gain much depth; the animal's skin was just too tough. The tree trunk looming close, I pulled out my blade, switched it to my right hand, and jabbed it into the right side of the creature's head, just behind its ear. It screamed once more, and as it did it turned its head into its right shoulder, guarding the sensitive region. This caused a change in its symmetry, and as a result it swerved off its intended course toward the right side of the gully. As its feet touched the sloping surface its momentum carried it partway up the right side of the gully. Now too close to the fallen tree, and too high to duck under it, the cat had no choice but to scale the remaining few feet of the side wall and leap over the trunk.

Back on level ground, the beast increased its momentum anew. I didn't afford it the chance to consider circling back for a second chance to scrape me against the log. My sword still buried behind its ear, I gave it a twist, and it had the same effect as before, resulting in the cat steering to the right. I freed my blade and passed it to my left hand, jammed it into the soft spot behind its left ear. The cat turned left. So this could work, I thought. Repeating this technique as needed, I began to cut a path to the dam. Shortly I heard Knox calling to me, and saw him appear, still mounted on his deer, from the trees to my left.

"Justin! What can I do to help?"

"Can't think of a lot right now…," I shouted back, "…I'm kind of winging it. Ever take one of these things down before?"

"Yeah, but it took all four of us," he said. "And we wore it down for a week."

"Encouraging," I said. Then, I had an idea. "Wait, I just thought of something. You have a net back at the dam? Like a big fishing net?"

"We do have a net, and it's pretty big. We use it to snare game sometimes. But I don't think it could hold...*that*."

"It's not for the cat," I said. "It's for me."

"Ok...Tell me what to do."

"Ride ahead," I said. "I can try to stall it but don't know how long I can keep it going in circles. So try to gain as much distance as possible. String the net up so that it forms a roadblock partway across the top of the dam. But do it quickly!"

"Got it," Knox said. "You sure you know what you're doing?"

"I'm driving a cat," I said. "So no." Knox sped on ahead, and soon passed out of sight. I didn't know how much longer the steering-through-pain technique would continue to work, and didn't really want to torment the poor animal any more than necessary, so I tried to make it count when I did give it a poke. This meant fewer, but more jarring turns, and I was beginning to lose sensation in my fingers where I gripped the creature's armor plating so tightly. I hoped we reached the dam soon, and I particularly hoped my zig-zagging course would afford Knox and the others enough time to set up the net. The cat was getting tired, its breath coming in rasping gulps. I couldn't afford for it to lose too much speed, or my plan would fail. I found the place where its armor joined in front of its hind legs, and dug my heels into the somewhat softer skin. I knew it wouldn't be enough to hurt the animal, but that wasn't my aim; I just needed it to stay mad. I guess nothing really likes to be kicked, and it seemed the act was sufficiently irritating to spur the cat on to renewed speed.

193

Suddenly the trees parted and we were beside the lake. Downstream the dam was just visible through the drifting mist created by the enormous volume of falling water. I gave the beast a jab, it moaned and started to turn to follow the lakeshore. The response was a bit slower this time, as it seemed to be resisting the natural urge to guard the place of injury. Perhaps it had the idea to drown me in the dark water. A second, more sincere stab and it came around. As we drew near the dam, I could see Knox, Corvus, and Kuro laboring to secure the net with ropes about two-thirds of the way across the top of the dam. The first rope holding one of the top corners was already in place, attached to one of the large towers on the face of the dam. Now they were pulling it taut around an abutment on the opposite side. The cat arrived at the dam and I dug my blade in once more. It reluctantly turned onto the road that would carry us across the dam to the far shore. I was hoping it would never reach the other side. The men had the other top rope in place now, but the bottom of the net swung freely. That wouldn't do at all. They struggled to tie off a third corner of the net, but we were coming on fast, and I couldn't conceive of any way to slow the creature enough to buy them time.

This was the plan: at the last possible moment before reaching the net, I would drive my sword into the side of the creature's neck with as much force as I could muster. This would cause it to veer off the face of the dam and plummet, I could only hope, to its death. A fraction of a second before it began its free-fall, I would jump away from the edge, landing in the net. The force of my feet pushing off from the creature's back would provide an extra measure of certainty that it would not be able to correct its path until it was too late. It required precision timing, but I thought I could pull it off.

We were almost upon the spot, and the rope from the last corner of the net was looped around the abutment, but not secured. The men had found it necessary to abandon the effort and take shelter, lest the beast trample them as well. Now came the moment of truth. I lifted myself to a crouched position on its back, raised my sword high, and stabbed it deep into the tender spot behind the great cat's right ear. It went deeper than before, and the animal shrieked with pain and stumbled, but didn't veer off course. Apparently it had the presence of mind to realize that whatever I could dole out was preferable to a suicide leap off the face of the dam. Too sure that the cat would do as I expected, I almost sprang anyway, but thankfully was able to drop back against the cat's hide without losing my grip. A second later it barreled through the net, tearing it easily from its moorings without losing momentum. The net tangled itself about the cat's body, effectively binding me to its back. My plan had failed, and now my situation had notably worsened. Unable to wield my sword and prevented from leaping free, it was now just a matter of time before the creature found something else to crush me against. I was about to give up hope.

Then I knew what I had to do. I don't know where the thought came from, but I knew exactly what to do, and somehow, I knew with absolute certainty that it would work. As the cat reached the end of the dam and made for the trees on the far side, I called a deer. Almost immediately one pulled alongside, matching the cat's pace. It showed no fear of the animal, and the cat made no move in its direction, indeed showed no sign of even being aware of its presence. "Muur-puurrha," I recited. I hummed the now-familiar monotone, and a vision appeared. It resembled the present reality, but minus the deer, the net, and me. I saw it from the cat's perspective; an unencumbered beast sprinting through a quiet wood. Gradually the path rose, grew more uneven. The animal had to slow its pace, take careful steps. The path became steeper yet, and a change in perspective revealed that it culminated at the edge of a cliff ahead. The cat slowed to a cautious stride, drew abreast of the drop-off, surveying a vast plain far below. Then it turned to seek an alternate course, and found to its surprise that there was no more path; it stood on a pillar of earth scarcely larger than its own body, towering a thousand feet above a yellow-grassed plain that stretched endlessly in every direction. It roared, a mournful, defeated sound that echoed off distant, unseen heights.

By this time I was mounting my deer as Knox sat on his own nearby, having recently cut me free of the net that held me. I was still humming. A large, confused-looking cat was turning about in place, bellowing occasionally to no one in particular. Making sure we started off in the direction opposite the way the cat was currently facing, we goaded our deer quickly to their top speed. I suppose at some point the great animal would have ceased to be under the control of my vision-trance, but it had excellent hearing, and I continued humming for quite some time. It was never going to hear the deer escaping, much less catch us.

20

"Sharing a vision with a non-human subject...," Kuro mused, "...Creating a vision out of pure imagination, not from any previously experienced memory..." He chuckled under his breath. "It's never been done. And not because nobody has tried – it *can't* be done! That's just not how the visions work." He shook his head, then looked skyward, raised his palms to the heavens. "What are you up to now?" he asked the sky, amused and just a bit exasperated. Then, turning back to me, "Knox has been telling me how you bested...," (Knox started coughing uncontrollably) "...uh, proved to be quite an excellent student for your first day of training! You'll continue training with him over the next few days. When you have demonstrated proficiency with all manner of swords and knives, singly and dually wielded, you will begin to work with Charr." I looked around, but didn't see Charr. "She will train you in hand-to-hand combat, though it seems you may have a head-start there as well." Knox was taken with another bout of coughing – perhaps he was having an allergic reaction to something we had encountered in the forest.

"Charr will also teach you ranged weapons; it may not be your primary mode of combat, but it's important to be able to land a well-placed shot should the need arise. Corvus will train you in stealth, and...well...*lethal* moves." The words were bitter in Kuro's mouth, as was evident from his expression. Apparently even he wasn't completely comfortable with the way Corvus operated, but found it to be an unfortunate necessity. Detachment, cruelty...these were not human virtues, but certainly enabled one to do on the battlefield that which "nobler" qualities such as empathy and compassion prevented others from doing. Whether that was ultimately a good thing or not remained to be seen. Corvus stood to Kuro's rear with head down, his dark hair falling over his good eye. He didn't look up when Kuro spoke of him, but his twisted lips displayed a grim smile.

"After Corvus," Kuro continued, "Kaire and Jager will have their time with you." I acknowledged the two members of Reya's camp standing to Kuro's side. "I suspect Jager's focus will be on strategy." Jager nodded silently. "That was always his favorite subject, and he's extremely good at it."

"Thank you, Master," Jager said modestly.

"Pah! The days when you must call me 'Master' are long past. I imagine you could teach me a few things now."

"I could have taught you a few things back then too, but you were too stubborn!" said Jager.

Kuro laughed heartily. "Well taken, old friend. But please dispense with the formalities henceforth." Jager nodded again, and Kuro went on. "Kaire, I must say that I don't know your strengths."

Kaire responded with a smile, "Neither does the enemy. That's what makes them strengths."

"Very good," he said. "Then I'll trust you to teach the boy in whatever manner you deem most appropriate." Kaire assured him she would do her best. "Good," he said. "That's all for now. Fire up the grills!" And he turned as if to head back into the dam.

"Wait," I said. "That animal…was it…sent?"

Kuro turned. "By Magus you mean? No, not unless it was disfigured in some way, had some kind of machinery attached to it. Did you see anything like that?"

"No," I said. I remembered the pitiable state of the puurr-deer in Reya's vision.

"Animals are not as easily swayed by magic as humans," Kuro said. "It is a weakness of our species."

"But what if it comes back? What if it is able to track us after all?"

Knox answered, "Not a concern, for a couple of reasons. First, humans are not the cats' natural prey. They have been known to attack deer, but they're extremely lucky if they can catch one, and they're in for one heck of a fight if they do. We surprised that one. We were on top of it before it saw us. Then it became a matter of pride. It couldn't flee without losing face." I thought he was joking about the pride bit, but he looked dead serious. "We also might have wandered too close to its den, and if there were young ones, that would make it act more defensively than usual. Granted, it might get the idea to hunt us down, you know, to settle the score, but we have defenses."

I scanned the dam, looking for something I might not have noticed before. I didn't see anything that looked like it would keep one of those cats away. And hadn't I just charged one straight across the top of the dam? "Defenses? Like what, some kind of hidden traps?"

"No, more subtle," he said. "Charr has designed an ingenious system of defense. There are motion sensors scattered in a broad perimeter around each end of the dam. Anything larger than a man will trigger the sensors, which then activate a second set of devices closer to the dam. These vibrate at a frequency that is incredibly irritating to the cats, and have so far been completely effective in keeping them at bay. All of the devices are solar-powered. The cats are pretty rare, anyway. On the few occasions that we've encountered one in the field, they've been easy enough to avoid, and didn't give chase."

"So what went wrong this time?" I asked. "Why didn't the defenses kick in?"

199

"I'm sure they did," Knox countered, "but your blade in the base of its skull must have been more bothersome than the sound."

Made sense. "Even that ceased to be irritating *enough* after a point," I mused. "But you said anything larger than a man triggers the system. What if the aggressor *is* man?"

"Well, usually they come in really loud, obvious contraptions, like helicopters," Knox teased. "But in truth, we really aren't all that well prepared for a human assault of any size. And it hasn't really been necessary; you're the first visitors we've had for as long as we've been here."

"Working on it." Charr's voice, from behind me. She and Maya had just ridden up and were dismounting. Maya was smiling broadly. I wasn't sure if it was because she was happy to see me or because of whatever Charr had shared with her during their day together. "I started thinking about additional defenses as soon as I heard that we might have some more company soon."

My pulse quickened as for a moment I thought she meant that Magus' troops were on the move. But then I realized she was referring to the possibility of Reya's camp joining us. I addressed Jager. "So what *is* the plan with regard to Reya's people?"

"I've discussed the matter at length with Kuro. The dam can't house all of Reya's people comfortably. But they're welcome to occupy the city below the dam, so long as they don't mind clearing the bodies. The dam will serve as a command center, and in an emergency, for a shorter period, they could retreat to the dam for shelter."

"Great," I said. "So how are we supposed to let them know we've found a place? We don't have the fuel for a return trip, and it may take time to find more. According to what Reya said, it's at least a

200

couple of days by deer. And it will take much longer for all of her people to move up here en masse; I hate to imagine how difficult the mountain crossing will be."

"Relax," Kaire said. "Reya already knows."

"What? How...?""

"The deer," she said. "They communicate with each other telepathically, remember?"

"Yes," I said, "But it was my understanding that they could only pass thoughts to other deer within close proximity."

"True," Jager replied, "But their range may be farther than you think. And it's not a matter of one deer here transmitting the message all the way to a deer at Reya's end. They pass it one to the next, and the puurr-deer are so abundant that if there isn't another close by, there will be soon enough, as they are constantly on the move, foraging and whatnot. It's not instantaneous, but it's pretty fast. We've already heard back from them."

"Wow." I was genuinely surprised. "So what did she say? Are they already on their way?"

"Not just yet," Jager continued. "She said she has a bit of business to take care of before they can come. But it will be soon, and she said she desires an audience with you immediately upon her arrival."

"Me? Why?"

"Apparently there has been a development that requires your attention." I knew Jager must have been referring to the matter of the traitor, but couldn't imagine what Reya wanted me to do about it. Did Jager know the details himself, speaking in non-specific

201

terms only to obscure his meaning to others now present? In my mind I had cleared Jager of suspicion of treachery, but could I have been too hasty? Yet, if he were the one, why would Reya risk sending the message through him? He might choose to change the nature of the message, or not relay it at all. Unless she didn't want him to know she suspected him. Ah, the more I thought about it, the more convoluted it became. I guess I'd just have to wait on Reya's communication. But I had let my guard down, I now realized. I resolved to be more vigilant going forward.

I looked at Maya, who had lost the smile. Naturally, she would have mixed feelings about her newly-discovered mother coming to town. And I now remembered, she had never had the chance to chat with Reya about it since the fateful moment she had found out through my blunder. I wondered how this might affect the new degree of intimacy we now shared.

Suddenly it occurred to me that not everyone was here. I asked Maya, "Where's Doog?"

"Oh, he's tinkering around on the chopper, naturally," she said. "Hey, we still have a little time before it gets dark. Wanna catch a movie?"

I tweaked one eyebrow, knew she must be kidding. "Sure, what's playing?"

"Does it matter?" she asked. "You can tell me about your day on the way there." Oh yeah. She and Charr would have no idea about the crazy events that had so recently transpired.

"How about we grab a bite first," I suggested. "I worked up quite an appetite today." We did so, and then I climbed onto a deer behind Maya, gripping her slender waist tightly. She leaned back into me just a little. The smell of her hair was like a soothing balm after the nightmare I had just experienced. This was easily the best ride of the day. She took us along the road from the dam, circling down through the woods toward the town below. After passing through a short span of forest, the edge of the road to our left fell off into a deep ravine spotted with diminutive fir trees. The road arced to the right, away from the edge of the ravine, and leveled out as we came upon a section of crumbling buildings. This was not the city proper, but a small satellite community still well above the town in elevation. It consisted of a handful of houses, the remains of a general store, and a little farther down, sitting all by itself some distance back from the road, a movie theater. A few cars and a rusted-out minivan held vigil in the overgrown parking lot. "You weren't kidding," I said.

"Of course not," she said. "You never take me out any more, so I had to take the initiative." I poked her in the ribs, just enough to make her jump. I dismounted, then made a dramatic display of my willingness to catch her as she descended. I expected her to slide down the deer's far side in a show of independence, but instead she swung her legs around and sprang off into my arms. I caught her readily and planted a kiss on her lips before setting her down. We approached the theater, or what remained of one. It had been a small deal, a single screen and a lobby. It had probably been the type of joint that would show one of the recently-popular movies a few weeks after its premiere in a bigger theater in the city. Most of the roof had caved in, but the stained and tattered screen still stood almost erect. The frames of the seats were there, their once-cushy upholstery weathered and shriveled. We located two seats side-by-side that didn't have too much debris lying around them, and sat. I glanced to our left, where the owners of one of the cars out front remained, their eyeless sockets staring at an eternally-looping reel of the same low-rate flick. No other skeletons were visible, probably now crushed to dust under chunks of fallen ceiling. Maya seemed unfazed by the grisly company.

I began to recount all that had come to pass since Knox had come knocking on our door so early in the morning, from my training session where I discovered that I possessed innate skills, to my near death experiences and subsequent victory over the great cat by means of some quick and fortuitous thinking. She leaned close and rested her head on my shoulder as I told the tale, listening with rapt attention but gazing out at the shredded screen as if watching the events unfold there. When I finished at last, she sighed deeply before sitting upright and adopting a scolding demeanor, complete with wagging index finger. "From now on you pack a lunch!" she commanded. "You would never have encountered that creature if you boys hadn't been out gallivanting about, looking for food."

"I hardly think what we were doing would qualify as 'gallivanting'," I retorted. "I'm not even sure how one *would* 'gallivant'." I saw her opening her mouth to say something, the index finger rising from the armrest, and I hastily changed my approach. "Anyway, I think Knox's idea was to provide me with a working lunch; that I would at least be working on riding and survival skills during the break. As it turned out, I got a whole lot more experience than I bargained for. But your point is well-taken. I will ask Knox if we can bring something along, just to be safe."

Maya relaxed noticeably, grabbed a handful of my shirt, pulled me close and kissed me, lingering for a long moment before whispering, "I just found you. Don't get lost." We decided to head back early so we could find a picturesque spot to take in the sunset before returning to base. We ended up below the dam, by the spillway where the water from the river above passed through the dam. We couldn't see the sun set over the horizon, but the effect of the late afternoon sunlight filtering through the mist was breathtaking as the vapor enveloped us in its cool embrace. We sat together on the point of a precipice that jutted out over the rift, our legs dangling in the void.

204

"So what did *you* do today?" I asked.

"Oh, so now suddenly you want to know about me?" she said. Then, ignoring my eye roll, added, "Only had the best day *ever*, that's all!"

"You mean, besides the day we met, and the days we went riding together, and that day at the canyon..."

"Oh...yeah...besides all *those* days, obviously!" she ribbed. "Yeah, so Charr took me to her workshop, down in the city. That in itself is an honor, as apparently she doesn't even let the others go there, except for Corvus on very rare occasions."

"Corvus? Why?" I asked. I could think of a lot of people I'd invite to my secret workshop before *that* guy.

"She didn't say. Just that she made something for him, and needed him to be present to test it out. Anyway, the whole place is surrounded by a series of clever traps, so don't try to show up there unexpectedly to pay me a surprise visit."

"I wouldn't think of it without a personal invitation from Charr," I said.

Maya went on. "The really exciting stuff was inside the shop. You wouldn't believe the kind of things she has made. A couple of them are secret, I can't tell you about them."

"C'mon, be a pal!" I taunted, as I reached around and tickled her just enough to make her hop a little closer.

"Quit it out!" she shrieked, apparently blending two phrases in her tickle-spasm. "You want to be retrieving me from those rocks down there?" I definitely didn't, and ceased with the juvenile behavior immediately, gripping her waist instead. Maya picked up her former thought. "One of the secrets you'll know about soon enough. It's *really* cool. But the other one…will *blow…your…mind.*"

"You're not exactly decreasing my desire to tickle it out of you, you know." She pinched her eyes shut and stuck out her tongue. "By the way," I said, "when do I get to actually *see* the city?"

"Oh, I understand that will happen soon as well. Charr plans to use the city, with its varied terrain and numerous hiding places, as her training ground when working with you. I guess Kuro has left it up to each of them to decide how best to train you."

"We could ride down there now," I suggested. "Find a nice restaurant, pick up some groceries for the house…"

Maya didn't supply the usual witty retort. Her eyes grew wide, unblinking, seemingly staring through me at some distant vista visible only to her. Then she cast her eyes downward, a look of wistful sadness claiming her face.

"What happened?" I asked, lifting her chin softly with a finger.

After a pause she answered, "I'll never do those things. We will never have that kind of carefree life. This is the only world I have ever known, or will know."

Her words chilled me, but I knew she needed me to stay positive right now. "You don't know that. If we manage to take this world back from Magus, we could begin to build a new one. If we can give the people hope…"

Maya looked up at me, her face brightening. "That's why you came, isn't it? To give hope back to our world?"

"Maybe," I said with a calming smile and an assurance that I didn't really feel. But somewhere in the back of my mind, a little voice said, *"Wait and see."*

208

Over the next few days I got to know a different Knox. Gone was the drill sergeant condescension I had seen the first day. He knew what I was capable of, and what I wasn't. And he played a more defensive game than before, not exposing himself as often by relying too heavily on his strength advantage. He also knew that each new weapon or fighting style would present me with a real, if brief, learning curve. His goal now was clearly not to demoralize me before I had the chance to acquaint myself with each new scenario, but to ensure that I learned what I needed in order to be an effective soldier. After all, on the battlefield we would need to watch each other's back; thus to train me poorly would have amounted to dulling his own sword, poking holes in his own armor. He actually offered words of encouragement when I evidenced facility with a given technique. It made training, if not enjoyable, then at least not altogether unpleasant. Truth be told, I started to like Knox, to appreciate his stoic determination. It became clear that the Knox of day one had been a façade of intimidation, and not the real Knox at all. And the more of himself that he allowed to show, the more I realized how difficult it must have been for him to play the part of that other man.

He trained me with daggers, scimitars, sabers, and broadswords, in addition to standard rapiers and swords of various lengths and weights, single- and dual-edged. He showed me how to fight differently with and without a shield. Lastly he taught me to wield two weapons simultaneously. To my surprise I discovered that this required a completely different set of skills. Confronted with his more cautious and reasoned approach, victory was not so easily claimed. One moment I would gain the advantage, only to be met with a cunning counter-attack, later to turn the tide once more. It was an exhilarating back and forth exchange, and with each passing day I grew more confident in my abilities. During a lunch break Knox told me that Magus' rank and file soldiers were good swordsmen, but not great. He was certain that I would be more than able to hold my own against them. He was careful to distinguish them from the assassins, for whose skills even he reserved a healthy degree of respect. He said that I could beat them, but that I should expect the fight of my life.

Each morning I would train with Knox, and each evening Maya and I would ride out in a new direction, discovering new wonders and ever more sublime panoramas. One day Knox cut me loose a little early, and I rode to meet Maya and Charr as they returned from the city via the winding road that skirted the ravine. I spotted them at a distance shortly after I passed the dilapidated cinema, and waited for them to reach the spot. After exchanging greetings, Charr thoughtfully rode ahead; out of earshot but still close enough to rush to our aid in the event of an ambush. I had Knox's training to thank for the change in my way of thinking that had me already starting to consider the potential military implications of all movements and decisions. "It isn't paranoia," he had told me, "it's survival."

Maya's deer at one point got a half pace ahead of mine, and I noticed that she had an unusual formed object strapped to her back. It wasn't a backpack, as it appeared to be a solid piece of material that hugged the curves of her back. Perhaps it was a piece of armor Charr had given her. I was studying it, noting the presence of several symmetrical grooves on its surface, and trying to guess their purpose. I was about to ask her, when I became aware of a sort of electrical buzzing sound, distant at first, but growing steadily in volume. It seemed to fill the air, frustrating my efforts to determine its source. As the noise crescendoed to a piercing scream, I turned my head suddenly. As I did, something big whizzed past my cheek, the breeze from its passage buffeting the side of my head. A huge insect the size of a watermelon braked suddenly and alighted upon Maya's back. Instinctively I drew my sword and shouted, "Maya!" Maya looked over her shoulder, saw my raised sword, and jerked her deer to the side, out

210

of my reach, just as I completed a slice that would have neatly separated the creepy thing's body from its legs.

"Justin, no!" Maya yelled, as the bug fitted its legs into the grooves on Maya's back and made itself comfortable. "This is Charr's gift."

My face exhibited a mix of revulsion and shock, as the thing's head rotated more than 180□ to focus one of its bulbous, wide-set eyes on me, several redundant pairs of mandibles twitching constantly. "Gift! Really? Why in the...I mean...if you don't know what to give, there's always...oh, I don't know...*flowers*, maybe?" I must have said it a bit too loudly, because Charr turned and scowled in my direction.

Maya laughed. "It's just that you don't know what it is. This is a hum-bug. Charr designed the docking harness and embedded it with tiny machines that attract hum-bugs through sound. It's like the ones that repel the armor-cats, only a different frequency. Once they land, they stay because they can sip nectar from a tiny hole in the harness. I actually forgot it was on; this is the first time I've drawn one!"

"That is...just...*so* great," I said with absolutely no sincerity. "Why exactly would you *want* to attract one, again?"

"They're telepathic, silly! They're not as smart as the puurr-deer, and they won't do something for nothing. But for a little bit of nectar, they'll perform simple tasks like carrying items for you."

I managed to suppress my horror enough to realize that such a thing might have its uses. But I wasn't convinced that it was worth wearing a giant bug backpack all the time. "Why couldn't we use one of those to send messages over distances, like to Reya?" I asked.

211

"Because of the range," Maya said. "They will forget what they were sent to do after only a short distance flying. And they won't pass it off to another bug. They're just not that complex."

That brought me right back to "Why?", but I decided not to press the matter. As I inspected the creature more closely, I determined that it looked most like a large cicada. It wasn't really that disgusting, in fact its translucent wings were quite beautiful. It was unsettling more for its many and frequent small, quick movements. I tried to ignore it and its nectar-sucking sounds, and pulled my deer up alongside Maya's. "So that's the first of the awesome, mind-blowing things Charr has in store for you. I can't wait to see the next one."

"You know," Maya said, "You're slated to begin training with Charr in a couple of days. It might be a good idea to chat with her, see if there's any preparation she'd like you to do beforehand."

"Yeah, OK," I said, and started to ride ahead.

"Hey," Maya said before I had gone too far. "I missed you." I smiled at her and went to catch up to Charr.

"So...," I said as I pulled next to her, "we're going to be working together soon...anything I should know?"

Ignoring my question, Charr said, "Knox has you wearing that accursed armor, I see."

"Uh...yeah. Is that a problem?"

"It is if I'm training you," she said. "I'm crafting something...more suitable. It will be ready by the time we begin. After you complete my training, you're free to choose for yourself, but I am confident you'll make...the right decision."

"So Maya has told me a lot about what you do," I said.

"Not too much, I hope."

"I'm looking forward to seeing your workshop."

"Sorry, no," she replied curtly. "I'm only contracted to train you. That entails no obligation to involve you in my private pursuits."

So. "Of course. I shouldn't have assumed...," I began.

"I understand Knox has opted to collect you at your quarters each morning," she said. "I shall do no such thing. I expect you to arrive in the city a half-hour past sunrise."

"OK, no problem," I said. "Where exactly?"

"Wherever I decide to be," she said. "Find me."

I snickered. She wasn't smiling. "What, in a whole city? You're serious? How am I supposed to find you?"

"There will be signs," she said. "Trust your senses. A city of the dead is not the same as a living city. The signs of life are more obvious than you realize. If you wish to do anything in preparation, try to become more aware of sensory perceptions during your remaining time with Knox."

I did that, and over the next couple of days I nearly convinced myself that I could tell when Knox was about to strike, and even the nature of the attack, based entirely on the subtle sounds of his armor plates sliding against each other, or the sole of his foot scraping against the ground by a couple of millimeters as he shifted his weight. Heck, I even thought I could detect the minute increase in perspiration he exuded as he tensed for a lunge. Charr's game of hide-and-seek would be the true test, of course. In any case, I fought hard, striving to learn as much as possible from Knox before our time ended, and I enjoyed the challenge. At the end, I thanked him sincerely, and in no small show of esteem, he welcomed me as a comrade.

The day arrived, and I stood in the middle of what appeared to be one of the main thoroughfares into the heart of the city. Charr had been correct, it was eerily silent. But it was not abandoned. Whatever had happened here had occurred so fast that the people had been going about their normal, daily routines: navigating traffic, pumping gas, hailing cabs, making deposits. The streets were filled with cars, most of which had slammed into other vehicles or swerved off the road into a pole or a building. For the most part the drivers, and sometimes the passengers, were still present in skeletal form. I had just stepped past a shattered bus stop where three partially mummified commuters had fallen against each other and appeared to be frozen in grisly mid-song, heads tilted back and mouths gaping. A fourth slept, curled into fetal position on the bench next to them. To my right a set of bones was slumped over a rusted food stand, its weathered skull watching me from the curb a little farther along. It was every post-apocalyptic scenario I had ever seen or read about in popular media. But far more disturbing with the knowledge that it represented a very real event already transpired.

Suddenly I didn't want to be alone, as I felt for a moment as if I really were the last person alive. I wanted to call out to Charr, just to make sure, before the hunt began. But I knew that wasn't what she wanted. So I listened instead. A chill breeze rattled the leaves of a dry tree on the roadside. When it stopped, only silence. I walked along a little farther, paused and listened. Nothing. A rustling ahead. I tiptoed forward, trying not to betray my presence. An overgrown lot, the top of a concrete fountain peeking over the tall grass near its center, neat rows of large trees having spawned a small forest from their wandering roots - what had been a park. The grasses rustled again, bending at the passage of something.

214

An emaciated cat emerged onto the street with a panicked look, spotted me and rocketed off down the street. Seconds later a huge rodent with long, slender legs and bared yellowish teeth came out of the grass behind it, whipped its head this way and that, its tiny eyes failing to notice me, then took off in pursuit of the cat. Life made its presence known.

Just then a familiar noise from my recent memory: the buzz of a humbug, sounding distant. I looked up and saw a tiny black shape, barely visible as it streaked across the dim, early morning sky. Was this one of Charr's "signs"? I watched its arcing flight path, breaking into a run as it passed overhead in an effort to try to triangulate its landing spot. It looked as though it ended up about six blocks ahead, and three or four to the right.

Reaching the neighborhood where I believed it to have gone, I stood between two big, sprawling structures. On one side, the backside of a strip mall, complete with an endless row of dumpsters. On the other, a huge apartment complex that couldn't have been well-maintained even when there were humans around. I hoped that wasn't where I'd find Charr. There was no sign of the humbug, visual or auditory. I continued to listen for a time, fruitlessly, then another sense was activated; I smelled smoke. There was no wind, but - wait - there was the faintest breeze. I calculated its direction, and walked upwind. At one point I couldn't smell it anymore, so I back-tracked until I could, then proceeded. Eventually I located its source - a smoldering bonfire in the corner of a parking lot belonging to an office supply superstore, but its creator had moved on. Dozens of shoppers never had, their desiccated remains lying in and around the cars that filled the lot, and no doubt in the aisles of the store as well.

In the periphery of my vision, I became aware of a flash of light that highlighted the low-hanging clouds in a corner of the sky with a momentary orange glow. That's where I headed next. Coming around the corner of a tall, angular building, I strolled into a once-

215

grand courtyard framed by concrete pillars set at regular intervals. The pillars still stood, but beds of moss and hardy tufts of weeds had claimed large sections of the paved courtyard. A heavily corroded iron gate stood slightly ajar at the back of the courtyard, the word "zoo" just visible amidst the coils of ivy that threatened to envelop it. The gate creaked and swung open, and there stood Charr in full armor, wielding a wicked crossbow. "Nicely played," she said. "Now you're 'it'." Without further delay, she cocked the weapon and fired a bolt directly at my chest. The armor deflected the tip, but the impact knocked me to the ground. By the time I got to my feet, she was readying the weapon once more. "I'd run," she suggested.

Seemed like a good idea. But ranged weapons were her specialty. She'd be as likely to hit me at a greater distance as she had from only a few paces. On the other hand, if I rushed her, she'd have at most one shot before I reached her. Even if she scored another hit and managed to knock me down, she'd be unable to reload again before I'd be on her. That's what I chose to do. Weaving back and forth as I ran, I closed the distance between us. Charr struggled to line up a shot with my erratic movements, and when she finally let one fly it glanced harmlessly off my shoulder. She was no fool; she knew she couldn't reload in time. Tossing the crossbow aside, she pulled a smaller, pistol-like weapon from her hip, aimed for my legs, and fired. The gun launched a weighted cord not unlike what Corvus had thrown by hand at our first encounter. It twisted itself around my ankles, tripping me so that I fell flat on my face just inches from her feet. She lifted a steeply-heeled boot and brought it down between my shoulder blades, pinning me. Without removing the foot, she asked, "What have you learned?"

"Not to expect a fair fight on the first day of training," I growled.

"Not to believe there is such a thing as a 'fair fight'," she corrected me. "More importantly, not to take unmeasured risks when you

216

do not know the strengths or equipment of your opponent." She permitted me to rise at last, then continued, "I will admit, I completely expected you to run *away*. In that you surprised me. But as you saw, even with that advantage I was able to counter you effectively."

"Was there a correct option I could have chosen?" I asked.

"Yours was not necessarily incorrect," she said. "Had you opted to dive for me when you got close, I probably would not have been able to stop you. Combat is a constant series of decisions. Only with great experience can you begin to make most of the right decisions, most of the time. On the other hand, as Knox has already learned, you are not a typical soldier. You have somehow come to possess certain innate skills that were never learned. Let's hope that this kind of intuitive thinking lies just beneath the surface as well. I am sorry for the rude awakening, but I've found that failure is a far better tutor than success. Now, let's even the score. By way of apology, I'll let you take the first swing." She dropped the pistol and assumed a stance more suited to fisticuffs.

Fully expecting another trap, I hesitated. "Come on!" she said. "Hit me!" My reservations had nothing to do with Charr's gender; I knew she was a battle-hardened warrior and I had no illusions about her ability to reintroduce me to the asphalt. Shelving my misgivings, I aimed a punch at her midriff, where her armor appeared to be layered slightly thinner to allow for increased mobility. She contacted my moving wrist with a fast downward grab, causing my fist to end up next to her waist. Then, holding it there firmly, she brought her opposite leg up in an anatomically dubious motion, contacting the side of my head. In spite of the enchanted helmet, I was dazed by the impact and dropped to my knees. She released her hold and stepped back to let me recover. "Now," she said, "let's get you into something more comfortable." She gave the rusty gate a good kick, and it swung open with a terrible creak to reveal...the strangest and most magnificent suit of armor I had ever seen.

It was black and not glossy, but somehow its surface absorbed the tones of ivy and iron, or whatever else happened to be nearby. Its texture was like leather, and it was as light as aluminum alloy, yet hard as steel. The design mocked symmetry, displaying an organic flow, with a short, wing-like appendage spreading over one shoulder, a curving enlargement of the opposite thigh. The whole thing had the appearance of having been formed of magma that curled and splashed as it cooled. The helmet was...well, it was awesome, stylized and highly-mobile – something straight off the pages of Japanese manga. I turned to Charr in disbelief and at a loss for words. She showed me an elusive smile and simply said, "You're welcome."

22

It fit like a dream. I must have been thirty percent larger in the armor, yet I actually felt somehow lighter, faster. Charr borrowed my sword to demonstrate its strength and shock-absorbing properties with a few well-placed blows that left not a mark on the surface of the suit. It was a further testament to her mastery of her craft that I could move freely in almost every plane of motion while wearing the armor. Charr assured me that it had other, "bonus" features as well, that she said would only become apparent with use. Small solar strips at the shoulders and the back of the helm led me to think that this might have something to do with hidden machinery. I hoped this wouldn't be the sort that invited large, segmented creatures to land on my back.

Charr taught me the use of bows, crossbows, throwing spears, and other, more specialized projectile weapons, like the ankle-binding pistol I had experienced earlier. One of the more interesting items was a rifle that launched a razor-sharp disc that would allegedly return to the gun's launching rail if it missed its mark. Not wanting to take part in the world's bloodiest game of Frisbee, I respectfully asked her not to demonstrate this one. She had a couple of rare functioning powder-based guns as well, but these she was loath to wield because of their propensity to jam. In between target practice sessions, she honed my skills in hand-to-hand combat. As with Knox, we soon discovered that I could hold my own with empty hands as well, drawing on a mysterious well of techniques and skills I had never performed before. Though I was strong with my fists and feet, I seemed to have had a more pronounced edge with the blades. Charr's style was a mixture of throws and holds that were reminiscent of my wrestling days, blended with airy kicks and strikes that had more of an eastern flair.

She didn't shoot *at* me anymore, a concession that was met with sincere appreciation. Instead, she showed me the differences in penetration of various projectiles through a variety of common materials. This was important not only so I would select the best weapon for the armor of my opponent, but also so I would know what was and was not safe to take cover behind when the enemy was doing the shooting. She also didn't make me perform a city-wide search for her after the first day, as that would have wasted too much valuable instruction time. From time to time she would pursue me, or I her, through the streets and alleys of the city, instructing me to use terrain and obstacles to my advantage. Whenever the predator would manage to catch up to its prey, a brawl would ensue. It was grueling, but refreshingly different from Knox's straightforward training.

As before, Maya and I would go riding in the evenings, or sometimes we would just walk to a quiet spot near the dam and talk, and enjoy each other. She informed me that Charr was allowing her to remain at her workshop during the day while we were training, but that her work there was still incredibly confidential for the time being. She would of course have to kill me if she told me, or so it was explained to me. Maya was incredibly impressed with the armor Charr had given me. Of course, she had already seen it while it was being fashioned, but refused to enlighten me on its hidden capabilities, if in fact she knew what they were. She did tell me that I looked really good in it. "But," she cautioned, "Just wait till you see the set she's making for me!"

"So that's the top secret project?" I asked.

"You wish!" she said. Even though Maya was working somewhere right there in the same city where we trained, I was never allowed to learn the location of the workshop. Instead, Maya would leave some time before I would finish lessons for the day and would be waiting at the dam when I got there.

The days passed, and I began to dread the next phase of my training, where I would be working with Corvus. I didn't imagine it would be a pleasant experience, as even his more amiable peers had put me through a bout of hazing on their respective first days. Corvus, I could safely say, had hated me since the moment he laid eyes on me. This struck me as a bit of a mystery, since he ostensibly belonged to a sect which hailed me as nothing less than a promised redeemer. Nevertheless, my time with both Knox and Charr had strengthened those relationships, and through my time with Corvus I hoped for, if not fondness, at least a stay of hostility.

On the last day of my training with Charr, she took me back to the ivy gate where I had first found – and fought – her. She brought out the armor I had been wearing that day. "It's yours if you want it back," she said. "But you'll have to relinquish that set."

"Are you kidding?" I said. "Not a chance. This is like the coolest thing I've ever owned."

"Are you sure?" she teased. "This one's imbued with magic, after all." She flicked it with her finger, and it made a tinny rattling sound that served to point up the facetious nature of her comment.

"I'm sure. And thank you again...for everything."

"Good. That one isn't enchanted with magic, but it *is* blessed by Chaer-Ul. I think you'll find that's an ace in the hole when all else is equal. Should you need any modifications or repair, you...well, you *don't* know where to find me, but just grab me when you see me." I assured her I would, and turned to leave. She halted me with another word, soft and imploring. "Justin...I know Corvus isn't kind…but he has a human side too. You don't know what he has endured. It would have destroyed most men. Give him time."

I grunted. I knew *I* wouldn't start anything, but so far, Corvus had been the aggressor. He may not have believed that I was the one called Martyr, but as far as I was concerned, *he* still had to prove himself to *me*.

Charr added in parting, "I'll be honored to fight by your side, when the time comes."

"Pray it is not too soon," was all I said.

When I found Maya at the dam, she was anxious to check on Doog, whom she'd seen but little of since we each started interning with the locals. She convinced me to accompany her to the helicopter to see what he was up to. When we got there, Doog was straddling the tail of the chopper, facing backward, trying to reach something near the tail rotor while hanging on for dear life with his other arm. I saw him turn his head and look over his shoulder before shaking his head to indicate a "no-go". A figure stepped out from behind the vehicle, caught the tool as Doog let it drop, and handed him another one. It was Corvus. Ugh. I was really not prepared to deal with him just yet. I knew one thing: if he made another go for Maya he was going to taste some of my new skills in a bad way.

Doog saw us first and waved with his support hand, falling to the grass with a thud. Corvus hurried over to help, then spotted us himself. As if embarrassed to have been caught doing something decent, he quickly heaved Doog to his feet then took a big step back. Maya skipped over to Doog, gave him a big hug and began chatting him up. I decided to make the best of it and approached Corvus, who was standing awkwardly by himself, clearly unsure how to act in this kind of situation. "Hey, Corvus," I said. Seeming a bit surprised that I spoke to him, he lifted his head, turning it just enough to watch me with his good eye. He said nothing, but stared at me with an expectant look, devoid of emotion, as one looks in the direction where he has just heard a sound for some clue to its cause. "What's the plan for tomorrow?" I finished.

"Training ground," he said at last. Then he brushed past me, striding swiftly in the direction of the dam.

"Yeah, OK," I said to his back. "How about time? Anything I should bring?"

"Show up if and when you want to train. I'll be there," he said without turning. "Bring your weapon of choice. It won't make a difference."

I let him go without further questioning, as I didn't expect him to give me any useful information anyway. I joined Maya as she was filling Doog in on all that we had been up to over the past couple of days. Except for the private bits, of course. I wanted to ask Doog if he had learned anything more about Corvus, or how he had even come to be helping him, but Doog was not the kind to talk behind someone's back. Or at all. Maya and I helped him finish up his work on the tail, and he fired her up just long enough to see that everything was turning in the right direction, then we called it a day and went to see if there was anything on the grill.

Kuro, Knox and Kaire were outside when we arrived, and Kuro as usual was quick to ensure that everyone had a juicy portion in hand before attending to other pressing matters. As I ate with Maya, Doog took over for Knox at the grill to give him a chance to eat. Kuro had a brief word with Kaire, then walked to where we were standing and requested a few moments of my time before I retired for the night. Maya and I finished, and I charged her to stick with Kaire for the time being, as I still didn't trust Corvus,

223

and not to wait up for me. She looked concerned for a second, but that quickly dissolved, as she knew I'd be safe with Kuro.

Kuro led me a short distance along the shore of the lake, away from the dam. The sun had set, but in its passing the sky still gave enough light for us to see each other clearly, if not for much longer. He reached behind his back and pulled out the weapon I had chosen during our first introduction to the armory. It was a bladed staff, the same type of weapon Tal-Makai had famously used and mastered. He handed it to me. "I need to see how you handle this," he said.

Suddenly curious, I asked, "What happened to the one Tal-Makai used in his final battle?"

"I think you know how that day ended," he said. "We didn't exactly have the opportunity to scour the battlefield for spoils of war. I have to assume Magus collected it. Probably keeps it over his throne as a trophy, or had it melted down to make a helmet for his inflated head. No way of knowing."

"You said 'we'," I pointed out. "You were there that day?"

"No, I simply meant 'we' as in the resistance. But everyone knows the tale of Tal-Makai's final battle. It has been told so many times that it can never be forgotten, down to the smallest details. And as he was my student, I was always eager to hear of his exploits, proud of the man he became. The day he fell was a sad day for all of the resistance, but a particularly devastating blow for me. He was like a son."

"I understand," I said. "I'm sorry. It was not my intention to reopen old wounds."

"Ah, I'm mostly scar tissue these days," he said. "Don't feel too much any more." His hastily averted eyes said otherwise.

"Anyway, show me what you've got." He carried no weapon but the wooden staff on which he leaned. This he drew into a defensive position as he broadened his stance. I held aloft the weapon he had given me, swung it in a couple of practice arcs, shrugged, and went on the offensive. Kuro was good with the staff; very good. He absorbed my attacks, one after another. It was not effortless for him, but it became clear that I could show him nothing that he had not seen before. The skills I now used were ones he had taught to one pupil after another for years, and like any good teacher, he raised no question to which he did not have a ready answer.

When he tired of playing defense, he took control of the fight, pushing me back. As he did he spoke to me. "You do well with that weapon. So much was expected." He issued another series of thrusts, one catching me in the ribs in what would have been a painful blow without the armor. I redoubled my defense, striving in vain to turn the tide back in my favor. "But I thought you'd be better," he continued. That one did manage to bruise my ego. "Something's not right."

Suddenly Charr stalked out of the shadows. She must have just returned from the city and heard the commotion. "Of course something's not right," she said. "That weapon was not designed for him. The balance is off." Kuro stopped, waiting for Charr to finish. "Justin, see that enlargement of your armor on your right thigh? Strike downward on the top of it with the butt of your hand. As I currently held the staff in that hand, I set it down and located the place she described, then jammed my hand down on it. A section of the armor snapped open on unseen hinges, and a shiny, metallic cylinder emerged. "Grab that," she said. As I did, something clicked and it released from the armor. As I pulled it free, I could see that the armor had concealed a surprisingly long, curving blade along one edge of the object. Immediately the cylinder expanded at both ends, forming a bladed staff similar to the one I had been using, but of exquisite workmanship. Like my

225

armor, it had almost no weight, and did indeed feel perfectly balanced in my hand. I grinned and prepared to continue the fight. "Wait," she said. "Strike your left elbow against your side." I slapped my arm against my side, but nothing happened. "No, like this," she said, turning her arm outward and driving her elbow straight into her ribs. When I imitated the action, the part that resembled a wing rotated outward from my shoulder and spiraled down my arm. As it did, another piece emerged from the forearm, fanning out to meet the wing and locking into it to form a stylized shield.

"*Sweet!*" I exclaimed, awestruck. By now even Kuro was smiling. Without delay and with renewed confidence I took up the attack, and soon the others were drawn to our location by the sheer energy of the fight. Kuro was an excellent foe, but I moved with a fluency and attacked with an intensity that was not long to be withstood. Minutes later he stood defeated, the severed halves of his staff in his hands. The few who had gathered cheered, and Maya ran into my arms. A lone figure in the shadows trudged off toward the dying fire at the dam.

"I go through more of these…," Kuro complained, holding up the remains of his staff before casting them into the lake. "I just carved that one today!" He walked to me and put his arm on my shoulder. "I've seen what I needed to see. You're ready." And then more quietly, only to me, "Don't worry about Corvus. He's been instructed to play fair." I had seen how well Corvus followed instructions.

The next morning I showed up at the training arena at dawn. I wasn't about to give Corvus anything to fault me for. My eye detected a subtle movement in the tower; a third figure had joined the straw dummies there. Corvus dropped to the ground, a distance that would have splintered a normal man's shins, but he landed lightly, and was immediately on his feet again. As he approached me out of the early morning shadows, I could see that

226

he was shirtless, sword in hand. "Lose the ridiculous armor," he snapped. It seemed only fair. I removed the helmet and slipped out of the upper body gear, setting it to my rear. Realizing that I would have no access to my weapon once I removed the leg coverings, I popped the thigh hatch and collected my staff. I wondered if Corvus had hoped I would not realize this, intending to leave me unarmed. He would have no such luck today. Once I had my blade, I removed the leg armor as well, leaving me only in trousers as he was.

Without hesitation he struck, batting my weapon aside and scoring a very real slice between my ribs on my left side. It burned with a searing intensity – his blade was poisoned!

"You cheat!" I shouted. "Kuro said you were supposed to play fair!"

Corvus laughed roughly. "Yeah, that's not exactly how he said it to me. He only told me not to try to kill you. I have no intention of doing anything of the sort. I have every confidence in your miraculous healing abilities, *Martyr*." He laughed again, derisively.

So that was how he was going to play. Fine. At least I knew what to expect. The sudden loss of the armor's weight, albeit minimal, had altered my reaction time in unexpected ways. I had been as careless as if my sides had been protected by the armor. It wouldn't happen again.

Corvus lunged again, and I parried. He laughed with sadistic glee, undeterred, hesitating not a moment before launching another attack, and another. He thought to wear me down, I saw. But I had not been doing nothing since our last encounter. I had been training hard, honing my skills. And I imagined he had not been training with anything like the same intensity, relying more on experience and over-confidence in his existing skills. My side still burned, but the pain was less than before. I didn't have to remove

227

my eyes from him to know that the healing process was already well underway.

He danced before me, trying to intimidate me with the unpredictability of his movements. But my senses were sharp, thanks in no small part to Charr. I knew instinctively which movements were feints, which were preludes to actual attacks. It was so obvious to me that I could almost allow myself to relax between true efforts, responding only to those actions that required a response. It was not that he wasn't good; he was – extremely. But simply put, I was better. I drew no vanity from the knowledge of this fact, as I knew only too well that I possessed it only as a function of incredible training coupled with an *unearned* innate skill set. Nevertheless, Corvus himself was slow to acknowledge this reality. And the moment when he began to do so could be documented by anyone watching his face. The contemptuous aggression gave way to something very much like fear, and as it did, his fighting style wavered, his strikes becoming clumsier, less intentional.

During one of these I saw an opportunity, and I switched to the offensive. Something in the back of my mind tried to remind me mid-swing that he did not possess the same healing abilities that I did, but it came too late. I wanted to make him feel what I had, to understand that the ability to recover from an injury in no way lessened the pain of the blow, and my weapon was more than willing to oblige. In fact, my attack was more severe than I had intended it to be, so that as my blade liberated a thick ribbon of flesh from his side, I was sickened by the realization of what I had done. This feeling lasted only for a moment.

The exposed tissue underneath undulated in an unnatural, rhythmic manner. I stared at its strangeness, momentarily entranced, before I realized what I was looking at. Tiny gears and pistons, their nature betrayed by the glint of shiny steel, moved within Corvus' flesh. "Metal...machinery...," I stammered,

228

dumbstruck. Then as understanding took hold, "This is what Charr did for you..." I stepped back, attempting to engage him in a human conversation. "Why?"

My question enraged him. Foregoing an answer, he growled and drove at me again. I brought my staff up to thwart him, and his blade met mine and continued to press. His occasional jerky spasms told me that he was feeling the injury. I held my ground. His face was inches from mine. He bared his teeth, and as I tried to avoid his vacant, icy glare he said, almost calmly, "You do know what a martyr is, don't you? You know what must happen in order for us to win?" A grin of pure hatred contorted his pain-wracked face.

"*Justin!* Corvus?" Jager's initial assessment had not made it altogether clear who was at fault in this conflict, but the blood evidence told him that things were not as they should be. At the sound of Jager's voice, Corvus broke off his attack. Suddenly self-conscious, Corvus clutched his side protectively and scampered off to retrieve his armor. Jager's news was for my ears, anyway. "Reya and her people have arrived. You won't...I mean...it's imperative that you speak with her at once!"

"Where's Maya?"' I demanded, suddenly concerned.

"Maya's fine," he said. "But...when she...oh, just *come!*"

I followed him back to the dam, riding as fast as the deer could manage. I couldn't imagine what could be so shocking about Reya's arrival, unless...unless Maya had already confronted her and it had not gone well. If that were the case, I wasn't sure that was a fight I wanted to, or should, mediate. I pushed my deer yet harder, and after what seemed an eternity, we reached the dam. As our deer sprinted across its top, I was shocked to see so many people standing on the far shore, where previously there had never been more than a few at any given time. It felt somehow like an invasion of our private sanctuary, even though I knew these people were friends. Reya was immediately recognizable as we rode up, though it seemed strange that she sat at the back of another rider that I soon perceived to be Denkel. His deer stood slightly to the fore of the others, and he looked at me with what appeared to be expectation. Of what, I wasn't sure. My eyes scanned to his right and I saw a number of other familiar faces, coming to rest at last upon one that I had somehow not managed to notice at first, but whose poise and confidence were unmistakable. But if Reya… My blood ran cold. My gaze whipped back to the figure seated behind Denkel, who could most certainly not *also* be Reya…a name formed on my lips. "Mana…" That's when I became aware of Maya, standing over near the dam, arms crossed, features drawn tight, one foot tapping. This was not good.

23

"Good to see you again. Nice armor," Reya said as she descended from her deer. "I understand you've made dramatic progress in your training since we parted."

"I've had some excellent teachers," I said.

She continued, "I also see that you are, in fact, acquainted with young Mana here. So...you knew my double in your own world. That almost seems like something you ought to have mentioned during one of our early conversations."

"Honestly, it didn't seem all that important. Everyone seemed a lot more interested in pointing out who *I* resembled."

"Point taken," said Reya. "Still..."

"Hah!" The exclamation came from Maya, stomping brazenly toward Reya, face burning. "You're one to lecture someone on things that *ought* to have been mentioned!"

Wow. She was going to do this right now, in front of everybody. Reya was caught unawares. She stood frozen, slack-jawed...then her head snapped in my direction.

"Don't you look at him...*Mother!*" she said, placing added emphasis on the last word. Her eyes were brimming. Reya approached her cautiously, and Maya, sobbing, took a step back. Reya closed the distance again, proffering a pleading embrace, and after a moment's hesitation, Maya permitted it.

I was close enough to hear Reya whisper, "I am so, so sorry. I need you to know there were reasons for what I did. Please give me the time to explain myself...later." Maya pulled away abruptly at the mention of a delay in her expected resolution, turned and marched back to her former spot, leaving Reya standing. Reya blinked several times in rapid succession, turned to me once more.

Denkel had helped Mana dismount, and she came up to stand beside Reya. The resemblance was undisputable, but surreal. Mana was younger, shorter, and more petite than Reya, but it was clearly the same person, so to speak. The correspondence was not that of a child to its mother, but of a different version of the same thing, as of a twin raised in drastically different circumstances and exposed to contrasting experiences. The same person, but from worlds apart. "Justin!" Mana said, and ran to embrace me, planting a kiss on my cheek. For the moment, I was glad my field of vision did not allow me to see Maya's face. I tried to appear as indifferent about the show of affection as possible, in case my body language were being monitored. "Oh, you don't know how good it feels to see a familiar face. Besides my own, of course!" Why was she still hanging on me like that?

Mercifully, Reya interrupted the embrace, pulled me aside. "This is the Mana you know?" she asked candidly.

"Yes," I said. "But what is she doing here? Where did you find her?"

"What are *you* doing here?" she replied. At first I thought she meant here, at the dam – an odd question coming from the one who had sent me in search of this place. Then I realized the question was rhetorical. "Chaer-Ul had a purpose for you. Obviously he has a plan for her as well. And forgive me for asking this, but...was she...your *lover*...in your own world?"

"What? No!" I said. "Why would you ask that?"

"Well, besides her recent display of fondness, I do have my daughter's feelings to consider. She's had enough heartbreak for one day, I think. Justin, *why* did you tell her?"

"It was an accident, I assure you," I said. "But think of it this way: I did the hard part for you." Her eyes became slits, and I thought I saw her hand sliding toward her dagger, so I quickly redirected, "Look, I think she's going to be OK with it, just tell her what you told me." She appeared to be considering what I said, and finally relaxed. "How did she come to be with you?" I asked.

"She found us," Reya said. "She was lucky not to have encountered anyone from Magus' party, as she apparently arrived a good distance to the east, and had wandered for several days before she found our camp. Chaer-Ul must have led her to us."

"So she just woke up in this world, like I did?"

"Well, found herself on a riverbank, as she tells it," Reya explained. "But the idea was the same. She was going about a normal day in her world when things just suddenly changed, and then it was the same, but different. She made her way toward what she expected to be a familiar highway to hail a ride, and it wasn't a road at all, but a rushing torrent. After that she just walked. She never passed out like you did. Women tend to be able to handle things like that better." She smiled. I pretended I didn't hear the last part. "Justin, we need to try to figure out what role Chaer-Ul has mapped out for her. It may be crucial in the war against Magus. I know it may create an uncomfortable situation for you and Maya, but I need you to try to spend as much time with Mana as possible. It may be that the connection you share with her through friendship may enable you to learn something I couldn't."

"You think she knows something she isn't saying?" I asked.

233

"No, I think she may know something she doesn't realize she knows," she replied. "Will you do this for me?"

I allowed myself to look at Maya at last. She had never looked more dejected. I shook my head, wanting to help, but fearing what it might do to Maya. "I'll do what I can," I said at last.

"Good," she said. "Now, let's return to the group. The next bit of news bears on everyone here." Reya strode to a place in front of her people, but facing Kuro and the others. I noticed that the assembled throng continued to swell as more of the people from Reya's camp completed their journey and fell in behind her, some on foot, a few on deer, nobody heavily encumbered, and all looking quite exhausted. Reya spoke loudly for all to hear. "On behalf of my people, I wish to express our gratitude at your willingness to receive us here. We are many in number, but we will work hard to minimize our burden to your space and resources."

Kuro closed his eyes and waved his hand in a magnanimous gesture that I knew did not reflect his growing discomfort with having to accommodate such a large host. The altruistic display was premature, as Reya continued, "That being said, I wish to entreat your hospitality yet a bit further." Kuro's anxiety began to show as his jaw tensed, fearful of what he would be asked to stomach now. Reya didn't keep him in suspense. "For too long we of the resistance have existed as scattered bands, ever susceptible to the coordinated attacks of Magus' raiders. Communication between camps is inconsistent and slow. There is no unifying goal or plan of attack, and no way of implementing it if there were. If Magus were to launch a series of simultaneous attacks on each of our major settlements, we would fall one by one. Individually, our bases are weak and vulnerable, merely existing, surviving. But united as one, we can formulate a plan to strike Magus where it counts, to destroy the source of his power and end this war once and for all." Kuro, perhaps anticipating what was coming next, opened his mouth to voice an objection, but Reya beat him to it.

234

"To that end I've been in communication with every resistance military base of which we are aware, and I've taken the liberty of inviting them to join us here."

Kuro squeezed his eyes shut once more and shook his head sadly side to side, utterly defeated. He ran his hand slowly through his silver-black hair, forced a more congenial expression upon the unwilling creases of his face, and croaked out, "Make yourselves at home." He then turned briskly on his heel and trudged toward the dam entrance.

Reya seemed surprised at his reaction, looking to me for explanation. "That's just Kuro," I said. "I'll talk to him. He'll be all right."

The crowd buzzed with chatter, sounds of excitement mingled with fear. Jager spoke next. "What about the matter of treason?" he asked. "Where does that stand? I trust you wouldn't have brought these people here unless that situation had been resolved?"

Reya nodded. "The traitor has been exposed and dealt with. Further detail need only be discussed among the leadership. It shall suffice to say that he or she presents no further danger to us."

Now Kaire. "But the other camps…if even *one* of them has been compromised, then we are essentially leading Magus right to our door, and now we'll be conveniently assembled for him to obliterate in one timely blow. Then all of this will have been in vain." She was visibly distressed. "Reya, this is something you should have discussed with all of us."

"And ideally, I would have," Reya said. "But given the circumstances, it was not possible. What I *can* tell you is that rigorous internal and external interviews have been conducted in an effort to eliminate the possibility of sabotage. And I am confident that this was the right move to make."

"How can you be so sure?" Maya demanded abruptly.

Reya simply smiled and answered calmly, "I have faith."

Maya turned and started in the direction Kuro had gone. I turned to Reya and said, "You know this isn't really about inviting the other camps, right?"

"I suppose not," she said. "I do want to talk to her, but just now…there are so many things I need to take care of. Leadership never rests."

"I know," I said. "But I know Maya. And you should make time soon." I turned and ran after Maya. Halfway to the door, I felt a tug on my sleeve. I turned to see Mana's smiling face.

"Hey Justin…can I have a minute?"

"You absolutely can," I said, "just not this one. I'm really sorry." I made to pull away, but she held my arm fast.

"Please. It's been such an awful few days, and I'm so scared." Tears were beginning to spill over the edges of her long lashes. "I need to talk to a friendly face." It was hard to believe that Reya or her people had been anything but friendly to her, but the truth was, I really had no idea what she had been through lately. I knew she needed me, but right now, Maya needed me more.

I pulled my arm free and placed my hand on her shoulder in an effort to comfort her. "I'm really sorry, Mana. I'll talk to you soon, I promise. I…I have to go now." I turned and hurried toward the dam. As I did, I heard Charr taking the initiative to provide some semblance of order in Kuro's absence.

236

"Most of you will be staying in the city you passed on the way up here. But clearing space will be a big job, and you must all rest and refresh yourselves first. I suggest you pitch your tents here for now, along the lakeshore. Food is another priority. Hunting parties will be chosen from among…" Her voice was muted by the door as it closed behind me.

I found Maya in our room, as I had expected. She was lying on the bed, face buried in her pillow. I realized belatedly that I hadn't thought about what I wanted to say to her. I had only known that I needed to comfort her. I cleared my head, then my throat, and opened my mouth to speak. I was interrupted by a jarring noise behind me, a rattling sound that made me jump forward so that I nearly fell on top of Maya on the bed. Whipping my head around as I reached for my weapon, I saw the humbug clinging to the wall above the door, now cleaning its forelimbs. Recovering, I said, "You can't be bringing that thing home with you!"

Without lifting her head Maya replied, her voice muffled by the pillow, "Why not? You brought your ex-girlfriend home!"

"Maya, that's really not fair," I said. "You know I had nothing to do with that and no knowledge of it. Besides, she was never my girlfriend."

"Because you didn't want that," she probed, "or because you hadn't worked up the nerve to ask her yet?" Well, no one could say she wasn't intuitive.

"What I may or may not have wanted then is of no consequence. I'm not the same person I once was. My life changed forever when I met you." I knew it sounded like a well-scripted line, but it was also the truth. I saw her relax. I think it was the "forever" that got her.

237

She turned to face me, propping herself up on one elbow. I could see that she had been crying. "Still, I don't like that she's here," she said. "Why would Chaer-Ul toss in a complication like this, just when things are going so well for us? It's hard enough to deal with my mother being here. I liked it better when it was just us."

"If you're referring to Mana, that's not a complication," I said. But I thought about Reya's request to spend time with Mana. How could I do that without bolstering Maya's insecurities? Sure, her concerns may have been unfounded, but I didn't want to cause her pain no matter how misguided her fears. "If she doesn't already know what you mean to me, she will soon enough," I finished.

"It's not just that," Maya continued. "All those people, from all the camps – they'll soon be here. No matter what kind of precautions may have been taken, there's no guarantee that someone among all of those hundreds of people won't wish us harm. At least when it was just the few of us, I knew who I could trust. I've literally never been among so many people before, and it scares me. I wish we could just go away somewhere, just you and I, and wait for it all to blow over."

"That would be nice," I said, "except that some of these people seem to think it won't 'blow over' without my direct involvement. Those people just *might* notice my absence." The color left Maya's face when I said this. I wondered what it was about what I had said that was so upsetting to her. "Maya, what is it? What are you really worried about?"

She shook her head, but I could tell that she was still shaken. I joined her on the bed, tried to read her. I liberated an errant tear from her lashes with my finger, then wrapped my arm around her and pulled her close. "I'm not going anywhere," I said. "The bug, on the other hand, has to go." She permitted a weak smile and

238

nodded acceptance. We held each other for a long while without speaking.

Later, I made a show of reacquainting myself with some of the members of Reya's tribe. But I was really looking for Kuro. Recent events had left questions in my mind, and I had a growing suspicion that he held some of the answers. After failing to find him in the immediate area around the dam, I checked upstream, where Reya and her people were setting up camp. There was no sign of him there, either. Charr, who would normally have been down at her workshop, was overseeing the establishment of the temporary camping ground. I asked her if she had seen Kuro.

"Try the rapids below the dam," she said. "That's usually a good bet."

Sure enough, as soon as I began to clamber down the rocky incline before the dam, I could make out a lone, tiny figure standing atop a boulder at the edge of the fast-moving stream far below. He was making a strange series of repeated motions with his arms. My mind conjured images of a sagacious sensei practicing his art. As I made my descent and drew closer I recognized the implement in his hands – a fly rod. Coming up from his side so as not to startle him I asked, "Any luck?"

"A fair amount," he said, focused entirely on the sinuous motion of his line and the dancing bit of fluff at its end. "No fish, though." He smiled, clearly pleased with himself.

"Kuro, can we talk?" I asked.

"I was of a mind that that was what we were already doing," he said.

I was really not in the mood for his verbal games, and addressed him bluntly. "I mean, face to face. I need your full attention."

239

"Son," he said plainly, "you are unlikely to find me in a more attentive state. Say what is on your mind."

Realizing this was all I was going to get, and grateful that we were at least far removed from the listening ears of those above, I asked my question. "Do the prophecies predict the death of the one called Martyr?"

Registering no emotion, Kuro began slowly to reel in his line, then turned to face me and lowered himself to a seated position on the rock, inviting me to do the same on a nearby stone. "Has Corvus been getting your goat?" he asked.

"He did say something," I replied. "But I've been getting similar vibes from other sources, not to mention the direction of my own thoughts."

"You must understand, first of all, that it was not the intention of the prophets to satisfy the curious yearnings of the faithful," Kuro began. "Thus was there no unambiguous description of what Martyr must do, nor of what he will in fact do. There is no clear intimation of the time or manner of Martyr's end, or even if he has an end. However…," he added, speaking carefully, "…*one* of the prophecies of Martyr ends with a mysterious statement that has been the subject of much interest. It reads, 'Through a veil may one time pass, a sacrifice for all.' The precise wording of this prophecy is known, as it was long ago immortalized in song. It's meaning, on the other hand, has been hotly contested for nearly as long. Some see it as a reference to Martyr's arrival, as accomplished by passing through the 'veil' between worlds. But then what is the nature of the 'sacrifice'? That has led many to interpret the words as referring rather to a future event. But then is there mystery surrounding the term 'veil'. One popular line of thought reasons that it signifies that barrier that stands between life and death. Others reject this view as being inconsistent with

240

the very nature of Martyr, who, they argue, cannot ultimately die, but is in a more transcendent sense 'perpetually dying' for his people. Still others say that the prophecy speaks not of Martyr at all, but of another sort of sacrifice entirely."

"And what do *you* believe?" I asked him.

"What I believe," he said, "Is that you are too important to the resistance, to the hope and future of our world, to leave us any time soon. I favor a method of interpretation that leaves room for a manner of fulfillment not anticipated prior to the actual event."

"Well, that suits me fine," I said. "I too prefer a fulfillment that doesn't involve my untimely demise."

"Nevertheless, you must understand that prophecy doesn't always unfold in the way we might expect, or hope," Kuro said. "The question you must ask yourself is, are you prepared to do *whatever* it is that Chaer-Ul may ask you to do, even potentially forfeiting your own life if he should ask it?"

"That is the question I must ask myself," I repeated. "But for now I have another question for you." Kuro raised an eyebrow. "What is Corvus' story?" I asked. "What happened to him? Why does he harbor so much hatred toward me? And why does he have *metal guts*? And those scars?"

Kuro moaned; a long, low, growling noise. He wasn't comfortable with this subject. "I would tell you that you need to ask him that question," he said, "but I think we both know where that would get you." He tugged on his sparse beard, gazed distractedly downstream. "I don't feel it's my place to talk about Corvus' past," he said at last. "But there is one he has been close to. I imagine you already suspect the one."

"I'll talk to her," I said.

"Justin, Corvus is recovering from his wounds. I don't blame you for what you did to him. You won't have to train with him again. I'd like to work with you some more myself, but I think the priority has shifted. Those people will need help clearing spaces to live in the city. Perhaps you can help Charr oversee that mess."

"Of course," I said. "And Kuro…I know how you feel about the impending mass immigration, and believe me, I empathize. But I've not known Reya to make rash decisions. I would urge you to hear her out. Remember, Tal-Makai loved her. That must count for something." He grunted, continued staring downriver. "Thanks," I said. He nodded silently, and I began the climb back up to the dam.

Charr wasn't where I'd last seen her. I thought I'd check inside the dam before heading for the city. In any case, I didn't know where to find her workshop, and would probably need Maya's help if I wanted to find her there. I pushed open the door that led to the lobby, and almost ran into Mana, who was just coming out. She grabbed me by both arms and made me back-step until I was standing outside again, then pulled me along by one wrist to a place several paces to the side of the door against the concrete bulk of the dam. There she positioned me, saying, "We're going to talk now." Her manner was playful, but it made me uncomfortable, especially as there were a number of people milling about, and I really didn't want one of them to be Maya just now.

"Mana," I started, "A *lot* of things have happened since I left class with you a few…" I hesitated. Had it been weeks? Months? The concept of time was definitely viewed in a different light here. "Anyway, I don't know how much you know about this world, but we're in the middle of a war here, and I…"

I didn't get to finish the thought, because Mana chose that moment to stop my mouth with her own, simultaneously pressing her body against mine and pinning my back against the cold concrete. I was too shocked to react, that is, until I felt her hands trying to explore other avenues. I pushed her away firmly but gently, as I knew she was emotionally distraught and no doubt also very confused. I half-expected Maya to emerge just then, but thankfully nobody seemed to have witnessed the uninvited advance. Mana had never acted this way back home. There was a time when I would have welcomed such a display, but those times, and those thoughts, were far from my mind now. "Mana...," I began, searching for words that would make the situation less awkward for both of us.

The door opened then, and sure enough, Maya stepped out. As she turned her head in our direction, Mana gasped loudly and slapped me hard across the face. Stunned, I blinked to clear the stars that were flashing before my eyes and tried to focus. "He just tried to kiss me!" Mana exclaimed.

"What?! No! Maya!" I said helplessly. Maya stomped determinedly in my direction, assessed me through fiery slits of eyes, then spun without warning and delivered such a backhand to Mana's face that it sent her staggering, clutching her already-swelling cheek.

"Justin would never do that to me," she said matter-of-factly. I couldn't help but feel a little sorry for Mana, not that she didn't have it coming. Maya wasn't a big girl by any means, but by way of contrast Mana appeared downright waifish. Anyway, now was definitely not the time to offer her words of comfort.

Maya took my hand and led me away from Mana, and as soon as we were out of earshot I said, "Maya, I need you to know that Mana kissed me. I don't know why she did and I was totally unprepared..."

Maya interrupted me. "I'm not surprised. I mean, I'm obviously not thrilled about it, but I kind of figured it was something like that. What I need *you* to know is that I would never give my heart to someone I didn't trust – completely."

I smiled. That trust meant more to me than she could possibly know, more than the faith of a thousand devotees. I was determined never to give her reason to think it was misplaced. "Hey, I need to have a word with your friend Charr. Do you know where I can find her?"

"I'll message her," she said. And with a screaming whirr her segmented friend took off from her back, arcing over the treetops.

245

24

Charr arranged to meet us at an old stadium that dominated the landscape in that part of the city. I spotted her standing at the very top of the structure, beside what would have been the announcer's booth. Maya and I hurried up the steps between rows of seats, which were largely devoid of skeletal remains; it had not been a game day, apparently. Maya had not indicated the reason for our visit beforehand, but Charr had anticipated it. After greetings were exchanged, she got right down to business.

"I feel on the one hand," she said, "that you have no right to information that Corvus himself has not seen fit to reveal." She paused, looking out across the city toward the glistening river. "On the other hand, I believe that a failure to comprehend Corvus' motivations may well put you at risk. I also hope your knowledge of these things may enable you to sympathize with what I know is on the surface a very unsympathetic being, and perhaps will help you to overlook, or at least forgive, some of his offenses." This would have to be a pretty good secret to elicit my sympathies for one who had recently viciously attacked me and had previously made similar threats to Maya's safety.

Charr continued. "Corvus did not spring from noble lineage. His family was poor, and his father was a controlling man with a penchant for violent outbursts. His mother suffered frequent injury at his hand." Ah, there it was. Poor Corvus had an abusive Daddy so everyone's supposed to excuse his being a jerk for the rest of his life. I had never thought that way, had never had much sympathy for those who never got past childhood trauma and learned to cope in human society. I hadn't grown up in a particularly nurturing family either, but I felt like I turned out OK. Charr would have to do better than that.

She went on. "He took a particularly dark turn when he discovered that his wife was pregnant. He accused her of infidelity, though she had never given him any reason to suspect that. I think he just didn't want a child because he was completely self-absorbed, and didn't wish to share his world with someone new. As it was, he seemed to resent his wife for taking up space in it. He hadn't chosen to become a father, and for him it became an issue of control - no such thing was going to happen without his having ordained it. He beat the poor woman brutally while the child grew in her womb, hoping, no doubt, to terminate the pregnancy. But she was remarkably resilient, as was the baby.

Sadly, she lacked either the wit, or the will, to leave for the sake of herself and the child. This was to prove a tragic mistake on her part. The beast let the child come full term, then, just as she was about to deliver, he rose in the night and drove a dagger deep into her belly. He let her bleed out slowly, screaming in agonizing convulsions as she died. The baby received a vicious gash but miraculously survived, to be rescued by a relative who happened by a short time later. The murderer had already left the scene."

"The baby was Corvus," I said.

"That much should be obvious," Charr replied. "Of perhaps greater interest is the identity of the father."

Maya went white. As usual, she arrived at the obvious conclusion just a few seconds before I did. Then it hit me as well. "Magus!" I said.

"Hmm…yes," said Charr. "Corvus is Magus' son."

It was a shocking realization, but something didn't quite click. "But, then, why the animosity toward me?" I asked. "I am certainly no friend of Magus. He wants to eliminate me just as he

247

tried to do with his son. I would think Corvus would see that as a point of solidarity, rather than a reason to hate me."

"Yes, but that's where it becomes complicated," Charr said. "Powerful emotions are involved. Although he hasn't said as much to me, I imagine that in some twisted way, Corvus is jealous of the attention his father is spending on you. It doesn't matter if that attention is focused on ending your life; right now, in Corvus' eyes, Magus is more interested in you than in him."

"That's positively idiotic!" I said.

"No, it isn't," said Maya. "Reya has hurt me. She has chosen not to be a part of my life for, well, *all* of it. I am angry, *really* angry, yet I desire nothing more than for her to love and embrace me, to tell me there were good reasons for her not being there, *even if I know they are lies!* In my heart, I've already forgiven her, even if she's not sorry. It's crazy, I know it, but that's how I feel. She's my *mother*. Somehow that's all I can see when I look at her." She was crying. I put my arm around her and began to dry her tears with my sleeve.

"You have to realize," Charr said, "that when something *that* traumatic happens to you, a part of you stops growing, stops maturing right there. Corvus is in so many ways still a child. A child that wishes for a relationship with a father who is incapable of giving him that kind of relationship, incapable of love. And as long as the two of them live, he will never stop hoping for that. At the same time, he sincerely wants to kill his father for what he did to his mother, for what he did to him. It's really quite sad, when you think about it."

"It is that," I said. "But maybe if I talk to him, try to make him see…"

"No!" said Charr sharply. "You must never speak to him of these things. I have told you this for your sakes only." There was no questioning her. That much was clear from her tone.

"So...the scars, the disfigurement...the result of that in utero attack," I said. Charr simply nodded. "Then I take it you had something to do with the subcutaneous gears."

"Yes," she said. "Corvus is a right-handed fighter, so it didn't interfere with his swordplay directly, but he had almost no use of his left arm. That will affect balance, not to mention defense. And two-handed weapons were not an option. I constructed mechanisms that would work with what little strength he still had on that side, amplify it, so to speak. I had never attempted anything like that before, but the results far surpassed my expectations. He is probably stronger now with his left hand than with his right. That is, if you haven't screwed him up too bad." I stared at my boots. "I doubt that very much," she continued. "I developed a very high-strength alloy. I imagine you will break before it does. And rumor has it you're unbreakable." She smiled, erasing it just as quickly.

"The question is, when push comes to shove, can I trust him?" I asked.

"When he's convinced that you are who we all need you to be," she said, "he will be your most loyal ally. Frighteningly so."

"*If* he's convinced," I corrected her. She shrugged, looked out once more at the river, meandering along the edge of the city in the shadow of the high cliffs leading to the dam. The scent of wood smoke on a passing breeze told us that Reya's people had begun to relocate to the city. When I looked more carefully I could make out the plumes of smoke from numerous small campsites rising skyward from between the buildings. As I continued to stare at the wavering columns of smoke, another

249

shape crossed the sky in the corner of my field of vision. Before my mind could interpret the image, a familiar and ever-startling buzz filled the air. A second later, Maya's humbug perched on my arm. I fought an instinctive urge to bat it away. "I think it missed its mark," I said, turning to Maya to offer her the bug.

As I did she turned her back to me, smiling over her shoulder, letting me see that her pet remained comfortably napping on her back. "That's not mine," she said. "Honestly, can't you tell? The face is totally different."

She was serious. "Face?" I asked. I forced myself to look at the creature's twitching head. "What am I supposed to..." Then, unexpectedly, I became aware of something. "Oh. Reya wants to speak with us right away. But I suppose you got that too..."

"No," said Maya. "It only told you." Interesting.

"She said she'll signal us with...oh, there!" I said, pointing to one particularly tall plume of smoke that was of a more bluish hue than the rest. "That's where we need to go."

Reya was standing near a roaring fire when we arrived. Denkel, Kaire, and Jager stood nearby. Here and there others were bustling about, mostly collecting bones and carrying them to an old gymnasium across the street. Reya, seeing the direction of our attention, explained, "They'll be stored there temporarily. Later, when things settle down, we'll give them the proper burial that the virus denied them. Obviously we can't dig that many individual graves, but a respectful mass burial will be better than leaving them to continue bleaching in the sun." I tried to imagine the scale of such an undertaking. There had to be tens of thousands of them. To even excavate an area large enough, without heavy machinery...the thought was overwhelming. But Reya seemed determined. "Follow me," she said. "I've managed to delegate tasks so that I may have a few moments alone with you few." She dismissed Denkel with a wave of her hand and he hurried off to attend to other duties. Jager and Kaire remained with us. "It's time to discuss the matter of the traitor," said Reya. "As I told you previously, the betrayer has been identified and dealt with, and poses no continuing threat to our security." We crossed the street and turned down another good-sized avenue. "However, we could not afford the luxury of a trial. More of Magus hell-hounds were spotted nearby, and though they too were eventually hunted down and eliminated, we knew they were getting close."

"How did you figure out who it was?" Maya asked.

"My officers are very observant. While nobody saw anyone actively engaged in suspicious activity, some began to notice the conspicuous absence on one person in particular, at times when they'd normally have been around. When I learned of this, I began to watch for myself. When I was fairly certain we had the right man, I tasked him with a special mission, completely fabricated. I sent along several others, one of my best men in command – a man by the name of Euthus. He was instructed to lead the others away in search of kindling, but to return silently and follow the suspect at a distance, unseen. Euthus excels at this sort of surveillance, and it played out exactly as we'd hoped. The traitor rode until he thought he was alone, then pulled out a device...," Reya reached into a pocket and withdrew a small object with several buttons, now conspicuously broken, revealing wires and fine metallic parts. It was not a phone, but looked like it could have served a similar purpose. "*This*," Reya said. "Euthus reports that he pressed a series of buttons, some code perhaps, then held it to his ear, and that it glowed with the same sort of orange lights that we've only seen associated with Magus' abysmal devices. Before he had spoken a word, Euthus burst from hiding and seized him, confiscating the device."

Reya had stopped in front of a broad, stone building with a façade of Romanesque pillars that were still intact. There was an

251

inscription above the pillars, but our close angle didn't permit me to read it. Reya waved us inside. After passing a large desk shielded by a cracked slab of thick glass, we stood before a row of cells. Feeble sunlight filtered through a row of small, barred windows high in the wall, scantly illuminating the dust-heavy air. It was a jail. Greda sat on a stool at the end of the hall, and waved when she saw us. I returned the gesture, then something caught my eye. A figure so emaciated that my eyes hadn't even detected him on a first pass leaned in the corner of one of the cells, head bent against the cold stone wall, and as I saw him I experienced a flash of déjà vu. After all, it was in such a cell that I had first met the man.

"Jeyt!" Kaire said. "Why?" He didn't even look up. I turned to Reya. "When you said you hadn't had time for a trial, I assumed you meant you had terminated the traitor. You marched him all the way here!"

Reya nodded. "I'd hope you know me well enough to realize I wouldn't put someone to death without a fair hearing."

"What does he say for himself?" Maya asked.

"So far, absolutely nothing," Reya replied. "His words have neither condemned nor vindicated him."

"So, do you think he was in Magus' employ even when we were being held together?" I asked. "If so, our whole escape could have been an elaborate ploy to lead Magus to the main camp."

"It's a possibility that I've had to consider," Reya said. I stared at Jeyt, positioned myself where he'd be more likely to see me, but he didn't move or acknowledge my presence. He seemed comatose, withdrawn into himself.

With a loud bang the dark interior of the jail was abruptly flooded with brighter light from outside. Someone had thrown open the door through which we had recently entered. A voice shouted, *"They've come!"*

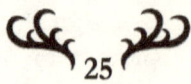

25

Running into the street, we were relieved to learn from a pair of overly excited children that the exclamation had referred to the arrival of the first of the other camps, and not, as we had feared in a panicked moment, to an ambush by Magus' troops. Once we reached the main thoroughfare once more, we could see the far end of the road obscured by billowing clouds of dust. They were emerging from the forest and pouring into the main street of the city, but it would still be some time before they reached our position.

"That is something I will need to deal with soon enough," said Reya. "But before I do, there is something else I wish to discuss with all of you. You two," indicating Jager and Kaire, "are already aware of this, but I think it's important to mention it while you are all together. When Tal was alive, he trained under Kuro, just as you have," she said, now looking at me. "As he trained, powerful bonds of friendship and camaraderie developed naturally between Tal and some of the people he had fought alongside. Out of these relationships, and those nurtured with other men from the camp, Chaer-Ul raised up a select band of warriors to lead the fight on behalf of all the others. The choice of who would constitute this elite squad came not from Tal, nor from a consideration of their respective skills, but came about naturally through the instrumentality of Chaer-Ul, and bore his stamp of authority. So clear was the selection that nobody questioned it nor sought to be included if they were not among those initially chosen. Both Jager and Kaire were among those who rode with Tal before. I know not whether Chaer-Ul would do a similar thing with you," she said. "Nor should we force it. But I would ask you to be watchful for signs of his leading in this regard."

"I can do that," I said.

"Incidentally, have you had a chance to interact further with Mana?" she asked.

I exchanged a knowing glance with Maya, and thought better of disclosing Mana's recent indiscretion in such mixed company. "Not yet," I said.

"Fine," Reya responded. "Then I must welcome the first of our guests. I would ask the rest of you to confer with Charr about how you can be most useful in the clearing and resettling efforts. We're about to need a whole lot more space." Reya turned and walked about three steps in the direction of the new arrivals, then stopped in place. I saw her drop her head, clench both her fists, then relax them. Finally she took a slow, deep breath and turned around. She addressed Maya. "May I please talk to you alone?"

As Reya led Maya away in search of a more private venue, I stopped one of the bone-gatherers and asked where we might find Charr. Soon I was busy helping to carry the remains of those long-deceased to their temporary resting place, and guiding new arrivals to not-yet-occupied dwelling places. Before long another camp arrived, and near day's end, two more whose paths here had intersected while passing through one of the gaps in the mountain range to the south. Interestingly, I received no complaints about having to clear dead bodies before beginning to settle in, despite the enormous distances I knew some of these people must have traveled to get here. Naturally some of them were short on good-natured small talk, but on the whole they were exceedingly gracious, and grateful, to their new hosts.

Maya reappeared over an hour later, grinning goofily and eyes puffy, but unwilling to say more than "It's good now." She quickly fell in alongside the other helpers, and together we all put in a good day's work. It was exhausting work, but of course we discussed the day's shocking revelations as we had opportunity, and occasionally teased each other to lighten what would

255

otherwise have been an entirely gruesome task. We met many new faces, and as the sun began to set over the dam, we had to agree that it had been a rewarding experience overall. When we left for home, nobody was without a place to lay his head.

Maya and I headed straight for bed, certainly hungry, but as we were a bit later than usual, too tired to fire up the now-cool grills to prepare something to eat. I sunk into a deep sleep quickly, the thought of getting up to do the same thing all over again tomorrow for a fresh new batch of guests only a distant reality in my mind. I dreamed.

I saw an endless plain, parched and cracked, where no living thing grew. As I watched, a great form passed across the sun, casting its shadow on the desiccated earth. I shielded my eyes and bore the sun's burning brightness to see a great bird, with wings of one substance with the sky itself. With a mighty stirring of dust it alighted upon the ground, and immediately began to pick at a piece of loose and crumbling sod. As it removed a piece of crust a moist shoot burst forth, unfurling emerald leaves. With a flick of its head the great bird snapped off the shoot at its root, then beating its celestial wings, rose into the sky once more. As soon as the bird reached a great height, the plant began to grow once more within its beak, so that a thorn pierced its eye. Just then a dove appeared from under the great raptor's wing, taking shape from its own flesh. Flying to a place near its head, the dove plucked the thorn from its eye and flew away with it. But the thorn had life in it yet, and now sent shoots out in every direction, encasing the smaller bird in a dense meshwork of twisting vines. These vines also produced thorns, which drove themselves into the dove's body and wings all about. The small bird fell from the sky and landed on the dry earth below, dead. Its diminutive body then melted into a crystalline pool, which the thirsty ground eagerly swallowed.

I woke with an unsettled feeling, eased none by the realization that Maya was not beside me. A sense of foreboding prompted me to don my armor before heading out. Passing through the lobby I picked up the scent of smoke, further intensifying my growing panic. My fears were quickly allayed, however, when I burst from the door into the cool morning air to find Maya stoking the coals of one of the grills. "Awww, you were supposed to sleep in!" she said. "I was going to bring you breakfast in bed."

"You mean *you* were hungry," I replied.

"That too. We'd better eat hearty though," she said. "Reya just informed me that another big group is slated to arrive this morning. They're gonna need all the help they can get."

The sight of Maya safe and sound, though welcome, did not completely erase the apprehension I was feeling. It must have shown on my face.

"Are you all right?" Maya asked.

"I'm not sure," I said. "Maybe I'm just being paranoid. I feel like something bad is going to happen. You stay close today, OK?"

"Now you're starting to scare me," she said. "Did you hear something?"

"No, nothing like that," I said. "Let's just try to stay together. Can we do that?

"Gee, let me think...," she teased, hooking two fingers over the top of my trouser and tugging me close for a kiss. Breaking it off abruptly she exclaimed, "Breakfast is burning!"

We stuffed ourselves, more than making up for the previous night's missed dinner. When we had finished and cleared the grill, Maya asked, "Ready to work?"

"Ugh, no," I groaned. "Now I need a nap!"

"Better to burn it off with a little menial labor," she said. "Come on." She got up to go, but I held her wrist.

"Hold on," I said. "I want to let Kuro know where we're going."

"Fine, but please hurry," she said. "I can already feel all that food turning into fat."

"Yeah, and I can *see* it," I said with what I hoped was a sufficient dose of sarcasm. She shook her fist at me in mock rage as I ducked back inside the dam in search of Kuro.

It took me a little longer to find him than I had expected, as he was not in his own quarters but in a small lounge around the corner sipping tea, or perhaps brandy. When I informed him of our intentions he raised his cup to me, wordlessly granting his approval. I wondered if I should mention my sense of unease, but decided that it would serve only to burden him unnecessarily, especially since I had no evidence that it was rooted in anything real. I hurried to meet up with Maya outside, but as I stepped out of the elevator and turned toward the lobby, a hand came to rest on my shoulder. Turning, I saw that it was Mana. I grasped her arm below the wrist and lowered it to her side. "Mana…," I said, "…this isn't going to happen."

"Actually, that's why I'm here," she said. "I wanted to apologize for the way I acted before."

"I appreciate it, but Maya's the one you ought to be apologizing to."

"See, you're right…," she squeaked through a sudden deluge of tears, "…I mean…I didn't know you two were together."

"Married, actually," I clarified.

"*Married?* You're…wow, that's just…well, anyway, I would never have…that wasn't even…me, really…and I wouldn't want to jeopardize the relationship we had before…I was just…*lost*…and you were a piece of home."

It was a little disjointed, but sounded sincere. How hard could I be on her? What she was saying resonated with me in a way that it couldn't with literally anyone else in this world. I had felt that way, exactly, except that there was nobody coming to my rescue, no familiar face – not one. "Mana, I understand how you're feeling, I do. And I'm sure it's little comfort now, but you will make other friends here…in time. I know it's scary and different, but there are many things in this world…"

" '*In time*'?!" The tears suddenly dried up. "I don't want to make friends here! I have no intention of growing to appreciate the many wonders this wasteland has to offer! Justin, that's what I wanted to talk to you about – I think I may have found a way that we can get back!"

"Back?"

"*Home*, Justin. Where we *belong*."

This wasn't something I wanted to hear just now. "Mana…if I'm ever going back…*where we came from* – and I'm not at all sure that I am – *this* is definitely not the time. There are things I have to do, things…I *need* to do, here."

259

"Oh my God," Mana said, her face a mixture of shock and amusement. "I had heard the rumors, but I never thought...Justin! You don't actually *believe* you are this messiah character these people are hoping for, this '*Martyr*', do you?"

"Maybe I'm starting to," I said.

"Justin! These people are crazy! They're nice, and hospitable, and, and...frickin' *nuts*! They have been looking for someone to volunteer to lead their armies in a war against impossible odds, and then to *die* for them, and...*guess what*?! Along comes Justin Mayer! Justin...I know how smart you are. You're smarter than this."

"Mana, I *have* changed. But I'm not stupid. Or crazy. And neither are these people. And I know what I want. Don't insult me. You've changed too, and I'm not so sure it's for the better. You're the new one here, and as much as I empathize with what you're going through, there's an awful lot at stake that you have absolutely *no* clue about."

"Oh, I think I can put the pieces together: you're all hot and bothered over a saucy new piece, and so you've adopted her religion and all it entails, even if that means you going on a suicide mission. Sound about right? Justin, when did you stop thinking for yourself?"

"Maybe when he started to care just a little bit more about others," Knox said as he stepped out of a nearby doorway. Mana was temporarily speechless. "Yeah," he said, "the walls are waterproof, but the doors aren't soundproof."

I was already walking. "Justin!" Mana shouted after me. "I'm sorry!" I just kept walking.

When I stepped outside once more, Maya was gone. A puurr-deer was standing nearby. Had she just called the deer for us to ride, only to be snatched up by something...or by someone? What part of "stay together" had given her the idea...*chitter*...*chitter-chit* – my thoughts were interrupted by a strange noise coming from behind and above me. When I turned to look I could see that it was a humbug, clinging to the wall of the dam above. Immediately it swooped down and landed on my shoulder. It gave me the message, "I've gone ahead. Surprise for you. Meet me at the gym." No sooner had I grasped the last word than it took flight, disappearing almost immediately among the trees. My concern was quickly eclipsed by anger, a cauldron that Mana had already started stirring. I jumped on the deer and took off, hoping to intercept Maya before she got too far. No such luck.

There were people on the road, lots of them. Most of the faces were unfamiliar. Some were ascending toward the dam; others, like myself, were making their way down to the city. Occasionally someone was seen riding a deer, and once I even saw a lone rider traversing a wooded ridge far below, probably sight-seeing, but he was going in the wrong direction; Maya was nowhere to be found. Moreover the pairs and clusters of people were getting thicker, further impeding my progress and frustrating my efforts to catch up to her. I was reintroduced to an experience I would as soon have forgotten, as more and more of the faces came to reflect something like reverent awe at the sight of me, and excited whispers were exchanged. More than a few times I heard among this chatter the hushed exclamation, "Martyr!" It appeared that my mythos had found its way to other camps as well, unless they had only heard of me after they came to this place. This seemed unlikely given the deep-seated emotion and personal ownership of the statements. I tried to steer wide of the larger groups, but the landscape was well nigh impassable on either side of the road, so I found it necessary to pick my way slowly, painstakingly, through the adoring crowd.

I finally reached the city, and it was a different place than when I had last seen it. Had it not been for the obvious signs of decay, I might almost have been able to believe that the plague had never struck here. The streets were teeming with people, and the buzz of a half-dozen conversations could be heard at any given time. It was alive. One could imagine that the city itself was happy to be occupied once again after such a long period of desolation. I heard the clang of metal cookware as I passed one house, the scent of a hearty stew tempting my nostrils. Here a man carried water jugs for washing, as his wife hung brightly-colored clothes to dry on newly-strung cords. There a child swept decades-old dust from a granite step before the door. I even passed a group of young girls playing a game like hop-scotch, skipping across chalk-drawn tiles hand in hand. Even as the remaining traces of the plague were slowly being erased, these glimpses of joy gave a piece of comfort, a sense of community.

I suppose the streets looked different, too, with so many people on them, for I soon found myself traveling an unfamiliar lane. I thought about retracing my steps, but the masses were thicker in that direction, so I decided to try to work my way in a more circuitous path in the general direction I thought I should be heading. Eventually this tactic succeeded, as I found myself passing the jailhouse from the direction opposite the way we had approached it previously. Noting that the door was slightly ajar, I dismounted, thinking to check in on Greda (or whoever was currently posted guard), and to hopefully have better luck drawing Jeyt into conversation. I wasn't prepared for what I found within.

Greda was dead. Gutted, her entrails spilling over her lap and onto the floor as she sat unmoving in her chair. Blood now pooled at her feet, and had spattered on the walls and ceiling with the violence of the attack that had taken her life. The cell door hung open. The prisoner, of course, was gone. Greda's face was contorted into a mask of horror, its many creases smoothed out as much as they'd ever be. I approached the body and closed her

262

eyelids and mouth, scanned the area quickly but saw no murder weapon or other indication of what had transpired. Suddenly I remembered the lone rider on the ridge.

I ran to the street, mounted my deer, then raced to the main road, turning toward the gym where I hoped Maya waited. Flying past curious onlookers, I drove the deer hard toward the large crowd assembled in the distance. As I drew near, an angel appeared before me in the middle of the road ahead.

This *had* to be Maya's new armor. Its design was similar to mine, with a few noticeable differences. It was all a pearlescent white, but when she moved, or the sun hit it just right, it shimmered with hidden color like an opal. The helm was falcon-like, complete with white tufted crests over both her ears. Like mine it sported a single wing, but over the right shoulder rather than the left. And she appeared to be in battle form, a matching white crossbow built into the suit's right arm, yet unlike mine the wing was persistent while armed. There was an outpouching on the side of her left thigh that mirrored the one on my leggings. It was a beautiful piece of work, and it probably did outshine mine just a bit, if only because of the luminosity of the materials out of which it was fashioned. I imagined it was every bit as strong, and as light, as mine, if not more so. But I didn't mind, as it suited her well.

In reality, I didn't have that long to appreciate its finer qualities. As I approached, she slapped both elbows against her sides simultaneously, and the armor split along multiple hidden fissures and folded within itself again and again, finally all but disappearing into a few discreet pieces attached to the back of her body, arms, and legs. In a few places the armor curled asymmetrically around the front of her limbs and body in a pattern that seemed more decorative than pragmatic. It occurred to me that the way these pearly tendrils fell might have allowed a less modest person to wear the armor sans underclothing. Maya wore it over her usual

263

blacks. The many-pocketed vest was missing, however. Perhaps that was the purpose of the receptacle on her thigh.

Maya's proudly beaming smile quickly dissolved when she saw the look on my face. "What happened?" she asked.

"Greda's dead. Jeyt is gone," I said. "Tell Reya and then *stay with her.* I think I can bring him back."

"I'm coming with you!" she said.

"No! *Listen* to me this time, *please!* Stay with Reya, you'll be safe. I will return with or without Jeyt, I promise."

"I can't lose you!" she implored.

"You won't," I said. "Now go, tell Reya what's happened. Tell her to wait here; I'll need to know where to find you both when I get back."

"Justin!"

"There's no time," I said, already turning my deer around. "If Jeyt gets away..." Maya nodded slowly as understanding dawned. I was off, racing through the streets of the city, weaving my way toward the outskirts that would lead to the wilderness. Larger buildings gave way to smaller ones, eventually tapering off into residential neighborhoods. Every time I had a choice between roads, I took the smaller one, until at last I spotted the tree-line at the end of a dead-end street. I prompted my deer to leap the weathered fence that stood between us and the forest, and we landed in a run on the far side. Almost immediately I steered to the north and west, the direction that I knew would lead to the place below the dam road where I had last seen the rider. After about ten minutes of riding I began to worry that I might have miscalculated, or gotten turned around in the dense wood.

Then, finally, the trees began to thin, and when we crossed a clearing I could see the cliffside rising sharply to my left, could even make out the tiny forms of tourists along its edge, making their way up and down the curving path between the dam and the city. I hurried on, reaching at last the place where I had seen the person I felt certain must have been Jeyt. But now what? I was racing in the direction I had last seen him moving, but there was no way of knowing if or when he may have deviated from that course, or how far he could have gone in the intervening time that it had taken me to work my way all the way down into the city and out again. I realized now that my plan hadn't actually covered what I would do once I reached this point. But then it came to me.

I spoke to the puurr-deer. "Show me any other deer that are nearby," I said. Instantly, an image formed before me. I saw men and women on deer traveling the dam road. "Are there any others?" I asked. The image changed, and then I saw Knox and Corvus, each mounted, riding into the clearing where the chopper sat, Doog sitting on the ground below it, enjoying a mid-morning snack. I re-framed the question. "Show me the last deer that passed this way." The image changed again, and now I saw Jeyt, mounted on a deer, riding through a shady valley. Good! But where was that place? It wasn't here, so I must have been seeing where he was *now*. I saw Jeyt turn his head to look over his shoulder toward something above. "Go back a little," I said, "and show me the scene through his eyes." Then I was Jeyt, pulling my deer to a halt and glancing back and up...at the dam road! He was checking to see if he had been noticed. The angle was different, but that enabled me to estimate approximately where he must be.

I hummed my deer into motion, and sped toward that place. Minutes passed, and then I saw the familiar valley from the vision rising on either side of us. Jeyt had not appeared to be in any

265

particular hurry, an odd choice for one who had recently committed murder and was almost certainly being hunted. The valley curved lazily north, finally opening onto a slate-strewn plain that rose like a ramp onto a high, broad plateau straight ahead. As my deer climbed over the apex of the slope, there stood Jeyt, facing away from us, having recently dismounted. His deer trotted past us, snorting a greeting before heading back the way we had come. I decided to dismount as well, and approached him on foot. As I walked, I performed the necessary actions to arm myself, the sound of which he must have heard. Yet he didn't turn, standing with the same despondent posture I had observed in the jail. He didn't appear to be armed. I could see now that he stood at the brink of a sheer drop, the unforgiving earth several hundred feet below. He spoke first.

"I didn't do it."

"Didn't do what, Jeyt?" I asked. "Brutally murder a dear friend and ally, or betray all of your people?"

"Either," he said. "I never betrayed them to Magus. Yes, I had the device. And yes, Magus gave it to me. I agreed to lead him to the camp. But I never actually did it."

"Why, Jeyt? Why would you help that demon? What did he offer you?"

"I'm not a brave man," he said. "I'm not a hero like you. I was tired of being afraid all the time. Magus told me he'd let me have a little piece of land where he'd leave me alone. I have a son, you know. He stays with his mother, far away from Magus' reach. But I knew one day the war would come there too. I thought maybe, if I did this, we could be together again and live in peace. This was a way I could save my little boy."

"Do you really think that justifies bringing a death sentence down on scores of others?" I demanded. "Some of them had families too, living with them in the camp. Did you think about them?"

"Of course I did!" he shouted. "That's why I never entered the full code. I started to, several times, but that thought always stopped me. That's what I was doing when Euthus jumped me."

"Oh, how *noble* of you," I said, "to stop *just short* of calling Magus' army down on dozens of innocents."

"I told you I'm no hero," Jeyt said. "That's why I'm here." He inched closer to the edge. I sheathed my weapon, preparing to grab him should he try it.

"Hold on," I said. "What about Greda? Are you saying you weren't the one who killed her?"

"Greda was like a second mother to me," he said. He turned at last to face me, and I could see that his scraggly beard was wet with the tears that had been streaming down his sallow cheeks. He took another step back. I poised myself for a lunging grab. "You should take a careful look at those closest to you."

That caught me off guard. "What do you mean? *Who did it?*" I demanded.

He stared blankly, seeming not to hear. "For what it's worth," he said in a rasping voice just above a whisper, "I believe you *are* Martyr. Take that demon out for us. *For my little boy.*" Even as he said the last words, he spun around and lurched over the edge, his arm twisting just out of my reach as I lunged, grasping only air. Jeyt was gone.

I leaned toward the edge, not out of morbid curiosity but only to visually confirm what I knew must have happened, and as I did I

267

almost followed him down, as the silence was abruptly shattered by a series of seismic explosions from the direction of the city. We were under attack.

26

The city was in chaos. Where previously the smoke of a handful of scattered campfires had scrolled lazily skyward, the air was now thick with black clouds, heavy with ash and cinders. Entire buildings were engulfed in flame. On the ground, people were scrambling in every direction, singly and in small groups, fleeing for their lives or desperately calling out the name of a missing loved one as they ran. I pushed forward amidst the anarchy, hoping to catch a glimpse of Maya's glistening armor through the searing haze, or to hear Reya shout a command to her troops. It was not immediately apparent who the aggressors were, though it could be safely assumed that Magus was behind the attack. The explosive entrance was all-too-reminiscent of the raid at Milltown. Corpses littered the street, invisible in the smoke until I was almost on top of them. These were not the parched bones or mummified husks of ancient plague victims, but fresh kills, twisted and torn and bloodied. My weapon leaped into my hand, shield at the ready as I continued my advance, more cautiously now.

A hollow roar was heard over the screams and the crackling of burning debris. Just then a stray gust of wind cleared the smoke from an area before me just long enough to display a scene of horrific violence. A family of pilgrims fled before one of Magus' black-clad assassins, mounted on an armor-cat that had been fitted with biomechanical restraints. An elderly matriarch failed to match the pace of the rest of the group, and the cat snatched her up in its massive jaws. With an effortless crunch, the beast rendered her fragile body limp, then tossed it aside and launched itself after the others. The glow of orange lights could still be seen for a second after the cat disappeared into the smoke with its rider. It roared again, and received distant replies from at least two more of its kind.

269

I decided it was best to stick to the shadows and alleys of the city buildings, rather than stumbling blindly down the main street, and possibly into the hungry jaws of one of those beasts. There were no deer to call – they tended to avoid the urban sprawl in favor of the wooded glens – and so there was no chance of repeating my mind trick on these cats. My strategy was to basically circle a block, then return to the main throughway long enough to see if I could spot one of my allies, and to try to assess the scale of the assault. I would then circle the next block in similar fashion. It was slow progress, but it was effective. Only once did I encounter an enemy off the main road. It was a lone assassin on foot, and upon seeing him I immediately flattened myself against the building next to me, but he never looked my way, turning instead to sprint toward an unfortunate couple leading a young child across the street a couple of blocks down. Upon seeing this I abandoned caution and shouted, "Hey!"

The soldier skidded to a halt and whipped about to face me. It took him only a moment to realize that I was not one of his own men, and he strode confidently in my direction, dragging the tip of his blade over the cracked asphalt as he came. I presumed that the reason he was not concerned about dulling its edge was because it was enchanted in the same way as his armor. His manner was casual, almost playful; as a predator toys with its still-living prey before snapping its neck. Clearly he was not accustomed to encountering much resistance from those he victimized. He was due for a surprise.

I stood my ground until he was almost upon me. When he finally attacked I swatted aside his first two half-hearted swings easily. Now I had his attention. He paused, then came at me with a much more sincere thrust, his body weight now behind it. I side-stepped at the last moment, then brought my staff up forcefully into the articulation between the armor plates of his arm and side, cleaving the limb cleanly at the joint and relieving him of that much extra weight amidst a shower of blood. Clutching the wound in

270

disbelief, he turned to run, underestimating the reach of my perfectly balanced weapon. With a broad, scything slash I invited his head to join his twitching arm in the dust, and his body flopped to the ground, pouring warm crimson into the cracks in the pavement.

Circling the next block, I returned to the main street once more, and as I did a stronger breeze momentarily cleared the smoke so that I could see to the end of the city and the forested hills beyond. There, in a large clearing at the base of one of the hills, a massive, dark, ellipsoid form hovered just above the yellow-grassed slope. A second shape, identical but smaller, or as I soon realized, more distant, appeared over the far-off mountain peaks beyond the foothills. My own-world cultural memory immediately conjured images of alien spacecraft, but context steered me toward a more reasonable conclusion: dirigibles. From the nearer vessel more dark troopers could be seen dropping the short distance to the ground, then vanishing into the trees that stood between the city and the hills.

I broke into a sprint, less concerned about encountering another mounted assassin and more about finding Maya and my friends before more of those death-dealers did. I hadn't run more than a couple of blocks when I heard sounds of battle from a side street off the other side of the main road. I crossed cautiously under cover of smoke and headed in that direction. Just as I reached the far side of the street, a bus-sized chunk of burning concrete and steel from somewhere high above crashed into the ground behind me, cracking the earth and throwing me off my feet. Heart in my throat, I picked myself up and re-oriented to the sounds of struggle – the ring of edged weapons clashing, the shouted commands, the cries of the fallen. As it turned out, the noises had seemed deceptively close; in fact, the site of the conflict was well away from the tall buildings of the old city center. In this forgotten place before the river's edge, deteriorated warehouses languished in the shadows of concrete colossi: a knot of looping remnants of overpasses and off-ramps that teetered precariously on crumbling legs. In a few places the years of erosion and disrepair had exposed a skeleton of rusted rebar. Beneath this firmament, a miniature war was waged.

I spotted Reya first, as she was never one to let others do her fighting for her. As I drew closer, I saw other faces I knew: Knox, back-to-back with Reya; Kuro and Jager, similarly paired; Kaire, a short distance away. Each warrior was facing off against one or more of the dark marauders, and appeared to be holding their own. They weren't the only rebels in the fray; numerous others I didn't recognize – most woefully under-equipped – fought the good fight as well. I scanned the dust- and smoke-obscured battlefield, and eventually located Charr, picking off unsuspecting foes with a traditional bow from an elevated position atop one of the warehouses. For a second I thought I saw Maya beside her, but it was Mana, who to my surprise was attempting to snipe bad guys with one of Charr's crossbows. I wondered how she could possibly hope to land a shot with no training on this kind of weapon, but before I finished the thought I saw one of her bolts find mooring in the soft spot at the base of an assassin's skull.

I couldn't reach any of my friends to ask after Maya, so I stalked the edges of the battlefield, hoping that a better angle might reveal her location. Here in the dusk and dark shadows, Maya's armor would not catch the sun's rays, and would offer no help in pointing up her location. As I traced a wide circle around the conflict, I was met by several of the dark soldiers who, upon spotting me, tore themselves free from the melee to oppose me. As my tutors had predicted, they presented a hearty challenge, but each time I was ultimately able to prevail against them and continue on my intended course. Finally I saw Maya, on the far side of the battlefield. But she wasn't embroiled in combat. Instead, she was running away, back in the direction of the main street via a narrow alleyway. I shouted to her, but it was impossible for her to hear me over the clamor. As I tried to make

272

my way to her last known position, I was intercepted by another dark soldier.

This one wasn't going down so easily. In fact, as we got into it, he gave me a few moments' uncertainty about the outcome of our fight, matching me blow-for-blow for the better part of ten minutes. An imperfectly-aimed attempt to dislodge his head sent his helmet flying instead, and I was unwillingly reminded that the enemy wore a human face. Oddly moved amid clashing blades, I asked him, "Why do you fight for him?"

His face registered not the expected anger, but consternation, bewilderment. At first I didn't think he was going to answer me, but as we continued to exchange blows he replied matter-of-factly, "He gives us freedom."

"Said the slave," I responded.

"*You're* the slave, fool!" he spat. "Magus shows us another way!" Now *I* was angry. As his sword came down, I shoved it aside with a powerful counter, and rammed my shield into his chest and up under his chin, pushing his entire body back as I pressed forward like an offensive lineman. Then I pulled my shield arm away suddenly, and without hesitation replaced it with the tip of my staff, driving it between his ribs and pressing it deep. He dropped his blade and stiffened, then fell at my feet. I braced my foot against his chest to withdraw my weapon, then completed my arc and slipped into the alley where I'd seen Maya go. As I did, the sounds of battle at my back muffled by the high walls, I heard another sound rising over the clash of swords and screams of men: a terrible chorus of bellowing roars. The armor-cats had arrived.

I didn't want to leave my friends and allies to fight them, but Maya was alone, and if she came face-to-face with one of those beasts...I wasn't sure how well her armor would hold up against

273

those crushing jaws. I increased my pace, dodging and leaping piles of scattered debris and the occasional set of human bones as I ran. Around a bend, and I startled a pack of grotesquely oversized rodents gnawing at the remains of one more recently fallen. I hurried on, emerging at last onto a proper street. I glanced quickly in both directions, but there was no sign of Maya. I stood in the middle of the block. Now I was unsure how to proceed. Maya could have disappeared around one of the corners to my left or right and down a side-street, but which way had she gone? I heard a roar behind me – one of the cats had followed me into the alley! Spotting another gap between buildings almost directly opposite my position, I bolted for it. I heard another roar, louder, but didn't dare to look back, hoping to be out of sight in the gap by the time the beast reached the street.

I slipped into the alley, heart pounding. The shadows fell deep, but I wasn't sure how well those cats could see – or smell. The alley turned left, and so did I, and nearly ran into a huge, vertical slab of concrete that had fallen across the gap, completely blocking further passage. I hurried back around the corner and toward the street, not wanting to give the cat a chance to trap me in a dead end. If I was going to go down fighting, I wanted room to swing my blade. As I neared the egress, I could see the beast and its rider standing just before the opening on the opposite side of the street. The creature was sniffing the air when I first saw it, but instantly snapped to center on me, lowered its head, and charged, bellowing as it came. I was still a short distance from the street, my senses restricted by the narrow slit of the alley to only that directly before me, and that – the terrible sight of that monster bearing down on me, its thunderous roar – was amplified to frightful effect. And so it was that I didn't hear another kind of a roar, rising quickly to swallow up the sound of the cat, until a great white shape, entering my field of vision from the right, slammed into the creature's side, flipping it up and over itself and launching its rider into the air. Only after it had passed by my spot and come to rest, purring, to the left of my view-slice, was I able

274

to identify the sound. I ran out into the street. The cat and its rider lay unmoving where they had fallen. I turned my head and saw...Maya...sitting atop a radiant two-wheeled steed.

To call it a motorcycle, a bike, would not do justice to the artistry of this vehicle. It was white and shimmering, of the same material as her armor. It appeared to have pairs of wings shielding its wheels on either side. As I watched, a third pair of wing-like blades that had been extended from the cycle's flanks folded themselves back into a more streamlined position along its sides, helping to protect the rider's legs. The rumble of its engine was music to a bike-lover's ears. So this was her big surprise. "Hurry, get on!" she shouted, and I complied. As she accelerated down the street, swerving to avoid the cat's body, she said, "I didn't want to hurt the cat, but time was of the essence. As you'll see," she said, flipping a switch between the handlebars, "it's equipped with the same type of deterrent devices as the dam. Under normal circumstances, that would be enough to scare away the cats." She rounded the next corner, steering back toward the river. As we turned, my peripheral vision detected a huge shadow passing up the side of the building to our left, but by the time I looked, whatever had cast it was gone.

We turned again, and now we could see the battlefield once again. Three more of the armor-cats were weaving in and out of the swarming masses, each occupying the efforts of at least six or eight combatants at any given time just to keep them at bay. The number of dead appeared to have grown, but it was darker now, the sun low in the sky, and it was difficult to tell how many of those fallen were friends. Just then a massive shape soared over the top of the building we had just passed, all but blotting out the sky. It was the second dirigible, and it seemed uninterested in the happenings on the ground, steering instead to follow the curve of the river upstream – it was headed for the dam! Maya saw it too, anticipated my question. "Nothing we can do about that right now, we have to help here." I nodded, and Maya throttled up,

275

speeding us straight into the middle of the fray. One by one, the three cats lifted their heads, shook them violently as if trying to dislodge something irritating, then began to lumber away from the field in frustration. Their riders dismounted unceremoniously by jumping clear and rolling, and hurried back to the fight. Maya steered for the biggest clusters of enemies, and careful not to include any resistance fighters in their sweep, deployed the blade-wings to great effect, shattering the shins of several of the dark assassins, cleanly slicing off the legs of a few. They were quick to adapt their tactics, however, and those that remained began to leap over the blades. Sadly for them, my staff was ready to dissect most of these in mid-air. Others tried to stay wide of our path, and when this failed, took to higher ground, climbing to the tops of nearby warehouses or into the branches of trees. These were readily dispatched by Charr and Mana, if not by Maya's own crossbow.

"The tide has turned in our favor," I said to Maya, "We should get to the dam."

"Not yet," she said. "One more thing we need to do first." Then she accelerated in the direction the cats had gone. I saw her reach up and flip the anti-cat switch the other way.

"Are you sure that's a good idea?" I asked.

"Normal armor-cats would be happy to be free of the riders and would return to the forest," she said. "But as long as these have Magus' machinery strapped to their backs, they'll come back. The riders will be able to mount them again and continue to harass us." The first cat was coming into view, running across the parking lot of an old pawn shop. "Because the repellers are off, they'll turn on us when we get close," she said, "but otherwise we wouldn't be able to get anywhere near them. Try to damage the machinery enough to break its control over them. If it doesn't work, we'll just have to kill them." This clearly wasn't her preferred option. She pulled alongside the beast as it ran, and tried to get close enough to give me a clean slice. As she did, it veered toward us, jaws snapping, and Maya hastily retreated out of reach. "That's not going to work," she said. "I'll see what I can do from a distance." Steering with one hand, she aimed her crossbow with the other. The first couple of shots glanced harmlessly off the machinery, or the cat's armor. "I can't get a steady shot this way. Can you reach past me and take the handlebars?"

"I'll try," I said. As I did so, she aimed again, steadying the weapon with her other hand. She fired, and one of the orange lights went out, sending forth sparks. Maya lined up a second shot, but before she could take it, the cat groaned deeply and went limp, burying its chin in the dust as it skidded to a halt. Maya shook her head.

"What happened?" I asked.

"Horrible man built in a fail-safe that kills the animal if the machinery is compromised." She took a deep breath. "We can't let them kill more of our people. It's unfortunate, but this makes our job easier." She sped up again, and soon the other two beasts appeared ahead, running together. Maya pulled up within firing range, handed off the controls again, and lined up her shot. The bolt went straight into the creature's eye, and presumably, its brain. It dropped soundlessly. Maya readied her next lethal shot.

"Wait!" I shouted. "I've done this before; let me try."

"Try what?" Maya asked.

"Just get me close," I said. "Once I'm clear, pull away before it tries for you."

"*Be careful!*" Maya ordered. She got me close as before, and as before, the cat snapped at us. But I was already in the air. I landed

277

on its back, and hanging onto the straps that held the machinery fast, I tried to examine the attachments. There appeared to be no mechanism that would be triggered by releasing the straps. After all, who would have expected someone to try to commandeer one of the cats? I slipped the end of my staff under the first set of straps, turned the weapon, and cleanly sliced through the straps. I did the same with the remaining attachments. Then I simply pushed the still-working device off one side of the cat and let it fall. Done! Now I was just riding a regular *wild* giant battle cat. Thankfully, I didn't have to wait for it to figure a way to scrape me off, as Maya was pulling back in. "Jump!" she said, and I did, but the cat lurched just as I leapt, and I landed not on the seat where I had intended, but on one of the blade-wings. "Hang on!" Maya screamed. She steered well away from the armor-cat, which didn't take up pursuit, but now ran blissfully to its forest home. I clung to the wing for dear life, its bladed edge drawing blood along my forearm, but my enhanced healing prevented it from doing more than surface damage. When we were safely clear, Maya stopped and helped me back onto the seat. "Nice work!" she said.

Just then Maya's humbug flew in. A second later Maya had its message. "Charr's on her way to the dam," she informed me. "The airship released several dark troopers on gliding wings. She was able to snipe a couple of them out of the sky, but two remain airborne, and are circling over the dam. She's not sure what they plan to do, but has ordered us back to the dam for immediate..." She was cut off by the sound of another huge explosion, followed shortly by a great rushing sound. "They've blown the dam!" she screamed. "We have to get there *fast!*"

Maya floored it, heading for the dam road by the shortest possible route. As we raced alongside the river, we could see that it was already swelling, creeping over its banks. Our route soon took us away from its course, but before long water was coursing along the edges of the streets, their drainage clogged by decades of silt and debris. We knew that in no time the streets would be completely submerged, and passage for a vehicle such as this would be impossible. We reached the main thoroughfare, and knew that from here it was nearly a straight shot to the dam road, and higher elevations. A thin blanket of water coated the street, and Maya was beginning to hydroplane now and then, a frightening thing on a two-wheeler. She pulled up over a curb onto the sidewalk, which was so far still dry, but this made for slightly slower progress, as we had to dodge fallen chunks of building and bump over the occasional pile of human remains. We reached the dam road at last, catching up to a growing number of pedestrians who had already started to evacuate. So much for the resettlement. It looked like the survivors would once again be camping by the dam.

When we arrived at the dam at last, there was a mad flurry of activity as people bustled about, squabbling over sharing of the now inadequate space and resources, and whispering anxiously about what was going to happen next. We could see to our relief that the entire dam had not been destroyed, but that a good-sized fissure had been hewn across its top, and there water was rushing through. Parts of the dam interior would be flooded as well, I realized. Charr was visible, standing on the brink of the dam, and as we watched she let an arrow fly, and a lone dark form plummeted out of the sky into the river below. That seemed to be the last of them.

Maya parked the bike near the dam entrance, and we walked together out to where Charr was standing. She had no words, shaking her head sadly as we walked back toward the main encampment. There we started to see others we knew, gathering out of the chaos to take stock of the damage and formulate a plan. Reya stood in the fore.

"What happened in the city?" I asked. "Are there more of Magus's men?"

"It was strange indeed," said Reya. "Of those that remained, some fled to the docked airship, and presumably escaped. Others made no attempt to avoid the rising waters, letting it simply overtake them. It was as though their prescribed role ended there, and nothing further had been written for them. Sad, really."

"That many less to kill," Kaire said.

"In truth this entire force represented but a tiny fraction of those at Magus' disposal," Reya continued. "And yet they've all but crippled us."

"Only because they caught us unprepared," said Knox.

"Yes, but *how* did that happen?" Reya asked. "The traitor was in custody. And I'm *certain* we weren't tracked when we came here. Yet Magus knew!"

"Quite obviously there is still a betrayer about," said Jager.

"I managed to get a few words out of Jeyt before he took his own life," I said. There were a couple of startled gasps, as apparently this news had not had time to make the rounds. "He implied that it might be someone in our inner circle of trust."

"Is everyone accounted for?" Charr asked.

"I spoke with Denkel and several of my officers a few moments ago," Reya offered.

"Where's Corvus?" I demanded suddenly.

Corvus stepped up from where he'd been standing behind some other people. "Right here, *ass*," he said.

Just then Kuro came out of the door and announced that the sleeping quarters were flooded and inaccessible. "I think that's everyone, now," said Jager.

Everyone…yes. *No. Mana!* "Where's Mana?" I asked. I turned to Charr.

"She *was* with me," said Charr, "but we got separated during the evacuation. I haven't seen her since."

"She's the traitor!" yelled Corvus. "That would explain how she just conveniently appeared, and now has just as conveniently disappeared!"

"Don't be stupid!" I retorted. "What possible motive would she have for betraying us to Magus? How would she even have had contact with him? We should be more concerned to rule out the possibility that she was either kidnapped by the assassins or lost in the flood."

"Justin's right," Reya said. "We should not rush to judgment at a time like this. Our first priority should be to determine what our losses are, and attend to the wounded. Second: to rethink our strategy. When Magus comes again – and he will – we must be prepared for him. This attack was undoubtedly meant to soften us up before the full assault. He won't be back tonight, or tomorrow, but he will be back – *in force*. I will ask each of the camps for volunteers to watch the perimeter throughout the night. Try to find a place to lay your heads tonight, as the morning comes quickly, and there will be much to do."

Maya and I looked at each other, feeling more than a little unsettled at having been unexpectedly ousted from our quarters. But as there was nothing to be done about it now, we started off to see if we could locate a spare tent. Reya caught us by the sleeves. "Not you two," she said. "You'll stay in the dam."

281

"But our room is flooded," said Maya.

"You can use one of the control rooms on the main floor," she said. "There are no beds, so you'll have to just lie on your clothes, but it will be safer there." Maya made a small sound like she was going to object. I suspected she wasn't happy with the idea of us resting comfortably in the dam while others had to lie on the cold, damp earth. But Reya shushed her, saying, "I haven't forgotten what's important. Justin, you mean everything to the resistance. You are our last and greatest hope. And hope is something we need now more than ever. And you Maya...well...you're my little girl." Maya blushed as Reya added, "Please do this for me." Maya blew out a slow, deep breath and reluctantly acquiesced. I was worried about Maya, who seemed shaken by more than just the change in sleeping arrangements. I was sure there was something else on her mind, but she wasn't voicing it. We started to walk away and Reya stopped us once more. Looking right at me she said, "We have something Magus doesn't. Chaer-Ul is with us, and he has sent you. We *can* defeat him." Yet there was fear behind her eyes. At the time, I wondered if it was really me she was trying to reassure, or herself.

27

Sleep didn't come easy. Staring at a strange ceiling, the rumble of water rushing overhead concealed the sound of countless imagined explosions, echoed the noise of weapons clashing, beasts roaring, men screaming. Maya was restless beside me as well, curling into me, then away, rolling back into me again. Several times I could feel her watching me in the darkness, and once or twice during these moments her fingers touched my cheek briefly before she would begin anew her restless pattern: rolling away, back again. When I tried to draw her out she gave no answer. The day's events had been traumatic enough, but this was a woman reared by war and conflict; something else roiled under the surface, disquieted her. I determined to ask her more pointedly at morning's light. I don't know how long we lay awake like this, but at some point the exhaustion that wracked my body claimed my mind as well, and I slept, in a place too deep for dreams to intrude.

When I finally awoke, Maya was gone again. If she had felt anything like the gnawing hunger that I now did, she'd be at the grills once more, preparing our breakfast. I dressed quickly and stepped out into a sun-bright morning. People were busying themselves with all manner of tasks: carrying materials to repair the breach in the dam, debating strategy and performing drills in preparation for the anticipated second assault, forming hunting and gathering parties to provide food and resources for the displaced populace. There was indeed food on the grill, but it was Knox, not Maya, who tended it. When I asked if he'd seen Maya, he said that he hadn't. I scanned the courtyard area and noted that her cycle was no longer parked where it had been the night before. As I still didn't know precisely where Charr's workshop stood, it was possible that it was still accessible and that she'd taken the bike there for a tune-up, or to talk to Charr. Making my way along the lakeshore, I spotted Reya talking with Jager. They hadn't seen

Maya either. Nor had Kuro or Kaire, who were a little farther upstream, overseeing the distribution of food rations from the latest successful hunt.

For all of this, I didn't begin to experience concern until I glanced back toward the dam and saw Charr ride up suddenly from the main road, exchange quick words with Knox, and then glance in my direction as he pointed. "Justin!" she shouted as she rode up to me. "Maya's gone! Her humbug just came to me with the message!"

"Wait, *what*? Where did she go? *What was the message?*"

"It said, 'I understand the prophecy. I know what you would do, and I mean to make it unnecessary. If I should fail, please forgive me - I did it because I love you.' I assume the message was for you."

"Charr, what does it mean? Do you know what she's planning to do? *Do you know where she's gone?*"

"I…don't *know*," she said, "not for sure…but…"

"Charr, if you know *anything, please!*"

"OK, well, I'd been working on something – a *weapon* – a dagger with a concealed mechanism that produces a modified electromagnetic field." She paused, ostensibly to ensure that I was following her so far, but seeing the near-hysteria in my face, she continued, speaking faster. "I may have intimated that it could theoretically neutralize a *magical* field in a limited application…but it wasn't tested of course; I have no idea if it will actually work."

"*So?*" I almost shouted.

"So a few days ago, Maya asked to borrow it, said she wanted to play around with it. Justin, I don't think she's playing."

"But what would she…," I began.

"Based on the words of this message," she said, "I fear…"

I gasped, finished the thought for her, "…*she's going to try to take out Magus by herself!* Charr, why would she do this? Why didn't she tell me?"

"Obviously she didn't want you to try to stop her," she said.

"But she had to know I would!" I stormed past her, toward the trees at the edge of the forest.

"Justin, wait!" said Charr. "You can't help her on your own. You don't even know how much of a lead she has, or which way she went!"

"That's what I'm about to find out," I replied. Then I formed the sound to summon a deer. The noise caught the attention of Reya and Jager, who started over to where I stood.

Soon a deer trotted up, just as Reya arrived and asked, "What's going on, Justin?"

"Maya's gone after Magus – *alone*."

"Alone? *No!* What is she *thinking?*"

"She's thinking she'll save me the trouble," I said. "She's trying to save me." Then I turned to the deer, scratched its chin, and said, "Show me where Maya went." The animal blinked its huge liquid-gold eyes once, then projected an image.

"What's happening?" Reya asked.

"Let all of these see as well," I added belatedly, and then we all watched as an aerial view of a nocturnal forest coalesced before us. We were soaring over the treetops, and then abruptly the trees ended at the edge of a cracked and overgrown ancient highway. Our view banked sharply to follow the road, and a white shape could be seen at the perimeter of our field of vision, racing toward a pre-dawn horizon. The view zoomed in, and there could be no question: it was Maya, tearing up the freeway on her angel-bike. "Show us Maya as she is now," I said. I had to blink against the sudden brightness of an instant sunrise, as the vision now showed Maya in full morning light, still riding hard. The forest had been replaced by scattered copses of trees and shrubs, and the surrounding landscape revealed smaller concourses and numerous interwoven side-streets, tracing their strange patterns among the many derelict houses that dotted the hilly plain. Straight ahead a vast metropolis stood, the end-point of the highway and Maya's apparent destination, terrible asymmetries darkly silhouetted against the early morning sun.

A line of darkly-clad figures came into view ahead, standing elbow-to-elbow across the highway. Directly behind them, the wrecked remains of several cars had been stacked to form a makeshift roadblock. Here the road had been hewn through sheer rock, its steep walls rendering passage around the blockade impossible. The blade-wings on Maya's bike snapped open as Maya accelerated toward the men, these not the highly-skilled assassins but some of Magus' general foot soldiers. As she reached their position she braked suddenly and cut the front wheel hard to the left, skidding out and bringing the rear of the bike and the right side blade-wing around, slicing the first soldier in two and tossing several others against the cars. Another came at her, sword drawn, and she dispatched him with a well-aimed crossbow bolt, even as she peeled out and sped back to a position well before the roadblock. Maya now retrieved a different-looking bolt

287

from a hidden compartment under the edge of her seat and reloaded. Taking aim at the base of the roadblock she fired, and the bolt exploded, toppling the cars and creating a bike-sized gap in the blockade. Now she came at them again full throttle, blade-wings tucked, picking off a couple of surviving soldiers as she slipped through the recently-created opening and resumed her race toward the looming city skyline. I banished the vision, was already starting to mount the deer.

"You'll never make it in time!" Reya said. "She's nearly to the city. That place is a hundred times the size of this town, and swarming with *tens of thousands* of Magus' troops. There's *nothing* you can do for her now."

"*We'll see about that!*" I snarled, and flipped my leg over the other side of the deer. I began to hum, and at that moment Reya hummed too, a little louder and with a bit more vibrato. The deer immediately sat down on its haunches, dumping me roughly on my back.

The next thing I knew, Reya was hauling me to my feet. I was astounded anew by her sheer physical prowess. "*Come with me,*" she insisted through gritted teeth. Hauling me out of earshot, Reya began, "Understand *this* before you go off half-cocked on some kind of macho suicide mission. First, that is *my daughter.* I almost lost her once, and I *will die* if anything happens to her. Please don't think for one second that you care about her more than I do. *Second,*" she barked, I've already lost Tal to that monster, and I believe you are here as a direct result of that fact, and specifically, *to do something about it.* I won't have you handing yourself to him on a platter prematurely by acting rashly.

"What...would you...suggest instead," I asked, choosing my words carefully to avoid unleashing my anger on her and thereby incurring more of hers.

"It's time for you to seek the face of Chaer-Ul," she said.

"Reya, surely you realize there's no time for this. If it's just me, or an army, we have to go after her *now*."

"I don't know if you heard me," Reya said. "Magus has *thousands upon thousands*. Have you looked at us recently? We number in the hundreds at best, and that was before last night's attack. You've become an amazingly powerful warrior, but that's not enough. We were never going to win this war by the numbers."

"And how exactly *are* we going to win this war?" I asked, sincerely, realizing for perhaps the first time just what the odds were.

"Chaer-Ul only knows," she said.

"*But...?*" I started to protest.

"It's what Maya would want you to do."

I knew she was right. "Not fair," I said.

"And I have little doubt it's what *she* did before taking this step," she added.

"Are you saying Chaer-Ul *told her* to do this?" I asked.

"No one can know what Chaer-Ul whispers in another ear," she said. "I'm only saying that Maya would have sought his counsel."

"Where can I find him?" I asked.

By this time Kuro had joined Charr and Jager, who had hurriedly briefed him on the situation. He jogged over to where we stood. "I may be able to help you with that," he said, having caught the tail end of our conversation. "Chaer-Ul is everywhere, at all times.

But when I first came here I found a place where it seems…well…just a bit easier to *hear*."

He led Reya and me across the top of the dam and off the other side, then off the road and down over the rocky cliffs that overlooked the river below. In the distance the smoke of still-burning fires rose over the treetops from the devastated city downstream. Our path took us along a narrow ledge where we were forced to inch along, hugging the cliffside for fear of plummeting to the jagged rocks and rushing currents below. Around a bend in this fashion, and then the path grew wider, and we had to cling to the trunk of a tree that had taken root in the meager topsoil here, swinging out over the chasm to get around it before regaining footing on the far side. As soon as I landed, I saw a cleft in the cliff face that had not been visible from the dam, or even from the other side of the tree. Kuro, landing after me, said, "That's your path."

"After you," I said thoughtfully.

" 'Fraid not," he replied. "The rest is up to you." And without releasing the tree trunk, he swung back around to the other side, where Reya waited to accompany him back to the dam. "We'll wait for you at the camp," he said, and I could hear them scuffling back along the narrow ledge. It seemed there was no arguing. I slipped into the shadowy cleft.

The crevice was pitch black and stifling, the scent of wet moss and mildew almost palpable in the stagnant air. A chill draft from deeper in the cleft told me that it was not a dead end, however, and I pushed forward. The way grew lighter, the air fresher, and I finally emerged onto another narrow ledge overlooking a scene that seemed to have been plucked from a surrealist painting. It was an enormous bowl the size of a football stadium, formed by high, arching cliffs on all sides. In its center was what appeared to be a massive, living sphere, covered with twisting vines of green

290

vegetation and hovering over a carpet of swirling clouds. A closer inspection revealed that it did in fact stand upon a slender pillar of stone, briefly visible between misty gusts, the rest of its support having been eroded away over millennia. What had seemed to be cloud was actually a dense mist caused by the roiling of underground springs that surfaced here briefly, the remnant of a much stronger current that had etched this wonder of stone. The globe, large as it was, stood directly in the center of the bowl, still some distance from any spot on the outer walls. But as there was scarcely space to stand on the ledge, I assumed that to be my intended destination.

Working my way along the ledge to my left, skirting the sphere, I came to a place where the ledge was notably wider, a stony extension jutting ever-so-slightly out over the abyss. Reaching that spot, I backed myself against the wall, then pushed off and performed the closest approximation of a running jump that I could manage with such a short runway. Luckily I didn't take the time to think about how I would get back, or I might have lost the nerve altogether. It was farther than it had seemed. As elongated microseconds passed, I thought I was going to fall short and plunge into the frigid cauldron below, but I managed to catch hold of a handful of vines on the underside of the sphere and arrest my descent. When my heart rate had returned to normal, I began to climb. The vines offered ample purchase, but it was still a formidable ascent; by the time I reached the top I was thoroughly spent. I bent, palms on my knees, panting, then stood and surveyed the view. I noted the location of the cleft from which I had emerged, of the springboard from which I had leapt. I couldn't see the mist from here. It felt as though I stood on top of a tiny world of my own making. But this was Chaer-Ul's world, I knew.

I pronounced his name, "*Chaer-Ul!*" Nothing happened. I tried again. "Chaer-Ul, I am here! Why don't you answer?"

291

After a moment's pause came the thunder, "You said nothing that required an answer." At the sound of his voice, a thousand hidden buds blossomed simultaneously into colorful bloom all over the surface of the sphere.

"I said your name," I countered.

"And it pleased me," he replied.

I was definitely not in the mood for his little games, but I dared not show my frustration; Maya's life was on the line. "How can I defeat Magus?" I asked.

"That's not what you want to know," he said.

He was right. "Can I save Maya?" I asked.

"Now that's more like it," he said. "*Yes*."

"*How?*" I asked, slightly irritated. "How can I save Maya?"

"What are you willing to do?"

"*Anything!*" I shouted. "I would do *anything* to save her!"

"Would you indeed? Even give your own life?"

"Without a second's hesitation," I said truthfully.

"So," he said. "And what about taking hers?"

"Of course I...uh...*what?*" I stammered, completely bewildered.

"If I asked it, would you let Maya die?" he clarified.

"How could I...why would you ask...*how could that possibly help her?*"

292

"You didn't ask how to help her," he rumbled calmly. "You asked how to *save* her."

"And that would save her - letting her *die?*" I asked in disbelief.

"I know what you are willing to do for *her*," Chaer-Ul said. "I seek to know what you would do for *me*."

"You can't ask that of me! This doesn't make any sense," I screamed.

"I see...so you wouldn't do it...if that were what I asked of you?"

"I can't...I don't see...," I mumbled.

"Would you let Maya die?" he asked once more.

"If that is the question...then...no. *No!* "

"I see. You're not yet ready," he said. Let's hope *her* faith is sufficient."

Then it was silent. Chaer-Ul was gone. And somehow I had the feeling that I had just failed the final test. I called out to him again, pleading for him to return, prepared to beg for Maya's life, as if I had anything with which to bargain. It was all in vain. No answer came. After a time I called out to Reya and Kuro as well, but I knew the sound would never reach their ears. Now I was trapped in this place, unable to even go after her, unable to fight, unable to do *anything*. I dropped to my knees, raised my hands, palms upward, and wept to the sky. Tears of frustration turned to tears of anger, at last to tears of despair.

A tepid breeze began to blow, softly at first, rising to become a temperate wind that buffeted my body, threatening to dislodge me from my lofty perch at the top of the world. The strangeness of shifting shadows before me compelled me to look to the heavens, where clouds were speeding across the sky as if in fast-forward. The wind persisted, howling and raging around the walls of the canyon, lifting the mist and carrying it up the sides of the bowl, around and around the globe like Saturn's rings. At last the wind began to push the sun itself, hurrying it toward its resting place beyond the westward mountains. Had I fallen asleep? Was I dreaming once more? Night's veil cast itself over the dome of the sky, as stars, scattered by an unseen sower, found their places in the firmament, burning more brightly than I could remember. I could see the light from those stars, and their beams curved toward me, becoming something almost tangible, like sinewy threads. I reached out to touch them, and the silken filaments of light danced on my fingertips before twisting together into two brilliant vortices, one suspended over each of my palms. Then, unexpectedly, the two points of light pierced my hands painlessly, their seemingly infinite wiry tails wiggling in the air until their entire substance disappeared beneath my skin.

Was this a vision? Instantly I felt my strength renewed, and something else: tracings of light spreading to define all the borders of my armor, my weapons becoming infused with it, saturated, so that they seemed almost to be made of only light. Then I felt a pervading warmth in my shoulders and back. A moment later the threads emerged there, bursting from the skin of my back, boring through my armor, and dividing again and again to form hundreds of fine, luminous tendrils that offered no resistance to touch, yet billowed and fluttered behind me as if moved by the wind. Turning my head, I saw these innumerable threads stretching out behind me almost to the rim of the great bowl. I watched as they allowed the wind to fill them, taking the form of a pair of vast, radiant wings. Before I could wonder why this was happening, a powerful gust caught the wings and carried me skyward. Fear found no place to dwell; I knew that these wings would carry me wherever I determined to go.

I stood high above the earth and surveyed the world below. By the light of a waxing moon I could see the dam and the place where it was damaged. Beyond that, the lake, and the diminutive shapes of tents along its shore. Through the trees I saw the hill where the chopper sat. And to the south and east, the still-smoldering and partially flooded city. I wasn't dreaming. I thought about landing in the clearing before the dam entrance, at the edge of the forest, and my wings took me there. As I landed, the wings folded themselves upon my back like a luminous cloak. There were few people outside when I set down, but these few rapidly swelled to a few dozen and more as excited whispers were exchanged and one person after another hastened away to wake a sleeping friend or loved one. Slowly the masses edged forward, those best known to me edging past the others to verify the reports. Kuro was first, all but shoving people aside to get to me, awe apparent on his well-lined face. Upon reaching me he dropped to his knees, head bowed low, and placed his weapon on the ground before me. Knox slipped in from behind him and did the same. Reya, smiling broadly, stepped forward and followed suit. Next came Jager, Kaire and Charr. Doog stepped from somewhere in the back and followed their example.

Then a hush fell over those gathered as Corvus strode up through the crowd. He stopped next to those bowed down and looked down at them, one by one. He made a small huffing sound that I took to be derision. Then he proceeded farther, walking right up to me. He paced in a slow circle around me, scrutinizing the places where light emanated from my armor, my weapons, and my wings. When he completed his circle he turned to face me, almost nose-to-nose. It was all I could do not to react, confronted so directly with his horribly scarred visage, that vacant, probing eye. He glared into my eyes for a long moment, then suddenly dropped to his knees, laying his sword at my feet. After Corvus paid homage, the entire assembled multitude did the same as one. No one moved or made a sound for what seemed an eternity. I began to wonder if I should say something, but as I thought over what I

295

might say, there came a soft, rustling sound from deep within the shadows of the forest.

One after another, puurr-deer emerged from the trees and took up positions around me until there were seven all told, forming a circle, their heads pointing inwardly. Then, as if in response to a silent signal, they all stretched out their front legs and bowed their heads low to the ground, eyes closed. The moment this action was completed my wings unfurled, arching high over the deer and men, showering them all with purest light. When this occurred, the deer began to change. At first it looked like a trick of shadows in the shimmering light, but soon it could not be denied. Their massive antlers grew smaller, many points merging into a few. A row of heavy scales started to appear on the upper surfaces of their snouts, cascading over the tops of their heads and all the way down their spines. When it reached their rumps, their thin tails swelled and grew into thick, muscular appendages that whipped about behind them in sinuous undulations. The scales completed their course, covering the upper part of the tails all the way to their tufted ends. The legs bulged with a thickening of muscle, fur overgrowing to form thick, wavy shocks over their hooves. The middle sets of legs then withdrew from the ground and folded back along their bodies, expanding and flattening to form the roots of what appeared to be vestigial wings. Their faces changed as well, subtly, as several pairs of oversized fangs overgrew the dimensions of their elongated mouths. Finally, and also simultaneously, they all appeared to be engulfed by tongues of blue-white flame, which circled their bodies constantly, licked off the tufts on their legs and tails, and ignited the wings, forming fiery plumage that moved and acted as real wings. A few characteristics remained very deer-like through the changes: the snowy-white fur evident under the scales and between the flames, their pointed hooves, and the knowing, liquid-gold orbs of their eyes.

296

When their transformation was complete, my own wings reassumed their tendrilly form, and individual threads stretched out over the heads of those gathered near. One of these alighted on Kuro's head, and without ever looking up or opening his eyes, he stood. Similarly, threads fell upon the heads of Charr, Jager, and Knox, who likewise stood. Lastly, a thread touched upon the head of Corvus, who joined those standing. These five, knowing without asking, opened their eyes and walked to five of the puurr-deer, or whatever it was they had become, and silently mounted them. When all of this was done I too mounted one of the creatures. When I did, Kuro asked me, "Who is to ride the other one?"

"I don't know," I said.

"Perhaps we should choose someone," Reya said from her place before the people.

"No," I said. "The choice is of Chaer-Ul." Then I spoke pointedly to Reya. "Assemble the army and be at the ready. I'll send you a sign."

"What happens now?" Charr asked.

"We're going to get Maya back," I said, "*And end this war once and for all!*" With that my mount launched itself into the sky on wings of flame, the others close behind. Far below, we could still hear the shouts and cheers of a few hundred people whose hopes now soared with us.

297

28

The first thing we saw, of course, was the tops of the ancient skyscrapers, outlined against the sky as they had been in the vision of Maya. But now in full daylight, having flown through the night, other features of the landscape made themselves known as well. Most striking was some sort of high wall or barrier that skirted the city in an arc several miles in diameter, presumably encircling it all around. Thankful for winged transport, I goaded my mount forward over the wall, and directed my companions to follow my lead. My beast displayed an uncharacteristic reluctance to obey, huffing and kicking at the air under its feet. We were all afraid, of course; why should it be any different with these creatures, who had seen the fate of some of their own kind at Magus' hand, and knew all too well the depths of cruelty that he was willing to plumb. I spurred my ride onward once more, and this time it complied, but with great uncertainty, head held low and twitching back and forth as it went. I stole a glance downward to confirm that we were almost directly over the wall now. Before I could right myself again I felt a clapping blow and my vision went suddenly black. I regained my senses only a second later, and as my eyes came to focus I could see a reflection of the city pulsing in liquid rhythm. My eyes cast about, seeking the true form that cast this wavering shadow. But it was no shadow. The air itself shimmered, giving evidence of a powerful magical field surrounding the city. I looked to my comrades, who hovered to the sides, having apparently seen my blunder in time to avoid a similar fate. I had been a fool to think Magus' defenses would be so readily thwarted.

I directed my mount to retreat to a safer distance, and began to study our situation. The height of the shield could not be known, and we could not risk a second trial – the first had nearly knocked me out. I examined the wall far below, turned to follow it toward the south. The other riders cautiously followed. After flying for

298

some distance an irregularity became visible, a possible breach in the wall's contour. As we came to a position more nearly above it, it was clear: there was a disruption of the wall in a place where another major highway led straight into the heart of the city. I signaled the others, and one by one we circled lower, until it could be seen that the opening was not barred. To my surprise there was no indication of any sort of guard or other defensive measures at or around the opening. It seemed as though this were the way Magus intended us to go – an open invitation. Fine. We'd play by his rules, for now.

I examined the area beyond the wall. Here all human structures had been reduced to rubble; a war-ravaged wasteland reminiscent of pictures I had seen of towns bombed during the second world war. Yet as far as the eye could see, nothing stirred. No dark armies marched, no treaded steel crawled over the pitted landscape. It occurred to me that the same magic that prevented our progress by air might also enchant the eyes, portraying a scene of desolation where in fact thousands of enemies lay in wait just beyond the wall. As far as I was concerned it mattered not; Maya was almost certainly inside those walls, and I was prepared to lay waste to Magus' thousands of thousands if need be to reach her. My weapons and armor glowed with untold power, imbuing me with certainty that I could manage whatever Magus had in store.

I signaled the others to follow my lead, and began a slow, gliding descent, finally landing a few hundred paces before the opening. The riderless creature fell in behind the others. We remained on our mounts, prodding them into a measured trot until we stood in the shadow of the great barrier wall. Now I could see the substance of the wall, and a chill seized me. It was composed of human remains. Not simply piled, but actually built, using some sort of mortar. I could see also that several large placards had been placed among the bodies, clearly meant to be viewed by the visitor, written in letters of no language I had ever seen. Corvus was beside me. "Can you understand it?" I asked him.

Corvus stared at the writing for a moment, then grunted, a sound that indicated revulsion at the content of the message. "Yes," he said. "Essentially, it translates, 'Behold the handiwork of god'."

Looking again, I saw that not all of the remains were skeletal. More recent dead were fitted in among them, and composed a sizeable portion of the wall's substance. "These aren't only those killed by the plague," I said. "Some of these were killed subsequently by Magus' men."

"I know," said Corvus. "Magus places responsibility for these deaths at Chaer-Ul's feet as well."

"Magus decided to butcher thousands more than those already claimed by the plague," I said. "How is that Chaer-Ul's fault?"

Charr answered. "He tells his people they are acting pre-emptively, that Chaer-Ul is amassing armies to exterminate those who would be free of his dominion. It's a message that tickles the ears of those who are already looking for a reason to fight."

"Do you think he actually believes that," I asked, "Or is it just what he tells his men to gain their obedience?"

Charr shook her head. "I don't really know. His mind is twisted, having given it over to the control of those...*beings*. I suppose it's possible he believes his own lies as well as theirs."

We pushed forward, passing between the foul walls of death that towered over us on either side. I half-expected them to crumble and come down on us in a horrific avalanche, revealing living soldiers hidden within. But no such thing happened. We traversed the plain of rubble, and still no attack came. Every so often we came to another sign, stuck in the ground beside the road or lashed to a rusty billboard from times forgotten. Often they were

300

decorated with more corpses, grimly posed or dangling from frayed and knotted cords. Corvus would translate. One said, "Who thinks for you?" Another read, "Let the wise man consider: god had a beginning." And a little farther along, "Every beginning has an end." Kuro groaned. We passed another sign reading, "God destroyed the world in seven days." And a short distance later, "Let us create it anew." Then we walked for a time without seeing any signs. When at last something came into view, it was a banner spread over the road we traveled, lynched cadavers hanging at regular intervals so that their gnarled toes tried to scrape our heads as we passed underneath. The banner read, "Are we not gods?"

A long time passed without further incident. At last we came to an intersection of roads. In its center was a roundabout, encircling a small, overgrown patch of turf. Rising out of the tangled mass of vines and saplings a statue had been erected. It appeared to be of recent design, though the stone pedestal upon which it stood may well have been original. The figure was roughly made, but clearly represented a cloaked person holding his hands aloft. There was a worn plaque at its feet. Knox approached the statue, bent and blew on the plaque to clear the dust that obscured its message. As he did, red flames burst from the palms of the figure, burning high into the sky before settling back to the height of a torch flame above each hand. The sudden conflagration sent Knox stumbling back, almost falling over the undergrowth at the base of the pedestal. Upon regaining his composure, he pointed to the plaque, where letters now glowed in the same fiery red. Magic, as it turned out, not natural fire. Corvus was already pushing past him to read aloud, "In this place, what you may become is limited only by you."

"Wow," I said, "He really went all out with the propaganda campaign."

"It's interesting…," mused Jager, "…that despite this promise of infinite potential, Magus seems to be the only one who has become more than a foot soldier."

"And the only one wielding god-like power," I added.

"Magus has grown unspeakably arrogant," Charr said. "He sees Chaer-Ul as a usurper and a fraud. That's because he assumes him to be the same kind of being as his dark whisperers, different only in that he was able to attain a greater degree of power. He believes…that Chaer-Ul was once a man."

"A man…," I repeated distractedly. Then, "The spirits that Magus speaks to – they were once men?" I asked.

"We think so," she replied. "But we believe Chaer-Ul is something else entirely. Both Magus and I begin with the same facts about Chaer-Ul. The difference lies in how we choose to interpret those facts."

"But how can you be sure your interpretation is correct?" I asked. "How do you know Chaer-Ul isn't just letting you see what he wants you to see, and deliberately concealing the rest?"

"Oh, I am certain he is," Charr answered. "And is that any different from what you do? What we all must do? How much do you ever *really* know someone, or let someone know you? What Chaer-Ul has allowed me to see is good; I choose to believe that for the most part that which remains hidden resembles the part I've seen."

The discussion intrigued me, and I'd have liked to pursue it further, but something else was starting to concern me. We had now traveled well beyond the statue and deep into the wasteland that stood between us and the city. Yet strangely, it didn't appear as though we had gotten any closer to the city itself. I looked

302

back, and the statue was barely visible as a tiny peg on the horizon. The wall of corpses could no longer be seen. Clearly we had covered a lot of ground, yet the skyline hadn't changed. Was it an optical illusion? I was struck with a sudden sense of unease. I put out my hand to stay the others, and my wings resumed their form. I didn't want to expose my mount to danger, in case there were another shield, or other unseen threat. Slowly I rose until I was high above the ground, then cautiously advanced. From this height I could see both the wall far behind and the concentration of towering buildings ahead. It was true; we had come a long way, but were not ostensibly closer to our goal. I glided onward, and as if by instinct several glowing tendrils separated from my wings and probed ahead of me, feeling for invisible hazards as I flew. Still seeing no change in the scene before me, I flew faster, accelerating until I was a virtual blur, a luminous comet streaking across the sky. My peripheral vision told me that aspects of the landscape were peeling away behind me, but when I stole a glance at the earth directly below, I was shocked to see my team, sitting in place upon their mounts, exactly where I had left them. This was no mirage; it was more of Magus' sorcery. I allowed myself to descend, alighting upon my mount once more.

Immediately I turned about to face my comrades, who had witnessed my unsuccessful attempt. "We're going to need another strategy," I said.

"What did you have in mind?" Jager asked.

"Well," I said, "If *I* couldn't get anywhere flying, I doubt we'd have any better luck on the deer. Is it deer? I don't really know what else to call them, now that they've changed."

"*Kirin*," said Kuro. "They're kirin."

"You've seen them like this before?" I asked, surprised.

303

"No, but there were old stories and songs that spoke of them," he said

"Oh...OK...*kirin*," I said. "In any case, we can't proceed by air, or by land. We couldn't get past the shield before either, until we figured out where Magus wanted us to go. He holds all the cards right now, so it seems we're just going to have to wait until he plays his next hand."

"I don't like it," said Corvus, an edge of panic in his voice that I hadn't heard before. "We're just walking into his web. We may as well have just waited for him to come back and wipe us all out at the dam."

"I know it looks that way," I said, "and I'm sure Magus thinks he is in control, but he's not." Corvus looked skeptical. The others shared his expression. "You have to trust me. No matter how bad it gets, we must persevere. I don't know how we're going to do it, but Magus is going down. *This ends today!*" The words didn't sound like my own, and then I realized they weren't – they were the last words of Tal-Makai. I shook off a chill at the thought. I really hoped I knew what I was doing.

Kuro started to speak, and I held up a hand to silence him. "Did you feel that?" I asked.

"Feel wha-," Knox started, but then we were all shaken by a violent rumbling. It passed, and then it came again, stronger. Were we not all seated on such massively stable beasts, we'd have been thrown to the ground. And it was a good thing we weren't, for soon small fissures began to appear in the earth at our feet, and then to spread, outward in every direction across the plain. As the shaking continued the cracks raced toward the periphery of the barren landscape, then grew wider. Now trails of black smoke issued from between them, first in a few places, and then more, and more, until the entire expanse of the plain was punctuated by

304

thousands of wavering columns of smoke like blades of scorched grass.

"*What is this?*" Jager demanded. The others were silent, eyes nervously darting this way and that as new tails of smoke appeared, wiggling into the few remaining spaces of cracked earth.

"*Ready yourselves,*" I said. One by one, the pillars of smoke slowly congealed into something more solid, as the fearfully familiar forms of black-armored soldiers set solid feet on the crumbling ground where the smoke had so recently emerged. First there were a few, and then more, and more, and more, like a deadly wave washing over the plain in a vast, sweeping arc, until thousands upon thousands stood around us on every side, plates of dark armor glistening with every subtle movement in the hazy midday sunlight, a shimmering sea of dark water. Then came a sound that would have instilled fear in the heart of the most dauntless warrior: the near-simultaneous unsheathing of thousands of deadly blades. I turned to issue a command, but found no words. Then, from somewhere amidst those swarming masses, the sound of a battle horn. The sea swelled, its tsunami waves inexorably encroaching upon our tiny island of calm, threatening to engulf it. Magus' army was charging.

29

This was my moment. We were but six in number, but one look at the fantastic beasts we rode, the pulsating glow of my armor, of my weapons, and I knew - numbers were not a factor here. Holding my staff high I shouted, "Follow me!" and rode out in a scything path that paralleled the ever-narrowing circle of the enemy's front line. I felt a surge of panic at the sight of that strangulating ring of death, the closing maw of a vast, undulating black beast, bristling with row upon row of razor-edged fangs. My response was instinctive; a primal cry that rang with authority and demanded obeisance, *"Back!"* The word shook the foundations of the earth and rebounded off the distant mountain peaks. The first few concentric rings of enemy combatants were blasted outward with an unseen shockwave that lifted them from their feet and tossed them limply into the bodies and onto the blades of their fellow men. The impact created a limited domino effect as the next dozen or more rows were staggered by the unexpected backlash. The result, while amusing, was quickly over as those that remained standing wasted no time clambering over their fallen friends and resuming the attack.

My mount stepped nimbly over the bodies and advanced to meet the new front line, pausing occasionally to deliver a killing blow with a sharply aimed hoof to the head of any of the fallen who attempted to rise. In its wake its thick tail whipped about viciously, taking down more with each pass. A glance to the rear showed me that the other creatures were following a similar pattern, including the unmanned beast. As we neared the leading edge of charging soldiers, I turned my mount sharply, bringing my bladed staff to bear on the dark army. Swinging my staff in a sweeping arc, I hoped to intimidate those leading the charge and quell their advance, if only for a moment. Instead, a blade of light extended from my weapon's edge and sliced deep into the ranks of dark warriors. Where it passed, heads were loosed from bodies, weapons cleft in two, limbs and bodies rent asunder. In all, fully two hundred men fell in that single slash. I eyed my gleaming blade with awe, glanced back at my companions, and smiled. Then I turned my attention to the next wave, rushing no less enthusiastically than their unfortunate peers to meet the tip of my staff.

Slash! Another hundred or so fell. Slash! A few dozen more. Now the beasts had an easier task finding those that needed finishing. I lifted my staff high over my head and brought it down with a chopping motion, its tip coming to rest low to the ground before me. Slash! A road appeared between rows of enemy soldiers, a path of bodies between dark waves as enemies were tossed to each side and piled high. My mount acted quickly, using the path as a runway of sorts, accelerating to its end and then leaping and soaring, landing in the midst of a fresh batch of troops. It landed with such force that its wings flared suddenly, a halo of real flame scorching outward with the heat of a blast furnace, roasting scores of Magus' men. As the smoke and the shimmering heat in the air began to clear, I lifted my eyes to survey the battlefield.

Still they came. Gathering courage, I tore into them anew. Slash! Another hundred or two. Slash! Slash! A few hundred more. When I was able, I turned to see how my comrades fared. They were scattered across the battlefield, each engaged in similar skirmishes, though without the aid of supernaturally-enhanced weaponry, of course. Corvus' beast was particularly aggressive, as if drawing something of its nature from the disposition of its rider. It snapped up men by threes and fours in its powerful jaws, crushing them until their armor buckled and snapped, their lifeblood dribbling down its chin and staining its breast. Meanwhile Corvus dispatched enemies individually with well-placed thrusts of his sword between the plates of their armor. Knox's mount preferred to charge headlong into groups of soldiers, barreling them over and leaving them for his rider to finish. Knox would frequently dismount, savoring the fairness of a face-to-face battle, until after defeating a few more foes his creature would nudge him with its vaguely deer-like snout, urging him to return to his place on its back. Charr's did more with its feet, repeatedly taking to the air and coming down with deadly scissoring kicks. Charr seized these moments of elevation to launch volleys of crossbow bolts into the ranks of enemy combatants. Kuro's beast used its wings of flame, spreading its fiery cloak over a group of men until they were gasping and smoldering, then moving on to find an as yet unburned spot. Jager's mount appeared more stoic, more deliberate, assaying the field to locate individuals among the swarming masses who appeared to possess leadership qualities, then soaring in for a decisive kill, leaving the surrounding men notably disheartened and confused. Jager would then cut these stragglers down in their stupor before they could think to reorganize.

It was fascinating to watch, but I couldn't afford to linger; the dark army came on, wave after ruthless wave. Slash! I cut another swath through the sea. Slash! Slash! Perhaps three hundred fell. On and on we fought, and every so often, when the soldiers would seem about to overwhelm us, I would shout again, *"Back!"* Many would fall, the area would be clear once more, and I would take up the fight anew. Slash! Slash! Slash! Thousands lay dead around us. It would have felt effortless if it wasn't so much work. I was starting to fatigue from the sheer monotony of it. Apparently my divine gifts offered no defense against exhaustion. I realized my team must be feeling it as well, so I decided to gain a better perspective on the situation. Kuro was nearby, doing battle with a group of enemy soldiers, so I addressed him, shouting over the noise. "I'm going up," I said. "Can you hold them for a minute?"

"We'll find out!" he said. I directed my mount to ascend, rising with great beats of its fiery wings in wide circles over the battle below. The shiny black armor of so many moving soldiers gave

308

the impression of countless cockroaches scurrying for cover under the sudden insult of a nocturnal light switch. But these insects inspired far greater terror, as they rushed toward the light, not away. I rose higher, scanning the distant plain in search of an end, a slice of untouched sand beyond this sea of chaos, but I searched in vain. There was no end, no finitude to the dark and storming masses, no glimmer of hope that with perseverance we might prevail. And that was not all.

I detected a stirring, a different sort of motion within the steady push of the endless masses. Here and there, quicker forms wove their way inward through the thickness of armored bodies, determinedly converging upon a single, central point: us. They moved with a swiftness and lightness that left little doubt as to their identity – assassins. And farther out, at a distance of perhaps a mile, larger shapes were moving among the greater swarm. I wasn't able to identify them at first, so I goaded my mount to glide to a position more nearly over them, and then it was clear. Not a few, but a hundred or more riders mounted on armor-cats. They were not the only representatives of the animal kingdom, either. Beyond them, lesser in number but an imposing force just the same, several dozen puur-deer. They, like the cats, bore the mechanical accoutrements and glowing orange lights of Magus' diabolical control. They lurched awkwardly forward, evidence of the mutilation of their natural forms to accommodate the biomechanical abominations. And there was something else.

So focused was I on the movement of troops on the ground that it was some time before I became aware of a darkening cloud rising in the distance, out of the ruined city. An entire fleet of dirigibles, drifting effortlessly over the battlefield and casting a dark shadow on the troops below. And from somewhere in their midst, the angular shapes of powered gliders appeared, assumed a multi-tiered V-formation, and preceded the balloons toward our position. I shook off a growing sensation of numbness and retrieved my dangling jaw in time to realize that the six of us

309

would not stand long against so great, and so diverse a force. We needed help.

Returning to the ground, I bellowed at the top of my lungs, *"Get back!"* and an invisible shockwave blasted the nearest soldiers back with such force that those on the leading edge were instantly killed, several more rows lifted high into the air and tossed like ragdolls deep into the ranks of their comrades, leaving a broad disc of earth untrodden between them and us. My riders were unaffected, and I quickly called them to gather at the center of the clearing. "We need reinforcements," I said. "It's time to call for Reya and the armies of the dam."

"What do you mean?" asked Jager. "They couldn't possibly get here in time to be of any assistance. We'll be overrun."

"He's right," Kuro echoed. "We're scarcely making a dent. Our only option is to retreat, and hope the way out of the city isn't barred. Then we can regroup outside the walls, and come up with a different strategy."

"Your powers are great," Charr added, "But there's just too many. We can't take them all at once. Maybe if we can funnel them through a natural bottleneck, like a valley, and take them down a few at a time."

"No!" The unexpected cry came from Corvus. All eyes turned to him. "Martyr will lead us, be it to victory or to death. It has been written. *Hear his voice!*"

I think we were all a little shocked, but no one offered further counsel, waiting instead for my next move.

"Gather the kirin here," I said. "Form a circle." The response was not immediate. "Now!" I shouted, "There isn't time to delay!" This got their attention, and they soon formed a tight circle. "No,

310

it needs to be wider," I said. The circle expanded, and I took my place as well, all seven beasts facing inwardly. "Now...show me Reya," I said to my mount. A sphere materialized in the center of our circle, and within it could be seen Reya, mounted on a puurr-deer and fully armed. Behind her we could see row upon row of her resistance army, standing at the ready. No two wore the same armor, and many had none, but almost all were exceptionally well-armed, thanks to Kuro's weapons stockpiles at the dam. I addressed the image of Reya. "Reya, are you ready?"

"She can't hear you," Kuro said, suppressing a chuckle despite the dire nature of our circumstances. "Their powers only produce an image. Sending a verbal message takes far..."

"We're ready!" came Reya's answer. Kuro nearly fell from his mount, the others looking equally amazed. When he recovered, he did laugh, not in mockery, but delight, a hearty sound that came from the gut. For a second, we almost forgot that Magus' dark army was rapidly closing in on our cozy circle of wonder.

I directed my mount to side-step until I was alongside Knox, creating a small gap in the circle, then I spoke clearly, "*Come through.*" All eyes turned to me, then slowly back to the sphere. No one spoke a word. A moment later, Reya's mount stepped out of the sphere, placing its feet tentatively upon the ground before us. Reya smiled warmly and offered a hasty greeting, then passed outside of our ring and turned to the side, taking stock of the battlefield. One after another her men followed, some on deer, most on foot. They came at first hesitantly, one at a time, but soon four and five were leaping out of the sphere at a time, taking up place with Reya outside of the circle.

As they continued to pour from the sphere, Reya, veteran warrior that she was, immediately started issuing commands to her troops, needing no direction from me. They fanned out to confront the advancing troops, forming small, delta-shaped legions flanked by

311

deer-mounted cavalry. These met the enemy lines at speed, staggering them and pushing them back several paces before reaching a sort of equilibrium where blade met enemy blade. After that, it began to get a bit messy, but the resistance fighters, still fresh to the battle, held a decisive advantage. Reya had prepared them exceedingly well in the little time they had had, and their tactics were markedly superior to the "mindless rush" strategy of the enemy.

As the last of Reya's troops emerged, the sphere dissolved, and I quickly rode up to her position near the front line. It took me a moment to catch up to her, as she was continuously racing along the rear guard of her battalion, shouting orders and modifying their tactics on-the-fly as the situation changed. When I reached her, I immediately informed her about the assassins I had seen. With a nod she began to address individuals within each of her legions who were specially skilled to meet this threat, instructing them to identify these particularly dangerous foes and intercept them before they could reach the rest of her soldiers. I watched as these men pulled back slightly from their current positions and began to scan the field before them. I saw one of these men locate an assassin, wait until he was only a few rows away, then signal his allies, who crouched to form a sort of human ramp. The man gained a running start and launched himself from their backs, soaring over the bristling tips of enemy weapons that jabbed at his passing in vain. He landed square in front of the assassin, delivering a jarring blow that halted his advance and staggered him briefly. Then ensued a display of exquisite swordsmanship from both warriors, who seemed about equally matched. The sea of dark soldiers surged past them undeterred, too single-minded or too respectful of the assassin's skill to interfere. This basic strategy was followed in the other legions as well, each time an assassin was identified. As needed I lent the aid of my field-leveling slash with more than the usual precision to create a path of retreat for one of Reya's warriors who had just defeated one of these deadly foes.

Now Jager joined my side. "And what would you have us do?" he asked. "Business as usual?"

"No," I said. "They're using beasts as well. Armor-cats and puurr-deer. They're too fast and too powerful for the regular troops to handle. I suggest we dismount here and let the kirin have a go at the cats. As strong as those things are, they're no match for our mounts in their present form. I'll take care of the puurr-deer myself." I spoke now to my mount. "Locate the armor-cats, and deal with their riders first. If possible, destroy only the machinery that controls them. Then they'll flee the battlefield of their own accord." I paused. "Failing this, kill them," I said at last. The creature bowed its terrible head, the golden orbs of its eyes registering understanding. It barked something to the others of its kind, who then quickly gathered near. The kirin waited for all of the riders to dismount, then all as one bellowed a chilling cry that must have meant "charge!", before barreling in various directions between Reya's legions and into the front lines of enemy troops. As they reached the dark masses they spread their wings and held them low to the ground, sweeping sheets of flame over the heads of row after row of dark soldiers. Those fortunate enough to escape the trampling hooves of the massive creatures were instantly incinerated under this suffocating cover.

Once the beasts were about their business, I said, "Kuro, you're in charge." Wordlessly he nodded. I had no cause to doubt the ability of these few, with or without their mounts. Then my own wings burst forth, and I rose high into the air, seeking the unmistakable pristine whiteness of the puurr-deer in the midst of all that black. Spotting one of the animals ambling through the sea of bodies, head held low, I tucked my wings and dove. The deer were riderless, and I suspected the reason - as in the vision of Tal-Makai's last battle, they were programmed for self-destruction. That meant two things. First, that since these machines were as much magical as mechanical, Magus couldn't be far off, must be overseeing their advance even now. And second, that they absolutely had to be stopped before they reached Reya's men, or mine. I had seen the destructive swath that one of these beasts, so equipped, could carve through human troops, and didn't fancy watching it happen to those under my watch.

I swooped in low, spreading my wings to brake at the last moment and alighting gently upon the creature's back. It scarcely seemed to notice the added weight, so encumbered was it already with the heft of metal machinations. I busied myself about the task of cutting the contraption free, well aware of the possible inclusion of a self-destruct that could be triggered by an attempted sabotage. To my mind it was a measured risk, given that I could almost certainly withstand any resultant blast, and my men just as surely could not. I managed at last to slide the blade of my staff under the straps that secured the device, and a quick slice later it fell harmlessly to the ground, as the grateful beast lowed its relief. One down, a whole bunch more to go. I instructed the free deer to make for the safety of the circle of ground currently held by Reya's men, certain that no forested land remained within the greater circle of the city's surrounding death-wall.

I took to the air again, located the nearest deer, and accelerated toward it, skimming just over the points of enemy weapons that could not respond quickly enough to my unexpected appearance. I hadn't cleared half the distance from the first deer to the second when I became aware of a shrill noise, rapidly growing in both pitch and intensity. Suddenly the orange lights on the sides of the deer flared fire-bright. An instant later a flash of light appeared over its head, bursting blindingly outward from within its many-pointed rack, and a cone of complete devastation spread before it, instantly killing all within its scope. Almost simultaneously a similar effect could be observed at various points across the battlefield, dropping nearly a quarter of the visible troops in a matter of seconds. Subsequently the deer also expired and fell, a mournful groan escaping their throats as they dropped. It was a

314

vulgar sight – the destruction of these gentle and possibly sacred beasts for no apparent purpose. Clearly Magus had seen what I was trying to do and had opted for the pointless deaths of not only these poor creatures, but of hundreds of his own men as well, over allowing me to set them free. What vile hatred, what absolute disdain for the value of so many lives, innocent or otherwise. I felt nauseous. Then a sickly familiar, ratcheting chuckle echoed across the battlefield, seemingly emanating from every direction at once. The very sound seemed to cast a dark shadow over the whole earth.

No, it wasn't the sound, it *was* a shadow; the very real shadow of the airships closing fast on my position and threatening to blot out the sky with their dark, unnatural forms. The gliding wings swooped and soared around and before the slower-moving dirigibles. All of them, no doubt, would be armed to the teeth with explosive payloads, even as they had been at the dam. As the sound of profane laughter faded away, it was replaced by the droning buzz of the motorized gliders, the swarming of angry wasps whose hive has been disturbed. Beating my luminous wings, I sped to intercept the first wave of these winged terrors. As I approached the first it banked sharply to the side, employing evasive maneuvers. Behind it, several more followed suit, peeling away to my left and right like two heads of a colossal hydra. In their wake the next wave was already ascending, trying to gain a height from which they could shower me with incendiary cocktails. They expected me to rise with them, competing for elevation. Instead I dove, rocketing behind them and all the subsequent waves of gliders. Then I shot up between the dirigibles that hovered behind them, spiraling up and over the gliders from behind. Now I chose a target at the head of their formation, tucked my wings and dove at it with the speed of a fighter jet. I tore through one silken wing of the glider, sending it spinning wildly toward the unforgiving earth. Pulling up, I took aim at a second bird, barreling into its wing support, which snapped like a

315

twig with the force of my impact. This one joined his fellow on the ground below.

A couple of the kirin, having dealt satisfactorily with the armor-cat threat, now joined me in this effort, apparently finding it quite good sport. One of them made a game of setting their wings ablaze with a touch of its own flaming appendages. The other preferred to drop its full weight on a glider from above, taking teasing snaps at its pilot as it forced the vehicle into an unrecoverable spin before pushing off to find its next playmate. I continued to do my part, slowly thinning the swarm. All the while its leading edge advanced inexorably toward a position over the place where my people waged war. The two kirin and I had polished off a dozen or more of the gliders, when suddenly I heard one of the creatures scream. I looked to see it fleetingly bathed in a reddish light, the beam of which originated from the undercarriage of one of the dirigibles. The kirin flew to a higher position, but the beam was redirected and fell upon it once more. Again it screamed, then turned and flew back in the direction of our army. I could see the crimson ray passing across the wings of gliders and the bulky forms of other airships, seeking the second beast. These vehicles and their riders seemed to suffer no ill at the beam's passing. I called to the remaining kirin telepathically, ordering it to retreat, which it did without question. I was about to target the source of that red light when all at once countless angular shapes dropped from beneath a number of the dirigibles - reinforcements in the from of about a hundred more gliding wings. These spread out quickly, blackening the sky like hungry bats at the appearance of night's first star. As I hung in the air for just a moment, pondering my options, a new sound reached my ears.

It was the rhythmic chop-chop-chop of a helicopter's rotor – Doog was here! I turned to look, just as he was coasting in for a landing in the clearing where the resistance fought valiantly against the endless surge of dark soldiers. As the chopper was about to touch down it turned, revealing what looked to be a massive-caliber Gatling cannon poking from its fuselage. I watched as Corvus ran and jumped into the open door on the chopper's side, taking up the gunner's position. Doog took the chopper up as soon as Corvus was aboard and settled into a hover opposite the approaching storm front of black airships. As I watched, the tail of the vehicle swung about, bringing Corvus' sights to bear on the enemy. With a mechanical whirr the cannon spun, unleashing a torrent of projectiles into the cluster of dark forms. The bullets rent the fabric of the dirigibles, tearing it to shreds and sending the airships plummeting toward the earth one after another, trailing ragged strips of sooty cloth. The gliders took evasive action, banking and diving every which way in an effort to escape the barrage of hot lead that sought them. But Corvus had unnatural sight in that one good eye, and having singled out a target, he would track the ill-fated glider through its loops and whirls, behind airships and against the sun's glare, before finally perforating its exposed rider with a fatal load of tiny missiles. One after another they went down, the sky offering no cover from the burning hail.

When at last the great fleet of airships was reduced to a small and scattered few, they began to slowly turn about, hoping to make a retreat. Corvus and Doog had other plans, and took up chase. At that moment a sonic shriek emanated from the distant city, and a crimson blade of light lanced into the sky from somewhere amidst its hulking buildings. The beam pointed toward the heavens for only a second, then sliced downward toward our position, splitting the sky in two. It passed through the cluster of fleeing airships, and cleanly sliced off the tip of the chopper's tail before slamming into the ground, crushing all who were unfortunate enough to be in its path. The metal bird went into an uncontrolled spin, as debris from the shattered airships rained down on those surviving soldiers below who had ceased their warring long enough to take in the sight. The helicopter banked sharply toward the earth as Doog struggled to regain balance. At last I saw it disappear into

317

the shade of some medium-sized structures on the city's south side. There was no tell-tale explosion, but after a tense moment I thought I could see a wisp of black smoke ascending from the place where it had gone down. To my surprise the dark army did not resume the struggle, but dropped to their knees as one, faces pressed to the dust in anticipation of what was to come.

The beam of red light had disappeared as soon as it completed its destructive slash, but now it reappeared , tracing the shape of a cone over the center of the city. It disappeared again. Then I heard another sound. It was sort of a hollow whistling, and I quickly ascertained that its source was a brisk wind that had begun suddenly and was now whipping across the plain and over the armor and swords of so many genuflected legions of soldiers. The wind blew with such force that the crouching enemy combatants could be seen to sway subtly as they struggled to hold their ground against its buffeting blows. Then, in the distance, a dark cyclone descended out of a cloudless sky and touched down in the midst of the city. It proceeded to bore into the ruined metropolis, carving out a goliath slab of stone and steel the size of a small mountain. This it lifted as if it had no weight, and as this unnatural island rose over the tops of the tallest buildings several monolithic skyscrapers collapsed inward upon each other amidst billowing clouds of dust. The vortex carried its load to a point just a few hundred paces short of our position, and deposited it unceremoniously on the heads of a few hundred enemy warriors, crushing them instantly. As we continued to stare on in abject horror, the funnel narrowed, focusing itself on a point atop the newly-formed plateau. Then the winds slowed, and the twisting vortex thinned itself, until all that remained was a halo of dark, wispy cloud, perpetually swirling around a single locus. At its center, seated on a concrete throne, sat the cloaked figure of Magus. Monumental steel beams, the twisted remains of fallen buildings, arched high over the throne on either side like the ribs of a massive, long dead beast. Before the throne, the prostrate form of a concrete giant – headless, handless – betrayed the

318

throne's original purpose: a monument to someone once deemed worthy of honor. A broader ring of the swirling halo enclosed two other figures, one on either side of the enthroned sorcerer, each slight by contrast. The figure on the left was Mana; on the right, still clad in her pearl-white armor, stood Maya.

30

"Maaar-tyrrrr..." The word reverberated unnaturally across the plain, a mocking, guttural moan that was barely spoken, but clearly heard from any point on the battlefield. A disembodied voice; there could be no doubt as to its origin.

"Magus!" I shouted, immediately disappointed with the anemic timbre of my own voice. I wondered if he had even heard me from where he sat. *"This ends now!"* I added, hoping to preempt his next jeering taunt, and perhaps to embolden my people, now face-to-face at last with the embodiment of all their fears, the mass murderer of their friends and loved ones.

"Well said...," the voice hissed, a near-whisper that bristled the hairs on the back of my neck. I tensed and crouched, poised to spread my wings and launch myself toward his position. As I bent, the fingertips of one hand pressed into the dust at my feet, I became aware of a reddish glow that had fallen across the wasted landscape. I looked up. At first it appeared as though the moon itself had taken on a crimson hue. But soon I realized that the light emanated from beyond the moon, as though the moon had just eclipsed a red sun that had somehow passed unnoticed until just now. The glow intensified on one side, carving a scarlet crescent around the moon's left side that gradually grew in brightness until at last a brilliant red fireball burst into view, streaking around the moon and burning a path toward the earth. It was soon clear that this was no random cosmological event, as the comet turned to describe an arc that would bring it certainly and most painfully to bear upon our exact location. The distasteful sound of wheezing laughter filled my ears. As the meteoroid blazed closer still its scale could be better comprehended, and it dawned on me that a projectile of this size would unquestionably extinguish all life within a very broad radius, erasing every trace of the resistance in a single act and leaving only a vast, smoldering

crater. I waited. The brightness was unbearable, and as I squeezed my eyes tightly shut against it I could still see only red, flaring as if to burn my eyes out of their sockets. Still I waited. The sweat poured down my face and drenched my clothes under my armor. I heard voices crying out in desperation and fear, "Chaer-Ul, have mercy!" I waited…a little bit longer…until the heat flared with such intensity that I was sure the hair on my head would ignite and my skin blister and peel. Then I focused my thoughts, and in reality, as in my mind's eye, the luminous threads erupted with explosive force from beneath the skin of my back, burst through my armor, and spread like a fountain of light, not just over me, but over all those under my protection, the entire resistance army. The strands formed a dome of light so complete that the heat of the fireball immediately dissipated under its shielding glow. Then, punctuated by the sound of a few hundred hastily indrawn breaths, the comet struck.

The earth underneath our feet shifted with such violent force that many of my comrades lost their footing and fell. Thankfully, my already crouched posture lent me greater stability and I was able to maintain the protective umbrella. Outside of its sheltering embrace, however, was chaos. At first all was brilliant red, as the meteorite dispensed its considerable payload of energy against my luminous shield in a single all-consuming blast, revealing its essence to consist of heat and light; there appeared to be no fragmentation of solid matter at the point of impact. That is not to say that it carried no force, however, as immediately following the flash of light the earth's crust buckled and cracked around us with a terrible shaking. The slab of rock under my guardian dome remained intact, a single monolithic disc heaving and crashing like a storm-tossed ship against the monumental plates of charred and fractured earth all around.

After several long moments the shaking stopped, and our vessel appeared to have reached a sort of stasis in the midst of the jagged and alien new landscape. The dust began to settle, and through the haze I was not surprised to see the silhouette of Magus' throne reappear, the ruined beams arching over him like great clawed fingers. I was also relieved to see that Maya and Mana still stood unharmed, albeit within his serpentine grasp. The sorcerer's rasping cackle filled the air once more. "I didn't expect to be rid of you so easily," he said. "Even the armor-cat likes to toy with its victim before *snapping its neck.*" The laughter resumed, joined by the snickers of his surviving soldiers, apparently untouched by the magical projectile, still bowed stupidly to the ground by the hundreds on their disparate slabs of tilting crust. "Truthfully," he continued as the chuckles abated, "I was curious to see whether your *benefactor* would step in personally to defend you. I can't say that I'm surprised he's sitting this one out...it seems even *he* is beginning to understand who holds the cards now." His self-confidence was unsettling. Could it be that he had actually managed to acquire power rivaling that of Chaer-Ul? True, I had managed to withstand his first strike...but I was not at all sure that I could return in kind. I certainly didn't know how to summon cosmic fireballs to smite my enemies. And even if I could I might be placing Maya and Mana at risk by attacking directly. I knew I had to figure out a way to beat Magus at his own game, but before I did, I had to figure out the rules. Luckily, he didn't leave me guessing for long. With an air of boredom mingled with impatience he muttered, "*God,* am I going to have to walk you through this?" He sighed deeply, then with a lilting, almost playful tone, he said, "This is the part where you are supposed to charge heroically up to me, rent me in twain with your magical god-sword, and rescue your two lovely lady-friends so the three of you can resume your uncomfortable love triangle. Meanwhile all of my followers, disillusioned by my unexpected demise, will join your noble cause or peacefully disperse to resume foraging the wasteland for edible scraps."

"Barring a couple of odd details, it sounds like a pretty good plan," I said. "But I'm guessing you want to tell me why it won't work."

323

"Smart boy…," he said. "Chaer-Ul really knows how to pick 'em. Hear me out; it will save a lot of unnecessary humiliation and bloodshed, not that I'm particularly averse to either. You see, I actually hope to *liberate* you. You've been led to believe certain things, and some of those things are…well…they're just…*not*…*true*."

"Don't listen to him!" The shout came from behind me, to my left. I turned to see Reya, a pleading look on her face. "He tries to poison your mind, he knows only lies – slit his throat before he can say another word!"

"Ah, yes, sweet Reya," Magus said calmly, addressing only me. "Her devotion to a heartless god cost her the life of her true love…and of countless others besides. She sees in you a second chance, and would repeat her mistake rather than learn from the past. She would have me silenced, but let me ask you this: is that truth which can only exist in the absence of opposing voices?"

"You should ask yourself the same question," came the accusing voice of Kuro. "You who slaughter all who oppose you!"

Magus was not riled. "Kuro, the wise old sage, interpreter of prophecy…," he began, still speaking to me. "He was there the day Tal-Makai died." Kuro said nothing, but shifted his stance uncomfortably. I heard Reya inhale as Magus continued. "Chaer-Ul had told him what was going to happen…he came to warn Tal-Makai…but he held his tongue…"

"What?!" Reya exclaimed, turning to face Kuro.

"It's true," said Kuro, head held low. "I knew Tal was going to die, but I misunderstood the prophecy. I thought his death was going to bring about the end of the war – the end of Magus and the salvation of many. I could have warned him, but I didn't. I

324

thought it was Chaer-Ul's will. Reya, I'm so sorry." He began to weep. Reya's answer came in the form of a hard slap across the old man's weathered cheek, her own eyes red with grief.

"You see?" said Magus. "Chaer-Ul is a cruel lord, playing men like pawns, toying with lives for his own questionable ends. Martyr...Justin Mayer...you had a name once. You're a man, not a hero. The very name he's given you is a mockery. What is a "martyr"? One who dies for a cause. What cause? Only Chaer-Ul knows. Has he even told you why he would have you die?"

"No!" I said sharply. But I wasn't talking to Magus. I was addressing Reya. "He's trying to divide us against ourselves, against Chaer-Ul." I put my arm around Reya, led her away from Kuro, and looked her in the eyes. "Tal made his own choices that day. As you showed me, you tried to warn Tal too, but he was intent on what he thought he had to do. There's no saying he would have heard Kuro, either. Kuro, like all of us, is only trying to do what he thinks is right. Truth isn't always black and white. I don't understand all of Chaer-Ul's motives, but Maya believes in him, and I believe in Maya! *She needs us now.*" After a moment Reya nodded reluctantly, and I paused to wipe a tear from her cheek before turning back to Magus. "Here's what I know, Magus. Your works deny your words. The walls of this city, not to mention the countless others you've slain without mercy, bear witness to your unfathomable cruelty. I've had enough of your preaching! Your way leads only to death. I'll take my chances with Chaer-Ul!"

"Fool!" Magus shouted. Come play your role, *Martyr!*"

Without hesitation I rocketed into the sky on wings of light. My staff and shield, my armor – Charr's gifts, blessed by Chaer-Ul, were at the ready. I hovered for just a second or two, deciding on a plan of attack, when suddenly, a whirring sound, and something whooshed over my right shoulder from behind. It was Maya's

325

hum-bug, and as it banked toward Maya the light glinted off something shiny held between its paired legs. As it came up just above Maya, it released its grip, and the object dropped, straight into Maya's hands. It hadn't occurred to me that Maya and Mana weren't bound hand and foot; apparently Magus felt no need to resort to such measures as he was protected by the swirling halo of dark smoke that stood between him and the ladies, even as it held them in close proximity to him.

I soared nearer, and recognized the object as the specialized dagger that Charr had made – the one that had gone missing from her workshop. Of course Magus' men would have searched the two women; Maya had exploited a loophole in his defenses by employing a post-search delivery bug. Magus had seen the hum-bug, of course, but didn't understand the nature of the delivery. Thinking it a common dagger, he laughed derisively, knowing his magical defenses to be more than a match for any physical threat. And so as he returned his attention to me, I swooped away from Maya, toward his other side, determined to give her the best possible chance. As predicted, Magus's focus stayed on me, and I stole just a quick glance back at Maya – long enough to see that the blade of the dagger had started spinning, silently creating a disruption, a focused thinning of the protective shield around Magus. I had to time my dive perfectly…and hope that the erosive effect of the dagger would be strong enough to allow my blade to penetrate. It was our only chance.

I saw a dark shape pull away from the wispy halo that encircled Magus and draw nearer to him. I dropped quickly until I was close enough to see what it was. The torso of a humanoid form composed of the same smoky substance as the shield had separated itself from the swirling mass and appeared to be conferring with him. Looking more closely, I realized to my horror that the shield itself was not in fact smoke, but hundreds of individual beings, dark spirits forming a living shield around the sorcerer – the very dark beings that lent him their power. It seemed they had become aware of the disruption and were presently informing Magus. Maya was in great danger and our window was about to close! Immediately, I dove. I aimed for the spot where the shield appeared thinner, near where Maya held the dagger. Because of my altitude, I was going to have to touch down before I delivered the strike, lest I risk injuring Maya in the process. I accelerated as much as I dared, then braked abruptly at the last moment, coming to a halt mere inches from the ground. Locating the weak spot in the shield, I drew back my blade, then thrust it with all of my strength toward the rapidly-narrowing gap, aiming for a spot under Magus' ribs.

Clang! Another blade met my own with staggering force, deflecting my weapon and causing me to miss my mark, as it threw me momentarily off balance. No! As I recovered, I lifted my eyes to meet the face of the enemy who had ruined my shot. At the far end of a long, metal staff stood Mana, a wicked sneer on her pretty face. "*What?*" I stammered. "Mana, why? What are you doing?!!?"

She laughed out loud, a sound soon echoed and overshadowed by that of her dark master. It was Magus who spoke. "That was the moment when I first truly understood that Chaer-Ul was not unique – that he had attained nothing that could not also be mine. That was the day I was able to pass between worlds for the first time. And mind you, since that day I have done so many, many times. It took many failed attempts before I was able to find the *right* world – one with a girl who resembled your Mana closely enough to gain your trust...but with the right...*qualities*...to do my bidding." Keeping her staff pointed at me, Mana back-stepped until she was pressed against Magus, then turned her head and exchanged a vulgar, full-tongued kiss with the sorcerer. I nearly gagged.

"What about the real Mana?" I asked, already afraid I knew the answer.

"*Dead*, of course," said Magus coldly. "I couldn't have her chancing into this world, screwing up my plans, now could I?" I felt a hard lump forming in my throat, anger and grief clouding my thoughts.

"And you can quit calling me 'Mana', idiot," she said. "My name is…"

"I don't *care* what your name is!" I interrupted, forcing the words out past the lump in my throat. "You betrayed the good people of this world into the hands of one of the most evil men that has ever lived! And for what, huh? What did he promise you?"

"We're going to live forever!" she squeaked with a mix of excitement and hysterical lunacy. "We're going to be *gods*!"

"You're going to be *dead* in a few minutes," I spat, "and nobody is *ever* going to care what your name was!" I turned to glare at the sorcerer. "And you're next, Magus!" At the threat to her lover the fake Mana's haughty smirk was replaced by a snarl, and she began to poke and jab with the end of her staff, forcing me to defend, pushing me away from Magus – and Maya. Her staff glowed ominously red, betraying its magical enhancement.

Just then I heard a shriek, and a kirin swooped in on flaming wings, alighting just behind my position. "Justin, what do you need me to do?"

I couldn't take my eyes off Mana's double long enough to look, but I knew the voice. "Corvus! You're ok! And Doog?"

"We'll talk about that later," he said. Then I saw him vaulting over my head, and with a powerful downward slash he drove the end of the impostor's staff into the ground. "I'll take care of this one for you," he said. Then he made eye contact with his foe. "Wait, isn't this…"

"No, it's not Mana," I said. "It just looks like her. But this one's with Magus. No time to explain, but anything you do to her is too good for her, trust me."

"If you say so," Corvus said. He continued to exchange blows with her, and though she was strong, he was equally strong, and faster. Much faster. The battle quickly turned in his favor.

"I thought maybe you'd want a crack at Magus…," I offered.

"Appreciate the thought," he said between slashes, "but I'm not sure I can kill my own father…even if he is the embodiment of evil. Anyway, I have a feeling Martyr is the only one who can finish him off for good. I'll lend support in any way I can."

Magus caught a slice of the conversation, and quickly deduced the facts. "So you're the bastard-child I left for dead, eh, Freakshow?" he jeered.

"Don't listen to him!" I said.

"Cut up the other half to match, love," Magus continued, "I hate to leave things unfinished. That *abomination* was never meant to live."

"Corvus," I began, "Don't let him…"

"Don't worry about me," said Corvus, channeling whatever anger he may have been feeling into an ever more spirited attack on his opponent, "just see what you can do about silencing that old fool for good!"

"I intend to," I said, and turned my attention back to Maya.

"Justin!" she yelled. "Here, maybe you'll have better luck with this." She raised the dagger over her head to throw it, and just as it left her hand a massive, bone-white blade sliced through the air and intercepted it, cleaving it in two amid a shower of sparks. The huge blade just hovered for several seconds in the air between Maya and Magus, then the space around it began to shimmer like rippling water, expanding to occupy an area twice Maya's height and several times as wide. Out of that space, its massive hands clutching a blade formed from the breastbone of a puurr-deer, stepped the monstrous stone golem I had seen in Reya's vision. It was a hulking colossus of granite, earth, and sinewy vines, and as it stepped from the shimmering portal and set foot firmly before me, the material that formed its face peeled away in gravelly layers to expose the never-decaying face of Tal-Makai, red eyes glowing in lifeless sockets.

"Anyone else getting a little déjà vu?" Magus taunted, followed by a disgusting cackle. The creature advanced toward me, and I took a step back, my first thought being to lure it as far away from Maya as possible. Off to the side, I could hear Corvus continuing to struggle with Mana's double, but didn't dare to take my eyes off this unnatural monstrosity long enough to see how he fared. Having drawn it to a safe distance I allowed it to engage me, meeting its blade with my own. As I sparred with it, my thoughts wandered. This thing had killed Tal-Makai, I knew, the evidence of which it perpetually carried around within its magically-animated frame. I had to defeat it, if possible, without destroying Tal's body – that much I owed to Reya. In an effort to suppress my growing fear I reminded myself that several factors were different this time around. First of all, I was theoretically immortal. That in itself gives no small amount of comfort in a situation like this. Furthermore, Tal had been surrounded. I thought of the assassins, bowed to the ground like the rest of Magus' army. But was there any guarantee they'd remain that way?

"Reya!" I shouted.

The answer came from close at hand. "We're all right here," she said. "Just waiting for you to tell us how we can help." Her voice was shaky, understandably. She was being forced to relive the most horrific memory of her life, and now potentially to watch the undead body of her true love be forced to kill his double. It was nothing short of incredible that she was still standing.

"Reya," I said, "It's going to be ok. It's not going to happen again."

"OK," she said, sounding tiny, and not at all convinced.

"All I need you to do is keep an eye on those soldiers and make sure I don't get surrounded. I'll do the rest. If worse comes to worse, I know what I need to do."

"And…what is that?" she asked in a barely audible voice.

"I'm getting Maya back," was all I said.

Magus was already putting the second phase of his plan into effect, wordlessly commanding his motionless soldiers to rise and converge on the remaining resistance forces. As anticipated, there were still assassins among them, trying to keep a low profile as they edged their way past their comrades and toward their target – me. Under Reya's able command, the best warriors resumed their task of identifying and eliminating these threats, a job made more difficult by the new contours and many hidden crevices of the remixed post-comet landscape.

I was able to concentrate on the golem. I parried its attacks with relative ease, as it was quite slow for all its strength. But I was afraid to go on the offensive. My blade might well be able to dismember the thing, maybe even decapitate it – but that would

331

damage Tal's body. If I were to kill Magus, his enchantments would likely die with him, but that was the real trick, wasn't it? He was still protected by his spiritual swarm, and I wasn't really sure how to take on a vortex of swirling demons. I took a couple of test swings with my staff, remembering the effect this had had on Magus' troops. It rattled the stones and some of the other organic parts that composed the creature. I slashed harder, and some of the smaller pieces were shaken free, but they rolled back and rejoined the monster's mass as quickly as they hit the ground. What about my wings, I wondered? Flight would offer me no advantage, except as a means to flee if I got in a tight spot. But could the tendrils serve another function? I concentrated, and the strands emerged from my body, then began to probe around the edges of the golem's body. The monster slashed at them with its blade, but the weapon simply passed through the tendrils without effect. Gradually I worked the threads into nearly every nook and cranny on the beast, all the while parrying its repeated attacks with my staff. Now I focused my energy into prying the thing apart. The threads exerted a supernatural force that came not from my muscle or bone, and with a great, prolonged rumbling, the golem flew apart into its respected parts, leaving only the body of Tal-Makai laid out upon a field strewn with bits of rubble and debris.

Reya ran to the body, but almost as soon as she did I saw a movement out of the corner of my eye and shouted, "Get back!" The pieces that had formed the golem were rolling and tumbling, reaching and seeking their unity once more. One by one the pieces converged upon the body of Tal-Makai, once again swallowing it within their roiling mass. I heard a pained shriek from Reya.

Magus' gleeful laughter filled the air as the golem came at me again, relentlessly, single-mindedly swinging its goliath blade at me. I parried, and I parried again. I dodged, and I side-stepped, and I parried, and when I tired of defense, I would slash once or twice, rattling its stones against each other, but for what? I began to feel tired. And what would happen when I was completely exhausted? What becomes of an immortal if he doesn't defend? Would it cut but not hurt? Would it miss every time? Magus could see it too, my response time slowed, my energy abating. "What happens now, Martyr?" he asked. "You can't hurt me or defeat my champion. My champion cannot destroy you. You've come all this way, and so many have died, yet you are no closer to your goal. You might as well just fulfill your destiny...give up...and...*die!*"

"You can't kill me, Magus! I fight with the power of Chaer-Ul. I can't die unless I choose to! And I choose to fight!" The words exuded great confidence, but I was beginning to wonder how long I could really go on, and what would happen when my strength was gone. I fought on, slashing and parrying, dodging the golem's blade, slashing again.

To my left, Corvus was struggling, playing a defensive game against an unexpectedly adept opponent. Apparently, what she lacked in speed she more than made up for in stamina. I heard Corvus grunting and breathing heavily as the imposter Mana lashed at him again and again with her glowing staff. She clearly understood that it would be game over if he got within sword-striking distance, and had no intention of letting that happen. He was managing to deflect her blows, barely. It was clear that he was fatigued, his defense crumbling. She struck his blade once, then her staff burned red with renewed intensity and she struck again more forcefully, sending his sword spinning through the air in a burst of crimson sparks. Her next slash was a clean cut across his thighs, dropping him to his knees. She followed up with an angled slice that opened his chest, exposing clockwork metal parts.

"What the...," she stammered, not sure what to make of what she was seeing.

"Corvus!" I shouted, trying to edge my way to where he had fallen even as I continued to deflect the golem's relentless onslaught.

The dark Mana's momentary confusion dissolved into devilish glee as a wicked grin snaked across her face. She drew back her spear, and with a mighty thrust jammed the tip in between the gears in Corvus' chest. The metal parts ground to a halt. "No!" I screamed, knowing I wouldn't reach him in time. Already the color was draining from his face. The imposter, triumphant, turned her head to regard Magus, seeking his approval for her clever win. As she did, a tiny, black-feathered dart appeared below her ear. Her hand immediately shot to her neck, clawing at it. As it fell free, a greyish pallor began to spread from the injection site, the veins on her neck visibly pulsating. Her eyes grew wide with horror, and any trace of a smile had vanished. She turned a pleading gaze upon her lover and lord, whose face revealed only cool detachment.

Corvus spat out a little hollow tube, the thing that had delivered the deadly projectile. "Sorry 'Dad'," he said, "looks like I've inconvenienced you again." He smiled, an expression easily mistaken for a snarl as his scar-stretched lip pulled back, revealing a single canine tooth. Then a peace came over him, his features relaxed, and his head dropped gently to his chest. Meanwhile, the poison continued to take its toll on Mana's double, making its way to her hands, her feet, her heart. She sank to the ground, lay her head on Corvus' lap, and slept.

Magus had been watching the scene unfold, and registered no emotion. Instead he spoke, slowly, deliberately. Though he never looked up, I knew it was me he addressed. "I cannot kill you," he said. "Perhaps this is true." He pulled a knife from his belt and wiped its blade carefully on the cloth at his thigh, first one side, then the other. "But I think I can give you a reason to die." And with that he stepped over to Maya, pulled back her head, and slit her throat.

"No!" I screamed. "Maya!" A crimson stain spread over her breast as her lifeblood gushed in spurts from the open gash at her neck. Behind me, Reya screamed uncontrollably.

I gasped for breath. The golem continued to swing at me mindlessly. With an exertion of sheer will I emitted a shockwave that blasted it into its component parts once more. Stumbling, I stepped past Tal's body and ran to where Maya's body hung, still suspended by Magus' enchantments. I clutched her body to myself and she fell, limp, into my arms. I crumbled to my knees. I sobbed, unaware and unconcerned about what was going on around me. When I managed to open my eyes once more, a shadow had fallen across me. I saw the tip of a bone-white blade emerge from my abdomen. Everything went white.

Minutes passed. Hours perhaps. The whiteness remained, but it had become warm, and it enveloped me in its warmth. Slowly I became certain that I could hear the rhythmic lapping of waves against a sandy shore. After endless time I heard a voice. It was deep as thunder and soft as a breath.

"You have done well. But it is not yet finished."

I received the words without question. The waves lapped against the shore. A long time passed. I felt warm and safe.

"Through a veil may one time pass, a sacrifice for all."

These were words I had heard before, words I knew. They had no meaning. They meant everything. The waves lapped the shore. The warmth gave way to a coolness that stirred my consciousness.

The words had meaning. The words required response. A long time passed.

"Will you do this for me?"

The words had meaning. I understood the meaning. The waves lapped the shore. The words required response. I mouthed the words.

("I will.") I tried to say, but I didn't hear my voice.

Then I felt a gentle breeze, and the whiteness was a mist, and the mist began to clear. And I saw the sand, and the waves that lapped against it, and the sun as it sparkled on the waves and the sand. And I saw her, clothed only in the mist, bare feet on the sand, raven hair flowing all about her.

"*I will*," she said.

("Maya....Maya, no!") I tried to shout. ("It's not supposed to be you!") But I didn't hear my voice.

I was on the battlefield again. The monstrous golem stood before me once more, but it wasn't facing me, it was looking at something else. I looked past it, to where Magus sat enthroned in the middle of a swirling vortex of shadowy forms. I watched him descend from his throne and go to examine Maya's body, which still hung suspended in the air, a crimson line across her neck. Gone was Magus' gloating smile, replaced by a look of wonder that melted as he looked at her into a mask of terror.

336

As I watched, Maya's body began to glow, as if illuminated from within. White light beamed from the seams in her armor and dissolved the bonds between them until the pieces of her armor fell like scales from her body. Her whole body glowed brightly with an inner light, and it shone from the tips of her fingers and toes. Tracings of light could be seen to define her eyelids, and it spread along the strands of her jet-black hair from root to tip until her hair was entirely white as if made of light. It flowed in slow-moving waves in an unfelt breeze, as if under water. Then, in one fluid motion, luminous wings burst from her back and stretched toward the heavens; not threads, but real, feathery wings, expanding outward in layer upon layer of light-giving plumage that seemed to fill the sky. We all gazed on in wonder, except for Magus, who had taken to shaking, and twitching, and shuddering in uncontrollable convulsions. Slowly, Maya's head turned toward him, an angel's face perched atop a long, graceful neck, and suddenly her lids flicked open, revealing huge, almond-shaped eyes, gateways into other-worldly wells of purest light. Magus screamed, and writhed in his skin, unable to bear the brightness of the light from those eyes, yet unable to flee. Then the feathers of Maya's wings began to vibrate and shimmer, and from somewhere within her breast came a rapid swelling of power, an intensifying of light and of energy, accompanied by the sound of a song that cannot be heard. Growing in pitch and in volume until it could not be contained, it burst in a supernova of infinite light and sound. For an endless time all of creation was bathed in its awesome, beautiful, terrible light. From this place the shadows fled away and were found no more, and Magus, the scourge of the earth, stiffened and fell dead. The shattered plain was peppered with the bodies of countless dead soldiers, clad in black armor and laying where they had stood. Finally the golem crumbled, surrendering the body of Tal-Makai at last. Having finished the work to which Chaer-Ul had called her, Maya turned her face to me, and in the midst of the exceeding brilliance I thought I saw her smile at me briefly. Then all of a sudden the glory departed, and Martyr too fell dead.

337

Dreams and visions. I see a long road. A caravan of war-weary travelers. A row of magnificent beasts with wings like fire, all but the first ridden by great warriors. The first bears a body, a black-haired angel bound in burial clothes and secured to the animal's back. Shattered buildings give way to grassy fields, to forests, to mountain heights. A dream. I sit on a mossy rock in a lush, green place, sunlight dappled through a leafy canopy. A crystalline stream trickles over polished stones. A figure sits on a stone on the other side. It is a man, but I cannot see his face. The brook is his voice.

"It's over," he said. "You did your part."

"But I didn't," I said. "Hers was my part. Now I have no part."

"Everyone plays the part they were meant to play," he said.

"But why did she have to die?" I asked. "Was there no other way?"

"Men will never understand. Death is nothing. It means nothing. Whether or when you die, that is not important."

"What *is* important?" I asked.

"Love," he said. "And love that will spend life for another, that is worth something."

"What is it worth?" I asked.

"Life," he said.

"Whose life?" I asked.

There was a long pause.... "When you spoke, you couldn't hear your voice," he said at last. "But I did. I know what you would have done. For her. For them. For *me*."

Mountains give way to hills, lowlands. A ravaged city, a river, an upward-curving road. A dam. Seven great white deer walking into the forest, disappearing among the trees.

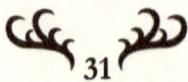

31

I stood in the sepulchre where Tal-Makai had been laid to rest, waiting for the others to pay their respects and file out. I was hoping to have a long overdue conversation with Reya, alone. Jager lingered for what seemed an eternity, then finally stood and left. "So," I said when he was gone, taking Reya's hands in mine, "that wasn't the whole truth about your daughter, now was it?"

"Not entirely," she admitted.

"Are you ready to tell me what really happened?" I asked.

"I suspect you've already figured it out, mostly," she said.

"It wasn't just a close call, was it?" I asked. "They really did take her. They...Magus' men...they killed your baby girl. So the Maya I know..."

Reya's eyes were welling up again.

"I'm sorry," I said. "It can wait."

"No, you deserve the truth." She pulled back her hands. Dabbing her eyes on her sleeve, she pressed on. "She was just like her, as much as she could possibly be. Chaer-Ul brought her."

"A double, from another world. Like me. And what about her real parents?" I asked.

"They had both just died tragically," Reya said. "She would have been an orphan."

"You didn't do anything wrong," I said. "Any parent would have done the same."

"She was my daughter," Reya said. "As much as she would have been otherwise."

"She was," I said. "And she knew it. She wouldn't have thought otherwise."

"I wonder if she'd understand," Reya said. "I hope she forgives me."

"You can tell her," I said. "I'm sure she'll hear you. I know she'd forgive you, if there were anything to forgive."

Reya smiled. "Yeah, I will, when I'm ready. It's waited *this* long…"

"We've got all the time in the world," I said. "This is a new beginning. We've all got to learn a new way, but we'll do it together."

Reya nodded, smiled warmly, and kissed me on the cheek. She stood, took one last look at the inscription, and left. After she was gone I read it again, then the one for Doog, and the one for Corvus. I allowed myself a moment to remember all that these men had done for us. Next there was one for Mana – the *real* Mana, though of course the box was empty. She had just been an unfortunate victim in a game she never knew she was playing. Finally I let my eyes drift to Maya's epitaph, but my vision blurred; I didn't want to read it again. This structure was a work in progress, of course; other names would be added before all the fallen were accounted for. So many good lives cut short…but maybe now the time of healing could begin.

My reverie was disrupted by a sound of feet scuffing the sand on the stone outside the arched entryway. Somebody cleared their throat softly. A pretty face tilted at an angle slid into view, the movement releasing a cascade of silky black hair that hung

341

halfway to the floor. "Maya!" I said. "You're supposed to be resting."

"I missed you!" she chirped as she stepped fully into the doorway. She was wearing something white, layered and flowy, not her usual utilitarian blacks. The indirect sunlight beaming down behind her imparted a downy glow to the edges of the garment, and hinted at the lean curves underneath. She had been here before, but somehow kept returning. Her nose wrinkled as she caught sight of the stone bearing her name. "Eeee, *creepy*...I hope they get rid of that soon."

"Yeah, I know," I said. "A bit premature, wasn't it?"

"You know, I always thought I'd be afraid when it was time to die," she said, "but there was no fear...I knew death wasn't the end. I'm just so grateful for this second chance." She looked at the other epitaphs and sighed, then came to sit beside me. "It does feel good that he's resting here with us, where he belongs," she said. She was obviously referring to her longtime friend. "I'm really going to miss him. He always knew the right thing to say." She blinked away the tears that tried to form, then sat in silence for a long time. Slowly her breathing became more regular. She leaned her head on my shoulder. I could feel her cheeks stretching into a smile before I looked down.

"*What...?*" I said playfully, trying to tease it out of her.

"Um...you know how you said we have to start rebuilding the world...?" she asked.

I didn't catch on immediately. "Yeah...so?" She smiled even bigger, drew her hand in an arcing motion under her belly, then lifted big chocolate-brown eyes to meet mine. "You don't mean....you're....we're... *Really?* Are you *sure?!!?*"

342

She shook her head up and down emphatically.

"Oh wow! But…Maya! What about your mother…will she be all right with this? I mean…you know…we should make it official…"

Maya stared blankly. "What are you talking about, Darling?" she said. "We're already married! Remember, at the dam?"

"Yes, I know," I said. "It's just that…there was no ceremony…"

"Silly! This isn't your world!" she said. "Do you need a ceremony to meet with Chaer-Ul?"

"Well, no, I guess not, but…"

Maya continued. "We were bound for life the moment Chaer-Ul brought us together. People mate for life. That's just how it happens. That's how it's always happened."

"Bound…for life," I repeated slowly, letting it process. In my own world, I had always been a bit wary of the whole marriage thing. It wasn't a fear of commitment; more a skepticism about the long-term prospects, based no doubt on my own cultural experience, my parents' marriage… But now that it was actually happening, had *already* happened…I found I wasn't afraid. It felt normal. And as I looked at Maya, 'life' didn't feel like a sentence. It felt…*right*. "So you and me…?"

"*Forever*," she said. "*No matter what*." Now I allowed myself to smile.

Then a furrow appeared over Maya's eyes. "Wait a second…you didn't think we were "*officially*" married? But you…*we*…you didn't think that I would have if…*Justin!*"

Mercifully, there came a rumbling sound outside the sepulchre, distant at first, then growing louder. Excited voices could be heard, multiplying as the rumbling grew to a steady roar. Suddenly Knox stuck his head into the doorway. "The last scouting party is back! And they've brought back…"

"My bike!" Maya finished for him, jumping up and down excitedly and forgetting what had upset her. She started toward the door, then turned back abruptly and placed a long, warm kiss on my lips before skipping out of the room, raven hair flowing out behind her.

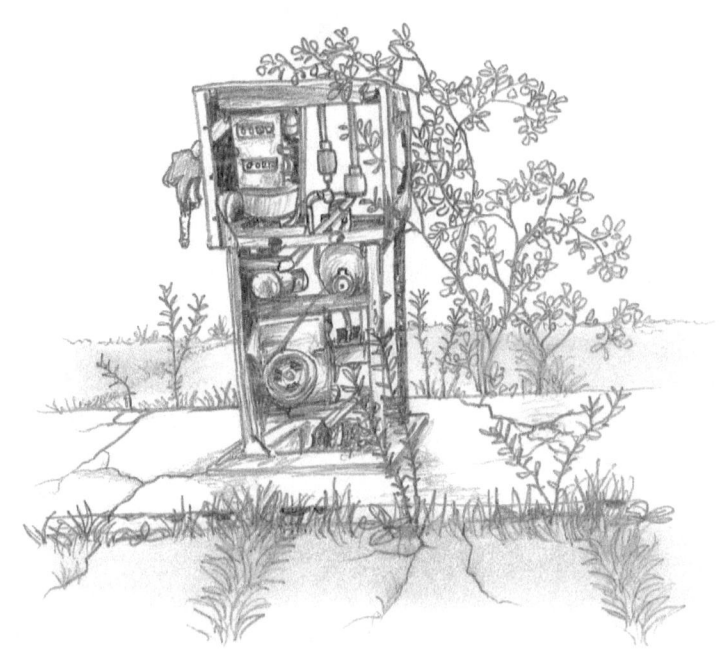

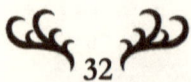

32

In a shadowy glade, a familiar-looking man awoke. Groggy, a bit confused, he sat up slowly, his head pounding. Slightly dazed, he looked around him. He recognized plants, grasses, trees. He was looking for something, some sort of confirmation. As he mused, an oversized, cicada-like insect alighted upon the trunk of a nearby tree, then immediately took flight again, a resounding buzz marking its passing. The man stared after it in wonder. "It worked. By God, it *worked!*" He lay back down, contemplating his next move as he rested, trying to regain strength. After some time a dark mist drifted imperceptibly out of the shadows and into the clearing, began to flow gently, inexorably toward the man. The mist surrounded and embraced this new arrival, and as the man inhaled deeply, the mist seemed to be taken into him, to become a part of him. The mist seemed to him like a welcome friend. The man was glad for the help; he had a lot to learn, and so very much to do…

About the Author

N. P. Beckwith is a professional chiropractor, former educator, casual artist, and undocumented theologian. Occasionally, on a dare, and at great risk to those he loves, he writes a novel. He believes that he who finds a wife finds a good thing, and that children are a heritage from the Lord. He is a world traveler, his conquests including Texas, Holland, India, Japan, and at least one alternate earth. He currently resides with his good thing and his heritage in his home state of Maine.